When The Fault Breaks

By Xavier Bruehler

Copyright © 2014

Facebook book page: https://www.facebook.com/
WhenTheFaultBreaks/

Table of Contents

Acknowledgment

This book would not have been possible if it had not been for the encouragement, I received by everyone important to me. The first one I want to thank is my sister Virginia; she has endured reading it from its inception and did several edits before I had even finished the skeleton of the book. The second person I want to thank is Susan Whitehorse for her insight on Native Americans language and customs. Her work gave Black Cloud the voice I couldn't have done.

I would also like to thank the many people from Facebook that gave me the needed feedback to find and fix many errors; your help was invaluable. I would also like to recognize Regina Carol for the inspiration on adding a chapter that I had been trying to figure out. Your input gave me the location for it.

I would further like to thank Kale Franklin for his support and promotion of *When The Fault Breaks* by spreading the word and posting it on his website. Additionally, I would like to thank Worth Schottlannder for the promotion he did as well. I would be amiss if I forgot to add a long-time friend Rob Sellers; he did incredible work, enhancing the cover photo. To my many other Facebook friends out there that gave me the feedback I needed and encouraged me I say thanks.

I would be amiss if I did not mention an influential person in my life, Professor Maynard Miller, he gave me additional encouragement to finish this book. He was the Leader of an expedition across the Juneau Icefield in 2006 with the Juneau Icefield Research Project, JIRP studying the effects of climate change. That is where the cover picture was taken from overlooking the Gilkey Trench. The year I participated was his fifty-eighth year in charge and the last time I saw him. I am happy to see his family has continued his legacy. May you rest in peace.

Dedication

Lastly and most importantly I want to dedicate the book to my loving wife Lee. Not only did she put up with my distraction from our time, she provided me encouragement and inspiration. Her unwavering support kept me from giving up when I had doubts and helped me realize I could complete the book even when I questioned my ability to do so.

Introduction

This pseudo-science fiction story is a blend of known geologic processes, and predictable behavior by a population in the aftermath of a massive catastrophic mega-geologic occurrence. It's based on known societal behavior from past epoch incidents in modern times, and how humanity reacted to those events. The geologic phenomenon depicted have been kept as accurate as possible though some writer's liberty has been taken, but in the end, it IS after all fiction.

Prologue

Ten years ago, the world shook as never before, at least as recorded by man. Ten years ago, an earthquake altered our existence in ways I would never have imagined. This is a chronicle of how life has changed for the survivors of The Great Quake. It is an account of those that lived through the catastrophe and rebuilt their lives anew. A story of a new, simpler world while keeping some choice twenty-first century innovations. Today is the tenth anniversary of that historic day. As I relax in my swing overlooking our little village below, I ponder the changes and sometimes wonder if it were for the better.

The Great Quake

Geologists tell us it started deep in the earth's crust off the coast of British Columbia, Canada. It was there that the Cascadia fault began to rupture. The rupture started just north of Vancouver as a low rumble that quickly became a loud roar as the seismic waves raced across the crust.

The rupture traveled south at an incredible velocity, violently shaking everything along its entire length. City after city felt the unimaginable power of the greatest megaquake felt in modern times. From its beginning in Canada to its end north of San Francisco, the fault had completely released. The seven hundred miles of the North American continent was uplifted as much as fifty feet as the quake roared along the fault.

Vancouver, BC was the first major city to be hit by the seismic waves. Given its proximity to the fault and its location in a basin, it did not fare well. Over fifty thousand people in downtown Vancouver died in the first nine minutes of the quake.

The landmark Alex Fraser Bridge tossed back and forth and then rolled for at least five minutes before breaking up and falling into the Fraser River below. North of the city the Capalano suspension bridge crashed to the ground killing tourists who had moments before been enjoying the amazing views.

There was panic in the Granville Island Market, as people ran for their lives, screaming as they watched the roadway above them crash to the ground. When the shaking finally stopped, almost everything had been destroyed and left in ruins. Most of Vancouver's skyscrapers lay in giant piles of rubble, having toppled and burying the streets and the people in them.

As the seismic waves continued south, they hit Seattle, the buildings began to sway violently. The brick facades on many of the old buildings crumbled, falling on the streets and people below. Pikes Place Market, which was built into the hillside like stair steps, couldn't withstand the shaking. It collapsed. The whole thing crumbled and slid down the steep slope with most of the shoppers still inside.

The Space Needle swayed heavily for several minutes; it was designed to take the force of a large quake, so it held up a long time. However, The Great Quake was too much, and the needle could no longer hold up. Suddenly, the Needle snapped off just above the top of the legs and crashed to the ground. It rolled onto the adjacent Pacific Science Center, nearly cutting it in two, trapping and killing scores of people inside. On the other side of town, the Columbia Center, Seattle's tallest building, was in trouble.

The Center had been swaying heavily for several minutes. It too was designed to withstand a large quake, but not this big a quake or for this long. Few had been able to get out of the tower because they couldn't walk as the floor was moving so violently. Near the top, people were screaming as the building was swaying side to side by several feet each way.

Then with one big sway, the tower began to topple over. It fell onto the building next to it, which had already been swaying as well and knocked it over too. The buildings looked like dominoes as one fell against the next, causing each in turn to fall. Once the Columbia Center fell, there was no hope for any of the remaining buildings along the direction of the fall.

The waterfront was a different picture. It had been built on garbage and fill from the hills above long ago, and so the area was prone to liquefaction. One building after another was swallowed up like they were in quicksand. Visitors of the Seattle Aquarium were tossed around like toys. When the glass on one of the large tanks shattered, tens of thousands of gallons of water washed the inhabitants and people through the Aquarium and into the Puget Sound.

Cars lay strewn everywhere. The buildings were not recognizable. There was nothing left of the waterfront. The ground had not even stopped shaking, when suddenly it dropped out from under everything. Not just one small area, but everywhere, the entire Puget Sound region subsided, the water rushed in and flooded all of it.

The release of stress caused the North American Plate where the Puget Sound lies to sink by around fifty feet. Every mile of the former waterfront in the Puget Sound now sits fifty feet below sea level.

The entire shoreline, and in some areas many miles inland were almost instantly submerged. When the water had finally settled, everything and everyone on the 2,500 miles of waterfront was gone, engulfed by the water. Over 4.3 million people had lived in close proximity of the shoreline. There was no time to run and nowhere to hide. And the destruction continued.

The rupture generated a series of Tsunamis that slammed into the northeast coast of the Puget Sound. Everything in its path was obliterated as the first wave washed miles inland. Tsunami waves don't recede, so the next wave washed in even further, this one...was far worse. It was over seventy-five feet tall and moving at almost one hundred miles an hour, so no one and nothing in the lower elevations could survive. Our home, Bellingham, Washington, was gone.

When the waves hit the foothills of the Cascade Mountains, they reflected, then ricocheted back and forth, down the Puget Sound until they lost their energy. Wave after wave washed into the Sound with the next couple being even larger than the ones before. The subsidence of the area allowed the waves to wash even further inland.

The Seattle waterfront, and everything else in the lowlands of the Puget Sound, were GONE. Destroyed by the shaking and falling buildings, then covered by the rising water then washed away by the waves. Few could survive the destruction that fell upon the Pacific Northwest that day.

But the devastation of the Puget Sound Region wasn't finished, Mount Rainier, a 14,411-foot volcano located southeast of Olympia, Washington, was about to come alive. It was the most heavily glaciated peak in the lower forty-eight states, covered with snow and ice year-round.

Its upper four thousand feet was made up of fragile hydro-thermally altered rock. The massive load of the ice and rock made it susceptible to movement and primed to collapse at any time.

Many scientists believed, like me, that a strong earthquake would cause the top of the mountain to fall away. It turned out we were correct. After more than nine minutes of shaking it could no longer hold up. The shaking caused the top four thousand feet of the volcano to collapse.

All that rock, ice, snow, water and other debris came crashing down, forming massive lahars that careened down the mountain. The 450-foot-high flows traveled all the way to the Puget Sound at over seventy miles an hour filling the valleys with a devastating wall of rock, mud, and debris.

When the top of the mountain gave way, it released the pressure on the magma chamber below. The drop-in pressure released the gases within the magma, sort of like taking the cap off a shaken bottle of soda, causing the volcano to explosively erupt. This resulting eruption made Mt. St. Helens look like a geologic burp by comparison.

A gigantic pyroclastic cloud filled the sky reaching over 50,000 feet high, blacking out the sky for miles around. Ash lightning filled the air as the cloud rose higher and higher before it collapsed under its own weight. The cloud then came crashing to the ground as several massive pyroclastic flows. They traveled at over 450 miles an hour and reaching temperatures of eighteen hundred degrees, obliterating everything in their paths.

The ash flows were followed by lava, exploding from the volcano that followed the same paths that the lahars and pyroclastic flows had already created. This filled the valleys and reached far into the Puget Sound. Thousands of lava bombs rained down on anyone within the blast zone. The eruptions continued for days, forming layer after layer before they subsided.

Finally, the shaking stopped, the waves subsided, and the volcano was no longer erupting. The entire region looked like it had been hit by hundreds of nuclear bombs. It was a wasteland. There were no trees left standing for hundreds of miles. Smoke and the smell of sulfur filled the air.

Xavier Bruehler

The sky was dark even at midday, and acid rain and ash fell non-stop for several more days. There was no life to be seen anywhere, no birds, no mammals, not a single human left for hundreds of miles. All ninety cities and towns that lined the shores were submerged.

The entire west coast of the United States, Canada, and part of Mexico was devastated. Many scientists had been expecting a major earthquake for years. We knew it was a matter of when, not if, it would happen. Everyone knew of the San Andreas fault, but for some reason only Geologists knew the dangers the Cascadia fault posed.

Many planners on the Oregon coast were aware of it, but none expected the fault to rupture along its entire length. Some Geologists had sounded the alarm, but few listened. But we knew this event was going to change the world. We knew it would in a profound way.

The changes that followed were far reaching, as none of the damage could ever be repaired. Every major city on the west coast was annihilated. The infrastructure that was needed to get help to survivors was gone. No one was able to get in to help.

All the freeways, bridges, and tunnels were impassable. The airport runways shattered, and rail lines had become twisted ribbons of steel. Every port was inoperative, so even ships couldn't be used to bring in help. Even if any of the infrastructure was intact the sheer volume of the devastation was impossible to overcome.

Nowhere was safe, as news of the destruction spread. Chaos and rioting made its way across the country and the world. It wasn't long before trading was halted on Wall Street. That sent the economy into a death spiral that only fed the panic.

With the world tied together by the global economy, most of the rest of the world's modern economies collapsed as well. Canada was able to keep some sort of order. China temporarily lost control of its billion people as their economy crumbled. It was able to regain limited control through sheer force.

Because of our flawed food distribution system, grocery shelves where picked clean in a day. Across the country, people were hording. Price gouging was rampant. For a short time, Washington was in control while the President tried to reassure everyone that we could rebuild.

Day by day, the news coming out of the disaster zone had gotten worse. Soon it became apparent it wasn't going to get better. Eventually the government came right out and said it was overwhelmed. They said there was no hope of getting any substantial help to the region. The people would have to fend for themselves for the unforeseeable future.

It was just as so many had predicted all along. We said that if something of this magnitude ever happened, the government wouldn't be able to deal with it. We predicted a complete breakdown of social rule in a short order. One only had to look back at New Orleans and Hurricane Katrina to see what was coming only on a larger scale.

This is the story of our survival and that of others we met along the way. The world would be a different place. Only the strong, prepared, and wise would be left to tell the story of what happened.

Chapter 1: The Beginning

I got up early that morning, ready for yet another beautiful day in our private, isolated paradise. The sun was rising over the canyon, and the view was astonishing. It was an incredible sunrise, just the two of us reveling in the splendor of it. I woke Ann so we could share the moment together.

My loving wife Ann is the strong type and just as smart as she is sexy. She is an avid animal lover who helped the alternative humane society. She was an animal behaviorist, before we left Washington having saved many dogs lives. Her love of animals was obvious as we traveled around the country with three dogs and two cats in our motor home. While me, I'm the strong not so silent type with an occasional goatee and a bit of extra baggage.

That fateful day, Ann and I spent most of the morning enjoying the sun and fishing. As usual, Ann was catching most of the fish. I was in a different cove when I heard, "Peter come quick I caught a big one." I took off in her direction only to see her line go slack and hear Ann screaming at the fish for getting away. It was the funniest sight and so typical of Ann.

Later that day as we were cooking the fish, we noticed strange events. Sometime after noon all the birds took flight at once. The dogs started running around barking acting like the sky was falling. Ann noticed their behavior and jokingly commented. "Looks like an earthquake coming."

Even before I had a chance to reply we heard a deep rumble. The ground started to roll, only slightly at first, but then it began to undulate like a wave! It wasn't a big wave for us more like a slight undulation. We were clearly amid a large earthquake.

I exclaimed, "It IS! a quake and this is lasting a long time.

With it lasting this long it MUST be Cascadia rupturing along its entire length."

Now frantic, Ann screamed, "Oh My God what about our kids? NO! NNOOOO."

There was nothing that I could possibly say or do. While we lived in Washington, we talked about what would happen and it was not good. We knew exactly what our kids were experiencing. All I could do was hold her while the shaking continued. We knew that our kids still lived in the Sound and didn't stand much of chance of making it.

We couldn't stop crying, knowing we just lost our babies. Our only hope for our kids was that we taught them what to do when it happened. We taught them where to go and how to get away. I remember telling my daughter to head for the Cascades and to join other refugees.

After several minutes Ann asked, "When is this going to end?"

"Soon baby soon."

After all the shaking had finished, we got up to find we were in good shape. Since we were a long distance from the fault, the quake only shook us up a bit. Even the satellite dish just needed a little tweaking for us to watch the news coming from undamaged areas.

Crying Ann sobbed, "Our kids are..."

I could no longer hold back my pain; I too was now crying. We held each other for what seemed like an eternity. I knew I had to be strong for the both of us. After we pulled ourselves together, we sat in awe. The news started coming in that every major city had been obliterated.

"Do you think we are going to still have this place to ourselves Peter?"

"I don't think so. Even though we're several miles off the beaten path others will find it the same as we did."

"So much for our peace and quiet."

"I know but it's not like we have any way of controlling who finds their way up here, let alone stop them. The best we can do is try to get to know them. Hopefully we can make friends, team up and pool our resources. Bottom line is there's safety in numbers if they're on your side."

"But how do we know who we can trust?" Then sarcastically, she answered herself,

"I know, nobody."

"The short answer to that is we can't, the only thing we have is our instinct. It has served us well our whole lives and we need to continue to trust it. The best thing we can do is develop a rapport with some. Maybe that will give us more strength against others."

"We can't accept just anyone that comes up here."

"You're right Ann we can't but we can't ignore them either. First off doing so will put us on the outside when others arrive. Secondly, we can't make it in this upside-down world alone. We will need lots of help from now on."

"I think you're wrong Peter, but I hope you're right, I hope your instinct does not fail us."

"Me too Ann, but I don't know what else we could do. Do you have any suggestions or alternatives?"

Ann quipped, "We could hook them up to a lie detector."

"Not a bad idea, or all we have to do is let you talk to them. You say you can tell if someone is lying most the time."

"Yeah their mouth is moving, you know me Peter, I'm a

cynic."

"I know Ann, and I NEVER want you to stop being that way especially now."

As we watched the news, bits and pieces of information came out of the harder hit zones by survivors that had made it out. They described images of absolute destruction; people looting stores and killing anyone for anything. The rest of the country was not directly affected by the quake, but it was devastated by the chaos that followed.

We were alone at our remote location, but that didn't stay that way long. As the news of the social deterioration continued, it became clear that the world we knew was no more. Social order had broken down and everyone was heading for the hills. Like rats running from a flood they came seeking the safety of the wilderness.

We had left Washington completely self-sufficient; with our own power and water, seeds for every fruit and vegetable, and weapons to hunt game or defend ourselves with. We were as ready as we could be to live in a remote area for our temporary home.

We had found the quiet and seclusion we always looked for but getting there wasn't easy. It wasn't possible to reach it by car, as the road was impassable to anything with a low clearance. That limited the number of people that could make it. Unfortunately, most of the new arrivals that did make it were under equipped and ill prepared for what was to come. Some came with only the clothes on their backs.

Chapter 2: The Influx!

They came in SUVs, trucks, and all sorts of recreational vehicles; they came in anything that could make it up the road. At first it was only one or two at a time but then they came in caravans.

Most people couldn't make it in their car and stopped at lower elevations; others continued on foot. There were families with small babies, couples, and single men and women; many had their pets with them. One group was a team of survivalist, armed to the teeth with no intention of letting others take their belongings. There was a wide range of ages including several elderly.

The influx of survivors only lasted a fairly short time. Fewer people were able to get gas let alone travel and the roads had become a no man's land. Abandoned and burnt cars littered every road; wrecked by the initial quake, abandoned because they ran out of gas, dead, or simply stolen. It was pure hell, it looked like something out of a Hollywood post-apocalyptic movie, unfortunately it was real.

The first to arrive were Beth and Ben, they were out camping on the river at a nearby National Park when the quake hit. Ben and Beth are very much like us. Ben was a stockbroker before the depression. He's a big guy easily 230 pounds but all muscle, he was clean-shaven but that didn't last long.

Ben is a funny man and like me has a quick wit and loves to use it, maybe that's why I liked him from the start. Beth is tall with incredible green eyes and as sweet as could be. They are a laid-back couple, it turns out they're our age as well, in their early fifties.

They had a simple motor home with all the comforts of

home and had some extras just in case. They were far better armed than we were but didn't have the food stores we did. We decided that first night that we would hook up with them and watch out for each other and share our resources. As we sat by the fire, I asked Ben where they came from and how they got there. Ben looked at Beth, shook his head slightly and with a long deep sigh he began.

"When my unemployment ran out, we decided to leave Salt Lake City and live full time in the motorhome as nomads working as camp hosts at various places to make ends meet. We had been staying at a nice park for a week when the quake hit, within days the park filled. Any place that you could fit anything was taken by the hordes of people that had left the surrounding cities to escape the disorder."

"Did the Park Rangers try to stop anyone from coming in?"

"No Peter, the Rangers were powerless to stop the influx, not that they even tried. Fortunately, I had topped off our motor home with diesel and propane before hitting the park so we decided to get out while we still could."

Ann asked, "So where did you go and how did you get here?"

"We headed south trying to get as far as we could from what was left of civilization, we came upon the forest service roads that led us here."

"Did you have any trouble getting here?"

Ben answered, "It was insane Ann; people were shooting anyone that got in their way or had what they wanted. I'm sure if we hadn't left when we had someone would have taken our home. As it was, we had to stand down a few people with our gun to make it out safely.

While we were passing near Monroe, Utah, we came upon a family of four by a small car that appeared to be broken down. They were outside their car with the hood up, roasting in the heat of the day when we pulled alongside them.

The guy waved us down and asked me for some water. By this time, we already knew not to trust anyone because of how desperate people had become, so Beth had got up grabbed the twelve-gauge shotgun and stood in front of the door at the ready."

Ann asked, "Were you scared Beth?"

"Yes, I was scared out of my mind, but I knew that if someone tried to come through the door, I was going to blow them away."

Ben continued, "You should've seen her, she was like Annie Oakley, standing there with that shot gun. While I was distracted talking to the guy, his wife came around the passenger side trying to sneak up on us. His wife opened the door of the motor home and found herself staring down the barrel of Beth's shotgun only inches from her face."

Beth laughed, "You should've seen her face, her jaw dropped, and she froze in her tracks. I told her to back the hell off or I would blow her head off. She backed off real fast crying about how sorry she was and that she was desperate to take care of her kids."

Ben continued, "After that they closed the hood, jumped in their car and sped away. Funny how suddenly their car worked just fine."

"You were lucky you didn't get killed."

Beth came back "No Peter, she was lucky she was not killed, if she had taken one more step it would have been her last."

Ben went on, "We found the more desperate people had become the more they were willing to commit acts of violence or deception to get what they wanted. You know the sad part was if they'd simply asked for help, we would've. After that we made our way out here."

It was getting late, and we retired to our motor homes and crashed for the night. Ann and I wondered who else would show up and what type of horror story they'd have.

About midday the next day an old class B Ford van showed up. Two girls stepped out and introduced themselves as Tammy and Sandy, they were maybe in their mid-thirties.

Sandy looked like a tomboy, with short hair, jeans and a tank top; I got the impression you didn't want to piss this girl off. Tammy seemed kind and sweet and more reserved.

We showed them around the camp then Ben and I helped Sandy get their camp set up. The rest of the girls got dinner ready by the fire. I thought to myself this was getting to be a routine and I was afraid it was going to happen many more times. That night while we were sitting around the fire, I asked them their story. Sandy decided to tell us their harrowing tale of their experiences and journey up here.

"The day before the quake we left Las Vegas to do some overdue camping. We were only planning on staying for two nights so we only had enough food for that time with only a little extra like chips and candy."

Tammy jumped in, "We had everything we needed for S'mores" and laughed lightly.

Sandy was not too happy about being interrupted; she looked at Tammy with the look you get from your mom when she didn't like what you did. Tammy pouted a little and ran her closed finger across her lips like she was zipping her lips closed.

Sandy continued, "I don't know what time it was, but I think it was after noon when the quake hit. Even as far from the fault as we were, we felt the ground shake quite a bit. It wasn't so bad that we couldn't stand on our feet, but Tammy did get sick from the motion, she always gets carsick while we drive.

"That old Ford van over there has a nice soft bed in back and a simple kitchen with a stove so we are warm and dry. There's no sleeping on the ground or cooking over the fire for us."

"Ford eh, a proud member of the order I see."

"What? What do you mean order?"

I looked at Sandy with this sly evil smile and began.

"I coined a new acronym for Ford, one that I think fits many Ford drivers so well."

"I've heard them all, Fix or repair..., Found on ..."

"Nope none of them, they are old and outdated, but still true. Mine is new and fits oh SOO well."

"Ford stands for, FORD, **F**raternal **O**rder of **R**etarded **D**rivers."

If looks could kill, Sandy gave me the coldest look. I guess she loves her Ford and didn't like being called retarded. Sandy shook her head with pursed lips in a disapproving way. It seems I was right, not someone you want pissed at you.

Sandy went on, "We were staying at Boulder Beach Campground on Lake Mead just off the highway, it filled up fast as people fled the cities. There was no order and at times we feared for our lives with drunks firing their guns and getting into fights.

Sometime on the second or third day after the quake, a large group rolled in and declared they're in charge. They said that everyone was to turn over anything of value including their keys, and that everyone now had to work for them or die.

That night they picked a bunch of girls and forced them to go with them. Tammy and I figured it was only a matter of time before they came for us. If those assholes even tried to tell us we were their property and that we had to "'service their needs'", I would've taken something completely off."

With that, we all laughed, and us guys grabbed ourselves and cringed knowing exactly what she meant.

"The next day we decided that we were not going to let that happen and made plans to get out. We waited for nightfall and when they picked their girls for that night, we figured it was time to go. I unbuttoned the top buttons of my shirt to distract the guard where they put our van, while Tammy snuck in to get it."

With this sly look in her eyes Tammy spoke up, "While I was there, I slashed every tire that I could so they couldn't come after us."

"Yeah that was good thinking on your part Tammy it probably saved our asses. I convinced the guard he was going to get lucky. I told him we had a bed in our van, with that he got our keys and we headed for it. He opened the big double doors on the passenger's side, and I got in first patting my hand on the bed. Meanwhile, I started unbuttoning more buttons on my shirt, and beckoned him to join me on the bed.

Before we got there, Tammy used our spare key to hide in front. He was so distracted by me when he climbed in, he didn't see Tammy, she hit him from behind and knocked him out. We stole his gun, tied him up, then dumped him on the ground like the trash he was. Tammy started the van and we took off. The men were so busy with the girls that they didn't hear us, so we were able to get out easily, never mess with an ex-cop."

Ann was not surprised that people could be that screwed up, she said, "You're so lucky to have gotten out of there; I sure hope none of them find us up here."

We continued to talk for a few more hours and even made some S'mores that the girls had brought.

It was around noon on the fifth day when a monster forty-foot diesel pusher pulled up. This average looking guy steps out and said his name was Ramon. My first impression of him was that he was a charismatic type, he said he was an artist. He was followed by a squirrelly looking guy who introduced himself as Sam.

Sam said he was a banker and it soon became clear that he was a bit of a loner. He kept to himself except around Ramon, maybe he was able to relate to him somehow. Both arrived from Albuquerque, after leaving town as soon as they heard the news about the west coast. Ramon said he knew it was Armageddon.

Ann suggested we catch fish for dinner that night and Ramon jumped up and exclaimed enthusiastically, "Fishing! I'll help." Sandy was all over that too so the three of us grabbed my gear and we headed to the lake to catch some. Ann took off with everyone else and they walked around the lake gathering whatever they could. Off the girls went talking about whatever girls do when they are alone.

You can learn a lot about someone waiting for a fish to bite. I've always felt I'm a good judge of character and I was finding I needed to rely on it more now. I got the feeling we could trust them. Besides, I'd have hated to tell Ann she was right. I would have heard her say I told you so, but did we really have any choice. It was something we were going to have to do much more from now on.

As the three of us returned to camp with only enough fish to feed us all, we passed by Ramon and Sam's rig. I was impressed by the look of it and saw a few things on the outside I didn't recognize. After handing the fish to Ann, I asked Ramon about what I saw on his rig.

I think Ramon was still unsure as to how much information he wanted to share with everyone, he simply responded he had made a few improvements, so I left it at that.

It turned out I was the only one there that ever gutted a fish before, and Ann never does it. We set up a nice prep line and cleaned the fish and handed them down line to get them ready to cook, everyone took their turn cutting them up.

It wasn't long before the incredible smell of trout cooking filled the air and my stomach started to growl. The eight of us worked well together that night, like we had known each other forever.

We enjoyed an unbelievable fish dinner that everyone chipped in on and enjoyed the quiet of the night. As I had with everyone else before, I asked Ramon and Sam if they would tell us their story.

Ramon began, "We don't have a horror story of our getting here. We have been Preppers for many years and have been planning for this for some time, including a couple dry runs to see how long it would take to get here. That bus behind us is a mobile Preppers unit set up for just this type of situation."

"What have you done to it?"

You could clearly see that Ramon was not comfortable

giving up top-secret information like that. I noticed and spoke up.

"I understand the need to keep as much information as possible from people you only just met today. It's important to keep good Op Sec on your rig, as us Navy boy's always say, "'lose lips sink ships.'"

Ramon replied, "You're right Peter I'm VERY hesitant to tell anyone about what I have in there, but this is different than before the quake. I would never see them again and never trusted my neighbor anyway he was an asshole.

Now it's eight of us out here needing to rely on each other much as we did tonight to make this great meal. We need to find a way to trust each other and in this situation that would mean showing each other what we have so we can better manage our resources."

"I couldn't agree with you more Ramon, Ann and I had this same conversation the night of the quake and came to an understanding, not necessarily an agreement."

Ann looked over at me with pursed lips and a scowl on her face.

Ramon smiled and said, "It's okay Peter oddly enough I agree with both of you. I don't like telling anyone what we have but, in this case, I believe I need to. Rather than telling you, it's easier to show you so follow me and I'll give you the grand tour."

Ramon turned and with a remote in his hand turned on the outside lights. It lit the area up like a Christmas tree. We got up and followed Ramon and Sam to their rig, Ramon began with the outside, as we walked down the passenger side Ramon lifted one of the underbelly storage compartments and the lights inside it came on automatically.

Ann poked at Ramon, "Show off."

"Thank you, Ann that was, what I was going for. This bay is my fuel cell. We installed this secondary underbelly mounted twenty-gallon propane tank. Here you see two more seven and a half gallon portable tanks all plumbed through these transfer valves."

Ben asked, "So how long will that propane last?"

"Without using the propane for hot water or heat, it will last over two years, longer if we cook outside on the grill or over the fire most of time. If we use it mostly for baking, it will last even longer."

Ramon pointed to the lower front corner of the bay and said, "The upside-down tote you see is a hybrid wind/hydro generator using a Fisher Paykel washing machine motor. It turns out that the motor that turns the drum makes a near perfect generator even at low speeds. I used the 80SP model because it starts producing at slower speeds and exceeds five hundred watts of power when it gets up to speed.

I asked, "What do you mean hybrid?"

Sam was the one who made it and replied, "The turbine is designed to use both wind or water to spin it. When mounted on the tote it can be placed anywhere like on a table or any flat surface. But if we're next to a stream with a three-foot fall, we use ever smaller three feet foot lengths of PVC pipe and shoot the water into a hydro turbine built into the same turbine that spins it in the wind."

I replied, "That's brilliant, you can use it anywhere then."

Ramon nodded and said, "That's right, and if we set it up at the top of a hill or cliff face, we get the roof effect and it runs even better. We made two of them so we can use one or the other, or both if conditions are right."

Ramon pointed to the roof and continued.

"That box on the roof contains five hundred watts of solar panels stored in it. The lid is a solar tracker that we can either use on top of the rig if we are in the sun or taken down and placed in full sun. We set the collectors up in a sunny location and the tracking system does the rest, plus there is five hundred more attached to the roof. As we continued around the back, the pole on the driver side is a telescoping Ham antenna, if there are no questions then let's go inside."

I was impressed, and put my hand on his back and said, "I like you...I think we could be good friends."

Ramon nodded his head slightly and put out his hand and as we shook hands said, "Thanks I'd like that."

As we entered his rig my eyes were drawn to the lights that were clearly, at least to me, part of an extensive control center. I raised my eyebrows and I grunted like a TV show tool guy.

Ramon noticed my response, smiled and said, "I see you noticed my command center."

"I did...WOW."

"Nice ain't she?"

As I stood there I tried to see if I could identify what I saw.

"Let's see now...this section monitors the power, with both analog and digital meters for voltage and amps, this one says solar at almost nothing coming in and batteries holding at a nice 13.4v DC. These ones are for wind, and this one is the hydro."

"Very impressive Ramon."

"Thanks Peter."

"How much total power do you produce?"

"Running at peak, with all three producing, it can exceed two kilowatts of power."

"Holy shit! That's enough to power three of our rigs, full time."

It seemed Ramon was starting to understand the need to work together and said,

"That's right...hey that gives me a thought. Why don't we circle the rigs like the pioneers did their wagon trains against the Indians, but in our case to keep out the zombies instead?"

We laughed so hard on that one. It felt good after the last few days.

As if we planned it, Ben and I said, "I'm game."

Sandy replied, "Hell yeah."

I continued going over the panel.

"Now I see this is your comm's area. Dude you have a Ranger RCI69FFB 400 watts Modulation SSB 10 Meter Radio."

"Yep it has over four hundred watts of USB, LSB, AM and FM radio."

"Nice...oh and a nice scanner too. I like that."

"It's the Uniden BCT 15X, it scans everything, air, ham, weather, all of it, over nine thousand channels."

"Sensors? You have this rig set up with sensors? Let's see now, there's motion, infrared, sound and light activated, and ...is that a radiation sensor? Really?"

"Of course, it is, I told you this is a serious Prepper's Rig."

"That may just come in handy sooner than later when one of those nuke plants out there fails and fail, they will."

"This thing is great Ramon; I bow to your greatness."

I bowed slightly with my hand out and we had a laugh at my expense.

We continued back.

"When we picked it out, we wanted bench seats instead of a dinette and made both benches insect and rodent proof. We have over a year's supply of staples like rice, flour and sugar. As you can see the refrigerator is a residential type and there's a pantry for the simple pleasures in life, like spices and tons of staples."

Ben asked, "But won't the refrigerator burn up your propane?"

"No because we produce all the power we need to keep it cold, with four massive absorbed glass mat scissor lift batteries for storage. Those batteries provide the power for two 2500w 240/120Vac inverters, so we don't need to ever run the generator."

Ben remarked, "But the batteries won't last for more than a few years."

"Not really Ben, the glass AGM's will last ten years with no maintenance except for checking the terminals."

"We installed a two-way chest freezer in one of the underbelly bays. The day of the quake we filled up the freezers before we took off, so we have a few months of meat, but it will run out soon enough. What sucks is I couldn't hit the broad side of a barn, so hunting is not much of an option. We hoped we would find other people with those resources or skills."

"Well Ramon you're in luck, Ben here has an arsenal so we will be able to defend ourselves; you have more staples than either of us, but we have the means and skills to get fresh meat. Plus, we have enough seeds for everything we need and then some."

Sandy said, "We don't have much like that to add but we sure can carry our weight, and you really don't want to be in front of Tammy with a rifle."

Ben said, "No matter who else finds their way up here, if eight of us stay together we will be just fine."

"Tomorrow let's get busy arranging our rigs in a large square with the fire pit in the middle."

Ben added, "Alright Peter, my bet is we are going to be here a while so maybe we could enclose all four rigs with logs from the ground up with only some windows exposed. We can even make shutters to cover the windows for storms and security."

Chapter 3: Circling The Wagons

I figured a simple design was the best, so I took the lead.

"We can use enough logs to completely enclose the exterior. Then fashion large log doors from saplings to complete the structure and finish the entire area like an old west fort."

Shaking her head Sandy said, "Boys always wanting to build something. What makes you think you can build something like that, it's not like you were around in those days?"

I smiled and looked over at Ann, she was smiling back with this little laugh.

Ann had to respond to that, "You don't know Peter very well, trust me if he says he can build something, he can."

Beth beamed, "And I'm so happy for that, these guys are going to build us a fort, how cool is that? What can us girls do to help?"

"You girls can start cutting a trench around the whole thing about two feet deep while the rest of us will go hunting for the right logs."

Four tall poles were set in the ground about six feet apart as a square in the middle to make a top center part of a simple roof structure. Next, we lashed those to four strong corner posts using smaller poles, then after some cross supports we covered the entire structure with tarps. A large opening was left in the center of the roof to allow smoke from the fire pit to escape. The four center poles also allowed us to suspend things over the fire at any height for cooking and smoking.

"Peter, I don't think we're going to have this place to ourselves for long. I'm sure if we found it so will others."

"Regrettably Tammy I'm certain you're correct that you guys will only be the first ones."

Over the next couple of days, we didn't see anyone new, but it was enough time to close in the fort. Then the influx started, some in groups others were alone. Most of the motorhomes were older ones, because many of the newer ones don't have the clearance to make it. There were several folks who arrived in those nice RV trailers with high clearance, but the road was just too much for most trailers. There sure were lots of tents.

Among the new arrivals was a small group of people on foot. Their leader was a big black guy who said his name was John, and that they were from Tucson, AZ. This guy had the deepest voice you have ever heard, and despite his intimidating look, in time we learned he was one of the kindest people we had ever met.

In his past life John was a cop before the quake and was on duty the day it hit. He had not been able to get to his family and lost them all, so he was alone. In his travels he met the others in his group and they just headed up far away from the mayhem.

John was standing watch over the road leading to camp with one of his fellow travelers, Allen. They had only been on watch for a few hours when he saw someone coming up the road. John told Allen to keep an eye on them while he came and got me. He came running up to our compound to tell us.

"Peter come quick we have some new arrivals and they look like they are in bad shape."

Thanks John, you return to your post and send Allen back with them, we will help them here in camp.

Before John could even turn around, Ann grabbed several containers of water and took off to help, with John trailing her. I stayed behind to get ready for our new guests.

Ann was the first to reach them, all they had was the clothes on their back, no food, no water, nothing, they were in bad shape.

"Hi, my name is Ann, and welcome to our little oases, first things first I bet you need some water."

They grabbed the water and inhaled it.

"Please follow me and I'll take you to what we like to call the fortress you see up there, you can get some food, more water and rest to start with."

"Hi Ann, my name is Allen, and this is my wife Sheryl, and these are our kids."

Allen stood a whopping five feet three with an attitude to match it; he had short brown hair and said he was a carpenter but hasn't seen much work these days, while Sheryl is a red head who towered over Allen. We soon learned that Sheryl had a short fuse.

Ann replied, "Nice to make your acquaintances we are almost at our compound where my husband Peter is getting some food ready for you, he will help you in any way he can."

"Thank you Ann."

"Don't thank me I haven't done anything but bring you some water."

Sheryl exclaimed, "That was the one thing we needed most."

It only took a few minutes for the new group to arrive. By then I had several MRE's pulled out for them to choose from. I opted for MRE's because they are quick and easy meals ready to eat, hence the name.

Ann introduced them to me, "Here they are Peter, this is Allen and his wife and kids."

"Hi, my name is Peter and we have several MRE's to pick from, feel free to dig in. They are not the best food in the world, but it is something quick."

Sheryl answered, "I don't care what it is as long as it is food, thank you. It has been several days since we had anything but water from a creek."

"After you have had a chance to get some food in you, we'll see what else we can do for you guys."

"Thank you, Ann, you're so kind."

"I think you will find that to be the case with most of the people here."

Sheryl was devouring ravioli in red sauce while sitting near the fire when she finally started to open a bit.

"Oh My God it feels so good to be warm again. It has been a week since we have had a fire. The last time we did, the fire caught the attention of others and we had to abandon our supplies when we heard a bunch of loud people approaching. Allen stayed back to see if they would move on, but they didn't so we took off."

"Well Sheryl you are safe for now and everyone here will help out as they can. Why don't I introduce everyone here? Going around the fire to my left is Ben and his wife Beth, Tammy and her wife Sandy, then there is Ramon and his wife Sam."

Clearly unhappy with my comment Sam was a bit taken back and quipped.

"We are not a couple; we are not that kind of friends."

"You protest way too much Sam."

"Funny guys, no we are really just lifelong friends."

"Okay so that's everyone in here at least, there are a whole bunch more outside our walls that you can meet later. Why don't you tell us a bit about you guys?"

"Well my name is Allen; I was a carpenter before this mess."

"This is my wife Sheryl."

Tammy replied, "It's nice to meet all of you."

Motioning to his left Allen went on, "Our three kids here are Ken, Kate and Karl; they are five, six and seven respectively."

"That is cool, each of them started with a K."

"Yeah Ann, it was Sheryl's idea."

Beth asked, "So how did you guys make it here? There're a lot of bad people out there you had to get past."

By this time word of their arrival made its way through the camp and the fort had filled up fast. Everyone wanted to hear the latest word from the outside. Many brought food and clothes to give to them.

Allen spoke up, "We were in Flagstaff Arizona when the quake hit, and it shook us up a bit and mostly destroyed our home. At least we were still able to be inside, so we had a place to stay and were able to get news of what had happened. I was shocked by the level of destruction that far away, when we heard that the west coast was gone for good, we knew we were in trouble.

It didn't take a rocket scientist to see that the country was not going to be able to make it through this intact, so we started planning our next move. Many in town had already looted the stores so most of them were already empty when we got there. We filled up the minivan with what we could find, we loaded our camping gear and anything else we could get in, or on the van.

We headed east on I-40 hoping to make our way to family in New Mexico when we came upon a roadblock near the Petrified Forest National Park. There was no way to get past the roadblock. I tried to turn around to get away from them but found they had come up behind us with AK47's pointed at us.

A large militia group had taken control of the parks headquarters and Visitors Center and stopped travelers on the highway as they approached it. Whenever anyone fell into their snare, they confiscated everything of value, and forced everyone into slave labor. There were always armed men standing over of us like a prison work detail.

The group was drafting any males over sixteen to become part of their army whether you wanted to or not. Everyone else was forced to work for them to support their army doing whatever their leader saw fit. I worked in the motor pool washing vehicles and doing other maintenance, I was making plans to get us out, to that end I made sure one truck was full of gas.

The truck was an old one with two fuel tanks and easy to hot wire. After a week there I saw an opportunity to get out. Late that night, like most nights, the men had been drinking heavily so most of them were drunk out of their minds. The day of our planned escape I was able to disable several vehicles to block the rest, this gave us enough of a head start on them that they couldn't catch us.

We made our way out of the main compound area and into the motor pool without being seen. Then we got in the truck that I had strategically parked facing the gate and we hauled ass out of there. We crashed the gate as we left the park, the men at the gate were firing at us but they were too drunk to hit anything.

We traveled east on Interstate 40 until just before daybreak when we reached Gallop, New Mexico. This was only a few miles from where our family lived but what we saw before we got there broke our hearts. The city lay in ruins, some buildings were still burning when we arrived, and there was not a soul to be found. Cars were strewn about the streets some of them burnt others laying on their tops or sides; whatever hit this town did so and moved on. It was an eerie place, like death had just passed through.

We found a residential area that had not been destroyed but was abandoned. A couple houses had gas cans for a mower, so we were able get some gas; we even found some canned food.

We spent the night there and rested, with no lights or fire; we figured someone could come along like us and we didn't want to be seen. Our brother lived north of Gallop, so we headed up US 491 only to find town after town in the same shape.

The next night as we approached a small town, we could see a dim light in one of the houses. We stopped several houses back and I approached quietly on foot to see who was inside. I almost messed myself when I looked in the window. Here was this gun right in my face and someone yelling at me to put my hands up, so I did as I was told. I could see he was not alone; his wife and kids were peeking around a corner. I told him I meant him no harm and asked only to be allowed to move on.

The man saw my wife and kids outside and lowered his gun and told us to get in quick and to put the truck out of sight in the garage. We shared some of the food we had, and we ate a nice meal that night. I asked him about the destruction we had seen, and he said most of it was by the people that lived there."

Allen described what John; the dad passed on to him.

"In city after city there was rioting; the stores were broken into, stripped of everything of value then set on fire. I was in Albuquerque when the quake hit, though we felt the quake, it only did minor damage.

Over the next couple of days, it became clear that the government had lost control and called out the National Guard. It turns out that the commander of the New Mexico National Guard was also the leader of the largest militia group in New Mexico. Long ago the leader of the militia joined the National Guard and became the commander of the local armory in order to gain access to the keys to the toys.

He ordered his followers to also join the Guard and all of them made up the local unit and slowly replaced any non-followers by lying and getting them kicked out. Then when the government called out the Guard there was no one to oppose them. They were both the Guard and the militia, which enabled them to take control of everything.

Tanks rolled into the city firing randomly and killing scores of people just trying to get away. The bridges in and out of the city had been destroyed, everyone that didn't make it out fast enough was stuck there.

It was difficult but we were able to get out in time. We headed as far away as we could and didn't care where we were going. That night we could see Albuquerque burning in the distance and knew at that time it was all over, the world we knew and loved was gone. Eventually we made our way north and here we are."

Allen continued their story,

"That night we took turns standing watch and got the first good night's sleep in a long time. We traveled by night without lights so not to be seen and continued north trying to reach my brother. We didn't get far before we could see lights at a roadblock ahead. We pulled off the highway and made a large loop around the roadblock the last few miles to my brother's home. When we arrived, we found it was burned to the ground and their house was gone. We could only hope they made it out safe.

We used to camp up here as kids so when we left my brother's we headed here. We made it part of the way before we ran out of gas and continued on foot. As we approached that big camp below here, we were able to see and hear the them before they saw us.

We easily made our way around them without being seen. I already knew what they were like and had no intention of getting involved with any marauders after that nightmare in the park. It took some time to make our way up here; we hoped it would be deserted."

Allen laughed and added, "I sure got that wrong," everyone else laughed as well.

Chapter 4: The Militia Has Arrived

The last to make it to our camp was what appeared to be a large paramilitary company wearing fatigues and riding on ATV's. Almost everyone here had encountered militia in their treks and most had to run for their lives to get away. That's why we took several precautions to be ready for them.

One of those precautions was to post a watch on the overlook scanning the valley below so we wouldn't be caught off guard. Ramon and Sam were on the afternoon watch that day, when Sam spotted something moving.

"Hey, Ramon, what's that over there on the switch back on the other side of the valley up by our mile marker four?"

"I can't tell Sam it's too far away, pass me the binoculars please."

"Ramon, please tell me I didn't see what I think I saw."

"Sorry Sam you're right, it's a convoy of ATV's carrying a bunch of guys in fatigues, sound the alarm Sam it looks like a militia is on the road to camp."

We had wired up a communication system with the lookout so that the watch could inform us if they saw something. It was an old sound powered phone that Ramon had as part of his Preppers gear. A Navy sound powered phone set up comes with two phones and spools of wire so you can rig it anywhere. It's powered by sound; no batteries are needed.

My stomach dropped when the growler we set up in our fort squawked to life telling me someone was calling; it was Sam informing us of the approaching column; Ben and I alerted everyone else. Everyone knew what to do because we practiced this for some time. We grabbed our weapons and headed down the road to the traps we set at choke points for just this event.

"Ben let's get to the observation point and see what we're up against."

"Alright Peter I will meet you there; I need to get my gun."

"Hey, grab both of mine, too will you?"

"Sure, will Peter."

When we got to the lookout, Ramon and Sam were watching the convoy. We had marked every mile of the trail on the opposite side of the valley to tell us how far away they were. The time it took for them to reach the next marker told us how fast they were moving based on travel time from one marker to the next.

"What do you have Ramon?"

"A convoy was passing mile marker four when we saw them. They are almost to mile marker five now Peter. That means they are going around ten miles per hour. That puts them at the bottom of the valley near dark."

"Thanks Ramon, you guys have done a great job. I figure they'll most likely stop and make camp and spend at least one night at the stream. We'll need to watch them to see when they leave. If they continue traveling at the same speed it will put them up here by midday if they leave the stream at first light. We'll need to keep a close eye on their movements including watching for scouts that may come up looking ahead of the column."

Sam said, "I would put money on that Ben because that is exactly what I would do."

As we expected they stopped for the night at the stream, we sent everyone back to camp.

"Ramon, I want you to go tell everyone to stand down, but to be back at their post first thing in the morning and to be ready at any time."

"Ok I'll take care of that Peter."

After a long night vigilantly watching the valley, Henry and Bill, who had the early watch, noticed movement below. Henry was a burly man with a jolly laugh. Before the quake Henry was a stonemason from just north of the Grand Canyon. Bill is a little guy with a cheesy smile from somewhere in Utah, before the quake he was janitor at a school.

Ben and I were already up so we grabbed Ramon and Sam and headed to the lookout to check if there was any activity below.

"Bill, what's happening down there?"

"We just saw the first movements a minute ago, so we didn't have time to call you before you got here. It looks like they just got up and don't appear to be getting ready to leave yet."

Ben said, "My bet is that they'll stay a couple of nights resting."

"You may be right Ben, but I bet they'll be sending scouts out during the day to see what is ahead of them."

Ben asked, "What do we do if the scouts make it here and see us Peter? If we detain them the rest will come looking for them and won't be happy. If they find us and go back, they may come in hot."

"That, my friend, is a good question, but one thing is certain, we can't harm them unless they strike first."

Henry called out, "Well Peter it's one we'll not have to wait long to find out, a couple ATV's are heading up. Wait, it looks like the entire column is heading out, seems we're all wrong."

"Well the good side of that is we don't have to deal with an advanced scout. They're moving slowly so we'll have at least a few hours before they make it up here. Get the word out so everyone can man their posts. Henry you and Dan head down to the rockslide trigger and get ready to release it if I give you the signal. Oh, and just in case you don't know, if they shoot me there is no need to wait for my signal."

We got a bit of a laugh out of that; it helps in tense situations. Just then we heard a large explosion, we looked down the valley and saw that they had blown up the bridge crossing the stream at the bottom of the valley. I looked at Ramon and told him to hurry and get everyone ready.

"Yes, sir we are on our way."

"Ben I'm glad you're here; I've dreaded this day. I hope we don't need to drop those boulders on them it wouldn't be a pretty sight."

"I know Peter, but we have to do what we have to do."

Every able body was given a weapon and formed a line down the road. They were hiding behind boulders we had placed along the road for that purpose.

As they were getting ready, I said, "We have both the high ground and the element of surprise on our side so let's use it wisely."

"Peter it looks like the scouts are about ten minutes ahead of the rest of them."

"Okay Ben let's get down to the first choke point to meet them, the rest will be in the kill zone and at least most of them will be inside the boulder fall trap."

"Alright Peter, are you ready for this?"

"I am; I just hope this doesn't turn into a blood bath for any of us."

"I second that Peter."

In the month or so before, we had plenty of time to rig the road as a kill zone. There was also a good choke point just below camp where we set explosives. A little further down, just past a small curve, we rigged tons of rock to fall along a hundred yards of the road. If triggered they'd fall and kill any intruders and prevent others from coming any further.

I stood just above the choke point with the explosives just below my position. As I stood there, I could hear the ATVs coming up the road. When they came into view, I saw a .50cal machine gun mounted on the front ATV. I stepped out on the road.

"Stop right there and identify yourself," I called out as I held out my hand in a stopping gesture.

The ATV stopped and I could see the front passenger speaking into a handheld radio while the back one stood up and manned the .50 cal.

A few minutes later another ATV pulled alongside the first one and stopped. That one also had a .50cal mounted on the roll bar. A few minutes later a third ATV pulled up and stopped. The rest of the column held back, luckily most of them were in the kill zone.

One guy got off the third ATV and made it a point for me to see him lay his weapon on the seat and started walking our way. First, he held up his jacket while turning around, then with his hands in the air he approached.

He called out, "As you can see, I'm unarmed, we come in

peace; we didn't think anyone else was up here."

I held my weapon above my head and motioned to Ben to come take it. He came down took it and returned to his post.

Before he left, I quietly said, "Ben, you know what to do if they shoot."

"I do, but please be careful Peter."

I laughed and asked in a sarcastic way, "You think? But thanks for stating the obvious."

I turned and headed toward the man, and in the same manner he used, showed him I was unarmed.

As I approached, I said, "I think we can both lower our hands now, no one is going to shoot if you really do come in peace."

We both dropped our hands and met halfway. I reached out my hand and introduced myself.

"Hi there, my name is Peter and I'm as close to a leader here as we have, to whom do I have the pleasure of talking to?"

The man replied, "My name is Fred, but my men address me as Sarg, but you can call me Fred any time I'm away from them."

Fred was average height, and like me, had a few extra pounds; on meeting, we shook hands.

"Well I would say it is nice to meet you Fred but under the circumstances I'm not sure it is nice for either of us."

There was something about Fred that made me feel relaxed, maybe it was the way he approached unarmed. I motioned for Ben to join us but to leave our weapons behind, as he arrived, I introduced him.

"This is my right-hand man and friend, Ben."

Fred reached out and shook Ben's hand.

I continued, "Almost everyone here has had bad encounters with militia in their travels, so they're edgy right now."

Fred nodded in acknowledgment and replied.

"I understand, we too have encountered some of them and have had to defend ourselves to get away. I promise you we want nothing to do with ordering anybody around or taking what you've got; my team and I just want to live our lives in peace."

Ben being the type to speak his mind just had to ask, "If you and your guys are not looking to take over anyone, then why, if you don't mind me asking, all the armament? And what made you decide to assemble a militia?"

Fred shook his head slightly, took a deep breath and replied.

"Where do I start? First off let me make this perfectly clear we're not a militia or army; we're just well-equipped Preppers prepared to defend ourselves."

Fred turned around and called out, "Brandon front and center, and leave your weapon behind."

A stocky guy in fatigues comes up, "Yes sir Sarg."

"This is Brandon; he is my right-hand man as well."

"Hi Brandon, my name is Peter, and this is my friend and second in command Ben."

Brandon reached out and shook both our hands; let me tell you this guy had a grip like a vice.

Fred continued, "We've known for a long time that society was frighteningly fragile. We were certain it wouldn't take much to push it over the edge and anarchy would rule. To plan for it we spent many years recruiting the right people that are of the same mind and we spent thousands of dollars for armaments. We spent even more on buying the gear we'd need to live out here for an indefinite period."

"You might be surprised to find that many of us up here were also of the same mind. Many have been preparing for it for years as well. You know Fred I think everyone here will be more at ease if we all lowered our weapons."

Ben spoke up, "I'm sure you're right Peter that everyone will feel much more at ease with out the guns being pointed at each other."

Fred nodded his head, then turned around and barked out, "Everyone lower your weapons and step away from the .50cal's."

They looked perplexed.

Clearly perturbed, Fred hollered out, "I said... lower.... your weapons... and don't make me say it a third time."

They complied.

I did the same, and everyone else lowered their weapons as well.

Fred started out, "We've come a long way and are awfully tired and we don't want any trouble. Is there somewhere the four of us can sit and talk? Then after we talk, if you still feel the same, we'll get back on our rigs and look for someplace else."

After a short pause Fred continued, "How about I make you an offer in good faith."

"What do you have in mind?"

"To show you we mean you no harm, I will order my men to leave their weapons on their ATVs and leave them behind. Your men can still have their weapons if it will put them more at ease; this is after all, your turf."

"Okay that sounds fair. How about you and Brandon, join Ben and I, back at our place where we can get to know each other?"

Fred nodded then keyed the mic on his shirt and said, "Bring up the column, and I want everyone to holster their weapons, and DO NOT, I REPEAT, DO NOT man the 50cal's."

It was a bit of an uneasy sight as one rig after another came around the corner. All of them had the .50cal mounts on them, but only a few had them in it. They came to a halt back with the rest. Now all of them were in the kill area.

Sarg turned to Brandon and told him, "You go down and pass the word to have everyone leave their weapons on their ATVs. I want them to get up, walk around, and mingle; I want them to try to get to know everyone because we could be here awhile. Then have Eric grab some cases of MRE's and hand them out to whoever wants some. Then you get back here, and we'll head up."

"Yes sir. I'll get right on it."

"Fred your men can run that up to camp on one of the ATV's if it will help."

"Thanks Peter, it'll make distributing them much easier. On second thought Brandon you ride that up and meet us at his place."

"Ben why don't you go with him while Fred and I walk up."

Brandon passed the orders to Eric and oversaw Fred's orders.

Eric called out to everyone, "Alright you goons dismount your rigs and leave your firearms on them. Ken you have your team bring up the food supply ATV to the camp and hand out the MRE'S to anyone that wants them. Randy and Cindy, you stand by and guard the rest of our gear."

Randy asked, "Should we be armed?"

Brandon grabbed his mic, "Brandon to Sarg...."

Sarg responded, "Go ahead."

"I need your opinion on an issue; do you want Randy and Cindy to be armed while they guard our gear?"

Fred looked over at me and I nodded telling him it was okay with me.

Fred keyed back, "Yes but don't fire unless you are fired upon."

Fred turned back to me and said, "Thank you for showing me the trust."

"You're welcome, let's get going." I then turned and called out to our guys.

"I don't expect anyone to use your weapon unless you are forced to. Everyone else head back to camp and show our guests around." Henry and Dan stayed behind at the trigger just in case.

Fred replied, "I'm sure that put many here at ease."

Then Fred and I turned and started walking up to our compound where Sandy, Tammy and Ann were anxiously waiting with the doors closed. As we approached, I called to them to open. We sat around the fire and started our détente.

"Where did you and your men come from?"

Fred replied, "Most of us lived in and around a small town outside of Flagstaff, Arizona, we hadn't planned on coming here, we expected to be somewhere else, somewhere even more remote."

It wasn't long before Brandon and Ben arrived. While the four of us talked, the girls put together some food. Then as we enjoyed a good hot meal, we continued our conversation.

"I bet it has been awhile since you have had a good home cooked meal Fred."

"You sure got that right Peter, MRE's are good to feed you but not comfort food... Ann everything was great I loved it all."

Brandon asked, "So Peter would it be too intrusive to ask your story?"

"No that's fine; I will make it short and simple. I'm retired Navy and have seen many things and places. We left Washington a few years ago and have been 'Free Birds' for a few years now."

Fred looked at me with a blank stare and asked, "Free Birds, what do you mean by that?"

I smiled and replied, "You know what Snowbirds are don't you?"

"Yeah it's the silver haired retirees spending their retirement riding around in their monster rigs."

"Right. Well we're doing the same thing except we don't have gray hair, so we are 'Free Birds' instead."

Fred smiled and replied, "Funny I like that."

"As I was saying, we were enjoying my retirement until this all hit."

"What about you Brandon, tell us a bit about you."

"Well I was a Sergeant in the Marines Special Forces for a few years and decided I didn't like some of the orders I was given. I carried them out then got out as soon as I could. And before any of you ask, no I don't care to elaborate."

"Not to worry Brandon, we won't ask."

As a sailor on a ship carrying nuclear weapons, I had the opportunity to work closely with marines. I knew one way to build camaraderie with them, so I decided to share a story of my time working with marines on the ship.

"As a Marine I think you will get a kick out of an experience I had with the Marine Detachment Captain on board my first ship. I got to know the First Lieutenant pretty good when I had to weld his safe back to the deck after it broke loose in heavy seas and chased him around his office.

Sometime later he called me at my shop and asked me to meet him in a certain passageway on board. The passageway we met in had an escape hatch for the nuclear warheads we stored (that is if we had them, I could neither confirm nor deny the presence of nukes on board our ship). The Marines regularly ran drills on someone trying to get to them and when they came running everyone else had to get out of their way.

I met the LT in the passageway, and he told me to kill as many Marines as I could and handed me a broom and said it was my weapon. I felt an evil smile come across my face and said sure. There was an open hatch in that same passage that went down into a berthing, so I hid behind it. The LT stood behind me and we waited. It wasn't long before we heard the call for the Marines to do their thing and we heard the clear sound of combat boots stomping as the Marine that was assigned to check on the escape hatch approached.

When the Marine made his way into the passage, I stood up with the broom aimed at him and called out, 'Bang you're dead'. The marine looked at me like I was nuts, but his Captain pointed at him and told him to drop to the deck where he stood. He did as he was told. Now he was supposed to radio in that the hatch was secure and when he didn't, they radioed him. Of course, there was no reply. It didn't take long to hear two more sets of boots hitting the deck.

This time they stopped and slowly peeked around the corner and when the one closest to me came into sight I pointed my trusty broom at him and said, 'Bang you're dead' then immediately turned to the other side said the same to the other Marine. Their Captain ordered both to drop right there which meant they had to lie in the middle of the passageway.

Before the slaughter was done, I had killed ten Marines, then I unexpectedly felt the barrel of an M16 poking me in my side from below. Needless to say, I dropped my broom and held up my hands. Those poor Marines, as I was leaving, I heard the LT screaming at them about how the hell did one stupid squid kill ten of them."

Everyone laughed but I thought Brandon was going to fall off his seat; Brandon said, "That sounds like something a Marine LT would do."

We continued to talk for a few hours, and I concluded that Fred was a visionary. Like many of us here he knew the day would come that the government would lose control, and he wasn't going to get caught with his pants down. He had recruited his band of like-minded people over the years and they had spent those years preparing for this time, just the type of person I wanted on our side.

Fred said, "I've another proposition for you Peter, one

that would be a benefit for all."

"I'm listening."

"From what I could see you weren't well-armed in comparison to any of the militia we have seen. It looks like you could use someone to help defend this incredible location if someone comes up here that is hell bent on taking it over."

"We're a bit more prepared than you know, but I'm interested in what you've got to offer."

"In return for you allowing us to join you here by the lake, but separate from the rest, we'll supplement your watches and help you defend it against invaders. We'll not be a drain on your food, as we have plenty of our own."

"That sounds like a hell of an offer, but I cannot make such a decision for everyone. As I said before our biggest fear is that some power-hungry militia would make their way up here and take over. Many here have lost friends or loved ones to groups and may not like your presence here."

"There is little I can do to quell that fear, but we sure can try."

Brandon spoke up, "That was what the militia down below wanted us to do; we wanted nothing to do with that, so we left. I'll tell you they're not too happy about how we departed either."

"That leads me to an important question that I'm sure many will want to hear. Fred, how did your team make their way up here with that group of thugs below?"

"That is a long story."

"Well we have all the time in the world." We laughed.

By now many of his men and our residents had already joined us in our compound and were listening closely to everything we talked about. The entire compound was filled with people eager to hear what was happening.

Fred started telling everyone their story, "We had planned for this for years and had found the perfect isolated location that we planned to go to when the shit hit the fan. We ran drills and knew every inch of the area so we would be ready when it happened. We spent years putting together the right men and women we'd need to make it without any outside aid and thought we were ready."

"What do you mean you 'thought' you were ready?"

"We'd made our way to our site and thought we'd be isolated, only to find that some other well-armed group had the exact same idea and had beaten us to it."

Sandy asked, "So why didn't you just stay there and team up with them."

"The other group wanted nothing to do with more people to deal with. When they saw us coming, they came out with their guns and told us to turn around or we would be shot, so we did."

Ben asked, "So why here?"

"Both of our alternate sites were also taken, and this was our last option."

Sandy, who was probably the biggest skeptic, didn't trust any militia. I don't think anyone could blame her, she wanted to know more, and she drilled Fred.

"How did you get here past the militia below, and did they follow you?"

Fred replied, "After we left our last site we headed here, when we came upon the group below, they wanted us to join them, but we had to follow their leader's orders. Those included holding people against their will and taking their belongings."

Brandon added, "Those assholes thought that this new world was for them to make as they pleased and to hell with anyone that didn't like it, they killed anyone that talked back. There was no way any of us were going to do that, we started to leave but they had different ideas. Fortunately for us we had practiced for this contingency and had our guns at the ready, so we could fight at a moment's notice."

Fred went on, "When they tried to stop us, we opened fire with the .50cals on them and took off. Brandon here, who always has my back, was riding shotgun with me, when they fired at us, he turned around and fired a grenade from his rifle into their arsenal. You should've seen it, there was a huge explosion which stopped them all in their tracks."

Excitedly Brandon exclaimed, "Sarg and I were in the last ATV and they were shooting at us because we were trying to leave. I stood up on the back of our ATV and trained my grenade launcher on their ammo dump and fired."

Fred continued, "It was quite the sight, (throwing his hands in the air) KABOOM their ammo started exploding, BOOM, BOOM. They started scrambling and taking cover because there was shrapnel flying everywhere and bullets going off in all directions."

"Did you kill them?"

"I don't know how many we got but they started it, all we wanted was to leave."

Sandy yelled out, "Good for you I hope you killed all of them."

Fred continued, "Anyway we hauled ass out of there and took a convoluted route up here. We found an alternate route up a different set of forest service roads that also met this one, so we made our way that way. To answer your second question Sandy, about if they followed us, I hope the answer is no, but it sure is going to be hard for them to get up here now, not impossible just hard."

Brandon added, "To make sure that we were the last to make it up we either blew up or otherwise destroyed the road behind us to ensure that groups or anyone else couldn't make it up here any time soon. We're well armed with lots of explosives, guns, and even a few RPGs. We are armed to the teeth, ready, willing and trained to defend ourselves or any group we feel a part of."

"We saw that; we saw you blow up that bridge at the bottom of the valley."

Sandy added, "I sure hope that is the case. If you truly want nothing to do with ordering us around you will be welcome here."

Fred replied, "If you guys welcome us, we'll do everything in our power to ensure that other groups NEVER make their way here while we are here; if they do, we will fight to the death to defend our ground."

We spent the rest of the night going over all sorts of things. We had a better understanding of where we were coming from. I called for a meeting the next day with everyone so we could go over if and how the newcomers would fit in. With any luck anyone that had encountered militia that wanted to dominate them would see that this was not the case. Hopefully I wasn't wrong about my sense of Fred's intentions.

That night Fred's men all slept on the ground by their ATVs in their sleeping bags and dined on MRE's. This was partly because it was late before it was decided they would even be staying and partly because of the amount of work it takes to set up even a temporary camp.

Chapter 5: Our First Vote

The next morning after breakfast everyone arrived so we could put Fred's proposition before the group and see how it would fly. It didn't take long for everyone to settle in for the meeting. You could hear all sorts of small conversations. The tension in the air was high, some were afraid that this was a prelude to occupation.

I called out, "Quiet please... can I have everyone's attention please?"

The area slowly fell quiet, Ben and I stood in front of the crowd with Fred and Brandon by our sides.

"I hope everyone has had a chance to get to know our guests. I personally believe that like us they're of the same mind as many here. They may dress like militia, but they're anything but militia, they too are Preppers. They felt our society was on borrowed time and took steps to be ready for it. After talking with them, I hope most of you've come to the same conclusion."

"What about the armament?"

"We'll take questions after I've finished going over what we've to talk about. But to answer your question Ramon, I'll ask a question. Who out there has their own arsenal now and wishes they had even more?"

I knew the answer to that question before I even asked it.

"If you had the money before this, many of you would also have lots more. Come on now don't be shy, let's see your hands."

Ben put up his hand and spoke up, "That includes me, how can you be upset about these guys being armed given many of you just used many of my weapons to defend us and still have them."

More and more put up their hands as they realized how hypocritical the question was.

"Ramon did that answer your question?"

I looked at Ben and mouthed, "Thanks Ben."

I turned back to the crowd.

"As I was about to say, they came here expecting it to be isolated and found us already here. It was just as much of a surprise for them finding us, as it was for us seeing that convoy of heavily armed men and women coming up the road.

We have come here looking for a safe place to survive and maybe build a better life in this new world. We know that life as we knew it is no more and we must make a new world on our own.

How many out there were more than happy to eat the MRE's they handed out? From my point of view these guys are no different than any of you. Ann and I had this place to ourselves, and now look at all of you. This same discussion as to who to trust has gone on each time someone new arrived.

You didn't see us telling any of you to go away, this is our lake. Instead we've helped clothe, house, and feed many of you, as you must those that have come after you when you could.

That has been the nature of our little community, we help those who come in and make them feel welcome. Now this well-equipped, and yes well-armed, group has asked to stay, and they have made a generous offer in return. I'll turn this over to Sarg now."

"Thanks Peter, first off let me thank you for coming and

hearing what we have to offer. I want to start out by saying that we're not a militia, we're simply well-equipped Preppers who've tried to be ready for anything."

Jade asked, "Then why do you wear those uniforms?"

"Uniforms serve a few uses; for one thing they create uniformity by everyone dressing equally. A more important reason is that it makes it easy to tell who is who, in a firefight.

I hope you'll find that our staying here is a win-win situation. In return for your generosity we'll defend this community with our lives the same, as you were willing to do. All we want in return is a location to set up our camp and live our lives in peace.

I understand that many of you've lost friends and loved ones to the militia groups out there and so have we. Like I said we're NOT a militia, we're just like many of you here now we are Preppers, that's it.

We knew life as we knew it was on borrowed time. My team and I spent years putting together everything and made plans to get out and live our lives in peace. Away from the people that would do anything to get to what you have. We're heavily armed because we want to stay alive same as you, like Ben already pointed out.

Like some of you we encountered that militia group below. They wanted us to join them and be a part of their army. We wanted nothing to do with that and told them so. That action cost several of our close friends their lives down there. We drove for days taking many back routes to get here and destroyed every bridge between there and here to ensure they couldn't find us.

Now we just want a place we can call home and are happy to build our camp on the other side of the lake, away from the camp here, if you'll have us. If not, we'll leave the first thing in the morning and continue looking for a place for us to live."

With Fred finished I figured I would open it up for questions,

"Alright then, are there any questions?"

You could hear many little conversations going on between groups of people, but no questions.

"If there are no questions, I put it up to a vote. Let me see the hands of those that are for allowing them to stay."

I was overwhelmed to see almost every hand go up.

"Those opposed?"

A small handful raised their hands.

"Then it's decided, Sarg you and your men are welcome to stay under the conditions we've already discussed."

A grateful Fred responded, "I thank every one of you for your hospitality and I promise you that you'll not regret your vote."

"All right everyone there are things that need to be done. Andy, I believe you're the section leader for watch tonight, can you come up here before you head out?"

Andy was a little guy with a big attitude, from Phoenix Arizona, and he made a great section leader. His life as a contractor enabled him to lead others.

"Sure Peter, I will as soon as I deal with something."

"Ramon I'd like to talk to you before you go, but I need to give Andy his marching orders for the night first."

"Okay I'll be right there."

"Andy I'd like for you to double up the watch tonight,

Sarg here will help you to make the arrangements. I'd like you to show him the ropes and he'll provide you with the other half of watch from now on. I want everyone to be armed the same as we are every night."

"But Peter do you really want to do that; we don't know any of them?"

"I know Andy but like I did with you I have a feeling I can trust them, and that they may someday save our bacon."

"Sure, thing Peter, I'll get right on that."

"Thank you, Andy, Sarg if you can have one of your leaders go with him to see what's needed to be ready for watch tonight, that'd be great."

Sarg replied, "That sounds like a plan Peter... Henry front and center."

Henry comes up to Sarg.

"Henry this is Andy; you work with him to set up the watch. He'll fill you in on the details. You two work together and make it happen, understand?"

"Yes Sir" and off they went.

"Whew!! Now with that done and out of the way, Ben can you go with Sarg and start checking out the other side of the lake for their camp?"

"Sure thing Peter."

Ramon was hanging out with some others talking, so I went over to him and put my arm around his shoulder in a guiding manner and said, Ramon lets you and I go for a walk."

"What's wrong Peter?"

"Nothing is wrong Ramon, first I want to say good job on catching that convoy coming down the other side of the valley, that was a good keen eye."

"Thanks Peter is that all?"

"No Ramon it's not, I noticed when I asked for hands of those opposed you raised your hand. May I inquire why you feel so strongly against them staying? I don't recall you telling me any horror stories about encountering any militia in your travels here."

"Can I be blunt with you Peter?"

"Always,"

"Then let me ask you a question? Why are you exposing us to this heavily armed group of people that we don't even know?"

"Well Ramon that is not an easy question to answer, I guess I can only call it instinct. I rely heavily on my instinct to get me through all kinds of stuff. I used it when everyone started to arrive here, I used it when Ann was ready to beat feet and get out of here for the same reason you just asked me. But here we are now with you being a total stranger to me not long ago and now I put my life in your hands today when we stood there on the road."

"But that is different you know me?"

"Not really, I didn't know you when you got here but I trusted you didn't I?"

"I guess so, but still how do we know if we can trust them?"

"We never really know we can trust anyone until the day comes that we have to put that trust to the test. That day truly came for you today Ramon and I'm happy I was right on trusting my gut with you, all we can do is take the leap and see how it goes."

"I guess I see where you are coming from, I'll give them the benefit of the doubt."

"Thanks Ramon, you have a nice night who knows you may find a friend among them. After all there are girls in his group," I said in a kidding manner.

"That's true Peter; I guess we'll see."

When I found Ben and Fred they were around the other side of the lake in a large clearing. We asked Fred if it would work and he said it would be fine.

When we returned to camp Fred brought his team to the spot and they started to get unloaded. Fred had his quartermaster Eric go over their setup with our guys while they helped unload the gear. Eric began by describing their ATVs.

"We have over a dozen custom ruggedized off-road vehicles; these things are decked out for rough off-road travel. They are like miniature pickups, some with a dump bed and all. All of them are equipped with snorkels on their intakes and risers on their exhausts for water travel.

Their suspensions are beefed up as well with a high clearance and extra-large tires to handle any terrain or large rocks in a stream. Most are four seaters, but a few are only made for two, most have trailers in tow. They all have a camouflage paint job to make them harder to spot from a distance, or from above.

All of them are equipped with winches in the front to pull them or others out of anything. There're great if they find themselves stuck or just want to go up or down a near vertical face. As you can see, they all have a mount for a .50cal machine gun, but we don't have enough for every one of them.

Every trailer carries at least 25 gallons of diesel in 5-gallon Jerry cans, so we have plenty of fuel. The engines can run on almost any type of fuel including used motor oil."

As Eric went on about the detailed information Fred turned to me and said,

"I hope you understand that this kind of information would be highly classified. You never tell anyone details about your operation, your assets or your strengths. I have instructed my guys to be open and honest with the people. I told them to answer their questions honestly in hopes of gaining their trust."

"I understand that makes you vulnerable, I think almost everyone will come around."

"Peter, we had several members of the team not make it before we left for whatever reason and lost a few getting here so we have some openings. Anyone that wants a job around here and does not have a good place to stay can have a job, food, and a warm bed in return for their assistance."

Several of the guys and a couple of the girls took him up on the offer. It took most of the day to get everything off loaded and set up but when it was done it looked like an Army command post.

I was curious about how Fred made his team. "So how did you pick your team?"

"It wasn't easy, but I found experts in every field we felt would be needed to make it in this crazy world. Most are ex-military; many seasoned Special Forces combat vets. We have a couple of medics, mechanics, scouts, and some snipers and of course some cooks; we even recruited a couple of doctors. My team is made up of both men and women but not in equal numbers and I made sure they were well qualified in their field.

As you can see some of the equipment includes three

modern military tents. They're the types that look like the old Quonset huts but made of a strong extra thick military grade vinyl. One unit is configured as a medical unit with the supplies needed to take care of almost any problem including combat surgery.

The second tent is my headquarters in the front half and quarters for Brandon and me in the back half. The third one is configured as a mess hall by day and a barracks for the team by night. They have cots to sleep on and zero degree sleeping bags."

"I bet this cost a fortune, where the hell did you come up with this stuff."

Sarg laughed and replied, "I got all three as a package deal, cheap from an army surplus auction. The tents came complete with the gear in hard shelled cases for easy transport, they even included multi-fueled heaters for each."

Ben asked, "But the heaters won't do you much good out here; they will run out of fuel."

Fred replied, "Sure they will, they even burn cut wood. Each tent and equipment fit into the trailers behind the ATVs for ease of transport. It's sort of like a rolling army post ready to be set up in less than a day."

I felt I was getting to know Fred and I was happy to have his team with us; I knew they would be an invaluable asset. Like any good leader I wanted them on our side and made sure that everyone made them feel welcome.

In the end more than a hundred people had made their way to our remote location, with the group made up of all sorts of people from every walk of life. Now sometimes I sit on my overlook watching the people going about their day and I wonder what I got myself into. They look to me for guidance and I have no idea what to tell them, I only know that the life we left back home was no more.

All of us are in the same boat and many have little but the clothes on their backs. Now the only thing we can do is try to work together to make our little corner of the world a livable place.

We knew we had to set some ground rules that would keep it livable for all, but I wanted nothing to do with being a cop. I had no problem explaining to people what we would need but I was not going to be a dictator and tell anyone what to do. We had no cops and no one telling anyone what they had to do or when to do it. And the one thing that Sarg and I never wanted to happen was for Sarg and his team to be cops. Their only function was to defend the camp from outsiders and help in hunting for food for all.

Ann and I decided to just concentrate on our little camp knowing that when or if the day ever came that someone wanted to take over and run the camp, as far as we were concerned it was theirs. We would just leave.

Chapter 6: Life in Camp

It seemed like an eternity had passed since the vote. Life in camp had settled down into a routine. Everyone went about their day doing whatever was needed to live. Time seemed to stop because there was no longer any reason to worry about what day it was anymore. Unfortunately, though, there were so many people living in camp it was becoming unpleasant.

One-night Fred, Ben, the girls and I were sitting around our fire just reminiscing about how things use to be.

"Fred things sure have changed since we first got here."

"I bet you're right Peter, it has changed even since I got here, I could only imagine what it was like before anyone else came here."

"It was like heaven; we were alone on this incredible heavily forested isolated lake with lots of fish and abundant wildlife surrounding it."

Ben added, "In some ways it still is, there're just a few more people."

"We're tens of miles off the beaten path with more twists and turns on this set of ever smaller forest service roads than I can count. Before the influx we figured we would stay here, it was an incredible location."

"We took so many roads to find this peace and quiet, we hoped this far back we wouldn't encounter anyone else. We would sit by the fire in the evening and could see the stars and enjoy the sounds of the night."

"I remember Peter some of the roads in were rough; it required us to disconnect the SUV instead of towing it to make it past them. We had to cross several streams with some sections that didn't even look like a road."

Ann added, "Us too Ben, you should've seen Peter he was walking in the stream several times to get us past them."

"Thanks Ann, that was something I could've forgotten and would never have missed it."

Ann quipped, "Stop whining you loved it here."

"Whining! No way, this is the kind of place you hope to find; and when you do you stay for as long possible. We were so happy when we made that last turn and there was the most beautiful lake we had ever seen, peeking through the trees."

Ben recalled, "The lake is not large, but it was so clear you could see the bottom twenty feet down. When we stood out on Fish Rock, we could see schools of trout swimming around; it made our mouths water just looking at them."

"You're so right but now the fish are almost gone, and you can't see the bottom anymore."

"I know Beth it's disgusting and the hunting, it used to be the deer would wander in and out of camp without any fear. It happened so much we called them pests because they would try to eat anything that may have been left out."

I added, "We had been here for almost a month enjoying fresh fish, lying naked in the sun during the day and watching the stars at night. Then you guys showed up Ben, and now we can't catch any more fish."

"Funny, I noticed you didn't say you couldn't lay around naked anymore, because you never stopped that."

"Why would we Ben, you and Beth were all over that? Beth loves to lay around naked in the sun as much as the rest of us."

Beth objected, "Really? You have to tell the world that we laid around naked here?"

"Oh, like you've ever had a problem showing off your body. I can't count how many times you said, 'let's find a nice nude beach.'"

Clearly unhappy Beth said, "Shut up Ben."

Ann barked out, "All right you guys stop fighting. It was so nice we would count the satellites we saw each night. We tried to see who could find the most as a sort of a game to pass the time on the warm summer nights. The sounds of frogs filled the air creating a symphony that would have been lost if the radio or TV was on."

"Yeah just like it was before we left our home in Washington, right Ann?"

Ann continued, "Bats filled the air at night feasting on the mosquitoes keeping their numbers down. Every night we could hear the owls hooting in the dark."

Fred added, "Well at least they are still out there eating the mosquitoes."

"They sure are."

"You know what I miss? Every now and then we even heard coyotes crying out in the night."

"Me too Ann."

Ben added, "Not me they used to scare the hell out of me."

I had to poke fun at him, "It's all right now, you're safe, I think they're gone or eaten."

"Funny, real funny." Ben added, "What I don't miss is the raccoons, if we didn't put everything up at night, we would find it scattered all over the next morning."

Beth teasingly added, "I can assure you they have been taken for dinner."

"Now when I stand on the overlook the scene is different, it's like something out of an Armageddon movie. Motor homes are circled like the old covered wagons arranged as a sort of barrier to the weather and walls of a compound. Inside the motor home circles are groups of tents with a large fire pit in the center."

"I know Fred it's so crowded now."

Ann added, "There're logs and rocks ringing the pits for seats. There're tarps tied everywhere covering the area, making it look like a big top. Some of the lucky ones were able to park their homes under trees and had made a sort of tarp house between the trees."

While we were talking Tammy and Sandy came in and sat with us by the fire.

I saw them and said, "Hi guys we are glad you joined us."

Tammy asked, "What're you guys talking about?"

Ann answered her, "We're just reminiscing about what it was like when we first got here and about how it's now."

A clearly irritated Sandy exclaimed, "I hate how things have changed since all these people have arrived. People are pigs, I hate them."

Tammy replied, "Yes, it's a shame even though this is now their home they treat it this way."

Fred added, "With this many people living here it has put a strain on the area, and it can't sustain the demand on it."

Ben made it clear how he felt, "I know Fred, to start with

we'll run out of food soon. Also, there's neither enough time to plant or grow the food, nor a place big enough for a garden for this many people. Additionally, we don't have enough seeds to grow the amount of food for everyone.

To make matters worse, even with everyone conserving, the fish will be gone in no time, and the wildlife has either headed for the hills or is already consumed. Even the raccoons left because many had turned to catching and eating them.

The entire area is covered with motor homes, tents and tarps. It looks like a tent city in the big cities with large numbers of homeless. Every night the smell of trash burning in the fires fills the air with a foul smell. There are fires in every site, meaning the wood is going fast."

I added, "I know and that's only the logistics issues, social issues are beginning to become a real problem. The sound of every type of music overwhelms the sounds of the night, it's no longer a peaceful or safe place. Gunfire erupts in the night as drunks' fire off shots in the sky.

People are stealing from each other and fights are erupting almost every night. Those fights are becoming more and more severe as fewer resources remain. One night a woman came stumbling into the fort in tears. Apparently, somebody had attacked her from behind when she went to go to the bathroom. The guy placed a bag over her head so she couldn't see his face then raped her and left her tied up."

Fred added, "It's really bad, some have asked me to assign armed men to patrol the area, but I've no intention of doing that. We have no desire to be police for the area but did add a roving night watch just to make people think twice before raping someone else. To be honest if we ever find who it was, he would be killed as there is no room for that crap here."

Tammy complained, "The waste generated by this

73

many people is impossible to manage. Even though we have dug several pits around outside the area and built enclosed outhouses, people still head out on their own to use whatever area they want.

Many complain that the outhouses are too far from their site, but there's no way to put enough in so that everyone is happy. Toilet paper litters the area as many won't even bury their waste or paper. At least the paper problem did go away on its own as everyone ran out of it."

I had heard enough; "All right everyone I got it, all in all the camp has become someplace we do not want to be. All these problems were the reason we did our best to find isolated locations to stay. We spent a fair amount of time as campground hosts in several state parks and found that in general, I hate people.

One time while were cleaning the women's bathhouse we found a big pile of shit in a shower stall, and more smeared on the walls. Here like there, we find trash and cigarettes butts everywhere, it's like they think the world is their ashtray. I never will understand that attitude. Why do they think they have the right to throw their butts anywhere?

I think the only answer is to find a different place to go. The first thing we need to do is to see if we can find someplace, one where we'll be able to cover our tracks getting there."

Ann asked, "Are we really talking about leaving?"

Fred was the first to chime in, "I sure am."

Beth asked, "Wait is this really what we want to do?"

Ann replied, "I don't know about you Beth, but I sure am ready to get the hell out of Dodge."

Ben cast his vote, "Me too Ann, we need to find someplace far away from here."

Fred spoke up again, "Ben has a point; we need to make it as far from here as we can. There are many reasons for it, first just from a logistics perspective. Then there is the social aspect, crime is on the rise, people are getting nasty and not the least of which the cleanliness issues we talked about earlier.

Luckily not everyone would want to leave, let alone have the means to. Before we find a location to go to, we need to figure out how many would be going. I know it's not a pleasant thought, but we need to figure out if we have to limit the number going."

"What are you saying Fred? You want to leave people behind?"

"Yes, that's exactly what I'm saying Beth, but I would bank money that most won't want to leave; it's likely that some won't want anyone to leave."

"I don't really care if someone wants us to stay, screw them. Things are getting out of hand here and we're running out of resources. If half the people left it would double the amount of time everyone that stays behind would have before their resources are gone."

We were so engrossed in our conversation we didn't even notice that Ramon had come in. He just sat quietly in the back listening to our conversation until he felt compelled to add his two cents.

"Peter is right, some may even try to force us to stay, they see us as their only hope and will be afraid to go it alone."

Beth asked, "Hey Ramon I never heard you come in when did you get here?"

"I've been here long enough; I agree we need to leave but I think some may try to use force to keep us from going."

Ann asked, "Where have you been?"

"I was hanging out with Sally."

Sally was a cute blond with deep blue eyes; she was one of the nurses that Fred recruited.

"You guys have been hanging out a lot these days is it getting serious?"

"Maybe Ann, but we'll see, it looks like I've missed out on a bunch, but from what I did hear it's not something you want everyone else knowing about yet."

"Hey Ramon before you sit down can you close the gate before you join us. We have been discussing options of what to do to deal with the overcrowding here and you may be right we don't want everyone knowing yet."

"That's easy we need to get out of here."

Everyone looked at Ramon and laughed.

"Are you sure you haven't been listening in on more of our conversations?"

"No Beth I haven't, I just know I'm not happy with the way things are here and have been looking for a way to tell everyone I was ready to leave for some time now."

By now I was thinking it was time to look further into it, "I guess the question now is where we go, and when do we get out of here. Fred do you have any thoughts on that?"

"I do, as a matter of fact, we've been unhappy and have already been looking at the maps, Brandon and I have some thoughts on where to go."

"Are you telling me that you've been planning on leaving without telling the rest of us?"

"No Peter I just wanted to come tell you in an informed manner, I never go into something like that without looking at my options first. Sorry it's one of my flaws, I have no intention of changing."

"Please never do, what conclusions have you come to?"

"We've found a valley over a hundred miles away that we'd like to go investigate. It's deep in the wilderness with absolutely no roads. It's several ranges away and there are no indications of human inhabits for at least a hundred miles around."

"How do we get there?"

"Well Ben, that's the crutch of it, it's SO remote it's going to be brutal to get to."

"That sounds like my kind of place. Have you already sent anyone that way looking?"

"No Peter, I wouldn't have gone that far before coming to you and discussing it with you."

"I'm glad to hear that Fred, but now that the ten of us have discussed it and are in agreement that we need to investigate it, we need to call a meeting on this and see how it goes."

"I say let's do it."

"I second that."

"Third here."

"Then it's done, let's get everyone to the fire circle tomorrow after dinner."

"I'll take care of that Peter."

"Thanks Ann, I can always count on you but don't tell them what the meeting is for."

Xavier Bruehler

The next night almost everyone gathered around the fire. Everyone was wondering why they were there, and all kinds of rumors were going around.

"I'd like to thank everyone for coming; the last time we met here like this was to vote on Sarg and his men to stay. That was a couple months ago and things around here have changed."

"That's for sure."

"Thanks for the support Tom, but I think I have this."

"Anytime."

"As I was saying, things have changed. I'm sure you will agree that life in camp has become overcrowded. It's getting harder to find game and we've had to go much further to find what little there is. Same goes with firewood, there's none left anywhere near here and winter is coming in a few months, so we'll need much more."

"After some soul searching and long discussions, we've concluded that some of us need to move on. Several of us have decided that we're going to scout out a possible new location, one that is far from here and as isolated as we can find."

"WHAT! Why are you leaving us?"

"REALLY! were you not hearing me? There're too many people living in this location to support us all, I know most of you know that. I'm sure there're also many more of you out there that want to move on as well and we would be happy to have you join us."

"What about the militia, are they going?"

That really pissed off Fred, he started yelling.

"I HAVE TOLD YOU OVER AND OVER WE ARE NOT A

78

MILITIA, we are Preppers we were just more prepared for this mess then you, but yes we are going too to get away from ignorant people like whoever it was that asked that."

"It's alright Sarg, yes, most of his team is going as well, some of them have made close friends here, and dare I say relationships, and don't want to leave. As he has said all along that none of his team is here against their will and they are free to stay.

I guess the first thing I need to know is how many of you want to go? But before we get a count, I want to make one thing abundantly clear. Many of the problems we have here have nothing to do with resources.

Many of the problems that led to our decision to leave were with some of the people's ethics here. Littering, destroying the natural beauty around us just because they can, the list goes on and on.

Anyone that wants to join us **MUST** to be willing to live by more civilized behavior. We will not take the problems we have here with us; we WILL NOT tolerate stealing. We WILL NOT tolerate rape, and to the rapist out there you know who you are, you are not welcome to come if you do and are caught you WILL be killed.

We won't allow any other sort of anti-social behavior. If you're willing to live by those higher standards and to help your neighbor than join us, if that's not your style than please stay here.

The repercussion for that type of anti-social behavior will be severe. Let me make this perfectly clear, we will be going to a completely remote location, hopefully one where no one has ever been before. If someone harms someone else and it cannot be made right the only option is death.

We couldn't allow someone to leave pissed off and bring

back help. I know it's severe but it's the only way. Over the last few months I've been able to get a grasp on your general nature and I know of several that WILL not be asked or allowed to join us. I'm sorry that is just the way it is."

Someone raised their hand to ask a question.

"This is not a vote or a question answer session. It's not a do we want to do this thing. This IS merely to inform the rest of you that some of us ARE leaving. It's an offer for some of you to join us. I know many of you have no desire to go and will never understand our reason for wanting to leave but it is what it is and that's it. If you want to go, gather over there by Ramon, raise your hand Ramon so they can see you."

Ramon called out, "Yo! Over here."

"If you already know you have no intention of leaving for whatever reason thank you for coming, you're free to go about your night. If you're still unsure or have any questions you're free to stay; I'll be happy to answer any you have."

"What about the rest of us, who is going to take care of us?"

"I don't know, you guys will have to find a leader, but it has never been my job to take care of any of you. You've been doing just fine taking care of yourselves. One thing you seem to be missing by us leaving is that many of you staying will now have a roof over your head for the first time in months. What more do you want?"

As I looked out over the crowd, I could see a bit more than half had left the fire circle. I thought to myself if this many come, we might be bringing many of the problems with us. I knew we needed to make sure we were on the same page.

"It's looking like more of you want to stay then wants to go, so it's not like we are leaving you ill prepared. I know there are some of you out there that are on the fence on if you want to go or not. I'll see if I can guide you one way or the other.

I said in the announcement that anyone that goes needs to be committed to life in a different world than you are used to, a world where we can live a peaceful life and provide for each other's needs. Given the nature of our plans only a handful of people will know where we are going; this way if someone overtakes this place none of you will know where we are.

But the flip side is if someone does come along and then can't live by those simple social standards the consequences will be severe."

"Who died and made you King?"

"To the asshole that doesn't have the balls to face me man to man and ask that, that's a perfect example of what I mean about anti-social behavior, no one did, it's simple if you don't want to live by standard social norms then stay here. That includes whoever you are that asked that question, we don't want or need your type of attitude around us."

Someone asked, "Does that mean death if the situation warrants it?"

Tammy answered that one.

"You're damn straight it does, and any reason that forces us to protect the whole."

"If any of you left out there can't deal with those strong standards. Enjoy your night. Now back to matters at hand, where we're heading, we won't be able to bring any motor homes or SUVs, we'll be leaving them for those that are staying. Maybe we'll trade them for some tents that some of you are living in."

"You can have your tent back Peter; we'll make do."

"Thanks Allen, but I hoped you would have been one that wanted to leave."

"No, I have three young kids and a hard trek is not for kids."

"There are other kids standing over there to go already, even a few babies."

"I know but Sheryl doesn't want to take them."

"I understand Allen, I guess I'll trade you the tent for our motor home, minus some of the stuff in it."

John called out, "You can use my horses to help find a new location."

"Thanks John does that mean you guys are going with us?"

John and Linda had come in on horseback with two extra horses and two mules for their gear; they are from Kanab, UT. John is a real cowboy type and Linda is your typical cowboy's wife. Both are nice people and enjoy life to its fullest.

"It sure does Peter; I wouldn't miss it for the world."

"All right then anyone who still wants to go, join Ramon there and we can start planning and figuring out what resources we have and what we'll need. As I said before the rest of you are free to go or you can hang around maybe you'll change your minds and want to go."

I heard someone call out, but I couldn't recognize the voice.

"That is highly unlikely Peter; I can't believe you are abandoning us like this. You should be ashamed of yourself."

"Please come up and talk to me like a man."

"Okay I will."

Coming forward was a tall man with long dark brown hair and a full beard and mustache. He spoke with a slight English accent and came to the U.S. from England many years ago. Before the quake he was a published writer.

"George, is that you? You must've been in the U.S. too long; you're losing your accent. I didn't recognize your voice."

"Yeah it's me, why are you just up and leaving us?"

"I'm not just up and leaving anyone, we made it an open invitation, anyone that doesn't want to go is free to stay, it's their choice, including yours my friend."

"I like it here; I have everything I need right here. Why go traipsing through the woods looking for something when we already have it here?"

"Look around you George; look at the filth, the crime, the lack of food, the lack of firewood, need I go on?"

"No, but even if you leave here it'll follow you wherever you go."

"Maybe, maybe not, we'll be trying to build a new community, one free of the crap we have here. Free of the crap we left behind before the quake, one where we don't have to worry about crime, one where we don't have to worry about nasty people, I hate nasty people."

You could see George processing it all; you could see he was thinking about it hard.

"I see your point; I guess I didn't understand Peter."

George smacked me in the arm and asked, "Why didn't you say so in the first place?"

"Because I didn't want to say that to the very people,

I felt that way about, it would have fallen on deaf ears. It would've been taken wrong by those who are not that way. Everything I said about the resources here is true, please join us George. You're one hell of a cook, we can use your skills and I know you don't want to stay here with this."

"Okay Peter than I'll join you, we'll help however we can."

"That's great George, you'll not regret coming with us. You'll be on the ground floor of making our own Utopia."

"Not like you have a pie in the sky view there do you Peter?"

"Nope, just hopeful thinking my friend, just hopeful thinking."

Chapter 7: The Search for a New Home

The next morning, we met at our fort, Fred and Brandon brought the maps of the area that they wanted to investigate further. We didn't make it an open meeting because we wanted the location to be classified. We knew we had much to resolve so we closed the fort doors and jumped into the task at hand.

Pointing to the maps, Fred was showing us what they had in mind.

"If you follow the ridge until you reach this pass, you can then drop down into this valley. It looks like it's a steep grade most of the way down and will be one that we have to rig the equipment down. When we get to the bottom we'll go north and follow the stream up to the headwaters; then over this pass looking down into the valley and see what lies beyond that."

Steve was one of Fred's men and has been involved with the planning from the start and added.

"We're going to have to be flexible on how we go to make sure that not only the horses can get there but the ATVs as well. If we don't, we'll have to carry everything the entire distance or not be able to bring as much."

Sarg added, "You're right Steve; it's something you have to try but not at the cost of not being able to find a good location for our new home."

"Thanks, from what I can tell from the map we should be able to make it a considerable distance with the ATVs. For one thing we can use their winches to transit some of the harder more vertical locations."

"Let's not get ahead of ourselves guys; first we need to

make it there on horseback."

"For sure Peter, my horses will be able to get us further than the ATVs, but we'll need to walk them at times, or take an alternative route for the horses."

"Thanks John, you're the most experienced rider, that's why I want you to lead this expedition."

Fred stepped over next to John, put his hand on John's shoulder and said.

"I assigned Andy and Steve to help you, they both know you'll be in charge. They're good working on their own and will be a great help finding the valley. I would advise you listen to their input, I have, that's how we made it here safe."

Andy is a young guy from Flagstaff in his mid-twenties he has this look about him, he seems to look right through you, but is really a good guy. Steve is also in his mid-twenties with a clean-shaven head, including his eyebrows. I turned back to John.

"Fred has assigned his two best scouts to accompany you in finding the location. These guys are seasoned Special Forces Ranger Scouts, they're as good as it gets, they know as much about scouting as you do about horses. I think you should work closely with them as they can help reach the valley successfully."

"I'll be happy to have them with me Peter, and thanks Sarg I'm sure they'll be a great help."

With that the three left to gather supplies and work out their own details. When they opened the door to leave, Dan, a big fat guy with red hair from Scottsdale AZ, burst through the door and started screaming something unintelligible at us. We stopped going over the maps to see what the commotion was.

I asked, "Dan what are you screaming about? We couldn't understand one word you said, talk to me man; tell me what's on your mind."

"Why are you screwing us over, by taking off like this. Out of the blue you're tired of the place and you're out of here just as fast as you can."

"Trust me it's not all of a sudden, we've had issues about the troubles here for some time."

"Of course, there's problems but nothing we can't deal with. You just decided you're gone and screw everyone?"

I could see this was not going well, Dan was just getting more and more angry. He kept raising his voice louder and louder. I was trying everything to calm him down, but it was to be to no avail. Fred became concerned and unsnapped his holster and put his hand on his weapon. That was a good thing for me because Dan had no intention of allowing us to go.

"You're not going anywhere Peter; you're staying here just like the rest of us. We all NEED to stay together to make it through this."

With that Dan pulled his gun, a Glock 9mm and pointed it at my head. Then he started screaming in that unintelligible manner again waving his gun in the air. I tried to calm him down, but he wasn't going to no matter what I said. Fred was certain Dan was going to shoot.

Fred could see Dan's finger tight against the trigger, that meant the safety was off, therefore the next time Dan waved his weapon away from my face Fred took his shot and hit Dan square in the temple. Dan dropped, dead before he hit the ground.

It was crazy, everyone was running around screaming. Ann ran over to me and squeezed me so tight I thought I was going to pop. I looked over at Fred and he was still standing there holding his weapon with this look of disbelief in his eyes.

"Are you alright Fred?"

Fred looked back still in disbelief and said in a questioning manner.

"Me!? I'm not the one that just had a 9mm pointed at my face. There was no doubt in my mind that he was going to shoot you. He was escalating more and more, and I didn't want to see you shot."

Ann ran over and hugged Fred tight around the neck, and said, "Thank you Fred, I didn't want to lose my best friend and husband either."

Then Ann returned to me.

Sandy also spoke up, "That nut case was going to kill Peter."

Sandy could see that Fred was shaken and walked over to him and took him in her arms. Fred fell into her arms and sobbed.

"It'll be alright Fred; you only did what you had to do. If you hadn't none of us think Peter would still be with us."

Fred told Sandy, "I've never killed someone before."

"But you spent so many years in the Army; you've never had to shoot anyone before?"

"No, I wasn't in a job that put me in that situation. I worked behind the lines."

By now I had regained my composure and went over to Fred. I put my arms around them and hugged them both.

"I don't have the words to say I'm sorry you had to do that, but if you hadn't, I'm sure it would be me laying there not Dan. You had no choice Fred; you had no choice."

"I know Peter but that doesn't change anything, well now I guess I can answer that question many Preppers ask themselves."

"What question is that Fred?"

"Would I be able to pull the trigger if I had too?"

Suddenly we heard a loud hysterical scream, and saw Becky running toward Dan.

"YOU KILLED HIM; YOU KILLED MY DAN."

Becky, Dan's girl friend from Phoenix, was crying and screaming while kneeling over his body.

"WHY, why did you kill him? WHY DID YOU KILL HIM?"
With that Ann exclaimed, "He was going to kill my husband! If Fred hadn't shot him Peter would be dead now."

"He would never kill anyone."

"Look in his hand Becky; look there, his gun is still in his hand."

Becky looked down and saw the weapon, she picked it up and started pointing it at Fred still crying and screaming you killed him.

Tammy walked over to her and stepped in front of the gun.

"Becky, give me the gun, you don't want to do this."

"Yes, I do, he killed Dan."

Tammy reached up took the barrel of the gun in her hand and gently removed it from Becky's hand. As she did,

Becky collapsed over Dan crying uncontrollably. Tammy took her in her arms and the two cried. I went over to Becky and she turned to me crying.

"I didn't know he was going to come after you Peter. Last night after the meeting I told him I wanted to go and would go even if he didn't, he just went nuts. He didn't want to go and didn't want me to either. He started screaming about how I betrayed him and that he was going to take care of it. He's the one that said that about being militia last night."

"It's all right Becky, there's no way you could've known what he was thinking. Like most of us he always had his weapon at his side. I keep thinking I could've said something different that may have calmed him down."

"There's no way Peter, if I couldn't get him to calm down, you didn't stand a chance of doing it. I'll understand if you don't want me to join you now."

"I'd never hold Dan's actions against you; you're definitely welcome to come with us still. Weren't you guys staying in a tent down by the lake?"

"Yes, we were but I don't want to go there now it'll be too hard without him there."

"Well you can stay with us until we leave, we'll be heading out soon."

"Thanks Peter, I'll take care of Dan, then my things and meet you and Ann back here."

With all that excitement we ended it for the day, plans were made for the section leaders to meet up again at my place the next day to finish figuring out where to go. It took most of the day, but we agreed about where to explore.

The next morning the three men started out staying on the trail that had been worn by all the daily traffic of hunting and gathering. They rode for several hours before they reached a point where no one had been before. From their vantage point they could see the valley below and the other side as well. They discussed their plans on how to proceed from there.

Their trek started out easy but that didn't last long. It required many changes in elevation both up and down and lots of bushwhacking. Every time they came upon heavy vegetation or thorny brush, they had to find a way around it or get off the horses and cut a path. On the third day in, Andy was riding in front, then his horse stumbled, sending him tumbling to the ground.

Steve was the first to reach him, "Are you alright Andy?"

"Yeah I'm okay but I think I dislocated my shoulder."

"That you did my friend, but I'm pretty sure I can reset it."

"I bet you can but that doesn't mean I'm going to like it."

Steve poked fun of him, "Oh stop whining you big baby."

"John, can you come over here. I need you to hold Andy so I can pull his arm back into position."

"Okay, how do you want me to hold him?"

"Wrap your reign around his chest and hold tight I'll be pulling fairly hard and twisting."

"Okay let's do this."

"Alright bud, do you need something to bite on for the pain?"

Ready for it to be over he snapped, "No just get on with it."

Steve grabbed Andy's arm and without any warning

pulled, you could see the relief in Andy's face as his arm popped back into place. Luckily for Andy, Fred had required his team to be Wilderness First Responder trained. Steve was able to get his shoulder back in with no problem. After Steve immobilized Andy's arm, they decided they were in as good a place as any to spend the night. Fortunately, the horse was not injured and just got up and stood there waiting for Andy.

The eighth day was a good day for them, after cresting a ridge they were able to see a promising valley below. They took a couple hours to figure out how to descend given that horses don't like going downhill, especially steep ones, but they did prevail. Though the area looked good from above it turned out it was not suitable for our needs. After close to two weeks of riding, with only a few days of resting to give the horses a break, they were on an overlook just above the valley floor.

Andy called out, "John, you've got to see this."

"I'll be right there."

Steve and John rode over and couldn't believe their eyes; the three of them sat there in awe.

"Oh my, look at it."

"It's beautiful. Is this the valley we are looking for?"

"I think so, but even if it isn't it sure as hell can be."

"Let's get down there and get a better look."

"I'm with you there Steve."

"Let's ride."

It was maybe another ten more miles away, deep in the wilderness and down in the bottom of a large broad valley. As they rode, they saw the location was perfect; there was ample wildlife to live off for a long time, clean fresh water, and almost unlimited wood. They continued down the valley and came to a large open clearing. Andy was in the lead when Steve and John heard a loud cry out, "YAHOOO!"

"Guys come quick."

John asked, "What have you found?"

"I think we found our new home; it looks like a cave."

"I think you're right Andy it is a cave, a nice large one, more than big enough for most of us to take shelter in if we need to."

"Steve check out the stream below."

As Steve leaned out over the edge of a large shelf, he exclaimed, "Hell yeah look at how clear the water is. Is that fish down there?"

"Yeah it is, big ones too."

"Well guys let's make camp here for a while and scout out the area downstream, but I think we found our home."

"I'm with you John, lets clear out an area under the overhang for the night in case it starts raining."

"The first thing tomorrow we'll head downstream on foot until midday then come back and go from there. But for now, I'm gonna catch me some fish for dinner tonight."

It had been nearly a month of scouting when they made it back to camp with the good news. All along the trip back they looked for the best way of getting the vehicles there without having to abandon them and they had marked it out as they went.

Back in camp Becky was the first to see them returning.

"THEY'RE HERE! The scouts have returned, hurry everyone the scouting party is back."

Loud cheers broke out as the three returned from their trek. Everyone was asking, "Whad'ya find? How far away is it? Can we all make it there?" The three were treated as heroes on their triumphant return; the crowd even helped them from their horses.

"Everyone, give them a chance to get settled in then they can tell us about everything they found."

"Thanks Peter, but it's okay everyone is excited to know what we found and we're just as excited to tell them. Y'all should have seen it; we found the perfect place to move to."

John said in his worst southern accent then he laughed.

"The location has everything we need and more than enough resources to take care of all of us even if everyone wanted to go."

"How long will it take for us to get there?"

"It took us close to three weeks, but it'll be considerably longer with the gear and provisions, not to mention the people."

"John, how hard is it going to be for us to get there?"

"It's going to be a major challenge and there's a good chance we'll lose someone in the process."

Steve added, "There're several locations where we'll have to rig every piece of equipment and even some of the less capable climbers to get past the steep elevation changes."

"Steve is right, I don't want to sugar coat this, it's going to be the hardest thing any of us have ever done, but in the end it'll be worth it."

Andy added, "The location is perfect, we found a large cave in the side of a cliff that we can close up for shelter from both the elements and intruders if they ever find it."

"Did you see any sign of people anywhere near it?"

"No, and we went a long way down valley with no signs of human activity, not even a piece of trash."

"Now you're fibbing," joked Becky.

"I'm not, it's the truth there wasn't any trash. We came into the valley from the side and found the cave down valley from there, but we only investigated up a limited distance. We figured we were far enough in and if there was no sign of human activity from below, then..., it may be that no man has ever been there, at least no modern man."

"All right everyone let's give them a chance to spend some time with their families, we can go over everything later on."

The crowd dispersed, then later that night we met at the fire ring where the three filled us in on the details of what they found. Now with a location found, and the details on what the trip would be like, everyone was given one last opportunity to either stay or go. Several backed out after hearing about the site, but a few more decided they were in.

We were ready for the long hard trip and knew that it would be even harder at our new home when we got there because we needed to get ready for winter as soon as we arrived. Even with that knowledge we were eager to get going; most had already begun to pack while waiting for the scouts to return so they were ready to go on a moment's notice.

Much of Sarg's camp was quickly broken down, the ATVs and trailers were loaded ready to go. All that was left was to break down the huts and load the rest in the ATVs.

We left two behind for the rest and get firewood and hunt for food further away. No one else knew where we were going, and no map was left because we didn't want anyone to find us.

The next morning, we gathered by the fire to go over details and hand out tasks that needed to be done. I wanted to make sure that everyone knew who was in charge.

I jumped up onto the bed of Fred's ATV with him and in a loud voice called out.

"CAN I HAVE YOUR ATTENTION PLEASE?"

The crowd quickly fell quiet, then after a bit of a pause I looked around and saw that they were watching. Then in a firm strong voice I continued.

"Thank you, now that I have your attention, I want to ensure you know Fred is in charge; he'll go over the details. I know we all can't wait to get going, and by now your personal gear should be ready to go, because it will be a long arduous trek."

Fred began, "Thanks for the confidence Peter, the way to our new location has no road to it, but I'm confident we can use the ATVs all the way fairly fast. We've begun stripping some of the motor homes of anything we can transport and use at our destination.

While the scouts were gone, we pulled the wires, pumps, and piping, then we removed every window we could and packed them for transport. There is a good stream flowing down the valley that we can harness for power. Generators will be given some priority, but they must be separated from the motor. As you strip your rigs remember, everything we bring needs to be moved piece by piece so be selective of what you take. Please remember to take what you need not what you want, think weight."

While Fred continued to go over the details, Allen motioned for me to come over.

"Peter let me show you what I made for the trip."

"What do you have their, Allen?"

"I took one of the ATV trailers and built a rolling chuck wagon. I used cabinets and other parts from some of the motor homes to build it. It comes complete with a sink and hot and cold running water heated by firewood of course. The work area has a pull-out cover and side walls, so the cook doesn't have to work in the rain. It also has two stoves with ovens for cooking."

"This is one hell of a trailer you have here Allen, I'm sure everyone will be glad to have it."

"I made it so it can be quickly broken down for transport."

"That's some smart thinking, I sure wish you were going with us."

"I'd love to go, but I think I'm needed here. At least I'll have your motor home and that sweet building you guys built around it. It should keep us warm through the winter. Besides I think many are looking at me as their new leader."

"I understand Allen and I'm sure you'll be fine, oh and good luck on your new job."

I noticed that Fred had finished imparting his knowledge on the crowd and everyone was mingling and pooling their ideas. When I got back, I jumped back onto the bed of his ATV again and called out.

"COULD I HAVE YOUR ATTENTION PLEASE?"

"I'm sure you know what is expected of you, and we have much to do before we head out in the morning. If there are no more questions we should take off, remember try to get a good night's sleep if you can."

The crowd broke up in all directions. That night we loaded the gear, ready to roll in the morning. We staged the vehicles just outside camp ready to go.

Chapter 8: The Migration

I was standing on the bed of my ATV, facing the gathering crowd with Fred next to me on his, with the trail behind us and the entire camp in front us. I had Ann hit the horn on our rig to get everyone's attention, the crowd slowly fell quiet.

"I'm happy to see I asked the right person to take the lead. Sarg is the most qualified to execute the move so I expect everyone to abide by his requests without question. It's the only way to keep us safe."

"Thanks Peter, I'll do my best to get everyone there safely. The migration will be carried out in a multi-phase operation. We have enough seats for everyone so we will be able to make good ground at times.

There'll be many times that we must set up rigging to either ferry everything up or down a cliff face or waterfalls. During those times we all will pitch in as needed. I want everyone to understand that what we're doing will be dangerous. It'll be of the utmost importance that EVERYONE follows directions and do exactly what I ask you to do, no questions about why."

Aaron asked, "How far are we going?"

"That's a good question, but for security reasons, we're not going to talk about where we're heading."

Matt asked, "What's it going to entail to get there Sarg?"

"It'll require a lot of work and cooperation. At times we'll be in open fields and other times we'll be driving down a stream."

"Why would we drive in a stream; why don't we just stay on the banks?"

"Yet another good and fair question, there're two reasons for that method. First in many ways it'll be easier to stay in the water because these vehicles are designed to do just that. But an even more important reason is that we want to leave as small a track as possible. That makes it difficult for someone to find us if this place is overrun by thugs."

We needed to get going so I stopped the Q and A.

"Alright, everyone has good questions, and I understand your desire to be more informed. However, we have things to do so let's get on with it, you can each ask him questions later."

Fred continued, "Thanks Peter, John and I will be riding point on my ATV with Peter and Ann beside us, we'll be in front, sometimes maybe a day ahead. Brandon, Andy and Sam will be at the back of the column making sure no one is left behind, as well as covering our tracks as much as possible. At times they may be as much as a week behind us."

"How long do you think it's going to take us to get there Sarg?"

"That's a valid question, one I have no answer for, other than it'll take as long as it takes too safely make it there. My bet is it will be at least a month."

"That'll be pushing it with the weather won't it?"

Fred replied, "Yes, but what other options do we have? None. That's why we have such a sense of urgency to get moving now. We'll still need to get our new home ready for winter before it hits us."

"How are we going to get the ATVs up and down the steep areas?"

"All the ATVs have winches with 100 feet of cable so we can use them to do the work. When we designed the ATVs, we addressed how to transfer them down steep faces. Simon, our engineer, designed an aluminum cantilevered tripod capable of holding the entire weight of the ATVs. The tripods can be easily set up and broken down. That also includes the trailers and a collapsible basket for people. We built three to enable more than one to be used at a time."

As Sarg finished I stood up one last time.

"It's time to leave, but I have one last word for everyone before we go. Ann and I had found this place many months ago, it was heaven. Since then the world around us has disintegrated and everyone here came looking for a safe place to live. A hundred people living here put too much pressure on our location and it shows. That's part of the reason we're leaving, it'll make things easier for the rest and hopefully allow you to make it through this coming winter.

For almost everyone staying, each of you now has a roof over your head and a bed to sleep in. No one will be sleeping in tents this winter. I'm sorry we can't tell you where we're going it's better that way. To all of you staying, I say adieu, to the rest I say mount up, let's roll."

With that, every ATV fired up, it was loud but exciting. There were cheers by all on their rigs and some in the crowd, but there were tears as well. It must've been quite the sight as we pulled away, we looked back and waved goodbye to those that stayed. As we pulled away, I called over to Fred and said, "Well Fred, are you ready for this?"

"I am, I was ready long before the scouts got back, I've grown tired of the conditions in camp."

"I think that goes for everyone in this caravan, we're all, ready to go."

"I'm certain you are right John."

"How far do you think we'll get today Fred?"

"I'm not sure Peter, the first ten miles to the pass are mostly flat. They've been traveled heavily by everyone collecting firewood and hunting game, so it's already clear.

When we reach the end of the path, we'll lower everything down several hundred feet, about one hundred feet at a time for a couple reasons. The horses will be taking the way they did the first time which is different from ours."

"Why is that?"

"Well Ben first off because there's no way to drive down the cliff because the path is too narrow for the ATVs to follow. But more importantly we want anyone that followed this path to think it was a dead end and turn back. If we lower everything down section by section with little impact, we can get to the bottom without anyone knowing we did. Any track left by the horses will fade away quickly."

Ben said, "That's a brilliant idea John."

"It was Fred's idea not mime."

"Alright then, it was a brilliant idea Fred." We laughed.

"Using the tripods, we should be able to reach the valley floor by night fall. Each step of the way we will leapfrog to get everybody down, then we'll transfer the equipment, so we won't leave much of a trail."

We finished getting everyone and the gear to the bottom faster than we planned. We decided to head up valley and get as far as we could before nightfall. This prevented anyone from above seeing any sign of us.

Over the next few days we traversed several valleys and over just as many passes. It must have been on the fourth day when our next descent was a steep cliff face. We were leapfrogging down when disaster struck.

Two of Sarg's team members had been lowering one of the ATVs over the cliff. They had cantilevered the tripod over the edge where it could be swung out to lower the gear. They'd already lowered several ATVs and trailers down and were lowering some of the gear.

"Henry, I need you to make sure that end of the tripod is secure to that tree, so it won't tilt when we lower the gear."

"I got it Sam; the back leg is chained to that big tree behind me."

"Good, that should hold it while I pay out the winch cable."

"Angie, I need you to guide the load over the edge while we let it out, but you really need to watch out for yourself, this is going to be a difficult task and it could go bad in a hurry."

"You got it Henry; I will be ready to jump at a moment's notice."

"Good because I don't care about the equipment; I do care about you."

Tom teased, "Ah that's so sweet."

"Bite me, you need to be careful too, you're in just as much danger."

Tom wanted to make sure Angie was ready "Okay, the load is ready to push out over the edge."

"I got it out, pay it out Tom."

"It's heading your way Henry."

Slowly the extra heavy load made its way to the bottom.

"It's almost there, give it some slack."

Everyone heard a loud pop, and the gear went crashing to the ground, the cable had given way. After breaking, the cable snapped back and hit Tom. While it could easily have cut his arm off, fortunately it was only a flesh wound.

No equipment had been lost and Doc was able to stitch Tom's arm. With Tom's injury and a broken cable, we decided to stay there that night to rest and figure out what went wrong. We concluded that the load was too heavy, so we made sure no loads were that heavy again.

The next morning John called out, "Now that we've rested, we'll head up the valley following the braided stream up to the next pass. The nice thing about braided streams is they're flat. Even if we drive along the banks, the first time it rains good the stream will rise and cover up our tracks."

Ann asked me, "How long can we follow the stream?"

"I'm pretty sure we can go another twenty miles before we have to rig any gear up for the steeper parts. It could take a week to reach the top of this valley."

The next six days went without any problems. The valley was incredible, beautiful plains with cattails, skunk cabbage, and fiddle ferns to name a few. Between the edible plants and wildlife, we were able to eat well for the first time in months.

The lush valley floor was almost flat for over twenty miles with an elevation gain of only one hundred feet over that distance. Not surprisingly, the easy going and need to rely on each other, helped us grow into a closer group. We began to think that maybe we COULD make a brave new world for ourselves.

On our tenth day of travel we approached our next

major obstacle. Ben was at the wheel, I was riding shotgun, and Fred was riding solo in the back seat looking at the map. Other than stopping to sleep, we had been traveling without rest, but we were still happy with our decision to leave.

As we rode along, Ben was looking around the valley taking in the beauty. "I'm so glad to be out of that camp and on our way to our new home."

I replied, "For sure for sure."

Ben was the first to see the change in the stream ahead,

"Hey Fred, look up. It looks like we're coming up on that first set of rapids you told me to look out for. If I remember right, you said we have to climb almost two hundred feet in under a half a mile."

"Yeah this won't be a vertical climb it'll be more like a set of steps with little plateaus."

I wondered just how hard it would be, "Sounds like it will be more challenging than coming down those faces."

Fred replied, "Much more so, not only do we have to go up but there are more dangers involved in dealing with fast moving water."

"Can't we go around and stay away from the water?"

"Maybe Ben but remember we don't want to leave any sign that we were ever here. If we drive in or near the water, it'll cover most of our tracks, making it harder to follow us."

As we arrived at the rapids Fred grabbed his radio and called for some of his men to join us.

"Sarg to Tom and Andy."

Tom is a smart looking man with well cut hair and brown eyes from Glendale AZ; he was a rigger at a metal yard before the quake. He was one of Sarg's men picked for his expertise in getting heavy things from one location to another.

"Tom here, what da ya need Sarg?" came crackling back.

"I need the two of you to come to the front of the column, we've reached the rapids I showed you on the map this morning."

"Yes sir Sarg, da ya want Henry, Bill, and Rick too?"

"Yeah you better have them come up too."

"Alright Sarg, we'll be there as soon as we can."

While we waited for the men to arrive, we looked around. Fred determined that it would be a great place to rest and I agreed. By then the rest of the convoy started to arrive so Fred stood up on the back of the ATV and called out.

"Let's get everyone up here and circle the rigs. I'm sure there are bear and cougar here so we may need some protection. This next part is going to take a while, that means we'll be spending a few nights here. To continue up we'll need to rig the equipment up a series of rapids to get to the next large plateau."

A couple minutes later the scouts arrived.

Andy exclaimed, "We're here Sarg, what's the plan?"

"I need you guys to do a quick scout out of the rapids. All I want you to do now is just check it out. Tomorrow we can start planning how to get past them."

Henry replied, "No problem, we'll find a safe way past these."

With that Fred turned back around and continued.

"As I said we'll be making camp here for a few nights, I need you to get started on that now."

Everyone formed a big ring around where we were going to be making camp and started unloading gear. It was mid-day; everyone began by either setting up camp or hunting and gathering for our stay. George and Christen prepared the camp kitchen while others put up tarps to cover the entire eating area.

As dinnertime approached, they made their way to the big fire we built on a large powdery soft sand bar. It was like our own little beach party. Jimmy Buffet's *Margaritaville* was playing loud and everyone was enjoying the down time on the beach with some skinny-dipping in the stream. Good thing too because some of us were getting rather ripe smelling.

That night we feasted on lots of grilled rainbow trout with a fresh elderberry sauce and all sorts of greens that were collected around us. Like we have so often, after dinner we relaxed by the fire socializing long into the night. We had turned off the music and were enjoying the relaxing sounds of nature. It was like a symphony of frogs, calling out for the mates and crickets chirping.

I decided it was time for a pep talk,

"I'm so happy to see us all here with no one getting badly hurt. The first thing I want to do is thank whoever it was that caught the fish for dinner tonight."

Someone yelled out, "That would be Michael, Susan, and Paul."

"Well thank you three for your hard work."

Paul replied, "It wasn't work Peter it was fun."

"Next I'd like to thank Christen and George for that de-licious meal they made for dinner tonight. And to everyone else, you've done an incredible job getting us this far. We've traveled at least thirty miles, which is a bit under a third of the journey, and we've made good time.

While we sit around this fire, I can't help but think about where we've been and where we're going. Many here remember how things were before the lake camp had become so overcrowded. Tonight, is the first time in a long time that we have enjoyed a good meal and a relaxing night with only the sounds of nature to fill the air."

"And we have you to thank for that Peter, if it had not been for you, we'd still be in that hell hole."

"Thanks, Phil, but you guys are who got us here not me. Every one of you has done your part in getting us past the obstacles. I hope this night will mark the beginning of a new life for us, one that we can be proud of."

"Most of you won't need to do anything tomorrow while we figure out how best to get everyone past the rapids above us. For now, everybody relax and enjoy the quiet and get a good night's sleep."

Over the next few hours almost everyone dispersed and went to their own tents. A few stayed up looking at the stars and socializing. Us original eight that built the fort at camp, stayed up late that night for our nightly fireside chat. Fred and Brandon had joined us as well and were officially welcomed into the fellowship.

I figured it was a good time to ask Fred about the plan for next day,

"We've been busy today and haven't had a chance to talk much. What's the word on getting past these rapids?"

"Well, the first two sets look fairly simple, with everyone being able to walk and leave no tracks. The last set is a different story. On the bright side there is another large sand bar like this one in between the second and third rapid so we can move camp there."

"That sounds great how long do you think it'll take to get past them?"

Brandon was the one making the plans and decided he was best to answer that,

"We figure it'll take a few days; I think we should stay here at least two nights and then set up camp on the higher plateau. We should stay there for a couple more days to get past the hard section. There's no reason to rush this one and take chances."

"Sounds like a plan to me."

Brandon inquired, "Hey Peter didn't you say you were retired Navy?"

"I did, twenty years of fun in the sun; I loved almost every year of it."

He continued, "What did you do?"

"Well that would take a while to go over, let's just say I wore many hats besides my Dixie Cup."

"Did you ever see any really nasty storms?"

"I did; I have ridden out several really big storms."

Sandy decided to join in, "What was the worst storm you ever went through? Or is it hard to remember any specific time?"

"No that is an easy question to answer."

Excitedly Tammy added, "Tell us about it, I have never heard any of your sea stories."

"Okay. I was riding the U.S.S. Nimitz around Cape Horn at the tip of South America."

Sandy replied, "Crap that is the roughest water on the planet."

"It is, and we transited in between two large tropical cyclones, it beat the shit out of us. I don't care what anyone thinks, I can tell you that even a ship as big as an eleven-hundred-foot long aircraft carrier can and does bounce around like a cork in the water.

The flight deck of a carrier is one hundred fifty foot off the water, and I watched wave after wave wash the length of the flight deck. The storm was so bad it sheared one-inch diameter steel stow pins we installed on our satellite antenna. The winds spun it round and round and ripped the wiring in it in two."

Fred asked, "Did you get sick squidley?"

"No, I never once got seasick and I have sailed around the world."

Sandy called foul, "I doubt that."

"Really, I've never gotten seasick. I came close once but never did. I was on my first ship the U.S.S. Canopus, a smaller six-hundred-foot sub tender standing watch. We were rolling back and forth extremely fast and I was watching the bubble that told me how much of an angle we were tilting. We were going back and forth from thirty degrees to thirty degrees. Watching that bubble made me feel a bit queasy so I got up and cleaned to take my mind off it.

Just as I started to feel better a roving watch burst through the door. He reached down and grabbed the new clean clear trash bag I just put in, stood up and barfed. The worst part was seeing it ooze down the bag. I yelled get out and almost lost it that time."

Everyone but Sandy started to laugh, instead Sandy

jumped in.

"HAAA!! You did get sick."

"No smarty, I never blew chucks not even in my mouth."

With that vivid picture we retired to our tents. The next day Fred sent his scouts to figure out how best to get the ATVs past the rapids. They spent the day exploring the options then briefed Fred and I on how best to move forward. That night, after dinner, we sat around the fire and filled everybody in on what was found and how to proceed.

"It'll be much more difficult and far more dangerous than descending the cliff faces, because of the proximity to the raging rapids. Everyone not actively transporting the equipment will be traveling on foot. Some of you will assist Sarg's team in rigging up the ATVs.

Sarg will continue to oversee the operation, I want everyone to listen closely to him tonight. I don't want anyone unsure of what their job is or how to do it. Now I'm going to turn this over to him, you're in his capable hands."

"We'll be splitting everyone into three groups. Some of you will be high lining the gear up the rapids using a series of cables and pulleys leapfrogging up stream. The next group will be rigging the ATVs over the rapids.

The rest of you will take whatever you can on foot to the plateau above. You'll be staying on a marked path to minimize our footprint as much as possible. You'll have to make several trips to get everything up there, but I'm sure we can do it."

"Angie, Tom, Sidney and Joe, I want you guys to divide everyone that's walking into four groups. Explain to them what they need to do to get the gear moved."

After everyone was assigned their jobs, and knew what

was expected of them, we were ready to call it a day. Just before retiring, I wanted everyone to be ready for the next day's tasks and shouted out one last message.

"It's getting late and I know everybody is ready to go. We have some hard work ahead of us, I want everyone to get a good night's sleep."

We had made it to the upper plateau between the second and third rapids with no problems and were almost past the last rapid. The first two days of that part went like clockwork with no problem. Everybody on foot made it safely to the top with their cargo and began setting up camp for the night. It was on the last leg of the last day when things changed for the worse.

Fred asked me. "What do you think the chances are it's going to rain today?"

"It rained some last night but seems to be clearing up now, but it looks like it is still raining up valley so that does concern me. Do you want to hold off today and see how things go?"

"We have one more ATV to get past the last rapid and it's in the middle of the stream so we can't just walk away from it. We need to keep moving and get it up to the top. We'll watch the stream level closely and continue, for now the stream level hasn't changed any."

"Okay Fred, I'll bow to your expertise on this matter, let's keep going then."

Fred continued calling out orders.

"Ramon, Henry, Alex, Ken you four get moving with bringing that last ATV up the final leg. I want you to pay close attention to the stream and be ready to abandon everything if the stream level starts to come up, even if it's only a little bit."

Ramon asked, "It's not raining now, why do we need to still watch out for the water level?"

"Because those clouds up valley look dark, I'm concerned it could be dumping up valley and will make its way down here."

"I see Sarg we'll be careful... who wants to take the plunge?"

Alex replied, "I will Ramon, everything will be fine, all we have left is to get this over that edge and we can take a break."

"Alright Alex jump in let's get this going." Alex jumped in the water and started pulling the cable and called out.

"Pay out the cable Henry."

"Alright it's all yours."

"Alex, pull the cable up stream then give it to Henry. Henry, wrapped it around the tree behind you and gave it a good tug." After hooking it to the tree Alex got in the ATV to help guide it.

"It's hooked up Ken, start pulling it up with the winch."

Ramon called out, "All is going good so far guys."

Just then they heard a few loud thuds, a couple of large boulders in the bottom of the stream came bouncing downstream.

Ramon yelled out, "Look out Alex some big rocks are heading your way."

"I hear them let's hope they don't hit me; I could be crushed."

Suddenly we heard a loud crash as a large boulder

smashed into the ATV and pinned it down. The force ripped the winch loose, which washed into the stream.

"Alex, get out of there."

"I'm trying to Ramon, but my leg is caught."

Ramon started stripping down.

Henry called back, "What are you doing Ramon?"

"What do you think I'm doing? I'm going in to free Alex."

"Are you nuts that could kill you!?"

"Whatever, he needs our help."

Ramon called out, "Hang on Alex, I'll get you out of there."

Alex hollered back, "No way Ramon stay out, I can get out myself."

Ramon had already made his way into the ATV and came up behind Alex. In a loud but soft and reassuring voice he said, "Too late I'm already here."

Henry called out, "Guys I hate to be the bearer of bad news, but the water is rising, fast."

Alex said, "Ramon he's right, the water is coming up and fast, you better get out of here before it's too late."

"No way, I'm going to get you free."

With the water coming in faster, Alex was struggling to keep his head out of the water. Meanwhile Ramon kept diving down to find what was holding him down. As Ramon dived down yet again the rushing water shifted the ATV. Alex popped free and was washed out.

"I'm free Ramon get out of there, Ramon. RAMON!? Where are you!?"

Alex tried to swim back into the ATV but couldn't swim against the faster current.

Alex was now screaming franticly, "RAMON, GET OUT OF THERE NOW!"

Kim, Alex's girlfriend, was watching it from the shore. She was pulling her hair and screaming at the top of her voice.

"Alex get out of there, you can't get to him."

Alex was not giving up, he fought the current but by the time he made it to the ATV it was fully under water, then it rolled and washed down stream. No one could believe their eyes. Ramon was gone; he died a hero saving Alex's life.

I stood there in disbelief as I watched it play out, "It's my fault, if I hadn't sent them in Ramon wouldn't have been there and wouldn't have lost his life."

Fred was standing next to me just as shocked, "It's not your fault, you asked me if it was safe to go and I made the decision that it was. If anyone is to blame here, it's me."

Soaking wet Alex came over to us, "Neither of you are at fault I was the one stuck in that damn thing. If I hadn't been there Ramon wouldn't have come out."

Ramon's girlfriend Sally was hysterical. She's a nurse from Colorado, who had come to us in one of the waves of people. After meeting Ramon, they had spent their time together at the lake camp. Not wanting to be far from Ramon, Sally demanded to watch from the shore as he worked on the ATVs, that meant she had seen the whole thing. She screamed at us.

"ALL OF YOU STOP IT. Ramon did what Ramon would have done for anyone. He jumped into the water knowing the danger. Alex you even told him to stay out."

"I know Sally but..."

"No buts he died saving your life, it was just who Ramon was, he would put his life at risk for anyone."

"But..."

Now clearly irritated Sally screamed, "I SAID NO BUTS any of you, and that includes you Peter. I don't care if you are in charge. Ramon is a hero; no one is at fault. You got it? NO ONE."

Fred went over to Sally and took her in his arms, and she collapsed in tears.

"You're right Sally, none of us can blame ourselves for losing Ramon, he is a hero and saved Alex's life. We're going to miss him."

Sobbing heavily, "I loved him Fred, we were going to be married when we reached the cave."

"I understand Sally we're going to miss him dearly; he was our friend too. There'll be a hole in our lives without him here."

Still crying even more, "You don't understand, we're going to have a baby, I'm pregnant, and we didn't want to tell anyone yet. We didn't want to worry anyone, so we kept it to ourselves. Now what am I going to do without him."

Sam came over and took over for Fred.

"Come here Sally, you are not alone, not now, not ever."

"I know Sam, but I LOVE HIM...."

"I did too Sally we were friends since we were kids. We loved him, he was a great person and easy to love."

It was almost impossible to console Sally, she cried for

the longest time, the only way to get her to sleep that night was to sedate her. The doc assured her it wouldn't hurt the baby to take a pill especially one time, she took it grudgingly. Sam walked off in the woods to be alone, I figured he needed the time but made sure he was safe. That night after dinner at our nightly campfire I had to break the news to anyone that had not already heard about Ramon.

"I'm sure by now everyone knows about Ramon, he was a great man and he gave his life to save Alex. He knew exactly what he was doing going in the water even after Alex told him to stay out. Now I want everyone to take a moment of silence to remember him. Many of us will miss him, our new home will just not be the same, but we have to move on."

"How did it happen?"

"Without going into the sequence of events, I'll simply say Alex was trapped in an ATV. Ramon went in to help him and lost his life doing so. Please no more questions.

We have reached the last plateau we were trying to reach, so tonight we rest and mourn our friend. But tomorrow when we start again, we need to keep our heads in the game. It should be fairly easy traveling for the next several days, but we'll still have a fair distance to go so everyone keep doing what you have done so well."

The rest of the way up was uneventful. We had traversed a couple more ranges when we found ourselves in a large valley. We were lucky that we came into it from the side where the stream was still braided, that made travel easy. After a few days we had managed to go two thirds of the way uphill by following the stream. From our vantage point we could see a long way down the west facing valley. I didn't like what I saw that day, the clouds were ominous.

Xavier Bruehler

Chapter 9: The Storm of the Millennium

I have seen a lot of storms in my life, one beat the shit out of a bunch of Boy Scouts I was leading. It made us abandon a one-hundred-mile hike around Glacier Peak in the North Cascades, but this storm was different. It was far darker than any I had seen before, and from our vantage point I could tell it was massive. You could see it drawing closer every minute and I could both smell and feel the electricity in the air. As I gazed down valley, I knew we needed to get ready for this storm. I called out.

"Hey guys can you come over here?"

Fred was talking to Ben and Brandon so the three of them came over to where I was standing.

Fred replied, "What's up?"

Without saying anything I pointed down valley. I was surprised after I saw Fred look at the sky. I had never seen him look like that; it was almost fear. I didn't think anything could scare him; he was always stone cold when it came to what he faced. I don't think Brandon had expected it either because he was clearly concerned by Fred's reaction.

Brandon exclaimed, "What's the big deal Fred, it just looks like a big storm to me?"

Fred replied, "That is NOT JUST a storm Brandon, that is a monster and it is heading our way. We need to get the tarps off the trees. Everything that can blow away needs to be stowed away and we need to find more shelter than just our tents. Ben can you go and start telling everyone to move everything far away from the stream. I don't want anything less than fifty feet up above the stream."

Ben asked, "Why? We have seen storms and never had to

take these kinds of precautions?"

Fred was clearly not in the mood to explain his orders and snapped back at Ben.

"Ben, we don't have time to go into why I need you to go and do as I ask, I'll explain it later if I still need to after this storm."

Ben could tell that Fred was not mad, he could see the concern in his eyes and replied.

"I'm sorry Fred, I'll get right on that."

Ben took off running and grabbed a few people on his way.

Brandon didn't need to be told twice he knew that if Fred snapped at someone that this storm scared him. I decided to start to figure out how to keep everyone safe from this monster. We were on a plateau well above the stream, that made it easy for his men to move the ATV's to high ground.

There were lots of trees laying down crisscrossing each other and I figured they would make a good place to take shelter. We tied the tarps around the outside of the pile and put more logs on top of them to help hold them down. There were a couple of those piles that we were able to make into makeshift shelters, enough for everyone to get inside of.

It was a good thing I had seen it when I did because we didn't have much time before the wind picked up and the air grew heavy. As we watched the lightning approach, I even became worried. Not only could we smell the rain we could smell the plasma from the lightning. The hairs on our arms started to stand up, you could almost taste the storm as it approached.

The clouds were so black that they lost definition; it

just looked like one massive wall of clouds with lightning going between them, with many more striking the ground. The rain hit us with such a force that it hurt to be smacked by the raindrops. As the storm progressed, we would see a flash and then hear the deafening explosion as the lighting ripped through the air.

If the rain had not been so heavy, I would have worried about fire, but there was no way fire was going to catch with that much water being dumped on us. The wind was blowing hard I was sure the tarps would be ripped off. The sound of the tarps flapping was almost unbearable.

The only good thing about the storm was that it was fast moving, it didn't take long for it to pass over us. I was amazed at how quickly the clouds were gone, but not the water. The stream was ripping by us so fast it even made me stand back. Boulders were being carried downstream like they were pebbles.

Ben had brought his weather station with us and didn't have time to look at it before we took shelter, but we checked it after it passed. The barometric pressure dropped below 25.50", which was far below the world's record low of 25.66" recorded during cyclone Tip in 1979. The anemometer was gone, but the meter recorded wind up to 125 mph before it broke.

Those kinds of lows never happened on land before. This storm was something different. It ripped past us in minutes and left trees down everywhere. When it calmed down and the stream subsided, we were amazed that we didn't lose a thing. Better still we didn't lose another of our friends.

I was looking out over the destruction the storm caused in the valley below us. We could see the result of the flood in the valley that just a few days before sheltered us. It was easy to see that the floodwaters went from one side of the valley to the other. If we had been down there when that storm barreled through, we would have died. As I stood there shaking my head in disbelief Fred came up to me.

"Well Peter what do you think of that storm?"

I replied, "I think that the changes in the climate we have been warning everyone about have happened. This storm was not like anything anyone has ever seen before and I don't think it will be the last nor do I think it will be the worst. I bet those sheep that believed that climate change was not real may be singing a different tune."

Fred laughed and he replied, "Well they can't blame that storm on the Democrats!"

We both got a laugh on that one too. But I had to reply anyway.

"Maybe not but I'm sure they will try."

With the storm from hell behind us we continued, after over a month on the move we reached the crest of the second to the last ridge that we needed to climb. Everyone looked in despair when we saw what was ahead. It looked like the hardest climb of all. We could see that the other side of the valley went a couple hundred feet higher than where we stood. At the same time, we were elated because we knew that the end was close. The next morning, we started down; it took two days to reach the bottom.

Ben turned to Fred and said, "I can't believe it, we made it to the bottom of the valley."

"I'm with you it was a hard trek, but not nearly as hard as I thought it was going to be."

"WHAT are you nuts? It was brutal. I thought we were going to die coming down that last face."

"Stop overreacting, it wasn't that bad."

"That's easy for you to say, you live for this stuff."

Rubbing his face like he was clearing away tears Fred teased, "BOO HOO would you like your diaper changed Ben?"

We couldn't stop laughing.

"Kiss my ass, I don't need your sarcasm Daniel Boone."

"Ouch... was that the best you have?"

Even more laughter.

I was worried Ben was getting upset so I intervened, "You two children knock it off."

"What! We are just having some fun."

It seemed I was right because Ben replied, "No you, were Fred, I was the butt of your fun."
"But you make such a good..."

"I said enough you two. We have way too much to do for you two to poke fun at each other. Besides if that is all you two have you need to go back to school, that's if there was still one to be found."

Ben pursed his lips and shook his head slightly and replied, "Party pooper."

Just then Fred called out, "Hey Brandon can you come over?"

"Sure, Fred what can I do for you?"

"Are you up to some hunting? We are going to spend at least a few days here to rest and give everyone time to just chill after nearly a month of hard travel. Besides we need to climb this side of the valley and down the other to reach the cave, I want everyone rested."

"Okay I'll grab a couple others and see what we can find."

Fred called out, "Wait for me Brandon, I have to get my bow."

"All right meet us at the creek over there," Brandon said as he pointed toward the creek.

Brandon looked around and saw just who he was looking for and called out.

"Henry, Doug, front and center."

Doug is a young cocky Iraq and Afghanistan war veteran from Prescott AZ. Fred selected him because he was one hell of a hunter both four and two legged. The two came trotting over.

"What do you need Brandon?"

"Hey, do you guys want to join Sarg and I hunting? We need to find some game because we're going to be here for some time."

Doug jumped up and said in his strong southern accent, "HELL YEAH..., let's go dooo... some huning."

Henry laughed and replied, "A little excited, are you?" More laughter.

Brandon replied, "Yeah he does like his hunting."

Henry laughed and said, "No you mean he likes his huning not hunting."

Doug flipped Henry off and said, "Goda hell ya asshole."

Just then Fred got back with his bow and Brandon filled him in on who he picked.

"Okay Henry you and Brandon head up stream and Doug, you and I'll head down."

With a sarcastic tone Fred turned to Doug and said, "Alright rookie let's get going."

"Rookie!? I'm not a rookie."

"Okay sorry then Rambo."

Fred challenged Doug, "If you think you're good, let's see who can bag the first one, but just don't shoot me."

"Alright old man let's get some fresh meat. Hey, the first one to bag some game, call out for the rest of us."

"Sounds like a plan Doug."

Fred turned to Doug and said, "Come on let's see if you can keep up with me young un."

"Do you want to put some money where your mouth is Old Man?"

"Sure, what do you have in mind?"

"The first one to bag something sizeable, I don't mean a rabbit or something, gets his meal brought to him by the other for a week."

"You're on, Little One; I'm looking forward to you serving me some venison for dinner tonight."

"Okay Fossil I'll take the left side of the stream you take the right and we'll see who is serving who."

Fred hollered across the stream, "See you later, may the best man or boy as the case may be win."

They left in four directions. Meanwhile down by the stream Tony came over to me and asked,

"How long do you think we'll be staying here?"

"We'll be here at least three days, I think. Why do you

ask?"

"Well if we have that much time, I'm going to set up the fish trap and see if we can catch some fish."

"That would be great, how long will it take to set it up?"

"Not long at all, we built it some time ago and made it so we can set it in the stream and catch fish right away. If there are fish in this stream, we'll be having fish tonight as well. Even if we don't have it tonight, we'll need to smoke some for the rest of the trip. Speaking of that, how much farther is it?"

"We are getting close; I'll be going over that tonight around the campfire after we eat."

"Alright I'll see you then."

It didn't take long before everyone heard Brandon yell, we knew Brandon got something. Everyone in the hunting party headed in his direction. Brandon got a nice twelve-point buck, all four cut up the deer and they each carried it back to camp to a happy crowd.

Someone called out, "Hale hale the mighty hunters have returned, and they bring us fresh meat."

Fred turned to Doug, "Well... I guess neither of us has to worry about the bet."

"You're lucky Sarg, I would've beaten you if Brandon hadn't gotten it first."

"We'll have to take this bet up again the next time we go hunting."

"You're on."

Everyone else went about setting up camp. Christine and George made an incredible meal with both the fish and venison as well as greens and berries others had gathered.

Later that night we met up around the fire. As always, I called out.

"Now that we're all here I want to start by saying we're close to our destination. The cave is over that ridge above us, then down to the bottom of the valley."

"Why don't we just stay here? It looks like a nice place to me, it has plenty of food and water, lots of trees what's the problem?"

"That is a fair question George, at first take it does look like an ideal location. It has all those things going for it and then some. But what it doesn't have trumps all of them. First what it doesn't have is a ready-made shelter. One large enough for most of us in the event of a severe storm, or an assault from outsiders, but more importantly it doesn't have enough flat open fields."

"The place we are going has lots of them, enough for everyone to build their own farm and have the fields we need to grow enough food for our needs. The stream is larger than this one and will provide a variety of options for its use; bottom line is it's worth making it over this last ridge."

George continued his line of questions, "Is the pass up this stream?"

"It starts out that way then we turn to go up the side of the valley. We'll go up the side just like we came down this last one. The climb up will be much harder, and it may take us even longer to go up than it did to get down."

After some needed rest and resupply of food we headed up. Finally, after several days of hard climbing we were able to look down into the valley that would become our new home. Ben was the first to see the valley, when he looked down, he couldn't believe his eyes.

"Everyone, come quick, you have got to see this, it's incredible! Is that going to be our new home Peter?"

"Yes, that's the valley we are going to call home for some time to come."

"Everyone, come on up here, we can see our new home from here."

We crowded on the pass looking down to the valley below.

Ben continued, "It looks like paradise. Hey, Peter, why don't we call it that, Paradise Valley?"

We heard him ask it and everyone called out that it was a great idea. So, our valley had a name before we even got there. I was sure it was going to be fitting.

Rick asked me, "Can you see the cave?"

"No and we wouldn't want that anyway, the cave is several miles down that valley around a few bends, but it sure is a sight to behold in any right."

"It looks like we have our work cut out for us on this one Peter."

"Why is that Fred?"

"Look down there three quarters of the way down, that is going to be difficult to get past with these," patting the ATV.

John added, "The horses had a hard time getting down there too; we had to walk them past it. It's only about five miles maybe seven down but the trip is treacherous. I have no idea how we are going to get them down, but we WILL find a way.

I had some concerns about what we were going to do and turned to Fred.

"It sounds like we need to make a plan."

"I suggest we spend at least one night here. It'll be a tough climb down, but at least we'll be able to drive part of the way. Then we're going to have to rig everything down again."

"I'll take care of letting everyone know."

"Thanks, but I'll address the riggers separately if you don't mind. We have a lot of detail to go over on how to get down and what to do with the gear. We don't need to bother everyone else with all that information."

"No problem buddy."

I jumped up on my ATV and addressed the group.

"All right folks we'll set up camp here for at least one night. If you look down, you will see the valley where we'll be living but you can't see the cave or even close to it. We have one last hard trek to get down and will only be able to drive part way. After that we will be rigging everything the rest of the way.

When we reach that point, we'll have to ferry every-thing by hand like we did a few times before, but this time it's to the end. The good news is this time we can walk the rest of the way there.

I know you're as excited as I am, but I need everyone try to be patient while we scout it out. That means we may still be a couple nights away from our new home. We've had to move people and gear more times than any of us can count. It's a great relief to see the light at the end of the tunnel and know it's not a fast approaching train."

That night we celebrated our achievements and rested. The group stayed put for several days while Ben, John, Fred and

I scouted out the best way down. We found a route that would take us a week or so to descend. Fred found a path that would allow us to only rig the equipment a couple hundred feet. You could feel the excitement as we drew closer to our home.

John and I were in the front seat when John saw one of his landmarks he set.

"I remember that mark, the upper plains will come into view just over that hill and around the bend."

"I think I see it; Oh My God it is unbelievable."

"See I told you that you'd love it Peter."

"You're right there, but love is an understatement."

As soon as Ben saw it, he was a loss for words, "WOW!"

I had to tease Ben. "Is that all you have to say?"

"Okay WOW WOW!"

Laughing, I turned to Fred and asked, "I guess, what do you think?"

"I think we've found our new home."

John replied, "Just wait until you see the rest of it."

It was the most incredible place we've seen. There were huge lush plains with vast open fields of grass, gently blowing in the breeze. There was a slow meandering stream with lots of fish flowing through it. We could see game tracks crisscrossing the fields and berries ripe and ready to eat. The stream leveled out into multiple terraces as it descended further into the valley with several ponds and a large oxbow lake along the way.

Pointing slightly up valley I called out to Ben.

"Hey Ben, look over there."

"Where?"

"Look you see that real long bend in the river?"

"Yeah."

"Follow up stream, do you see that falls it must be at least fifteen feet."

"Yeah I see it."

"Now follow it a bit more, look at that clearing, it must be at least two acres with almost no trees, it's on a nice plateau, it's perfect for our garden."

"Dude you found the perfect site."

"We're not there yet, we have a long way to go and the biggest hurdle in front of us. Hey, Ben, could you do me a favor?"

"Sure, what do you need?"

"I know when we get back here, I'll be in the front of the column, I won't be able to show this to the girls. Can you make sure they see this? I know they would love to from this vantage point."

"You got it."

John came up and said, "If you two ladies are done follow me, the cave is not far from here, maybe two or three miles downstream. Better still is that it's an easy walk the rest of the way."

"Well lead the way, I know I can't wait to see the rest."

When the four of us finally reached the cave there was no question, John and the rest of the scouting party had found our new home. We were in a hurry to get back and bring the rest of the group down, we just spent one night at the cave and returned to give everyone the great news.

It took us a couple days to get back and everyone was ready to go right away so off we went. We had made it to the point where everyone had to descend on foot, which was when we lost our second life.

Megan and Lucy were crossing the shale field at the back of the pack.

Megan asked, "What is the first thing you want to do when we get there Lucy?"

"We're going to build a nice cabin and have a small garden, one big enough to grow all the peas I can eat. I love to pick them as fast as they ripen then I never have any to can."

"Now you sound like me Megan, I love to eat them like that. Hey Megan watch that shale field it's really loose."

No sooner did the words escape Lucy's lips when the large shale slate Megan was stepping on slid out from under her feet.

"MEGAN!! MEEGANN!!" Lucy screamed.

As she fell, she hit a large rock and both her and the rock careened down the face of the steep slope. Wendell, Megan's boyfriend was at the bottom already when it happened.

This time, because I was at the back of the pack, I heard the scream. Wendell heard it as well and we both took off to see what happened. There were a few people already down the hillside working over Megan. By the time we got there they had put her on a makeshift skid and were covering her.

Lucy exclaimed, "What about Megan we can't just leave her there!?"

"We won't leave her; we already have people down there getting her off the slope and bringing her down. We'll take care of her; you don't have to do anything except be there for Wendell."

By now the rest of the group was off the hillside and making their way to the cave or wherever they were going to stay. Unlike in modern day life, there was no time for a long wake or services. We had to quickly say good-bye to Megan, otherwise predators would get to her.

They brought Megan off the hillside and took her to an open field not far from the trail to lay her to rest. The mourners made their way back up to the first clearing, which was close to where she was to be buried. The group was small because Megan was a loner and only had a few friends.

Those close to her were there for the simple ceremony. Each of them said something and tossed a hand full of dirt on her grave before walking away crying. The loss of Megan was going to affect everyone for a long time to come. Though she wasn't well known her loss will be hard to get past.

It had been a difficult day and the hard descent made for a long morning. Eventually most of our new residents had made it to the bottom. The only ones left were some of Fred's team who were getting the last of the ATV's off the face. As the last ATV hit the ground, Fred called me over.

"This is the last one, my guys will be down here in a few and we can meet up with the rest at the cave. But first I have something for you."

"What you got?"

Patting his hand on the ATV Fred said, "This, she is all yours."

"Mine? Really?"

"Yep, I know you'll need it and you deserve it."

"Holy crap I can't believe it; this'll make things much

easier than if we had to do everything by hand."

"There's more, the trailer is yours too."

I couldn't believe what he did for me, no one ever did anything like that before. I jumped in the driver's seat with Fred next to me. As we drove, we went over some of the things still ahead of us for that day and enjoyed the ride down what was fast becoming a road.

When we reached the first group, I filled them in on what had happened to Megan and that her friends didn't want a large wake or religious service. They wanted to be alone with her and say their goodbyes in private. They said that everyone else was welcome to say their goodbyes.

It was easy to find the rest of the people, there was a nice easy to follow path from the ATV's. I had left Ann on the ATV we rode there, when we pulled up with me driving Ann was understandably thrown.

"What are you doing driving that thing?"

With a bit of a snicker I replied, "Check out my new ride baby."

Surprised Ann replied, "What? It's yours?"

"Hell yeah, Fred just gave it to me as we got it off the hill, he gave us the trailer too. We left it above to get on the way up."

Ann leaned into the ATV and gave Fred a hug and said, "I can't thank you enough Fred, you have to at least come by for dinner tomorrow night to let us thank you. We'll have our campsite decked out before nights' end tonight."

Fred replied, "I have a ton to do but I know better than to say no to you, I'd be happy to."

"Great, we'll see you then."

Ann turned to me and said, "I can't believe what happened to Megan and less than two miles from here. Are you alright Peter?"

"I am Ann. I'm just upset, I just can't believe we were so close when she fell, and we lost her. It's just not the best note on which to start out our new life. Hey I just remembered. I think we need to do something to remember both her and Ramon, maybe put up some sort of memorial."

"I think that is a great idea Peter, I'll get with Sally, Wendell, and Lucy to see if they would like to work on it or have someone else. We don't want to forget our friends that didn't make it here."

"That sounds like a great idea, I almost forgot, did Ben show you the overlook we saw when we were down here before?"

"Yes, he did."

"I was hoping you got a chance to see it from above. I need to make sure everyone is settled in, then we need to get started on the cave. Then I'm going to help Fred find their new home as well. Maybe if we're lucky, we can find our way up to our site tonight.

"Okay; I'll meet you back at the cave when you're done. See you soon."

Later that night after everyone else was good to go, I picked up Ben and the girls from the cave and we headed back up stream to go find our home. It was easy to get back to the point we came down but as we passed Megan's grave site, we stopped so Ann and everyone else could pay their respect before we continued up. The rest of the trip was a different story.

There was no trail to follow, now we were on virgin ground. We had to cut a new path through some heavy brush.

About half mile up we hit the open field we saw from the bluff above, after that it was smooth driving, well bumpy but no obstacles in our way. As it came into view, we couldn't believe our eyes.

Ann looked in awe and exclaimed, "OH MY GOD!!! Look at it, it's beautiful."

I looked at my wife and with a sly smile said, "It is my sweet but not nearly as beautiful as you."

Ben decided he wanted to be a smart ass, "Do you have any wine to go with that cheese."

Beth was none too happy with Ben's response and reached back and smacked him upside the back of his head.

"Serves you right Ben, sometimes the ladies like to be told you think they are hot."

Now Sandy spoke up, "Where are we going to stay to-night?"

"I think over there in the grove of trees is the best choice. We can tie out the tarps and make a covered shelter with side walls while we figure out what and how we will build."

"It's perfect, let's get started."

That night we set up our temporary home. While the girls made dinner Ben and I set out the blue tarps so that we could collect the water and be out of the rain that started to fall on us. Funny it must be a universal thing because as soon as we set them up it stopped raining.

We collected some rainwater off the tarp before it stopped but didn't really need it for drinking because the stream was crystal clear and sure to be safe to drink. After making a nice fire and having dinner we were tired and went to sleep. The next day we headed back down to the cave.

Chapter 10: The Cave

When we arrived what we found looked little like a cave. Hundreds of years of growth had allowed the forest to take over the opening. Vines covered every surface including the roof and walls. Trees and brush had grown well inside the opening, and huge chunks of the rock from the roof had collapsed to the floor below. Large trees stood guard like sentinels in front of the entrance almost completely obscuring its very existence. That morning for breakfast we gathered outside. With everyone milling around I called out,

"We have a huge undertaking ahead of us here. The first thing we need to do is to clear the vegetation growing in and around the cave. But for now, do not cut down any trees in front, just the brush, vines and weeds. Oh, by the way save all of it, we will use most of it for something."

Henry asked, "Why do we want to leave the trees standing Peter?"

"Because we may use some of them as structural support, but we won't know for sure until we get a better view of the rock without that pesky vegetation in the way."

"Stack any large flat rocks in one pile near the front on the right side. Next the smaller ones between six and twelve inches in a stack near the front on the left side. All the rest should be put in a pile somewhere out of the way, nothing gets wasted."

Henry came up to me and said, "I think this is going to be a hell of a shelter."

"It is; did you find your own site yet or are you going to be staying here?"

"I kind of like this for now, it looks like it has potential

Xavier Bruehler

to be really decked out."

"What kind of things do you have in mind?"

Henry replied, "I would build a one-foot-thick solid rock wall to the top of the cave."

I pointed to the ceiling at the entrance.

"Hey, Henry, do you see that black line?"

"Yeah."

"That is rock varnish. It's black manganese oxide deposits, which is the point where the water drips off and no longer moves inside. If we build behind it a bit, it will stop the rain and drips."

Henry continued, "Thanks I will keep the wall behind it, I would build a large fireplace on one end of the front wall. It would serve as the cooking area including a wood fired oven for baking and a hot box to heat water."

"You have some great ideas Henry; how would you feel about me handing over the task of designing and building the structure to you? Feel free to use your own judgment, it sounds like you won't need my help in designing or building it."

"I don't know if I want you to walk away from it all, but sure."

"I'll be around checking on everyone else, if you have any questions or simply want a second opinion on something feel free to ask."

Henry reached out and enthusiastically shook my hand and said, "You got it Peter."

Then he stepped in and gave me a manly hug and said, "Thanks for entrusting me with such an important task, I promise you I won't let you down."

"I'm sure you won't, I'm sure I put the task in the right hands."

Fred had just arrived and was anxious to begin checking out the location for the fort. As I headed out with him, I heard Henry calling out to the rest of the people working on the cave.

"Peter has tasked me with getting the structure done, what do you say we get started, all right?"

"Way to go Henry we're here for you, what do you want us to do?" Brian said in a supporting manner

"That's what I like to hear."

Susan added, "We're behind you Henry, we know you can do it."

Henry started giving out directions, "I'll mark the trees in front that I want saved. Make everything else here that is green go away. The opening of the cave is almost due south, because we want the sun shining into the cave from sunrise to sun set in the winter."

Susan inquired, "Why is that important?"

"Because with the higher sun in the summer, the over-hang from the roof and the remaining trees, will block the direct sun. But in the winter the sun will be lower in the sky and shine inside all day long and help with heat. Now with everyone's help it won't take long to clear out the growth from inside the cave."

Everyone worked hard to get the clean-up phase completed. After it was done, we were finally able to step back and see what we really had.

The cave had been carved out of limestone much like

the sandstone used by the Mogollon that built the Gila Cliff Dwellings and many other cliff dwellings long ago. The opening was almost seventy feet wide and the cave went back at least thirty feet. The floor was mostly flat but had a couple terraces inside which made it nice for dividing it into smaller areas and sleeping platforms. The shape was perfect to build a single front wall to completely enclose the cave from the weather or intruders.

The floor jetted out well beyond the roof of the cave. It was twenty feet above the stream, that made a good overlook of the stream below. That overlook provided good protection from flooding and allowed us to watch for game from a high point as they came in for a drink.

Henry and his crew continued working on the cave.

"Now that it's clean and prepped we need to start to build. The first thing we need to do before we close it in is to support the roof."

Tom asked, "Hey Henry why don't we do that after we get it closed in, we don't have to worry about the weather?"

"For one thing it'll be harder to bring in the logs and beams we will need if it is closed in Tom."

Maria, a pretty Latino, with black hair, from Flagstaff, AZ. was standing next to Henry as he was describing what was needed and felt she had good idea.

"May I make a suggestion?"

"Sure, anyone is always welcome to put their two cents worth in, especially if they will be living in it, please let's hear it."

"We have already knocked down the loose limestone from the roof, this way it won't fall on our heads. What if some of us work on the front wall, while others work on the inside supports you want?"

Henry replied, "That's a great idea Maria."

"Gracias."

Henry continued, "We can make the front like they did at Mesa Verde stacking and cementing rock together."

Inside the cave, workers took dozens of small two-inch diameter poles laid them flat and tied them to larger poles making large squares. Old tarps were put on top of the squares, which were then raised to the roof and held up by even larger poles. The grid of squares covered the entire roof making it look cool, and the tarps provided the additional benefit of preventing the dust from falling on us.

Meanwhile a team was hard at work outside the cave making the front wall.

"We need to use medium to large river rocks to make the front wall, then we can use the limestone slabs we removed from the cave and the ceiling to make the fireplace."

Kenny asked, "Just how do you plan on holding it together?"

"We're going to make our own cement, much like the Romans did for the coliseum."

Henry reached down and picked up a hand full of sand and small bits of limestone and replied.

"We take these little bits of limestone and sand, smash it to dust then cook it in the fire for several hours. Then we scoop it from the fire, including some of the ash, mix it with gravel and a few other ingredients, and add some water and you have cement. There's a bit more to it than that but it's not important right now."

By the time Henry and his team collected the materials

for the internal structure, the wall team had laid out the outline of the wall and fireplace and had started baking the limestone. Over the next few days the concrete was ready, and the interior walls were taking shape.

Many of the upright poles that support the roof structure were also used to make the inside walls. This method worked to both, reduce the trees that needed to be cut, and to act as cross supports for the roof. The interior walls were designed to provide the families staying in the cave with some privacy, but remained open enough to allow for heat circulation

After the concrete formula was worked out, the outside walls were built, which included a few of the RV windows with reinforced insulated shutters inside and out. The front door was constructed from crossed layers of four-inch diameter limbs that were trimmed to be flat. I tell you it made one hell of a door. It stopped a .50 cal round from a Desert Eagle test fired at it at close range.

Chapter 11: The Fort

I had turned my attention to Fred and his team. We didn't need everyone working on the cave and Fred's team needed to get their camp set up, subsequently they had a place to live. They needed a location big enough for the Command Center and two small barracks, one for the men and one for the women. While the cave was under construction by everyone else, including most of Fred's team, a few formed a scouting party to find a location.

Fred turned to his men and called out.

"All right guys, the cave dwelling is under way, but we need a place for us to live. Bradley, I want you to take Allen and Paul and head down valley to find a good spot to build the compound. The rest of you keep working on the cave until we find a location, after that most of you will get to work on ours."

Bradley responded, "Yes sir Sarg, how far down valley do you want us to look?"

"I don't want you to go too far, but I also don't want to be close to the cave either, maybe a mile max."

"Yes sir, we're on it."

Fred stopped Bradley before he took off and said, "There are some precise criteria I want you to look for. First and foremost, it needs to be defendable, that means high ground. I don't want the structure to be able to be seen from down valley, it needs to be tucked into the forest.

The location needs to be near the stream for several reasons, but it also needs to be high enough above the stream to ensure it won't be flooded during rainy season. It needs to be on a large plain, and if possible, one full of Aspens to build the fort with."

"Yes sir Sarg."

Fred added, "Make sure to take your bows with you, that way you can bring back some game when you return."

Bradley turned and called out, "Yes sir ... Paul... Allen, get over here."

Paul and Allen stopped what they were working on and came running over and stood in front of Bradley.

Paul answered, "What's up Brad, what do you need."

"I want you two to get your day packs together, we are heading out on a scouting mission, oh and make sure to bring your bows for hunting, be back here in a half hour ready to go."

Together they responded, "Hell yeah," and off they went.

Bradley turned back to Sarg.

"Sarg, I'll get my gear ready and we'll set out in about a half hour."

"Thanks Bradley I know I have the right guys on the task and that you understand how important finding the right place is for everyone."

"I do Sarg, we'll find a good spot. We'll be back as soon as we can."

Sarg and I headed back to the cave to check on how it was coming along.

"I hope they find a good spot Fred."

"I have Bradley on it Peter, if anyone can find what we are looking for he will."

"You seem confident in him."

"That's because Bradley was the one that found the place, we were planning on being. He has an eye for seeing past the trees and knowing how it will look when the trees are gone."

"That's a good skill to have, it seems you picked out the right guys for your team."

"That I did."

Off they went looking for their new fort, they headed downstream looking for the perfect location. Finding the perfect place was important, and Bradley, Paul, and Allen knew how critical it really was. They hadn't been gone long when Allen stepped out from some heavy brush and saw it.

"Brad, come quick, I think I found the place."

Bradley came running over and so did Paul, Allen pointed out a large grove of Aspens on the inside of a large bend in the stream. It was sitting on the second terrace above the stream and unlike the terrace below, it didn't have recent signs of flooding. Most of the plain was covered by aspens about a foot in diameter and they were perfect for building the fort walls and buildings.

Bradley said, "Well Allen it looks like you found our new home."

"Thanks, but I don't want to settle in yet, Sarg still has to come look at it and give the go ahead."

"Trust me, he will give the go ahead, let's not keep everybody waiting, let's go get Sarg and see what he thinks."
Paul asked, "Hey Brad, should we find some dinner?"

"That's not a bad idea, why don't the two of you stay here and see if you can bag a buck and I'll go get Sarg."

"You got it, come on Allen lets go get some fresh meat."

"I'm with you, you take point."

While they were hunting Paul asked Allen, "Why don't we get with a couple others and build a cabin down here for us? One not too far from the fort, that way we don't have far to go but a nice place, then we have some privacy and quiet."

"That sounds like a great idea. I think I saw the perfect place a bit down valley of here on the other side of the stream."

"How did you get there?"

"There is a huge log down over the stream that we can just walk across."

"Let's head that way looking for a buck."

"Okay, who do we want to stay with us?"

"Well I don't know about you, but I have my eye on that blond Kathy."

"The one from camp?!"

"Yeah that's the one. We've been spending a fair amount of time together whenever we can. We've taken several long walks as we made our way down here. What about you, do you have someone you are interested in?"

"As a matter as a fact I do, its Jenny."

"Our Jenny?!"

"Yes, we have been close friends since long before the quake. We never hooked up before but now we are in a different situation and everything has changed. There are far fewer girls than guys in this new community and I don't want to be one of the ones that are alone. I think this may be the perfect way to see if she is interested in me that way."

"Go Paul go," Allen laughed.

"What do you mean, you are trying to hook up too," Paul laughed.

Allen and Paul continued their trek through the woods for a short bit when they came upon a small clearing. It was a nice spot, not big just a nice flat area for a cabin with lots of trees. It overlooked a small beaver pond not far from it.

"There it is Paul it's not big, but it will work for a nice cabin. I would bet you everything that there's fish in that pond."

"That is not a bet I would wager against," Paul laughed.

"It looks like it would be a good place to call home."

"I sure hope so, because it's not like we have many options."

"Okay Allen you head west, and I'll head the east, and give you a holler after the kill."

"Alright Paul, I'll see you when you come running to help me with my buck."

"Yeah right it's more like you will be coming to me Bro."

While Paul and Allen were out looking for some game, Bradley had already headed back to the cave to give Sarg the news. He was sure they had found the perfect place for the fort; it was about a mile from the cave. The location was far enough away that they wouldn't disturb the others, but close enough to protect everyone.

Fred and I were still near the cave supervising the progress when Bradley came up to Sarg.

Sarg asked, "What are you doing here, you should be down valley looking for a site for us?"

"I think we've already found the perfect spot."

"That fast? That's great news, how far away is it?"

"Maybe a mile Sarg."

Fred turned to me and asked, "Hey do you want to join me to go look at the location?"

"Sure... Hey Ben why don't you come too?"

"Okay, I'll be right there."

Fred called out, "Tom, put someone else in charge of your crew and you come with us too."

"Okay Sarg... Tony you take over here while we go check it out."

We jumped on an ATV and started cutting a road to the location. We were headed down valley and maybe halfway there when we heard Paul's yell echo up the valley "WOO Allen I got a BIG buck."

We continued down as far as we could on the ATV and only had a short way on foot before Bradley could show us the spot they had found.

Sarg looked around and asked Tom, "What do you think?"

"Hell, guys you hit the jack pot here, it's just right. Look at all those trees and they are all almost the same size. Perfect just perfect."

Fred added, "It's just right Bradley, we'll be able to build a large fort here. Well Bradley you did it again."

"Sorry Sarg I don't get to take credit for this find, Allen was the one that found it. He just came on it and knew as soon as he saw it that this was the right place."

"Well he was right."

I added, "Sarg we have plenty of people working on the cave and most of the clearing is done, there is no reason that you can't take most of your guys off it. It looks like you have a bigger job here then they do there."

"Thanks Peter I think we will finish out helping today and I'll start our guys on the fort tomorrow. In the meantime, Tom, I want you to go back and have anyone that is not actively hands on working on the cave to pack up our gear and bring it here. We're going to be staying here from now on. Oh, by the way, have a couple of them cut some of the obstacles out of the way for the road down here."

"I'll get right on that Sarg."

And off he went. Just then Paul and Allen came in the clearing dragging a big buck.

"Hey, Sarg, looks like it's a good day today. Is this a good spot for the fort?" Paul said in a proud manner.

"It is Paul, and that's a nice buck you nailed there, and Allen you did a hell of a job finding it. Why don't you guys stay here while the gear is brought down and prep that buck for roasting tonight. Find a good spot to make a fire pit and get that going. I'll have your gear brought to both of you. ... Good job guys."

"Alright Sarg, by the time you guys get back we will have the fire going and the buck roasting on a spit. Hey Sarg, do you want a piece of the heart when we get it out?"

"No, that honor belongs to the two of you. However, I'd love a nice big piece of backstrap."

Fred asked Bradley, "How much further down valley did you guys go?"

"This is as far down as I have been, but I think Paul and Allen have both gone further down. Why do you ask?"

"No real reason I just wondered, we'll need to scout even further down before long."

I added, "That's not a bad idea Sarg let me know when you go and Ben and I'll join you, that's if you are game Ben."

"I'd be happy to have you guys with me, but I don't think it'll be until after we have this place well under way. One of the things we'll be looking for is a place to build a couple of blinds."

"Another good idea Fred, ones you can see far down the valley."

"That's the idea."

Sarg left Bradley behind with Paul and Allen. Tom had already taken off to give the rest of his team their marching orders. Meanwhile, Fred, Ben and I continued to look around the area to get a feel for the site. We were headed off to the west of the stream and found a good spot to set up their generator.

They didn't need a field for growing because others would be providing their produce for them in return for meat. It looked like it would be a good place to build a large fort. One big enough for everyone to take shelter in if some group came in making trouble, at least for a short period of time.

By now it was getting late and I still hadn't even started working on my ranch. The girls had stayed there and were staking out where they wanted the cabins built. By the time I made it back they were finishing up dinner. I would be starting work on ours the next day.

That night everyone stayed where they were sure to

spend many more years. This was the second night in this new land for of us, but for the first time everyone felt like it was home. It was a somber night.

The next day the cave crew continued working on the cave while others began working on their own sites. At the same time Fred's team attacked the grove of trees with a passion. Fred put Tom in charge of getting everyone going on clearing the site.

Tom called out, "All right everyone let's get moving on this, you're going to be divided into four groups of four, and each group will be responsible for a different task. Paul you and Allen are in charge of two. Henry, you and Doug are in charge of the other two. All four of you select your teams and get started."

Tom brought Paul over to a tree and explained to him what he wanted.

"Okay Paul I need you to attach this big pulley to the bottom of this tree. Then attach one end of the hundred-foot cable as high up the tree in front of it as you can. Feed it back through the pulley and attach it to the winch on the ATV. Then winch in the cable until you see the dirt on the opposite side of the tree being pulled start to move."

"We'll be using the winches to pull down the trees, then we don't have stumps to deal with. Then Allen's team takes over for a bit, I'll mark out the perimeter."

Tom continued, "Allen, Doug, you guys take your teams and shovel away the dirt around the base of each tree exposing the roots. Start by cutting the roots on the same side as the winch, and then cut the rest of them working your way back."

"Paul after the roots on the winch side are cut put more strain on the cable and start pulling the tree down. As soon as the rest of the roots have been cut you should be able to just pull over the tree, stump and all."

"Henry after the tree is down your guys start to limb it and cut it from the stump."

"Allen we'll need more men to cut them to be able to keep up with them."

"Alright Henry go ahead and get as many as you feel you need to do it."

Allen said, "I think it'll take at least twelve to cut them up and haul it into a big pile. Nothing will be burned every-thing will be used for other purposes."

Tom went on, "Everyone else, if you're not working on the cave today then just jump in and help wherever you can. We'll do this over and over until the trees in this entire area are down and the area is clear. I want everyone to pay close at-tention to what is happening around you, I don't want any one hurt."

Everyone jumped to it. They worked feverishly to get the trees down, cut up, stacked and hauled to the pile. It was an amazing sight as tree after tree came crashing down. Henry's team attacked the trees like ants, cutting them up and moving on to the next. Some of them cut branches while others cut the trees into different lengths as needed. Every-thing was going great; they had cleared most of the area when Allen cried out.

"MEDIC!!! I need a medic quick."

Tom had assigned one of the medic teams and had the doctor on scene accordingly they could respond in a flash.

Karl, one of the medics, was first on the scene, "What happened?"

"David was cutting a root under too much tension when

it sprang up and hit him in the head."

"It's okay Allen, I have it now, step back and let me work."

David was bleeding badly from his forehead and was unconscious. It was a good thing that Susan, one of the doctors was close behind Karl and took over the care. The two of them were able to get the bleeding under control with clotting powder but she had some concern that he was still out.

Susan didn't want to move David, and the medical tent had not yet been erected. The team improvised and set up a tent. They provided a cot on site and a warm sleeping bag to make David as comfortable as possible.

Karl and Susan kept a close eye on David. It was several hours before he finally woke up and Susan could perform a complete exam. After checking him over completely, Susan determined that David had a severe concussion. He would need to rest for several days without being moved, but he would eventually recover.

With David in good hands, the group continued pulling down trees. Everyone was motivated as they wanted to be able to sleep in their cots again. Their highest priority was clearing a spot for the barracks tent and they worked long and hard to make it happen. And while Fred's men were working on the fort, Ben and I had started on building our cabins.

Chapter 12: The X Bar Ranch

We built our cabin about a mile upstream from the point where we entered the valley. Our chosen site sits on a large plain with several drops between us and the cave. Our plan was to build a cabin for Ben and Beth, and a cabin that Ann and I would share with Sandy and Tammy.

Ann asked, "What do have in mind for our home?"

"I'll build a palace for you my dear."

"I hope not, I want a nice simple house we can be happy in, one that keeps us warm and dry, that's it."

"I know my sweet, I was just kidding."

Sandy chimed in, "You know you two are not the only ones that are going to be living in it remember, do we get a say?"

"Of course you do Sandy, you and Tammy will be there too, and I wouldn't have it any other way."

Ben snickered and sarcastically said, "You better not, because we know who's in charge in a house full of women, and that sure as hell isn't you."

"What're you laughing about Ben, you don't even have a house full of women and you're not in charge."

Ben replied, "Ouch that one hurt," we laughed at that one.

"Now you boys stop beating your chests and let's get busy here."

Bowing and rolling our heads while kicking the dirt with a pathetic pouting face, like a couple of schoolboys, we both said at the same time, "YES DEAR."

We turned to each other, surprised we did and said the same thing, and high fived each other.

"All right let's get started on yours first Ben, it'll be a lot smaller."

Beth, of course, jumped right in on that.

"I want a simple cabin with just one room for the kitchen and living room, and one for the bedroom. We don't need anything more than that."

Ann replied, "Well Beth if the last few months are any indication, you'll be spending most of your time with us and eating with us any way, at least I hope that's still the case."

"I'm sure you're right Ann, I don't think any of us want it any other way."

"That goes for all of us Beth, none of us want to change the way things have been, you guys are all the family we have now."

"We love you guys too Ann."

Ben started rubbing two fingers together like a violin and humming. That stopped fast when the girls gave him that look. If he had a tail, he would have tucked it between his legs as he lumbered off.

Their cabin has a simple river rock fireplace mortared together with Henry's cement and a couple of the RV windows for light. It has a loft for an extra bedroom with a simple ladder to get up to it. It's a quaint place well laid out and easy to heat. Being small and simple we had it closed in a bit more than a week. It also served as a great place to stay while we built ours.

Ours is a much larger cabin with a post and beam wood frame and river rock exterior to resist fire if attacked. It took us almost a month to close the structure, but we did it before winter hit. It was bare bones inside with a dirt floor but with it closed we could work on the inside all winter.

"Guys here's the plan, before the ground freezes Ben and I need to dig our well up hill of both the cabins, this ensures the septic system won't contaminate our water."

Sandy jumped in, "Hey ladies why don't we work on the garden while the men folk work on their projects?"

Beth replied, "I'm game."

Ann said, "Count me in too."

"Great let's get on it."

We dug the well first and piped it into both cabins, This way we would have water inside even after winter set in. Then we dug the septic tank and lined the walls with river rock mortared with a modified version of the cement. It took us a week to get the well and septic tank built and for the ladies to do the first tilling on the garden. It was none too soon either because the ground was getting hard to dig in, therefore we moved inside.

"Our next task will be to build the fireplaces. We should build yours first Ben because it'll be smaller and simple to build, that way you have a warm place when you're there. Then we can work on ours, it will be a large double-sided fireplace in the center, with one side in the living room and the other in the kitchen. The dual stack will go up through the roof with heat channels built into the chimney."

Ben asked, "What are the channels for?"

"The channels tap off the waste heat that would otherwise be lost as the smoke flows out the chimney. The fireplace will also have channels in the fire bed to feed heat into the bedrooms. The embers will heat the air inside the channels and convective currents will cycle the heat into the bedrooms."

Sandy replied, "That's all well and good Peter but these RV windows don't hold out much cold. Why don't I start working on shutters while most of you work on the fireplace?"

Ann replied, "I want to help you Sandy; I get cold easily."

"That sounds great Ann, I could use your help."

The girls made some great tight-fitting shutters both inside and out. They could close at night or during storms to limit the heat loss. All the rock around the house and fireplace made for good thermo storage and let off heat well into the evening, that way it stayed warm at night even after the fire went out.

The ranch had a great view of the valley and we were high enough above the stream and set back a bit on the limestone cut bank, we didn't have to worry about flooding. Our new home was comfortable and provided a nice place to live.

We had both cabins done with Ben and Beth mostly finished before winter hit. Our cabin required much more work and took us most of the winter to get the floor built and separate bedrooms made. At least we had the fireplace finished before winter, that made it comfortable to work in.

Chapter 13: The First Winter

By late October most of the cabins were built and the cave was buttoned up and fully stocked for the winter. Several cords of wood were stacked close by and the aqueduct was covered and buried to ensure a supply of water. Anybody that had not finished getting their own cabin done, would be staying in the cave at least until they could close theirs.

Our little farm was well stocked and had more than enough wood. It was stacked in an attached woodshed with its own inside access, that way we didn't have to go outside to get it. The root cellar was fully stocked with salted meats, fish. It had all the food we collected while there, we were as ready as we could be. Everyone had done their part to prepare for the coming winter.

The fort walls were finished, and the fort was also well stocked for the winter. They had more than enough wood for heat from the trees they cleared from the site as well as logs recovered from the lower flood terrace that way they were already seasoned. The Command Center walls were up, and it wouldn't take long before the roof would be on and ready for use.

We started to see signs that fall was ending and knew that with winter close behind Paradise Valley would be a different place. When we looked down valley from the ranch, we could see the leaves changing, it was an incredible sight.

The aspens looked like a rainbow of colors and when the wind blew the colors shifted like waves. We had a short Indian summer that lasted about two weeks and gave everyone a nice reprieve from what we knew was to come. The nice weather also allowed for a small rush of outside construction.

It wasn't long after our bit of good weather that the

snow started to fall. At first lightly but over the next month it became heavier. Winter had settled in on our little community and many spent a fair amount of time in the cave or working in their homes.

In the back of the cave a storage room was carved out of the limestone with the cutout blocks making the front wall to act as a root cellar. This allowed the stores to be reached without going out in the cold or being buried under the snow.

Ample supplies of deer, elk and other wild game including pheasant had been smoked, dried or salted. We would have plenty of meat when we couldn't go out. There were a couple ranchers that had captured some of the wild game for breeding to ensure a long-term supply of meat throughout the winter without depleting the wild stock. Every effort was made to finish their barns before winter.

After winter set in even more game would be processed and placed in the cold storage facilities that had been built for that purpose. That same storage would be used well into the year by cutting blocks of ice from the nearby oxbow lake after it froze. This same technique had been used for centuries before the invention of freezers. Everyone that wanted ice for their freezers did their part in cutting it from the lake or ponds.

The lake had frozen about a month into winter and the ice was thick enough to walk on. Several ice-fishing huts were built with runners over the fall. We were able to slide them out on the ice this allowed us to ice fish without freezing.

The hut we built was big enough for four with a covered access hole in the middle to get to the ice. The seats went all the way around and had a couple of windows with shutters to provide light. It had a small clay and stone fireplace for heat that we could cook the fish on. That meant we could spend the weekend in it to maximize our haul.

It had a cleaning station to clean the fish and bench seats that opened to expose the ice. With the ice chest we could keep the fish fresh inside. The benches also doubled as beds if we chose to stay longer. I remember a weekend in late December when Fred was hanging out at our cabin. Ben and I were talking with Fred and Tony.

Tony is a real nice guy from San Antonio Texas but a witty smart ass. He's also as devious as can be, not someone to mess with if you can't take the heat. After living with Tony, his wife Penny can handle anything.

Tony asked, "Hey guys are you guys up to hitting the ice cabin for an overnight fishing trip?"

Ben decided he was going to have some fun on Tony's behalf and said, "Hell yeah I'm always up to fish Tony... but do you think Penny will let you go fishing with us...overnight?"

We laughed.

"Funny Ben, and I don't need Penny's permission."

Somehow wives have this incredible selective hearing even when they are on the other side of the room.

"You don't need my permission for what?" asks Penny as she crossed the room.

Us guys looked at each other, shook our heads, smiled and laughed.

"The guys are going fishing tomorrow and we'll be staying overnight in the fish house. Do you mind?"

"No go fishing, bring us home some good fish mighty hunter."

Yet again we laughed, then Ben shook his hand in the air like he was cracking a whip and made the sound of a whip being cracked. Tony warned, "Ha Ha Ha that's right Ben get your jokes out, but just beware I will get you back."

Now all of us laughed including Tony and Penny.

"Fred, what time do you want to head out fishing tomorrow?"

"After breakfast sounds good to me."

Ben jumped in, "You're welcome to crash in our loft if you like Fred."

"That sounds great, thanks, it'll get me out of the fort for a spell."

Ann spoke up, "We'll make breakfast for everyone while you get your gear ready to go. Then Penny you can stay with us girls and we can a have a girl's night here."

Tammy loved the idea and enthusiastically responded.

"That sounds like a great idea, I haven't had a girl's night in years."

Ben quipped, "That sounds more like your style Tony you sure you don't want to stay with the rest of the girls." We laughed... AGAIN.

"You're dead meat dude. I WILL get you back for that."

"Bring it on, bring it on."

It was funny watching them and I added, "I have a feeling this is going to be a fun outing."

Fred replied, "I think you're right."

Ann added, "It sounds like we're all set then. Maybe we'll see you guys, say about seven?"

Fred started out the detente, "Well I was thinking of getting started by six and out of here by seven. It's a half hour walk to the lake in this snow."

There was no way I wanted to get up that early, "SIX! Are you nuts? I was thinking we could get out of here around nine. That leaves plenty of time to spend on the ice and we can fish the early ones the next morning."

Ben called out, "I second that."

"I third it" came Tony then he added, "Then nine it is."

Ann spoke up, "Then if you're here by seven you'll have enough time to get ready and we girls can get breakfast for you."

Sandy jumped in, "Don't expect to include me in the cooking thing I won't be up until eight, but I'm all for the whole girl's night thing that sounds fun."

The next morning everyone arrived a bit before seven. They let themselves in and the girls were busy making breakfast, except Sandy of course, she was sleeping in. Fred and Tony were out back with Ben while I was getting the ice fishing gear together.

The smell of elk bacon cooking on the stove wafted through the air and made us hungry. We hurried to get everything ready so we could get inside to eat breakfast. The smell must have gotten to Sandy too because she was out by seven thirty following her nose and snitching a piece of bacon.

After we finished eating, we left for our weekend of fishing and stomped our way through the snow. The trek out was hard because the snow was deep, but it was well worth it. When we reached the fish house the snow had drifted up and blocked the door, that meant we had to dig our way in.

Chapter 14: The Ice House

The first thing we did when we got in was to fire up the heater that way it would be warm. Then we chipped away the ice for the opening and put that ice in the fish boxes. It didn't take long to make the hole in the ice, and we couldn't wait to drop our lines in. We were having fun laughing and joking about things when Fred pulled out a quart size mason jar of clear liquid.

"Hey guys look what I have."

"Is that what I think it is?" Tony asked.

Fred answered, "If you think it's moonshine then you would be right."

Tony exclaimed, "Hell yeah now it's time to separate the men from the boys."

Ben chimed in, "Well that will leave you out Tony."

"Well Ben, I guess we'll see who says uncle first and I can promise you it won't be me."

"OOHHH that sounds like a challenge." Ben replied

"You're damn straight it is boy."

"Bring it on."

Ben reached over and took the first hit, he replied, "Lame, your turn Tony."

Ben handed the jar to Tony.

Tony took his hit coughed a bit then said, "WHOA."

I reached up and took a swig, then shook my head a bit and blew out, goose pimples formed on my arms as effect of the white lightning washed over my body.

"Damn that is some good stuff."

I handed the bottle to Fred. He took a hit with no reaction and handed it back to Ben.

Ben took his second hit, made a strange sound, shook his head and said,

"DAAMMNN...."

Tony said, "Never talk shit when you can't back it up."

Ben bantered back, "Go for it Tony, but don't cough up a lung."

Tony took the jar and took a big swig. He shook his whole body and said, "Oh My God" but that was it. Tony handed me the jar for my second hit.

"I've had all I'm going to have, I guess I'm the biggest loser in this battle, here Fred."

He took another hit; it didn't seem to faze him and handed it back to Ben again.

Ben looked at it, paused, Tony jumped on that and said, "What's the matter lightweight can't you take it?"

Ben replied by slamming back a big hit, you could see his face turn red instantly.
Then acting like a real tough guy, he said.

"This stuff isn't that bad ass."

With that said he went to stand up. You should have seen it, with one fluid motion Ben stood up then fell flat on his face, passed out. He nearly fell into the hole in the ice. After the initial concern for his safety passed, we all started laughing when we saw he was ok, he was just passed out.

Tony looked at Fred and asked, "Do you want another

hit?"

"Nope I'm good."

With that Tony capped the jar without his third hit either. We laughed about it for a while and laid Ben out on the bench and made sure he didn't choke.

After a slow start we started hauling in fish after fish. We had filled the fish boxes under the benches and still they kept coming. Before the end of the night we had so many fish we decided to just stop fishing and call it quits. We put the cover over the ice hole to keep it warmer in the hut and had some fresh fish for dinner. Tony really got Ben that night. While he was passed out Tony painted huge eyebrows and a big L on Ben's forehead. There was no way any of us was going to tell Ben about it.

Later that evening we took turns telling stories and laughing long into the night.

Tony inquired, "Hey Peter, tell us another one of your sea stories."

Fred replied, "Yeah squid let's hear another one, something funny this time."

"Okay, I had only been on my first ship stationed in Spain for about a month, and already had to see the Executive Officer. I had XO's mast a couple times, that meant he knew who I was. One day I was in the shop and my second class came in with a double female fire hose fitting and told me and Woody to come with him.

We followed him to a head not far from the bridge. Once there he pointed to a pipe below a urinal and told me to hook the fitting to the pipe and the fire hose that was on the deck. I started to ask him 'but', then he barked back, 'DON'T BUT ME'. I was going to ask about checking valve settings on the line like they taught us in school.

Then he told Woody to follow the fire hose to the hose station the next deck down. He told me to stand on a ladder between decks and tell Woody to turn on the water when we were ready. I hollered down to him to turn on the water and watched as the fire hose filled.

Soon after the water started rushing through the hose, I heard a blood-curdling scream from the Executive Officers office. I could see in his office from the stairs and could see into his head. Looking in the direction of the scream, I saw the XO come flying out of his stall with his pants down. That's when I saw a column of water slamming into the over-head above the toilet. As I watched the XO running, I started screaming at the top of my lungs. 'Woody SHUT IT OFF, SHUT IT OFF.' As soon as the XO spotted me, he screamed out 'BREST ERRR!!!'

I looked at the XO and pointed at the second class and hollered he told us to do it. The XO was not too happy but really all he could do was tell us to clean it up. That second class looked at both Woody and I and told us to get in there and clean it up. The XO stopped us and told our boss the second class to clean it up. The force of the water was so great it had stuck turds to the overhead.

It was everything we could do not to laugh while we were still in front of the XO. As soon as we were down a couple decks Woody and I fell to the deck laughing our brains out. We had to see what the fire main pressure was for that hose and it was almost one hundred fifty pounds of pressure. I can only imagine what it did when it hit his ass."

Fred and Tony couldn't stop laughing. Fred asked, "Why didn't it all go down the drain?"

"Because it turned out a valve was left closed after a

drill. The only other thing on that drain line besides the urinal was the XO's toilet, all that pressure hit him in the ass. It was hilarious, I remember it vividly still today.

I asked Fred, "Fred what about you, do you have any good stories for us? Come on soldier boy it's your turn."

"Okay, I have a good funny one too. I was stationed at Luke Air Force Base teaching for a few years in the early eighties. One day I was returning from the mess hall and was crossing a parade field and came upon an Air Force officer. As it turned out I didn't see the guy, but he did me. I heard "'SOL-DIER.'"

I turned and replied, yes sir. He snapped back, 'Don't you salute a superior officer when you see one?' Without even thinking I replied, "'yes sir when I see one.'" Just as the words escaped my lips, I realized what I said and didn't have a chance to clarify it before he went off on me.

He made me give him my Staff Sergeants' number, my name and reamed my ass. By the time I got back to my office my Staff Sergeant called me into his office. He was standing there with his arms crossed and this pissed off look. I told him my side of the story and he told me not to let it happen again. I promised him it wouldn't and that was that, at least he thought so.

I decided that arrogant ass of an Air Force officer needed to be taught a lesson. You don't treat a jarhead like that without consequences. I told my students about what had happened and told them the next time we see him we would pay him back. You see we normally went to lunch together and would pass this officer. I told my students that the next time we spotted him we needed to space out the group. The plan was to walk in a drawn-out column over ten feet apart.

It wasn't long before we saw him, and I yelled out nice

and loud 'FAN OUT HUT'. We separated into this long line that required him to salute each of us one at a time raising and lowering his arm each time as he passed us. I just smiled as I saluted him and said, 'good afternoon sir'. He was clearly irritated by it but what could he do but salute all of us.

This happened a few times before he stopped me as he approached me. He told me to stop doing it, and I replied that I thought he loved to be saluted I just gave him more opportunities. He wasn't too happy and said not to do it again and said it was an order.

When I got back to my office my Staff Sergeant again called me into his office and had yet another talk with me. He told me not to do it again and I promised him I would stop. As I was starting to walk away, he leaned into me and quietly said, "'Good job I hate that guy.'"

Tony couldn't stop laughing, and neither could I for that matter.

Fred and I spent more time making fun of Air Force Officers, well most officers for that matter and told a few more stories of some of the idiots we had encountered over our years.

After a few more hours we finally crashed. Poor Ben, he missed out on all the good fishing and fun. When we got home the next morning Ann looked at Ben then looked at us and we shook our heads no and put our fingers to our mouths. Shhhh.

Beth came in, looked at Ben and asked, "What the hell is that?"

We stood there with this innocent look, held up our hands and shrugged our shoulders all innocent like, Beth held up a mirror to Ben and he wasn't happy.

Tony turned to Ben and gloated, "I told you not to mess

with fire boy you might get burned."

We got a good laugh out of it including Ben and spent the rest of the day sitting by our fire.

Many fish were caught over the winter in those ice fishing houses and everyone was welcome to use any of them and they did. Before spring the houses were removed from the ice, that way they wouldn't fall through and be lost.

We had been having a mild winter for some time, but we knew that would end soon. One night in the middle of February we were hit by a monster of a winter storm. The weeks leading up to it were already bad enough, but this storm was different. The skies had darkened early in the day and from our vantage point we could see ominous clouds creeping up the valley.

Tony asked me. "Have you seen the snow out there?"

"I sure did it's crazy."

It started out as freezing rain and lasted like that for several hours then it started to slowly turn to snow, lightly at first, then it really started to fall hard.

Tammy was amazed by what she saw, "I've never seen snowflakes that large; they're the size of softballs. Look at that, it's unbelievable. Have you ever seen it before Peter?"

"Sort of; I saw it snow like this in The Great Christmas Blizzard of 88 in Denver. It's not that uncommon to get golf ball size snowflakes this far up in the mountains but this storm is different. I'm worried about the combined weight of the ice and snow on the tree branches they could come crashing down tree after tree soon."

Ben said, "I bet everyone living in the cabins is happy that no trees were left standing within falling distance of any house."

"Of that you can be sure, this is a blizzard from hell that everyone will remember."

The storm lasted for what seemed like a year, but in reality, it was almost a week before the snow stop falling. When we were finally able to get out and check out the damage, we were in awe. Eight feet of snow had fallen on the ground and there were drifts up and over many homes. That was also when we learned that we lost John in the storm. He was trying to keep his door clear of snow when a giant mountain of snow slid off his roof and killed him.

The cave fared well in the storm with no damage or loss of life, and everyone else made it through warm and well. Some of the residents needed to remove snow from the entry way every day to ensure they didn't get buried.

Over the course of winter, the ham radio transmissions we had been listening to ended, even the ones from Salt Lake. We figured that couldn't be a good thing, as it meant that many remaining bits of civilization were now more than likely gone. We had decided never to transmit because we didn't want anyone to find us by the signal. We also didn't have any arrivals from the time we arrived or throughout the winter. For now, we were alone and isolated from the rest of the world.

We were happy with our seclusion, though, as the cave made for a warm inviting atmosphere where we were able to make plans for the spring. The cave worked great as a shelter, and except for John, we didn't lose anyone to the cold or from starvation.

Despite the circumstances that led us to the valley it was like a Norman Rockwell setting. The views were breathtaking even though the snow covered the area and looked foreboding. Icicles hung from everywhere and the stream was frozen over. It was a good thing we closed in the aqueduct that supplied the water to the cave. Our handiwork provided the water that was needed throughout the winter.

Looking out at the snow we could see little paths between the cabins and the cave that looked like a maze for rats. It was clear there was a great deal of travel back and forth between the cave and people's places. We had really become a tight-knit community with everyone making sure others were warm and well fed.

Winter in this part of the country lasts at least three months consequently we spent a lot of time inside the cave. There was something about the quiet that made us feel like all would be well. At the same time, we knew we were there because everything we ever knew was gone. We figured that we would never see any of our family again.

Chapter 15: The Council

We were in the cave having dinner and celebrating the coming spring, when Liz asked me about establishing a council. Its purpose would be to streamline the decisions that needed to be made about the village and give everyone a voice about it. We'd already agreed that it needed to be done. we decided that was a good a time as any. With no warning Fred stood to speak.

With his glass and knife in hand Fred tapped the side of his glass a few times. CLING, CLING, CLING.

"Can I have everyone's attention?"

The cave slowly fell quiet.

"First off what I'd like to say is welcome, and I hope everyone is enjoying themselves tonight."

A large overwhelming yes was heard.

"That's great, it's been a cold winter, but I hear that everyone is doing well. I'd like to take a moment of silence for the loss of John last month, he'll not be forgotten."

The room fell silent and everyone bowed their heads.

Fred motioned his hand toward Liz and said, "Liz here has brought up a topic that has been tossed around for a while now and I think this is the best time to talk about it seeing that we are ALL here."

"She suggested we form a council. I think it's not a matter of should we do it, but more who should be on it. But before we get to that, I wanted to take a moment and personally thank Peter for all he's done. If it hadn't been for him NONE of this would be here. It's been his vision for this community that has brought it about."

"Thanks Fred, but that's not the case, I couldn't have made this myself, all of you built it."

"That may well be the case Peter, but I still thank you for the vision."

By now I had stood up next to Fred and Liz and shook Fred's hand,

"Thanks again Fred, and we all thank you for everything you and your team have done, there's no way we would've made it here without your guidance.

Now let's get to the business at hand. There are forty-seven of us here today not counting the newborns. We need a fair representation of the different groups that arrived at the lake camp. I think that four members is a good starting point for a council. If we ever get more, we can add to it to represent them as well. Does anyone have any opposing thoughts or feelings on the number of members?"

I looked around the cave and saw many simply nodding their heads in agreement.

"Ok then four it is. I'll be the first to nominate someone for one of those positions. I think for the sake of fairness no one can nominate more than one. My nomination is Fred, besides representing his team he is levelheaded and makes decisions based on what is needed not on emotions."

Ben spoke up, "I second that, all in favor raise their hands."

From what we could tell everyone raised their hands.

"Then Fred is the first member of the council, now keep in mind the order elected means nothing."

This time Sandy spoke up, "I nominate Ben to be a member, as far as I'm concerned, he can represent us up on the hill and he is a good man."

"All in favor?"

Again, it seemed like all hands went up.

"Okay Ben you are number two, why don't you two get up and stand over there by the fireplace while we figure out the rest of the council."

The two got up and stood by the fireplace shaking hands and congratulating each other in a playful sort of mocking manner.

Fred spoke up and asked, "Is it appropriate for a member to nominate another, I would have before I was selected."

"I don't see any reason why not, who do you have in mind?"

"I think that Becky is a good choice."

"All in favor?"

Yet again all hands went up.

"Okay that makes three we need one more, any nominations?"

Ann spoke up this time, "I think we need to have equal numbers of men and women on the council. I nominate Cindy, she seems to speak for those guys that came in that second large group, it should be her."

Cindy responded, "I don't think I would make a good councilwoman, I'm nowhere near as smart as the rest of them."

Sam, one of the people that came in with her stood up.

"Not only are you as smart as the rest of them, I think that you are the best choice of all. All in favor?"

One last time all hands went up, and with a big cheer

from her followers we now had our council.

"All right then why don't you join them Cindy and let's see our new council."

The four stood in front of the rest of the community while everyone clapped and cheered for them. It was an emotional sight one that will stay with us for a long time. From the crowd we heard "SPEECH SPEECH." They looked at each other and nodded in Fred's direction, Fred reluctantly shook his head and agreed.

"You have elected the four of us as the council to keep things in order or deal with the bad things that may come up. I know the four of us will do so in a fair and sensible manner that will make you proud. I think the first act of this council will be to nominate a Chairman. (With a sly smile he added) Someone that can act as a leader for us and keep us from abusing this great power we now have."

Laughter rang out by all.

"The Chairman will also act as a tie breaker for when the four of us are divided over an issue. I'm certain that every person in this room would pick the same person for that position, as I'm about to nominate. And I think that one person is Peter, he's been the driving force for us and the only real choice. Let's see the hands of those in favor."

With a VERY LOUD cheer every hand in the place went up and, in many cases, both hands.

"Now I think that given the nature of this position, I'll ask is there anyone opposed."

To every one's surprise one hand went up, it was mine.

Ann responded, "You don't have a say in this Peter, the people have spoken, and it's you, now shut up and say thank you."

I dipped my head and rolled it slightly while kicking the floor and replied, "Yes Dear. Thank you," then looked up with a sly smile.

Then in unison "SPEECH, SPEECH." I shook my head again and took a deep breath.

"You know I have no desire to be anybody's leader, but it seems that you all do, I'll graciously accept it and will do the best job I can. Seeing how we're here I think the first order of business for our new leadership would be to give our community a name. Several people have asked about it and it has been put off mostly because we had bigger fish to fry. Now I think we should do it. The question is how to come up with a name?"

Susie, a little six-year-old that joined us from Phoenix, spoke up in a little timid voice and asked.

"Why don't we put out some names now and vote on one?"

Joking I said, "Funny the things that come out of the mouths of babies."

Clearly irritated Susie stomped her foot and with her hands on her hips and exclaimed, "I'm not a baby."

"I'm sorry Susie it was just a figure of speech, please continue." Timid my ass.

Thanks Peter, I say we call it Little Haven because this IS our haven."

"You know Susie I really like that one. Does anyone else have one?"

Frank asked, "How about Eagles Nest?"

"That's a nice one too."

Becky spoke up, "I say we call it The Valley."

"Nice ... Are there any other ideas out there?"

I looked around and didn't hear anyone or see anyone raise their hand, I said, "Well then I'll start with the last one first, all in favor of The Valley raise your hand."

I looked out and saw a few of Becky's friend's hands go up.

"Okay then, how about Eagles Nest? All in favor?"

Franks' friend's hands went up for that one but not a lot.

"Well then, all that is left is Little Haven, all in favor."

The vast majority raised their hands including Becky.

"Well it seems there won't be a need for a recount, our little home will be known as Little Haven."

Everyone was happy with our new name. We felt it described where we were and how we saw our new lives.

The rest of the winter was mostly mild and seemed to ebb away. Spring was just around the corner and we were looking forward to getting out more.

Chapter 16: Spring Has Sprung

It was early in the season and the spring thaw was well under way when we were hit by heavy rains. This was followed by heavy snow then again by a wet snow. The next couple days were also exceptionally warm which caused a tremendously heavy snowmelt. All that water came rushing down the valley and flooded everything.

Almost everyone had been careful about where they had built their home but the Jones. They had fallen in love with the site and were confident it was far enough from a high cut bank that they were safe. They built their house almost two hundred feet back from the stream in the belief it would be ok.

It turned out that it was not the case. They were comfy in their cabin when they heard a horrendous sound and felt their cabin shake violently.

Cindy, Moe's wife asked, "What is that Moe"?

"I don't know Cindy; it sounds like a freight train rumbling past. Katie, look out that window and tell me what you see."

As Katie looked out the window you could only imagine the terror in her eyes.

She screamed, "DADDY!!!... DAAADDDDYYYY!!!"

Moe came running over and Katie pointed out the window hysterical and said, "Look daddy the river is really close to the house."

Moe looked out the window expecting to simply see floodwater but that was not what he saw. He started screaming to his family.

"Cindy, grab Jason and get out, most of the yard is gone

and the river is only a few feet from the house."

"Do you mean it flooded?"

Moe answered, "No."

The river had cut almost the entire bank out and eliminated most of the back yard now the river was less than ten feet from the house.

Frantically Moe screamed, "The river is taking out the yard we need to get out of here."

Moe grabbed Katie and they ran to their neighbors the Franses. Scared they spent the rest of the night there hoping they wouldn't lose their house. Luckily the river had taken as much of the bank as it was going to that night.

After nearly losing their lives, Moe decided he needed to move their house to a safer place. As soon as the flood was gone, we took his house apart and moved it on to higher ground and rebuilt it in less than a week. They loved the new site and were positive that the stream wouldn't reach them this time.

As spring moved in, we were able to spend more time outside. The stream continued to flow heavy and flood the fields we had prepared before winter hit. We knew if we flooded the fields from the stream properly, we could both fertilize them naturally and prevent flooding where we didn't want it, it worked great.

Back at our ranch, before winter we had cleared the area of any vegetation and tilled the ground. We fertilized the soil and built a retaining wall for the expected flood waters before the first snow and waited. As the floodwaters receded, we were glad to see our plans had worked. The floodwaters were gone but our retaining field still held almost two feet of floodwater.

"Look Ann, now that the silt has settled, we can see the bottom of the field again. That means we are ready to slowly let out the water."

"Peter look, we can see fish in the water."

"That's right Ann when the water level was higher the fish got trapped behind the wall just like the silt did."

"YEAH! Look at all that fish, and we don't even have to catch them. Now what do we do with them?"

"We make a fish trap at the out flow to catch them as we drain the field."

"Okay I got it Peter. I'm only taking out just enough rocks to lower it bit by bit."

Ever so slowly the water level dropped, the water continued to drop with the removal of more rocks until it was almost gone. Then we were able to corral the fish into the trap, it was easy to catch them.

"It worked Peter, look at the fields, look at the silt left behind by the stream as the water flowed out, it must be six inches thick."

"That's right Ann, that silt contains the minerals that plants need to thrive."

"Once the fields are dry, we can till in the compost we've been saving, and the plants will grow like mad."

"Hey Peter, why did we drain the fields, I thought we were using some for rice?"

"Those fields are also drained that way we can plow and fertilize them as well. Then we'll smooth them out with logs and flood them when we are ready to plant the rice seedlings, we have been growing the last month or so. Then we open the fish trap and return the fish to the flooded field. They will both fertilize it and keep pests out."

"But why do we need all that water?"

"Well first it is the ideal way of growing rice, and second it prevents the weeds from growing and lastly it keeps out vermin, it the best way to grow rice. A bit before harvest time we will drain the fields again to let it dry then we can harvest it easier and we also harvest the fish."

It was an amazing sight to behold. All the fields we prepared in the fall were now green with little seedlings sprouting up and reaching for the sun. We held a meeting where the council divided up the seeds, we had to ensure everyone had what they needed and to coordinate the crops.

We had a little of almost everything at our ranch so that if something happened, we always had a second source. This method ensured we didn't lose any variety of seeds. As the weather warmed, we started on the barn for our ranch. It wasn't going to be a big one, but it was going to be multi-purpose.

It was an impressive sight, every member of Little Haven showed up to help. We fell trees and hewed the lumber to the shape we needed for framing. The chain saws made short work out of that task. Then in a flurry of craziness the frame was up. It was amazing, we raised the barn in just less than three days.

Many barns were built that spring as we went from farm to farm building one after another. After a spell we got down our parts and we were able to build them even faster. In the end every farm that wanted a barn had one.

Chapter 17: The First Arrivals

We were well into spring and everything was almost completely thawed. You could see the spring flowers poking through the snow and the stream had receded back in its banks. Life had fallen into a blissful routine when they arrived; I remember the day well. From our ranch we could see where we came off the mountain. Ann was outside working when I heard.

"Peter, come quick."

I took off in her direction calling out, "What is it Ann?"

"Someone is coming down the mountain."

I turned to Ann and told her, "Hurry go get Ben and have him bring both our guns."

"I'm already on my way," she said as she disappeared around the cabin.

Ann returned with Ben and our guns, Ben and I took off on the ATV. As we came around a switchback, I was the first to see them.

"Oh my God, is that you Allen?"

"It is Peter; it seems you are always finding me in quite the mess."

"Where is Karl?"

Allen stood there for the longest time and dropped his head. You could see tears welling up in their eyes as Allen told us he was gone.

"You guys are in bad shape, let's get you up to our ranch and take care of whatever you need."

"Thanks Ben."

I felt we needed to hurry beside the girls were probably worried about us, I said. "Let's get going, you can throw your gear in the back."

"Thanks, again, you are life savers."

Everyone jumped on the ATV and we headed back up to the X Bar. As we came around the last bend the ranch came into view.

"Holy shit Peter, is this your spread? We saw this from up above and was hoping it was."

"Well sort of, it belongs to the six of us, Ben and Beth, and Tammy and Sandy, we built it together."

We got to the ranch and were unloading when Ann came running up. She threw her arms around Sheryl, both started crying like babies.

Through the tears Ann asked, "Are you alright?"

Still crying Sheryl got out, "We are better now that we found you guys."

Ann asked, "What the hell happened to you?"

I turned to Allen and I asked, "What did happen up there?"

"It was hell, just plain hell."

Beth had kept a clear head and barked out, "We can go over that later when they are warm, dry, fed and rested. For now, let's get you guys some food and warm clothes.

"Okay but let's get you guys a seat first."

Allen replied, "Now that is something I would love."

As word made its way to the rest of the community everyone made their way to the ranch. Most came with food both cooked and not, clothes, all sorts of stuff.

Later that night, after the kids went to bed in Ben and Beth's loft, we were sitting by the fire with only their friends, the rest returned home. Allen decided it was time to tell us what had happened. Everyone fell silent because they wanted to hear the story.

"Some time after you all left, we saw a large group of nomads on foot making their way up the road from the valley below. First it was a couple of scouts that bolted when they saw us. Randell took them both out with two shots as they started running back down the hill. Of course, their friends heard the shots and when their guys didn't return, they came up fast."

"Did the road trap work at all?"

"Yeah Greg it worked well, it wiped out a large number, but not all of them; that really pissed them off. Killing that many of their friends fueled a rage in them that we couldn't defeat. They came at us so hard and fast we couldn't stop them, and they had no intention of letting anyone live.

They tore through the camp shooting and burning everything. Karl was in your home Peter when they got there. They didn't even look to see if anyone was inside, they just started burning the whole thing all the way around.

Sheryl and I were on the opposite side of the lake with Ken and Kate fishing when they arrived, so they didn't see us. We watched in horror as our home burned to the ground knowing Karl was still inside."

We could see tears rolling off everybody's faces as Allen told us the horrific story, there was not a dry eye in the room.

Pushing through tears myself I told Allen, "You don't need to go on, everyone here would understand."

"It's alright I'll go on. We watched as the group made their way around the lake toward the RV fort we built after you left, but everyone in there fought back. They lost many more of their men trying to take the fort. Then we heard a large explosion as one of the nomads fired an RPG into the gate and blew it to pieces. It wasn't long after that that the fort fell, but not before we killed even more of them.

Sheryl and I knew there was nothing we could do for anyone and we had to go. We took off in the direction you guys left and headed down the way the horses did. We stopped at a good vantage point to see if anyone had followed us but saw no one. We concluded that no one had seen us.

I can't tell you how happy we were that you guys had put that bugout stash where you did. We were able to get to it before we headed down the valley. We made the MRE's in it last a while and all the rest of the stuff saved our asses. You did a really good job of covering your tracks. If I had not been there when you were going over the plan, I wouldn't have had a clue on where to go.

We were about halfway here when we found a small cave not far from a creek. Thanks to the skills y'all taught us we were able to find food and make fire. We knew winter would be upon us soon enough so when we saw the cave, we decided to hold up there until spring.

We closed most of the opening but left a few inches at the top open for ventilation and blocked the opening to divert the wind and made it hard to see the cave. We made a small fireplace with stacked rocks mudded together for heat. Our bed was made with moss and other stuff and slept together to keep warm. All and all it wasn't a bad little shelter, and as you can see, we made it through the winter.

Every now and then we'd find a sign of your travels and

I knew what valley you were heading to, so we headed there ourselves."

Ben said, "Wow I can't believe you made it through last winter, we were hammered in February."

"We were never slammed by any storm; it must have passed us by."

I spoke up, "Well it's getting late and the kids are asleep next door. Allen you and Sheryl can stay with us in our loft. We're tired I think we're calling it a night, tomorrow we'll show you around Little Haven."

"You named it?"

"Yeah a cute little girl came up with the name."

Before Becky left, she turned to Sheryl and said, "When they bring you down in the morning there is room in the cave for all of you if you are interested. I can assure you it is far nicer than the one you stayed in over the winter."

"Thanks, we'd be happy to come check it out tomorrow."

"It's my pleasure, we would love to share our home with you."

Our new guests were clearly tired, and the kids were long since asleep when Allen and Sheryl went to sleep, they crashed hard and slept in.

"Morning sleepy heads, it's about time you got up."

"What time is it?"

"It's almost noon, you must have been exhausted from your travels."

Allen replied, "I guess, thanks for letting us sleep. Peter, when do we get the dime tour of this place?"

"Well now is just as good a time as any."

Ann spoke up, "But wouldn't you like some bacon and eggs first?"

"Are you kidding? HELL YEAH."

"Great while the girls get that ready, we can look around. Our place is simple. We're standing in the living room; the three doors you see on my right are the two bedrooms with a common bath in between. It's a full bath with a flush toilet, sink and a large garden tub."

Allen exclaimed, "Bathroom...it has a flush toilet!? How can you make a flush toilet out here without pipe?"

"The Romans didn't have plastics, but they had flush toilets. They made pipe out of ceramics or wood and so did we. When we were building, we dug the pit between both cabins to make a simple septic system. When the pipe tiles are done, we can flush the toilet. The system will serve dual duty by also producing methane for the stoves. And we have the pipe from the RV's for the gas to the stoves."

"How did you come up with that idea?"
"I don't get credit for this one, the pipe is Roman, and the Chinese have generated methane this way for their homes for cooking and heating for generations."

The girls were already in the kitchen when we arrived.

"Wow look at this kitchen, it looks like you have all the comforts of home from before the quake."

"We do have a few, as you can see the back side of the fireplace doubles as both a wood fired stove with its own contained fire chamber and a wood fired oven next to it."

Allen's eyes lit up and he licked his lips as he asked, "Does that mean pizza tonight"?

"I don't see why not, I make one hell of a pizza, several as a matter as of fact. Just place your order and I'll see what I can do."

We continued the tour and met the girls coming out of the bathroom laughing. The girls chipped in and made a feast for breakfast and everyone pigged out. Several people came up wanting to know when they were going to be at the cave, off we went to show them the rest of Little Haven.

Chapter 18: The Grand Tour

As we made our way down, we stopped at several farms and chatted with their residents. Most of them followed us to the cave like little ducklings. When we reached the cave, Becky was there waiting to greet her new guests.

Allen stood outside looking in awe at the front of the cave and said, "This looks like one hell of a cave Becky, definitely more than we had last winter."

Beaming with pride, Becky enthusiastically replied, "Thanks but you haven't seen anything yet, let's go inside and I'll show you the place."

Sheryl excitedly replied, "I can't wait."

As they entered Becky began to describe the cave.

"We call this the great room, it serves as the kitchen, living room, and sitting area. The doors on my right are some of the bedrooms." She turned as she, "The ones on my left are the rest of the bedrooms, there are five in all. If you look up, you will notice you don't see any rock. That is because all that wood keeps it up there and not raining down on us in here."

Sheryl exclaimed, "Holy shit this must have taken months to build, how did you get it done before winter?"

"We didn't, all we got done before winter was the ceiling, front wall and the fireplace. We got the water in here too, but that was about all we were able to do in time. Much of what you see was built over the winter while we were held up inside. We built the bedroom walls out of Alder saplings, which we were able to get even in the snow.

When we get the floor built, channels will carry heat from a chamber in the fireplace and feed it into the bedrooms. The fireplace already heats the water and gives us hot water for washing and baths, in time we'll build a drain to take out the wastewater."

As they made their way through, Becky showed them what would be their room. Sheryl was happy.

"This is far more then what we had over the winter, it'll be great, we'll take it. How much is the rent, and does it include subletting options?"

Everyone in the cave loved that and laughed.

Becky continued, "The four of you will have to share one bedroom for a bit, but Sidney and Angie are almost done with their cabin and will be moving out in less than a month."

Angie chimed in, "Three weeks' tops Becky, we're not waiting until it's done, we'll finish it while we live in it like everyone else has."

Sheryl replied, "This will be fine Becky, but I'm not sure about how long we want to stay in here. It's not that it's not a great place because it is, it's just not something I could do for long."

Allen asked me, "So how do we go about building a place of our own?"

"Well in many ways that's the easy part, finding the right place that's a bit more challenging because you have many options. But before we talk about setting down roots, we need to talk about some expectations and conditions."

"What do you mean?"

"Do you remember the conditions we talked about before we left the lake?"

"I do."

"Everyone living here in the valley has agreed to them

in order to be welcome here, not the least of it is that we help each other which includes building the cabins. Along with that we share the produce and game. It's evenly distributed, and no one goes hungry."

Allen interjected, "It sounds like socialism to me."

"In many ways you are right, but in other ways it's not. In socialism everyone gets a piece of the pie even if someone is lazy and don't carry their load. That does not happen here, at least it has not yet. Though we don't have ANY classes here we also not have rulers. We don't have anyone dictating anything.

The sole purpose of the council is to resolve questions that can't be resolved on their own. Besides we have been a socialist nation for many generations. We didn't have multiple classes in this country anymore before the quake it was the filthy rich or the poor with a few lucky souls in the middle.

Despite poplar belief we haven't even elected our president since who knows when. That's was done by the fat cats that screwed us over and caused the Depression. But I don't want to get into that anymore. It's in the past, now we live happy and free. Now, where was I?"

"Oh, if you want to build a cabin you find a place you like, and we all help you build it. If you want to grow food, we will provide you with seeds and help if needed and the harvest is divided for all. It maybe you pick one type of thing to grow like wheat, rice or sugar, or maybe a variety of things, that's your choice. You could also do like some of the other ranchers, they have captured animals like deer, ducks, pheasants or rabbit and are breeding them for everyone."

Sheryl asked, "I want to make sure I understand this, in return for what we do we get things we need like meat or produce that we need but didn't grow?"

"Yes, Sheryl that is correct, everybody's needs are met, no one ends up rich, but we live our lives happy and well provided for."

"That sounds like utopia."

"That's funny, Allen called it socialism and you called it utopia. I wish, if it were utopia we wouldn't have to worry about the other side of things."

"What things do you mean?"

"So far Allen we haven't had any, but at some point, people will be people, and someone will decide that something that isn't theirs is. theirs, or someone will hurt someone else. Maybe they'll figure what's the point of working hard everything will just be given to me like a handout. That's not an option."

"I remember, what happens then?"

"Well that depends on what it is. Either the victim or his or her family or friends decide what is justice. If someone commits something that physically harms another, then the only option is death."

Sheryl exclaimed, "WHAT!? What do you mean death? Isn't that a bit harsh? Who decides that?"

"Like I said the family or friends do. Remember we talked about this at the lake."

"Well I didn't pay any attention because we weren't coming. Why don't you just send them away?"

"Where? If they leave, they could bring back the friends, pissed off for being exiled."

Allen responded, "Well Peter, you won't have to worry about us hurting anyone."

"I know but telling you all the expectations is something I needed to go over with you."

Sheryl said, "It sounds like there are lots of rules to live by here."

"Not really, no one tells you what you to believe, no one crams their beliefs down your throat and threatens you with eternal damnation. No one tells you where to live or how to live. You live your life as you wish provided it does not harm others. Let's continue down valley because we need to go to the fort next."

"Ok let's go we can talk more as we walk Peter."

Off we went and continued our talk as we walked.

Sheryl asked, "I heard something that surprised me, and I want to know if it's true."

"What was that?"

"We heard that Wendell and Lucy lost Meagan on the trail here."

"That is correct, it happened a bit more than a mile from here."

"I also heard she was carrying his baby. I remember when Wendell and Lucy came to the camp he was married to Lucy. How was Meagan pregnant with his baby if he was married to Lucy?"

"That is a good question Sheryl. I said we don't tell people what to believe or how to live their lives. Wendell was married to Lucy before they came here, they both met Megan, and both fell in love with her. They were quiet about their relationship in camp for fear of being judged, but when we left camp, they no longer had that fear with us."

That got Allen's attention.

"Let me make sure I got this straight, Wendell was living with two women and it's all cool?"

"Yep that's right Allen. He was married to Lucy and fathered both babies. No one has the right to judge them for living the way they wish."

Allen smiled and replied, "I think I'm going to like living here."

Sheryl sneered at Allen and said, "Don't even think about it, you are mine and only mine."

We laughed.

Allen asked, "Hey what about you Peter, you're living with three women does that mean you have your own harem?"

More Laughing.

"No Sandy and Tammy are married and not into guys."

As we approached, the fort came into view. It looked much like one out of the old west. From the outside all you could see were the twenty-foot high walls with no windows, but as we entered that was a different story.

Fred was standing by the gate waiting to greet everyone.

"Welcome Allen it's really nice to see you again, we missed you here."

"We missed you too Fred. I only wish I had decided to come with you in the first place, but we are here now, and we'll make the best of it."

"Well let me show you around the fort. Front and center here is our command center, as you can see it is not built out of logs. It's built almost entirely of river rock cemented together with a log backbone inside.

The roof is a sod covering on a log structure and non-flammable material that won't burn if it's hit by fire."

Allen asked, "What is that they are building out of the command center?"

"It's a tower of its own in the center that will be forty feet high when finished."

"Can we go inside?"

Fred replied, "Sure let's go."

As we entered Fred continued his description of the Command Center.

"In the back corner on the opposite end from the bed-rooms is the galley. It has a fully equipped kitchen including a refrigerator two stoves/ovens taken from the chuck wagon you made. The cooking equipment from the mess hut has been moved here that way the cooks have everything they need to make the meals. On the other end are two bedrooms with my office in between them.

As you can see, it has a large center area set up. Everyone can sit to eat, and orders for the day given out. The fireplace on the front wall to one side of the main entryway. It was built like the rest incorporating the ability to heat both the air and water."

We headed back out to finish the tour of the fort.

Fred continued, "To your left and right you can see the beginning of the two barracks going up, and behind them is the beginning of the south towers. Under that left tower they are digging a forty-foot deep well that will be lined with con-crete. Under the right one will be an ammo dump."

Allen exclaimed, "Wow you have one hell of an operation going here."

"We do now, all we could do was the basics before winter hit. Now we have plenty of time, by next winter the fort will be done. We'll no longer need any of the tents and we will be ready for whatever comes our way. When we're done it'll have four towers like the old west, and we'll mount the .50cal's in each."

Allen jokingly said, "Well it's nice to know you're in the neighborhood."

After we were finished with the tour of the fort, Ann brought Allen and his family up to the cave to get ready for lunch. Fred and I went over some additional issues.

"Hey Fred, are you ready to move into your new home?"

"I already have, we moved in long before the rest of the building was done so we could get out of that tent. I have had enough bunking with this guy."

Fred points to Brandon.

"Thanks buddy. Does this mean the honeymoon is over?"

"Sorry but that ended when you farted so loud it rattled the tent walls."

We laughed.

"I'm broken hearted Fred, I thought we were happy."

"All right ladies that's enough, what's your plans for your tent?"

"We figure we can use it for emergencies, or if we go somewhere."

"What about the rest of your team what are their plans?"

"There are several groups that are building their own cabins, that way they can live in their own homes. It's only a matter of time before the barracks are finished for whoever is left. That way they don't have to spend more than the one winter in the tents."

"Will the barracks be finished before winter?"

"Most definitely."

"It sounds like you have worked out the details Fred, I guess it's now just a matter of time."

In all, ten of his men and women wanted to move out and into their own homes. To everyone's surprise Sarg was not opposed to their request, in fact he supported it. Sarg knew that by them building their own homes they would protect it with more determination then if they didn't feel it was theirs.

He made sure everyone knew they still had to be in the fort during their duty hours and were not to go home even for a meal. Everyone was fine with that and each found their own location, either as groups, couples, or alone.

By the time I got back to the cave it was lunchtime and folks had gathered at the cave to see their old friends. It was a festive day with several families bringing food and drink, enough that it started to look like an impromptu potluck. Since everyone wanted to hear if there was news from the out-side world, we decided to call for a real potluck at the cave that night.

That night at the potluck I called out to everyone pre-sent,

"Now that everyone has eaten and been able to get re-acquainted, we know why we are here, let's get started. First,

I want to thank everybody for coming to this potluck for our old friends. I want to officially welcome Allen and his clan back to our family."

There were cheers all around with several people yelling out a welcome of their own.

"I know they are good folks and are of the same mind as the rest of us. I know many of you want to know if they know anything about the outside world. I will turn this over to Allen."

I turned to Allen and said, "All right Allen, the floor is yours."

"We only had one other couple make their way to the camp before it was overrun.
They told us what had been happening in other parts of the country. They said the United States was no more. There was no central government and almost three hundred million in the United States alone died, billions worldwide were gone.

Anyone left in the large cities was hiding underground in subways and sewers. Eating scraps of food or rats and rummaging abandoned homes or stores for anything they could use. Even that didn't last long before it was picked over and the rats gone.

Many of the large militias that had formed in the years leading up to the quake had taken control of some of the cities. Wars broke out between them as one tried to take control of the other. Some had taken over nuclear power plants but horded the power or used it to blackmail the residents of the small cities that survived to comply.

The problem was when the militia had taken over the plants, they killed most of the people that knew how to operate them. Plus, there was no hope of getting needed parts to keep them up and running, that meant they shut down as well.

Several nuclear power plants along the west coast were destroyed by the quake but shut down automatically preventing radiation from contaminating everything for hundreds of miles. In time some of the plants all over the country either melted down or shut down so large areas of the country are now uninhabitable.

It was clear that there was nowhere safe anywhere near any city. In fact, many cities were completely abandoned, long since stripped of anything useful with much of them burned to the ground. Every major city on the entire west coast was obliterated. Nothing was left of any of the large cities, they looked like they were hit by nuclear weapons."

"Did you hear anything about New York City?"

"I did but it's not good, though. New York had not been hit by the quake, but we heard it was gone. After Wall Street shut down because of the news of the destruction of the west coast the city went into total chaos. Beyond that we didn't hear much.

Chicago had not folded. It's become a sort of new capital for what is now a new government called the Eastern States of America known as the ESA. Even that partial government didn't include every eastern state. Most of the southern states followed their own idea of how things should be and that varied greatly from the northern states. Atlanta is their capital and there are isolated pockets of slavery again though it was not just blacks that are being put to work.

The ESA had no influence over anything west of the Mississippi and no one knew anything about the military or who they answered to if anyone. They couldn't function too long without any means to resupply them. This is hard to talk about and we're tired, can I finish this later?"

"That's a scary picture, now I wish I never heard it."

"My bet is there are many out there that feel that way Peter."

"I'm sure you're right Fred, but you can't put the cat back in the bag once you let it out."

"You have that right."

We returned to our ranch for the night. The next morning, I had one more thing to show Allen. Sheryl and the kids stayed at the ranch with the girls while Ben, Fred and I showed Allen our next great endeavor, the mill.

Chapter 19: The Mill

As we approached the area there was nothing special to be seen. We were looking at a clearing with a large pile of stacked logs lying not far from the creek.

Allen asked, "What are you planning on building here?"

"We'll be building a mill. We started working on it before winter. We cut and hauled logs and piled them up; that way we would be ready in the spring to start building. As the spring thaw came on, we watched to see how the river flooded to ensure we built it in a way it wouldn't be harmed from the spring floods."

"What is it going to mill?"

Ben chimed in, "It's most important purpose will be to grind grains like wheat, corn and rice but it will grind anything we wish. There are forty-seven, wait now fifty-one of us here with you guys. We'll need to process of it for breads and things."

Beth reminded me, "Peter there are sixty here when you count the kids now sixty-four."

"Thanks Beth I keep forgetting them."

"Now where was I, oh yeah, we'll be damming up the river over there and will channel it down to the wheel. By doing it like that we can ensure the flow would always be the same even at high waters like a flood. The dam simply overflows and continues downstream for irrigation."

"What else will the wheel drive?"

Ben answered, "The primary shaft will drive the stone grinding wheels, and a couple secondary shafts will drive things like a generator. Over there we will build a sawmill it will drive as well. Eventually it will also drive a bellows for a forge when we are ready for that."

"Allen, how would you feel about being in charge of building the mill and adding your own ideas and skills?"

"It'll give me something productive to do so I can feel I give something to Little Haven. I'm not much of a farmer, I couldn't hit the broad side of a barn, so hunting is not an option for me, and I don't know anything about raising animals. I'm at my best fixing and building things."

Fred responded to that, "We had the pleasure of using some of your handy work on our way here Allen, that camp kitchen you made for the trip here was invaluable."

"Thanks, it was my pleasure. Hey by the way what ever happened to that?"

Fred answered, "It made it all the way here intact and was used to feed us the entire time. Now it has been distributed to various homes."

I turned to Allen, put my hand on his shoulder, "Well I think this is the perfect job for you. Then after the mill is built it'll need someone to operate it and grind the grains. Are you also up to that? You would be the caretaker; everyone would bring their grains to you for processing. You wouldn't be alone on it, there are several others that'll help you out."

"Who's going to be building this monster?"

Ben replied, "That is the easy part, like the way we will build your cabin and every other building here, we'll have a raising to get it built, after that everything else can be built inside. We hope to have it done before winter and I'm pretty sure we can do it."

"Well I'm in, but first I need to find a site for my cabin."

I continued, "That won't be a problem. Your cabin can be part of the mill structure."

Allen was excited by the idea. He took my hand shaking it and replied, "When do we start?"

"Well in a way we already have, we have located where the dam will be and how to divert the water with its own flow. The building will be going up some time later this month, but that will only be the beginning."

"That's for sure it'll be a major challenge to make all the parts work. It'll take much longer to get the rest done than it will to build the structure. I'll make it happen Peter, thanks for trusting me with such an important project."

"I know you will Allen."

It took less than a month to get the structure built. The inner workings that make a mill work are intricate and took some time to make, but in the end the mill was turning, and the stones were grinding together to work before harvest time. We knew that with the freeze there would be no water flow but that by the time of our first real harvest, the mill would be done.

Chapter 20: Change of Command

It was well into July of our second year, the fort was finished and many of Fred's team had built their own homes around the fort. Now that things were settled in Fred decided it was time for a change.

"Hey, Peter, do you have a minute I need to talk to you about an important matter."

"Sure, what's up?"

"I was thinking, now that the fort is mostly done, I think I'm going to change a few things."

"What do you have in mind?"

"First, I'm going to drop the Sarg, I don't want the title anymore. We'll still need to maintain a well-trained security team, but I don't want the job anymore, I'm tired of it. You know I'm not getting any younger, it's time for someone younger to take over. And I've grown tired of having to deal with the trouble of supervising these people."

"I understand, who do you have in mind?"

Fred Pointed to Brandon.

"Brandon and I have been talking about a change of command at the fort. I started training him from the beginning to take over in the event something happened to me, he is already ready. I think he'll make a great leader."

"I think you're right, what do you plan on doing with your newfound freedom?"

"Rest my friend, go fishing and sleep in every day. Need I say more?"

I turned to Brandon and asked, "How do you feel about

that?"

"Excited, I've been asking Fred for some time now to give me more responsibility. I'm ready to take the reins."

"I bet you are. Have you guys said anything to your team yet?"

Fred replied, "No I wanted to talk it over with you first, I didn't want it coming from someone else."

"Thanks, will you still be staying in the fort?"

"No and I haven't found a place yet but I'm looking."

"There is one site near mine if you are only looking for a place to build a cabin and not do any farming or anything."

"I know; I remember you showing it to me some time back."

"Hell Fred, now you'll be my neighbor, it'll make hanging out even easier."

"I'm happy to hear you say that, I was thinking about how nice it will be to hang out with you guys in the hot tub with four women." Fred said with a smirk.

"Well I'm sure they'll have something to say about that, but my bet is it will be jump in."

It didn't take long for everyone to get Fred's cabin built and it was not even a quarter mile from our ranch. Fred wanted a simple one-room cabin with his bed only slightly enclosed from the rest. He used logs instead of rocks and a heater from one of the tents to heat it, that meant there was no need for a fireplace.

Fred helped us in our garden, that way he didn't need to have one of his own, but he did have a small herb garden. He hunted most of his own game and ate a lot of fish that he smoked. We were happy to call him our neighbor.

Chapter 21: The Second to Arrive

Months before we had set up a remote monitoring outpost down valley. By day we used Semaphore flags and by night Morse code with flashlights in order to maintain radio silence. The outposts were placed far enough down valley it was impossible to see the smoke from the village because of the turn in the valley. Our system allowed for plenty of warning if someone was coming up the valley.

One day in early summer it was put to the test when a small group of people had made their way to the valley. Aaron and Sam were on watch the day when Sam spotted something.

"Aaron, take a look down valley I think I see something moving."

"Where do you think you saw it?"

"There, just past mile marker four on the right near the stream."

"There it is, I see them too, signal the alarm."

Aaron signaled the outposts up valley and it was relayed to the fort, that triggered an alert, and everyone mustered at their rally point. Fred was at the cave, that meant he reached the outpost first with Brandon close behind him.

"Report," Fred barked out.

"Belay that, Fred you gave up the job let me handle this okay?"

"I'm sorry Brandon force of habit, I'll step back."

"You heard the man report."

"About ten minutes ago some people were seen just past mile marker four. It looks like they may have made camp there because they have not moved any since they got there."

"Alright Sam you and Aaron grab the response packs and your weapons and start heading down that way. Don't approach their position in the light, wait until after dark to try to get in range to find out if you can get any intelligence."

"Yes sir, we won't let you down."

"I know you won't, now get."

I was confident Brandon had it under control and added, "Okay we have drilled these enough times we should have it down pat. Are you staying here Fred?"

"Nope Brandon has a handle on it and it's his job now, I don't need to stay, but I'll return in the morning if that's okay with the boss here."

Brandon replied, "Of course it is Fred, I still value your input."

"Thanks, I appreciate that."

"Peter if you are heading up to the fort can you have half the response team go home and have the other half stay the night in standby."

"I sure can Brandon, you watch over us now okay?"

"I will buddy."

Later that night Sam returned to the lowest outpost to update Brandon on what they heard and saw and left Aaron below to keep an eye on them.

"Back already? Well what did you find out?"

"From what we could tell its group of ten that have been traveling for some time looking for someplace safe to stay. I didn't hear any talk about attacks or anything like that."

"Did you see if they are armed?"

"Yes sir, it looks like all of them have a variety of weapons but nothing heavy."

"Does it look like they are staying the night?"

"Yes sir, they are. They had set up camp and were making dinner when I left."

"Okay you return to Aaron and keep an eye on them, and we'll be sending down a response team before light."

"Yes sir."

He departed downhill.

Part of the training included responding to this very situation, teams were always at the ready to respond. This time the team included Tom, the leader, with Alex and Scott filling out the team. The next morning, I met up with Tom and Fred, as well as Brandon and the rest of his team as they were heading down for the encounter. We were armed with P90's and various other side arms.

As we walked, we talked about the importance of not going off half-cocked. We didn't want anyone shooting someone before we knew who they were or their intent. When we got to the outpost Brandon gave the team their marching orders and off, we went.

Approaching an armed group of ten people like that is a dangerous thing, and it needs to be done with extreme caution. We surrounded their position while they slept and waited. I was sure glad we had night vision goggles.

Tom took charge, "Alright Alex you and Fred split up and surround the right flank. Scott you and Peter split up and take the left, and Brandon and I will come up the middle. When everyone is in position stay put. I'll approach the group in the morning after they are up, and we can see everyone. I'll give them one warning shot. If any of them go for their weapons, or if they point one at me, shoot em."

"Okay Tom we have your back."

As Tom approach the group he came in with his hands in the air. He turned around and called out for them not to pick up their weapons because there are guns trained on each one of them.

"My name is Tom and I'm not here to harm you. Please do not even reach for your weapons because my team will shoot if you do, with no additional warnings. As you can see, I'm not armed, I just want to talk. You're a long way from anything, and we just want to know where you are from and where you are heading."

An average looking guy with a beard approached Tom, with his hands up, and called out for everyone not to touch their weapons. He repeated Tom's action with his hands up and turned around.

"My name is Floyd and we're tired, cold and hungry, we mean no one any harm. We're not looking for a fight; we saw smoke rising above the ridge as we rounded the pass from the south. We followed the river up and here we are."

Surprised Tom asked Floyd, "You saw our smoke from the valley below?"

"No, we saw it when we were on top of the ridge above us, and we came down to check it out."

Tom replied, "I see, well my leaders will want to know who you are and where you're going. Before they come in, we will have to temporally take your weapons."

Tom motioned for us to enter. The team had their weapons at the ready with the safety off, but Fred, Brandon and I stayed back. They cautiously walked around and picked up every weapon they saw and placed them in a pile near Tom. None of the strangers made any move or complaint, as weapons were collected. With that Brandon, Fred and I entered the area.

"Hi, my name is Brandon. I'm the leader of the men that have their weapons trained on you. We're not a militia, but we are well trained and will shoot if we feel threatened."

Floyd's wife Alice was a tough lady; she was not too keen on guns being pointed at them and exclaimed, "Threatened?!! You are not the ones with the guns pointed at you."

Floyd put his hands out toward Alice and said, "I have this, there is no need to make things worse."

Brandon nodded and said, "She is right Floyd."

Tom turned and called out to his team.

"Everyone, safety your weapons and lower them."

Our team lowered their weapons but still held them at the ready. Brandon continued,

"Okay now, Alice? Was that your name?"

"YES."

"Why don't you join us over here and we can sit down and talk. Okay?"

Hesitantly Alice walked over to where Brandon, Tom, and I were and took a seat by Floyd at their fire. The rest of their party stood by and listened intently.

Brandon said, "Now that everyone seems a bit more at ease let me introduce you to our leader, to my left here is Peter. He has led us through some tough times, and I'm sure you'll find he can be a good friend if you are as you say you are."

"Thanks Brandon, that's some introduction, first off, why don't the rest of you
join us around the fire and stay warm."

Everyone moved around until we were around the fire with Alex and Scott still standing on the outside with their weapons.

I continued, "I think the first order of business should be taking care of your needs, I heard you say you were hungry. Scott, bring over our MRE's and hand them out to these people."

Scott retrieved the MRE's and handed them out to the strangers. Everyone attacked them like they had not eaten in days. Brandon and I just had some instant coffee and gave them the rest of ours.

Floyd spoke first, "Thank you for the food it has been a spell since we have eaten anything but fish and berries."

I replied, "It seems to be a standard practice for us, feeding strangers we find. Why don't we go around and introduce ourselves and tell everyone where we came from? I'll start, my name is Peter and I'm originally from Bellingham, Washington. I had been traveling and living full time in a motor home with my wife Ann for about three years when the quake hit."

Floyd spoke up, "Holy shit! We're neighbors, we are from just outside Concrete, Washington."

"Then you and I'll have to have a one on one talk at some point. Anyway, we were in northwest Arizona when the quake hit. To my right is Brandon."

"Hi, I'm Brandon, I'm the leader of the security force here."

"My name is Tom, and I'm just a foot soldier."

"No Tom you are far more than that."

"My name is Fred and I used to be their leader."

"Well I'm Floyd, my right hand here is Alice my wife." Gesturing to his left Floyd held out his hand. We could be at this all day, I'm just going to go from my left here and give you everyone's name, if that is okay with everybody.

"I'm good with that."

"Alright, this is Mark and his wife Kate, Bill and Ed, Hank and Ted, and John and Edith. We came from different parts of the country and all of us have made our way out of a zone of destruction. As I said before, Alice and I made our way out of the Pacific Northwest. I'll let everyone else tell you their stories, but I really don't want to get into those details here and now."

I said, "I'm with you there Floyd, I know you're tired, and I'm certain that everyone else would like to hear more about what is happening outside the valley."

"It's not just you guys here?"

Brandon replied, "No Mark not by a long shot, but before we go over that we need to know your intentions."

Floyd added, "I don't think we really have any intentions except to stay alive. The only guns we have are the ones your men have, and some more pistols in our packs. We have very little food but if you need some, you're welcome to it. We're just looking for someplace safe to live, away from anyone that wants to do us any harm.

We're simple people and want rest. I get the feeling that you guys feel the same or you would have already killed us in our sleep and taken everything from us. Please tell me I'm right about my impression of you."

I spoke up, "You're righter than you could ever know. We live in a settlement up valley from here. We're a community of like-minded people that made our own little utopia, for lack of a better word. It has been our way to bring people in from the cold and make them part of our world, but you would be expected to comply with our social standards and to do your part for the whole.

If you're all in agreement with that we will take you to our settlement and find you a place to live. We will help you get settled in, then you will be given a chance to tell everyone else of your travels."

Mark was still not sure he trusted us, "And what if we don't want to join you, will you let us leave here?"

I replied, "We will, but I'll warn you that if you make that choice, then think you can pretend to leave and try to return with hostile intentions, you won't make it within a mile of our compound."

"Is that a threat?"

"No Mark I'm just saying."

We went over the rest of the conditions to join us. Floyd looked around at his traveling companions who were nodding their heads in agreement.

"Well it looks like it's hell yeah."

I said, "Okay then if you are each in agreement then raise your hands."

Before Mark raised his hands, he asked, "What did you say about what happens to people that break the golden rule?"

I replied, "Well so far so good, we have not had to ever deal with that, but if it does the person will be dealt with in an appropriate way depending on what happened. Something like rape or murder will be fatal, and on from there. Those are some very interesting questions you have Mark. Why would those be the questions you ask in this situation?"

"It's simple Peter, you're not the first group that we have met that had guns that wanted us as slave labor."

I added, "You're right Mark, many in our home have had the same experiences and have been just as suspicious, that's a good sense to have."

"Do you have a name for your little home?"

"Yes, we do, it's Little Haven."

I called out, "Let's see a show of hands."

Everyone's hands went up fast except Mark. He had this cautious look on his face and looked at the rest of his traveling companions. He noted that had their hands up and were looking back at him with an are you nuts look. Finally, Mark slowly raised his hand too.

With that we returned their weapons to them and collected their belongings and started up the valley. This was the first time I had gone up the valley from below since everything was built. I smiled as it started to come into view. Now I was sure Paradise Valley was the perfect name for the valley.

That day everyone showed them around and our new guests were surprised at how nice a place we had built. We showed them the outside of the fort and the cave, then we brought them by the mill and on to other places. We knew the cave wouldn't hold everyone. We invited Floyd and Alice to stay in our loft until they could get a cabin built, the rest were split up between the cave and others in the community.

That evening we met at the cave for a potluck dinner and meeting. We had a nice fire going in the fire ring outside.

Everyone wanted to hear about the outside world, I wanted to hear about home, I asked Floyd and Alice to be first. I was being selfish but sometimes I deserve the perk of being the Chairman. What Floyd related could only be described as an apocalyptic scene.

Chapter 22: The Pacific Northwest

"The devastation was complete, absolutely nothing of the green lush land we loved remained, none of it. Vancouver, BC was hard hit and Canada abandoned it. I'm sorry to tell you Peter and Ann but Bellingham, Washington was completely washed away by multiple waves."

"To be honest Floyd I expected that, we both did."

"Ash from Mt.Baker fell nonstop for days, it was dark even at noon, many more days. After the ash fall slowed and it wasn't as dark, we decided we needed to check out the lowlands to see the damage. The only news of the quake we had was from the few people that had made it up from the Skagit Valley below.

We were not sure why we had not seen anyone from Anacortes, Sedro Woolley or any of the lowland cities at the bottom of our valley. If anyone had made it up, they would've had to follow Highway 20 to get away from the damage.

I needed to find out what went on down there, to that end my neighbors and I put together a scouting party of four guys. We headed west down Hwy 20 to get a look at the destruction but didn't get far before we started finding it. The highway was covered by over a foot of ash in places and it was getting deeper. Cars littered the highway having smashed into each from the ground shaking violently. They were completely covered with ash; most had left their doors open as they fled.

Further down we came upon the most unsettling sight. Some thirty miles inland from the Puget Sound was a long pile of rubble. All of it laying haphazardly and intermingled with everything under the sun. The pile was only a couple feet tall but went as far as we could see in both directions. I immediately knew what it was because we could see cars, boats, and the remains of houses left behind as a wave must have made it that far than lost its energy.

We could see the tangled mess we were standing on top of must have been the high-water point for the biggest tsunami wave. In front of us was an obliterated wasteland, completely covered in gray ash. Behind us everything was also covered in ash but still mostly intact. It was the most disturbing sight I've ever seen; the odor was almost overpowering, the smell of death hung in the air.

In the distance we could see bands of mounds coming up the valley with nothing between them. They were clearly the same type of debris lines from smaller waves. The waves washed all the way up the Skagit Valleys to the base of the Cascades.

It looked like a wasteland. There were no trees, no buildings, no vehicles, nothing. The ground was mostly flat and covered with small debris. Every so often we could see the foundation of houses and the posts from various signs, but the signs were gone.

As we made our way further down, less and less was found between the mounds. Even the foundations and poles were gone, and we saw fewer bodies. The smell of the rotting flesh was horrendous.

It took us a couple of days before we got down to what we expected to be the lowlands, but there was none. All we saw was water, saltwater washing ashore in small lapping waves. What used to be corn, berries and tulip fields was now the shallow tidelands of the Sound. It was impossible to tell exactly where we were because there were no landmarks left. It must have been low tide when we arrived because we could see sign of human habitation were the water was clearly there just hours before. There was also no ash on any of it.

We couldn't get further south subsequently we couldn't check on Seattle. We knew that no one below where we stood survived, it was most likely also the case in Seattle too. We made our way back home and decided it was time to get out of there. There was nothing left of the region and no hope of ever getting any help, we had to fend for ourselves.

We lived at a higher elevation outside of Concrete up near Baker Lake. That area escaped the waves but had lost everything to the shaking. There was no power, water or anything. Many had bugged out right away even though they had little hope of getting far. The bridges east of town were all destroyed and there was no west anymore.

We had a ham radio but heard little about the Sound, as there were no local radio signals to be found. However, we were able to pick up others further away. Listening to those broadcasts we picked up limited reports about other parts of the country and learned that nothing would ever be restored. After a few days the sheriff and his deputies feared for their families; they went home to protect them, with that chaos ruled.

We made our way back and decided that it was clear that our world was not going to make it, we packed up our gear and headed out. We wanted to make sure we could still travel.

We put the topper on the back of our 4x4 pickup and packed it with everything we could fit in it then headed east. We took the portable gas pump from my toy hauler to use to get gas from underground tanks at gas stations. We filled the truck with gas and then filled several 5-gallon cans with enough fuel to fill the truck twice more on the road. With that we would be able to go over eight hundred miles.

I had customized my truck with a high clearance and big

meaty tires. Everyone used to ask me why I had done that to my pickup, but now it was clear. Any time we came across a wiped-out bridge we just went around it. With the extra high clearance and tires we were able to cross the streams even if we had to find a better spot to cross.

As we passed through Eastern Washington, we found that area had faired the quake well, with many people still in their homes. There was ash everywhere but not so much that they couldn't survive. But those areas where overtaken by militia or looted and burned afterwards, one group had taken control of the National Guard facilities and their equipment. Many of the men assigned, knew the government was done. They simply followed the militia's orders in hopes of protecting their own families. Many civilians were killed disobeying them.

We avoided every major city trying to get south. We traveled by night as much as possible to avoid the roving militia patrols looking for '"volunteers"' and anything they could use. We ended up in Arizona in a remote section of the Kaibab National Forrest. That was where we met Kate and Mark, they were on the rim of a canyon west of the Colorado River. They had a nice camp and we were relieved when they invited us to join forces with them."

Everyone thanked Floyd for telling us about their harrowing experiences and he thanked us for listening.

Chapter 23: Las Vegas

Next up was Mark, a tall skinny guy with a little mustache and no hair. It was clear he was intelligent and had no problem thinking on his feet. Kate was also tall, skinny and seemed like a perfect match for Mark. The two of them seemed to know what the other was thinking.

"We were in Las Vegas when the quake hit and could really feel the shaking. As soon as we heard the news about the scope of the quake, and that it had affected the entire west coast, we knew everything was going to change and fast. We knew that we needed to get out of town quick before all hell broke loose.

Luckily, I'd inherited a ton of money from my grandfather, money wasn't an issue. We swung by my buddy Ned and his wife Amanda's place and picked them up. Then we headed to the stores to get the last of the gear we felt we would need. The four of us had been great friends, we had done several practice runs, bugging out over the years. We were sure we were ready for anything.

We'd been prepping for years, that meant I already had a fully loaded diesel Land Rover with a snorkel and exhaust riser. You can drive down the middle of streams with water over the hood. It also had a high clearance and big meaty tires for even the roughest terrain. We hooked up the large military trailer, to transport more gear.

We hit an Army Surplus store first and bought everything we could from there. Next, was one of those big sporting goods stores to load up on more gear. Now the truck had all the gear we could fit.

It had a nice chuck wagon kitchen with cast iron skillets, and everything needed for an extended time in the woods. All that was left to focus on was food, then guns and ammo, and a few comfort items. Next, came every case of freeze-dried food in the place as well as every MRE they had. When we walked out, there was no food left in the store. Then we decided we needed to get lightweight gear for when we no longer had the Rover.

We picked up one of those expedition style backpacking tents that could hold up in any wind. After that we got four lightweight down sleeping bags good down to negative ten degrees and all kinds of cold weather clothes. Next, we got a couple of small multi-fuel backpacking cooking stoves and two lightweight titanium cook sets.

We picked up every Sayer mini filter straw they had; each one is good for 100,000 gallons of water for drinking. We got two large backpacks and two smaller ones for the girls that allowed us to carry everything. We were as ready as we could be.

Before we headed out of town, we loaded up two dozen five-gallon yellow Jerry cans with diesel in the trailer, that meant we had plenty of fuel. We picked up topographical maps of the entire southwest region to make sure we were covered wherever we went.

We headed west into the Kaibab National Forrest, where we had already scouted a remote section of it. The plan was to get as far from people as possible in hopes of staying away from those that would want what we had. We reached our destination late the first night and set up camp. We only set up a quick camp and left everything else in the trailer and Rover in case we needed to get away fast.

We hoped we would have the place to ourselves, but we were not that lucky. We'd been there a week when a small group showed up. Kate and I were in camp while Ned and Amanda were off fishing when the group surprised them on foot. Before we knew it, the bastards killed them both. Kate and I took off in the Rover and were able to get away. I wanted to kill all of them, but Kate convinced me we needed to get away instead. I'm going to miss them; Ned was my best friend since grade school."

That was hard for Mark to recall, the tears welled up in his eyes as well as many in the crowd. I told him he didn't need to continue but he insisted. Kate went over to him and held his hand and that seemed to ease his pain some. Mark regained his composure and continued.

"After a few more days of travel we reached a spot high above the Colorado River. From our new location we could see the river below and had plenty of water from a small stream passing through camp. Whenever someone new showed up we would hear about the mayhem we left behind. We learned that the government flat out stated they couldn't help anyone on the west coast and that everyone had to fend for themselves.

In time a fair amount of people showed up, that painted a grave picture of what was happening and proved I was right about what to expect. I'm not sure how long we had been there when Floyd and Alice showed up and joined our little camp."

Ann said, "We were swamped where we were, I wonder why you didn't get as many people at your camp."

"I have no idea Ann, maybe because when Las Vegas fell not many people made it out of town, it's anybody's guess."

Chapter 24: The Great Flood

Mark continued....

"It was only a few days, maybe a week, after Floyd and Alice arrived that we felt a strong aftershock. It wasn't much, but after that we heard a loud roar coming from the canyon. Everyone rushed to the edge of the canyon to see what the noise was. We couldn't believe our eyes; a massive wall of water, trees, rocks and mud was rushing down the canyon obliterating everything in its path. Looking down on the scene, I could only imagine what had happened up stream.

Later we heard that the violent shaking from the quake had damaged the Glen Canyon dam. That had weakened it leaving it in a vulnerable state and primed for failure. Fleeing the surrounding cities many had migrated up the Colorado River and settled on its banks. Unfortunately, there was no one to tell them about the state of the dam above them.

The aftershock put more stress and pressure on the already undermined dam, and it gave way. It must have made some eerie sounds before it gave way. The force of that water was punishing the dam. When the dam gave way giant chunks of concrete, steel, and silt-laden water careened down the valley.

We watched in astonishment from above as the water rushed down the valley floor below us. It was horrible; the people down there had set up a hell of a settlement, as they were getting ready for the winter.

None of the settlers ever imagined they were sitting below a failed dam. Or that they were in the path of a wall of water that would reach over a hundred foot tall. The water carried all the debris from the dam and everything it picked up along the way. It came crashing down the valley fast, no one had a chance of getting out of its path, everyone perished. Even more disheartening, we knew the water was on its way to Lake Mead. The worst part was that there was more on its shores, and below the Hoover Dam, we could only assume the worst was still to come.

All that debris and water did indeed make its way to Lake Mead and the Hoover Dam. Unlike Lake Powel above, Lake Mead was over a hundred fifty feet below its normal level. Most of the people out of Las Vegas had made camp as close to the water as they could and as far up the river as possible. Huge numbers of people had made their homes on the shore of Lake Mead above the Hoover Dam. Even more for miles along the bank of the Colorado River below the Hoover Dam.

Like the people below Glen Canyon, they too had no warning about the impending doom heading their way. When the waters from Lake Powel, and the debris, reached Lake Mead it instantly raised the water above the normal level and killed the people along the shores.

Hoover Dam was also damaged by the quake and aftershocks, that meant it was weakened as well. When the flood hit Lake Mead it filled so fast that the Hoover Damn couldn't take any more. Suddenly, the dam ruptured. A giant wall of water, concrete, and steel exploded, and the entire upper face of the dam blew apart with a tremendous force.

More and more chunks broke away until most of the dam gave way and Lake Meade spilled out into the canyon below. As the water rushed downstream it obliterated everything in its path. Everyone living on its banks were gone, crushed by the power of the water and the debris or just washed away.

The water continued to make its way down the entire length of the Colorado River taking out every dam and bridge along the way to the coast. It eliminated every man-made obstacle along its entire length. It took some time before the flood ended but when it did the river flowed free again all the way to the Gulf of California. It was the first time in more than a hundred years.

As odd as it sounds though, while this was a tragedy for everyone killed, it was a blessing for the four of us. After the water receded it left an easy path to follow up the Colorado River. We found it left wide flat barren banks on both sides since everything along it had been washed away.

By now the place we were at was overcrowded, it was no longer a nice place, accordingly we began preparing to leave. We decided that we were going to take advantage of the disaster and make our way up the river as far as we could. We figured if we drove on the flat, we could stay off the roads and avoid most of the people.

We thought that the only ones that knew about this new route were those in our camp, we figured it would be smooth sailing. I still had most of my diesel left in my Land Rover and the full Jerry cans, we headed back to ALT 89 and down to the river below.

However, it turned out that we were not the only ones to have found this new superhighway. Many others had discovered it as well and were making their way up it too. But because we had the Land Rover and extra fuel, we were able to make it much further than anyone else before we would run out of diesel.

As we went along, we discovered that the river had changed course in many locations and had formed large lakes now teaming with fish. Many of the people that had headed up the river opted to stay along these lakes, the number of travelers dwindled quickly. We had also stopped for a while and enjoyed some good fishing before continuing along the new path. We found traveling to be easy going all the way up the river as far as the base of the ruins of the Glen Canyon dam.

The ruins were a strangely beautiful sight. The rubble and debris formed what looked like a giant fan that made a perfect ramp. There was a large waterfall cascading down the middle as the stream washed away the fan down the center. We had no problem getting past it because the sediment was still behind the dam in much the same fashion.

Standing on the broken base of the dam, we could see the devastation below us, and we could also see way up valley. It was an eerie scene ahead of us, there was no life to be seen. Everything was this dreary grayish color with countless large broken tree trunks as far as the eye could see. Let me tell you it is a strange feeling walking where a lake used to be not long ago.

We made it all the way past what used to á Lake Powell, and well into Utah, when we came upon a large confluence from the north. I could tell from the map that this branch came out of the canyon lands and the desert, we decided to continue east toward Colorado, deep into Navajo Nation territory.

We were a couple days into the reservation, camping on a nice plateau, when we saw a line of men on the edge of the canyon above us. Then we heard splashing coming from the river and it was clearly getting closer. As we looked in that direction it was like something out of a Hollywood movie.

Materializing slowly and approaching us was what appeared to be a band of Navaho warriors on horseback. Our adrenaline started pumping as we realized it wasn't just a band of warriors, but a war party, complete with painted horses, men wearing war shirts, and all with painted faces and carrying rifles or AK-47's. I immediately told everyone in my group to not move.

The men circled us on horseback and what looked like the oldest of the warriors dismounted. I noticed that these warriors had short unevenly cut hair as if chopped off with a knife.

Watching the warrior's approach, I remembered reading how when traditional Navahos lost someone close to them, they cut their hair to show they were in mourning. The men had short cropped hair, which also increased my level of fear.

The older man walked to within an arms-length of us, turned, then signaled his warriors to dismount. As the old man climbed off his horse, I could see he was wearing a painted war shirt that was soiled and had traces of blood. The old man was about six feet tall and built like a tree stump. His face was etched with a road map of wrinkles showing a difficult life outdoors. I found myself stretching to my full height and introduced myself as Mark."

Chapter 25: The New Navajo Nation

"As this old man looked me up and down, with a face that was unreadable, he said",

"'My name is Black Cloud and I'm the chief of the Navaho Nation. **You** are trespassing on **Our** land.'"

To Black Cloud I said, "We mean no disrespect. We only want to pass through your land. If we have overstepped our bounds, we ask your forgiveness. We would be grateful if you would accept our generosity in extending some of our provisions to you in exchange for passage through your land.

I then told Floyd to grab a case of freeze-dried ice cream. In his haste Floyd quickly reached into the Land Rover. As he did, we heard the unmistakable sound of rifles being cocked. Floyd's face was as white as a sheet and he became as stiff, rigid, and unmoving as the freeze-dried ice cream. We looked around and we laughed so hard. As soon as Black Cloud saw Floyd's response he and his warriors also joined in on the laughter.

As Floyd stepped away from the Rover, his adrenaline still pumping, with the case of freeze-dried ice cream in his hands, he whined."

Floyd spoke up on that, "Yeah I bet you wouldn't have thought it funny if it was you, they had their guns trained on."

"Sorry Floyd it was kind of funny. Anyway, Floyd slowly placed the case at Black Clouds feet, and I pulled one out, opened it, and handed it to him to eat. He took a bite of it and stood there for the longest moment when he took a second bite, the corners of his mouth turned up in what looked like a slight smile."

"What is this stuff? It tastes like chocolate ice cream."

He asked.

"I smiled and told him. It's freeze-dried ice cream. We have several cases of it as well as other foods. Black Cloud, why don't you and your men join us for a feast?"

"Yes, but I want some more of the ice cream first."

"Of course, that case is yours, we have lots more.

With that for an ice breaker, no pun intended, he motioned to his men to lay down their weapons. I then also invited Black Cloud's warriors to join us as well. He nodded and sat down by the fire with us and continued to eat his freeze-dried ice cream. I had Floyd pull out cases of MRE's and we feasted, so to speak. Later that night we sat around the fire eating ice cream in the middle of the desert, it was quite the odd sight and we developed a bond with Black Cloud and his men.

Black Cloud motioned to one of his warriors to bring his pipe to him; I couldn't believe it when he lit up a bong. We had a long talk with Black Cloud about what had gone on, and about some of our harrowing experiences.

I asked him how he felt about the fall of the government that had taken their land. He paused for some time on that one and with a slight sigh he spoke in a soft almost emotional voice.

"It was long ago that the Bilaganna took our land, Dinetah, from our ancestors and much has changed. Through education our native language has once again returned to our people. Most of our people are now bi-lingual, speaking our Native language and English as well.

The tribe paid for my law degree from Harvard. In return I represented the tribe on litigation involving our disputed land and treaty rights. I had practiced for 10 years in your courts and saw many injustices. I found that what the

Bilagaana calls justice and what we call justice are two very different things

After completing my agreement for my tribe to represent my people, the Dine, in your injustice system, I decided I wanted nothing more to do with your world with its injustices and misinterpretations of the law. I returned home twenty years ago to live my life here amongst my people, and here I will remain. The more I lived amongst the Bilaganna, the more I understood their life, the more distrust I had for other people. At least my people rattle first.

Your government was run by a few rich men driven by the lure of easy money, they spoke of morals but lived an immoral life. All of them were rotten, starting with the bankers who were the worst, then followed by the corporations, Congress, Senate, and not the least among them, the President. None of them could be trusted, because they each had their own agenda and it wasn't our best interests."

"I'd like to say that I understand, but that would diminish your feelings. I can say that I've also wished for so long that things would be different, much in the same way as you have. In the end, I respect your feelings and views. It hurt to see our country run by unknown, unseen faces."

"Now the world we once knew is no longer. Your government no longer runs our lives or anyone else's. But this may not be such a good thing. Now there's no order or law. Large groups of heavily armed people are attempting to control their small parcel of land and will kill anyone in their way."

"This is just one, of the reasons that we traveled to your land, Black Cloud. We're trying to stay away from those areas with rampant anarchy. If we passed through them, they would take everything we have left if given a chance."

"What makes you think we, won't? We have you out-numbered, and you're on our land."

"We knew as soon as we made the decision to enter your land that we would be virtually at your mercy. We only hoped that you'd allow us to pass through, that way we could avoid passing through the militia's lands. Like you said earlier, at least you guys rattle before you strike!"

"You're correct, at least we're talking before we shoot," he laughed but without humor.

Now with a more serious look he said,

"You asked how I felt about the events that have led you here. The U.S. government took our land many generations ago and now we have it back, need I say more. Many Dine have returned to our native land, Dinetah, since the fall of your government and now we will fight to the death to keep it. This time there are no armies, armed forces, or an organized government with unlimited arsenals to again take our land.

There are only unorganized groups of people spread over this vast land. We know our land as we know ourselves. It's living and breathing as we are. To outsiders this land is unknown and hostile terrain. They'll fight to take what isn't theirs and we'll fight to keep what is ours. I ask you, who'll fight harder?

As an Iraq war veteran, I'm saddened at the loss of a great nation, but as the Chief of the Navajo Nation, I'm overjoyed. Our Nation was once able to live in harmony on our land before the Bilagaana stole it, bringing their treachery and their religion. Now we're still a nation, and this isn't the case for the white man! You too said you were unhappy with how things were."

"I was, unhappy. But what could I do? You had the

option of coming back home, to your land and leading your people. I didn't have that option! (I said slowly working around the lump in my throat.) I fought in the Gulf war, stood by and watched two sons risk their lives fighting another war to defend our freedom. It was insanity!

I had only wanted the country to become a bit more humane, not to be destroyed. But I have also learned that sometimes before things are able to change, destruction is necessary, and there is no other way.

We were exactly what some wanted to be as a nation, driven by the moral minorities and money. We lived with great abandon not caring about the ultimate outcome, only caring about our personal gain."

"Mark, there is one important factor that defines the differences between our survival and our ability to thrive. They could destroy our lands but not our connection to this land or our spirit."

"You're absolutely right Black Cloud. Most people today have lost the ability to survive in anything other than their house. If there was food in the fridge, people didn't care. They lost the ability to survive in adversity, without hot and cold running water, electricity and heat. If they're put in a situation of having to survive, their faces would go blank with the deer-in-the-headlight stare. They would panic or remain in denial with their heads in the sand, most do not even know how to make fire without a lighter."

"That is true Mark, you hit the nail on the head. You seem to be faring well in this new world."

"That's because most of us here are of the same mind. We've spent many years honing our survival skills backpacking or camping. We know how to make fire and treat water; we can hunt and fish without modern gear. I've personally ensured I'd be ready no matter what, even if I hadn't been able to get the things I did.

It'll be those without skills that could be the most dangerous, but they're also the ones that are going to die in large numbers as time goes by, and all the store shelves are empty. Billions will perish around the world, lost to the elements and lack of food.

Sensing that some catastrophic event was inevitable, due to the raping of this earth, I've always had basic survival gear ready. Anyone that paid attention to the direction this country has been heading would've been able to see it. However, in this case the moment the quake hit I knew this was it. I didn't wait for any signs that the apocalypse was coming before acting.

Most of the militias have known for a long time that this day was coming. Therefore, they have stockpiled huge arsenals of weapons and built well-defended compounds that many have lived on for years, expecting a catastrophe long ago. The difference between them and me, or us, is they decided it is ok to just take what they want, and we don't see it that way"

Floyd asked, "Were you here on your lands when the quake hit Chief?"

"Yes, I was."

I asked him, "Have you traveled outside your land lately to witness what's happening in the rest of the country?"

"No."

Black Cloud hesitated, closing his eyes before continuing to answer further. He'd seen the destruction and chaos in a vision. He was drawn out of his silence by me again asking if he'd seen what had happened outside his land.

"Mark, I've not left Dinetah and have no desire to leave. There's nothing out there that we need. I know what's going on in the rest of the country, there's complete unrest almost everywhere. I didn't have to leave here to know."

"What have you heard?"

"Well Mark, some of my people were able to make it here from Denver, they said they barely made it here alive. There was rioting everywhere and total chaos in the streets. All of the stores had been looted and set on fire."

"Was there anything left of it?"

"I was told that most of the outlying area survived being burned, but there was still rioting and looting. Lawlessness prevailed and there was no food or water for people, which will certainly increase the turmoil. Many in their haste to get away from the mayhem headed for the mountains. They left as soon as the shit hit the fan, trying to get away from death, but without any provisions. It didn't take long before the roads into the Rockies were blocked by abandoned cars, and hordes of people on foot just trying to get away.

Some of my people were in Aurora, Colorado when mayhem broke out. They headed south as soon as the quake hit, and they were able to stay ahead of the hoards. Knowing they'd be safe and welcome here, the men headed in this direction. Since the quake, we had blocked the roads in and out expecting our people to arrive here looking for safety."

"Tell me. How was it we were able to make it this far onto your land unseen?"

"You didn't make it unseen. The second you stepped foot on our land our scouts sent word of your trespassing. The scouts were instructed to observe only. To watch and to listen, and to report back to me. I wanted to see who was smart enough to use the rivers rather than roads. Since you were watched from your first step onto our land, I believed you had no intention of stealing from us. Had it been different, you wouldn't be here."

"What about others, I'm sure there'll be more trying to come in the same way we did."

"I don't doubt that for a minute, which is why we now have warriors down by the river to stop anyone from entering our land."

We planned to head on in the morning. We won't be able to travel much further up the river in our vehicle, as we expect the terrain will be impassable even in the Land Rover. Given that, I'd like to make a trade with you. How about six horses for the Land Rover, trailer, and fuel.

There's still quite a bit of fuel in the trailer. The Rover has been modified to run on many different fuels including vegetable oil and clean used motor oil. You could make your own and never run out. And how about I sweeten the deal, literally, I'll throw in a couple of cases of that freeze-dried ice cream you seem to like."

He laughed and said, "Sounds like a fair trade to me, we'll ride with you as far as you can go in your truck then we'll make the trade.

We spent the rest of the night talking about many things including philosophy, religion and even a little politics before we called it a night. The next day we headed up stream as a large caravan.

When we had gone as far as the Land Rover would take us, we transferred as much gear as we could to the horses. When we finished loading what the horses could safely carry, one of Black Clouds men started to get into the Rover. I quickly yelled, 'STOP!"

"WHAT are you doing!? Why did you stop him from taking the Rover? We had a deal."

Black Cloud's man immediately stopped in his tracks reacting to the commotion.

"I wasn't stopping him from taking the Rover, I was saving his life. I booby trapped the Rover with explosives. I jogged over to the Rover and disarmed it removing the explosives. I planned to take them with us just in case we'd need it.

Black Cloud nodded his head, letting out a long-held breath. He then thanked me for everything, and we reciprocated with thanks to him and his warriors. Black Cloud then said that when we could no longer travel with the horses, to just let them go and they'd return home.

We'd come to know each other in such a short time but given the circumstances it was not surprising that good comrades were made in times of adversity. We then began to say our good-byes, but before we left, I had one final request of Black Cloud.

Black Cloud anticipated my request and said that he had every intention of watching our backs and wouldn't allow anyone on his land, or to follow us for that matter as we had become more than friends. We were brothers. We then rode off, hopefully towards some safety.

Black Cloud told us the river would take us past a small town called Mexican Hat. We hoped to avoid people, we made sure to pass it in the dark of night. After a couple of days of travel, we reached Mexican Hat. As Black Cloud mentioned, we found a bridge through the middle of town.

While we were resting under that bridge, we heard a car coming and it came to a stop on top of the bridge. We heard a couple guys talking about filling up their water jugs and spending the night there. We grabbed our weapons and got ready for what we expected to be a fire fight."

Pointing over to Bill and Ed, "It was then that these two came into view. You should have seen them, I thought they both were going to crap themselves when they saw us."

Bill spoke up, "You would've too Mark if it was you climbing down that embankment, expecting it to be deserted, and seen four guns pointed at you."

"Anyway, that night the six of us talked and decided to allow the two of them to continue up stream with us."

This time Ed responded, "And we're glad you did, there's no telling what would've happened to us if we had not found you guys."

Ann asked, "Where are you guys from?"

Bill replied, "We're from San Francisco, we both lived there our whole lives and met each other in grade school."

Tammy asked, "Did you guys know you were gay that early in life?"

Surprised she knew, Ed replied, "We never said we were gay, what makes you think we are?"

Tammy quipped, "Oh please, it takes one to know one, and in this case, it's easy to see."

Bill continued, "Anyway we left The Bay Area about a week after the quake."

I jumped in, "So far you're the only ones from that area that made it through the quake. Are you guys up to telling us your experiences?"

Bill responded, "I can't speak for Ed but I am."

Ed replied, "I'm okay, but I'm going to let you do most of

Xavier Bruehler

it."

"That's fine."

Chapter 26: The Bay Area

"We weren't in San Francisco, when the quake hit. We were in the Golden Gate National Recreation Area across the bay, enjoying a nice picnic, when the ground began to shake. We couldn't believe what we were seeing as the city we both loved was being leveled before our eyes."

"It was our favorite spot because of the magnificent views. At night the lights of the city and bridge made an incredible sight. From our vantage point we could see the entire length of the bridge, and out over the expanse of San Francisco. That day we sat in disbelief and watched in horror as the magnitude of it unfolded in front of us."

Bill and Ed's eyes began to fill with tears as Bill told us what they saw next.

"It started out like any other quake, but we knew in seconds that this one was different. When you live in an active quake zone you get used to them, but this quake was the biggest and strongest we ever felt. When it hadn't ended after a minute, we knew it was different from any other quake we had lived through. I kept asking why it wasn't ending.

We watched as the bridge began to sway before the full force of the quake had reached it. Cars were being thrown from side to side and drivers stopped to avoid going on the bridge. People all around us were screaming 'Oh My God look at the bridge.'

We couldn't believe what we were seeing. It was difficult for us to even stay on our feet, after a bit it was impossible. Ed and I sat on the ground, hanging on to what was left of a light pole, and were stunned as we saw the bridge was being shaken apart.

As the full force of the quake hit the bridge, we could see

cars being thrown off and large chunks of the structure breaking apart and crashing to the water below. Watching was horrible, as we knew people were falling to their deaths.

The quake had been going on for over five minutes when I commented to Ed that this had to be 'The Big One' we've always been warned about. Ed said he was happy to see that the bridge had not completely collapsed even though parts were broken away and cars had been shaken off.

Moments later we heard what sounded like an explosion. Then we saw the main center tower begin to crumble. Even before the top of the tower hit the deck, we could see the cables, that hold it up, begin to break free as the bridge started to fall apart.

Any cars that had remained, fell into the water below as the entire surface of the road collapsed and crashed into the bay. It was a terrible sight and we both had to close our eyes because we couldn't watch anymore. We couldn't believe what was happening to our city."

Bills eyes began welling up as he described what he saw, but he wasn't alone, almost everyone there was already crying or holding their mouths.

"Because we'd been watching the bridge so closely, we hadn't been watching the city. When we looked out at our beloved city, we could see the landscape had already changed. I kept looking for the Trans-America Tower, but I couldn't find it. That was where I worked, many of my friends and co-workers were in the tower when the quake hit.

We both had tears running from our eyes as we watched in disbelief as our home was being destroyed. We could see building-by-building falling, with dust and smoke enveloping the city. It wasn't long before we couldn't even see the city anymore.

The ground continued to shake for over nine minutes, we knew this was not 'The Big One' we had been told to expect. We had both lived through the Loma Prieta quake back in 1989. We knew that when the Loma Prieta or the San Andreas Fault gave way, it only lasted for a few seconds to a minute; this was clearly not one of them. We also knew from having lived through countless other quakes that the ground didn't move like this.

When it finally stopped, we fell into each other's arms and cried, but to our horror after only a few seconds the ground started shaking again. This time it felt more like the quakes we both had grown up with, living in the Bay area. This one was another strong one, but it wasn't bouncing us around on the ground like the last one did. Additionally, it only lasted for a couple of minutes and it was over.

We knew we couldn't get back to the city across the Golden Gate Bridge. However, we were frantic to find out about our family and friends. Everyone around us was crying and screaming in disbelief and not knowing what to do. We started to head for our car when we came across a police officer. He was surrounded by people who were trying to find out what happened.

He told everyone he had lost contact with the station and that it was best for everyone to remain calm and stay where we were. Ed would have nothing to do with that, he started screaming at me to get in our car and go. We ignored the advice of the police officer and got in our car.

Unfortunately, everyone else had ignored him as well. We didn't even get out of the park before we were halted by traffic. Ed and I spent a day in the park sleeping in our car before the road cleared up enough for us to get out.

We were elated as we made our way to Oakland because

we could see that the new Oakland Bay Bridge was still intact. But our joy was short lived as we started to approach the exit to the bridge. We were stopped by a roadblock. No one was being allowed to enter the city and the bridge was only one way, out.

Again, we were crushed; it had been three days and we hadn't heard from any of our family or friends, we feared the worst. We remembered a friend that lived nearby in Oakland, we decided to head there.

They had a nice bay view house, set back a bit from the water. It was at least thirty feet above sea level, and not near any tall buildings. It had been built after the last quake, that meant it was designed to survive the big one.

As we pulled into their neighborhood, we couldn't believe our eyes, all the houses were gone, washed away by a huge wave. All we could do was cry. A police officer driving the area came to investigate who we were and what we wanted. We told him about our friend's house. All he would say was he was sorry for your loss, and that we had to leave the area.

He told us there were refugee camps being formed east of the city and that San Francisco and Oakland were being evacuated. Maybe we could find our friends at the camp east of Oakland, it turned out to be a FEMA camp.

We spent a few more days looking for anyone we knew in the camps but there was no hope. By now things had started to deteriorate, mobs were forming to get what little food that was left. There were no additional relief groups, no red cross except the local group, and no one was coming in from anywhere. That was when we knew we needed to leave because it wasn't safe there anymore. We traded my grandpa's gold watch for a tank of gas and headed to Reno where we heard we could find help.

When we made it to Tahoe, we learned that Reno was a dangerous place. There was no law and no hope of finding any food or shelter. After that disappointment we headed south because we heard about settlements forming along the shores of the Colorado River.

We headed toward Las Vegas by night, following state roads and staying away from large populations to avoid people. We topped off the tank a couple times from some gas cans we found in abandoned homes and made it around Las Vegas into the Grand Canyon National Monument area.

We couldn't believe what we saw the first time the Colorado came into view, it looked like a wasteland, there was no life, no trees, just a barren land with the river passing through.

We figured that since we were heading downhill, we should take advantage of it and turn off the engine. Ed let the car just roll down the mountain. We were able to go most of the way to the bottom of the valley before we hit an uphill big enough to stop us.

Driving a dead car like that is a challenge, when you have no power steering or breaks you must really work at controlling the car. At one point we almost crashed. As we came around an almost hairpin bend in the road, we didn't see a car in the road ahead of us, and on our side, until it was nearly too late.

Fortunately, Ed reacted fast and was able to make it around the car but just barely. It was crazy. We had an adrenalin rush from the close call, all we could do was laugh about it for the next several miles.

Once we reached the lower elevation, we could make out the valley floor. It was stripped clean, there were no trees, nothing for as far as we could see in either direction. We followed the road the rest of the way down until we reached what used to be a bridge. We decided to stay there for a while, that was where we met up with Floyd, Alice Mark and Kate. The six of us spent several nights at the bridge when a couple of guys showed up, that would be these guys (pointing to) Hank and Ted."

Hank has a medium build, about five foot six, two hundred pounds and balding on top. He's a pretty easy-going type guy but the type you wouldn't want to piss off. Ted is a bit shorter and a good fifty pounds lighter, with long blond hair and clean-shaven. He's the quiet type unless you get him going, then hang on to your shorts.

"Hi, my name is Shelly; I hate to interrupt but it's time to eat. We have everything set up along the counter, please help yourselves."

"Thank you, Shelly, could our new guests come on up and go first please, oh and don't expect this kind of service every time. We can pick this up again in an hour or so."

Everyone devoured the food and mingled in and outside the cave. Someone had lit a fire, and people were gathering around it.

I spoke up, "It's a nice night out tonight, it's a bit crowded and stuffy in there, why don't we stay outside? If you are up to it, you're up Ted."

"Thanks, I think I am."

Chapter 27: The Mormon Wars

"Though we lived for many years in Provo, Utah before the quake, we were never really a part of their community because we're not Mormons. We loved it there because it was so close to the mountains. We could be on them in just minutes, skiing in the winter and hiking from spring to fall. One of our favorite activities was exploring Timpanagos Caves.

We were kicked back having a couple of burgers and brews, at our favorite pub in Provo, when the quake struck. It didn't feel like a major quake, but everyone was commenting on how long it was lasting. Bottles fell from the shelves and smashed on the floor and Hank joked that it was alcohol abuse. I was wondering why it was lasting so long, as it was several minutes before the shaking stopped

We had been watching a game when the quake started, we stayed glued to the set after it had stopped, hoping to hear news of what happened. When it finally came, the news was limited, all that was said was that an earthquake had occurred somewhere on the west coast. It was funny everyone in the pub was laughing at the news guys for stating the obvious. In all fairness it took a long time before anyone had any idea what the hell had happened.

It sounds like many of you here are like us, we knew this couldn't be a good thing. We were not like some of you and prepared and ready to go, but it didn't take someone knocking me up-a-side the head to figure it out, fast. I was surprised at how quickly the thugs attempted to take control of the city, but the Mormons weren't willing to give up their homes or their lives.

Mormons are the most prepared people in the country. They've taught their children to be prepared from their churches very beginning. The Mormons have their own factories for canning dried foods. Their church strongly recommends at least one year's supply of canned, not frozen supplies in order to be prepared for hard times.

The Salt Lake City region, including Provo, is predominantly Mormons, therefore most of the people had supplies. The problem for them was that the groups knew about those supplies. Many people that had not taken any precautions before the quake wanted that food and water for themselves.

What the groups had not counted on were the Mormons fighting for their homes. They were surprised at how many didn't turn the other cheek and roll over. Many had guns and didn't hesitate for a second to use them to defend themselves. Many live-in organized neighborhoods, others were just part of the fabric of the city. The groups never knew when to expect someone to fight back.

They couldn't just go in and wipe everyone out, because that would also mean they would destroy what they were trying to get in the first place. To counter that threat, they would go into a neighborhood, search every house and set fire to it as they left killing anyone that resisted.

This slaughter went on for days, gunfire rang out every night and fires raged with no firefighters to put them out. In the end everyone lost, the Mormons lost their supplies to either fire or thieves. The groups lost because many of the supplies they went after were lost as fires spread to homes that had supplies. It turned out that Salt Lake City was a hot bed of Preppers, ready to fight to the death for what they had, and those that didn't fight bugged out.

Luckily for us we loved to backpack, that meant we already had everything we needed to make it in the mountains. We had a friend that was Mormon, and he had a shit load of dried foods and was willing to turn us on to some. With that we got what we could and headed for the hills. We hung out in the mountain over the area for some time watching the city burn.

Many of the residents from the cities packed their supplies in their cars and went to live with families far from the populated areas. When the scavengers went looking for what they could, they found house after house already empty. Out of spite they burned those houses down as well. When it was over, little was left of the entire region, no one stayed. Eventually we decided to leave our sanctuary. It was getting crowded in the mountains and people were starting to go after each other even up there.

We traded some gold for a tank of gas and made our way east across the mountains. Then we headed south staying on forest service and smaller county roads as much as possible. With that, and by traveling mostly at night with no headlights, we were able to make it deep into the Canyon Lands without detection before running out of gas. From there we had to backpack, it was easier to remain invisible on foot, we ended up by the bridge where we ran into these guys.

I can't tell you how worried we were when we came upon the bridge and there were already people there. We announced ourselves and came in with our hands in plain sight."

Floyd said, "Unlike Bill and Ed we didn't hear them coming; we didn't have our guns at the ready. We were actually surprised by them."

Bill replied, "It was better than us coming in firing Floyd."

Hank added, "And we were happy that you guys didn't open fire on us."

Hank said, "We headed out the next morning."

Chapter 28: The Trip Upstream

Hank continued the story.

"Thankfully, these guys welcomed us in their group, now Ted and I made eight. We started out traveling on the road at night as much as possible, traveling along a riverbed is hard work. We were always on the lookout for others and did our best to avoid them. One day after we'd been on the road for a few hours we heard a big truck coming down the hill.

We could hear it getting closer, we took off for the stream and took cover wherever we could. There was a bend in the road where the stream and road parted, we headed up stream a bit. We figured we were safe and hoped they would just drive by, but that was not the case. With the squeal of metal on metal the truck stopped just past the bend and everyone jumped out. There were four scraggly looking guys and all of them were carrying assault weapons.

They were all drunk as a skunk; yelling at each other, and laughing at stupid stuff like drunks do, and they were heading for the stream. We feared we would be seen for sure.

One guy yelled out at another, 'Hey Andy, were the hell is my lighter?'

His friend yelled back, 'It's in ya shirt pocket ya dumb shit.'

They thought that was funny and started laughing at him. He even thought it was funny and started laughing too. The four men stood by the streams edge and took a piss, and then one bent down right where he stood, cupped a bunch of water in his hands took a drink. Then he splashed it on his face. Proof that in-breeding produces stupid people.

We figured we were had but we stayed quiet until they

got back in their truck and drove off. Every one of us looked at each other in disbelief, we couldn't believe he did that. We just sat there and laughed about them."

Everyone broke out laughing.

"Seeing that the stream parted from the road for as far as we could see, we stayed in the stream bed for several days before we came upon anything. We found an old empty farmhouse that we stayed in for a night. We chose not to stay longer because we figured the idiots in the truck could easily come along, we left in the morning. There was nothing of use in that old house, but it was a good place to sleep.

The next few days we didn't run into anything or anybody, but we did find a nice fishing hole that we could see huge trout swimming around in. We spent a couple nights there fishing and smoking the fish, that meant we had some food for the next few nights.

Even more time passed, we switched back and forth between the road and the stream depending on which we felt best about. At times we decided to travel at night on the road because the stream was impossible to travel. In the light we wouldn't have any real places to hide if someone came along.

After a while we were deep into the wilderness. Wildlife was abundant and there were not many people. We spent weeks walking up the streams following one tributary after another. We occasionally found a few old farmhouses where we would spend the night and then move on. At some point we realized that we hadn't seen people for some time, nor were we seeing any sign of recent human activity.

We had left the last road behind some time before. We traveled at least fifty miles up ever smaller streams when we came upon a small cabin in the woods. I was the first to approach it while the rest stayed back. I had my handgun at the ready and started calling out, is there anybody there? Nothing, again I called but this time a bit louder, IS THERE ANYBODY THERE? Then we heard the unmistakable sound of a 12-gauge shotgun being cocked from the cabin, we saw a gun barrel poke out of one of the shutters and a shot rang out followed by that sound again.

'GET THE HELL OFF MY LAND' a guy yelled, then he fired a second warning shot, over our heads. I yelled out we mean you no harm, I laid my gun down and asked again can we come up? The guy in the cabin answered that clearly, he fired a third round this time at my feet. The guy yelled out that was your last warning, now get out of here.

With that I told him okay we're going to just continue our way and leave him alone. We kept our eyes on the gun as we backed away. We did so until we were out of sight of the cabin. To be sure we wanted to be nowhere near that guy's cabin, we went way up stream that night.

We had no idea how long or how far we traveled, only that it felt like months. Every time we started to run out of fresh food, we'd stop for however long it took to catch more fish and game then smoke it, that way we'd have it on the trail. Bill is good at identifying edible plants as well, that meant we had plenty to eat.

Who would have thought that roasted trout with skunk cabbage and cattails would taste good? I suppose the seasoning salt had something to do with it. Bill and Ed were great cooks and always found ways to make something different and tasty for meals."

Ed added, "The only thing that meal was missing was a nice white wine."

"Fall was closing in on us and we could tell it was getting colder at night. It had been so long since we passed that cabin that we barely remembered it. We hoped it wouldn't be the last one we found and continued our trek up stream. One day we came upon a confluence that looked good both directions.

There was no way to tell which was the main stream, or which was the tributary. We stopped for the night to rest and scout out our options. Mark and Ed went up one leg and Bill and Floyd took the other leg. Everyone agreed that they would go up as far as they could and still be able to make it back to camp by nightfall. Besides them not having shelter, there were animals out there that would be happy to eat them.

It hadn't been more than a few hours when Floyd and Bill came rushing back to camp. They were both excited, they had found an old intact cabin that appeared to be empty. The best part was that it was only a few miles upstream, therefore we were only a few hours away from it. Alice took off up the other stream with Floyd to find Mark and Ed while Bill led me and the girls up to the cabin."

Chapter 29: The Mine

"The walk upstream was easy; it only took about an hour to reach our destination. We couldn't believe our eyes when we saw the cabin. It was large by cabin standards, better still it was built up against the face of a steep cliff and looked like it was in great shape.

As soon as the cabin came into view, we started calling out to see if anyone was there, but we didn't hear a thing. As we approached, we could see a big chimney in the roof, we hoped we would be warm that night. We even saw a wood-shed with at least a cord of wood stacked in it. There was a nice fiberglass axe embedded in a large round with a splitting wedge next to it next to a large pile of un-split rounds.

The whole work area was covered and partially en-closed for working in inclement weather. Talk about hitting the jackpot, we couldn't believe it, we crossed our fingers it was abandoned.

I approached the door and knocked, no answer. I knocked again this time a bit harder, still no answer. I reached down and tried the doorknob and it wasn't locked. I opened the door and called out to see if anyone was home, still noth-ing. Everyone else stayed outside as I slowly walked in calling out as I did, still no answer. It didn't take long to check out the whole place. When I returned to the group and told them it was empty, everyone was elated.

We went in to check out our new digs. We hoped this was going to be our place for some time to come, at least I hoped so. It was clear winter was getting close, subsequently this was going to be our home for at least that long. When we began exploring the cabin the surprises continued. There was a fully stocked kitchen with plenty of pots and pans and everything else we would need. The kitchen had a nice electric stove and a full-size refrigerator, we knew there was power here. I opened the refrigerator and almost blew chunks when the smell hit me. I wondered why they had left it full of food and without power.

To our surprise we even found a fully stocked pantry with all the dry goods we could want, it looked like real pancakes for breakfast. The place had two bedrooms with nice soft queen size beds and a loft over the kitchen area.

Continuing to look around, I noticed a big double door on the back wall, the one that was up against the cliff face. I almost fell over when I opened the door and realized it was the entrance to a mine. There was a light switch by the door, though it didn't work, but at least I knew it had lighting. We found a couple of flashlights by the door and headed into the mine. It went back quite a way and branched off.

At the far end of one of the tunnels we found digging gear stacked up like it had been placed there yesterday. It was almost too good to be true. We'd found an abandoned cabin and mine, miles from anywhere and everything. We knew now we would make it through the winter.

We made our way back out of the mine and decided to check out the grounds. About that time everyone else showed up, they were excited to check it out. While the rest went inside, Bill and I decided to continue looking around.

I remembered the lights in the mine and kitchen and decided we needed to figure out where the power came from. It wasn't hard to do because when we made our way to one side of the cabin, I could see a large wire coming out and heading up hill.

We followed the wires up and were happy when we saw where they went. They came from a box that was attached to a water wheel in a dried-up streambed. Without flowing water, the wheel wouldn't turn, that meant there was no power now, but there clearly had been power in the past. I spun the wheel by hand and found it turned freely.

We wandered up the stream to investigate what had happened to the water. There was a large boulder that had fallen into the channel and blocked the stream. From the looks of it, the channel for the generator was a man-made diversion, running parallel to the main stream.

It was easy to move the boulder and the water began to flow down that channel. Now that the wheel was turning, we figured there was power to the cabin again. We were anxious to return and check it out.

On our way back we came across a bunch of chickens running loose. There was at least a couple dozen of them running free, just as happy as could be. Bill cried out, 'hot dam chicken for dinner tonight.' We both laughed and he took off trying to catch a couple while I continued down.

When I got back to the cabin, everyone else was coming out excited. While they were in the mine the lights came on. All this was unreal after the last few months of hell. It was the first time any of us had felt this happy and at ease in a very, very long time. That night, we ate the biggest chicken dinner you've ever seen. It was great, we feasted on fried chicken, fresh bread, mashed potatoes with chicken gravy, and much more.

After dinner, Bill, Floyd and I, decided to check out the mine further since it was now well lit. This time we headed down a different tunnel. It started out like the other, but later didn't seem to be as complete as the first. We thought that perhaps they hadn't gotten to that part yet, but as we continued, we encountered what looked like a cave-in.

We decided to leave it alone for now and to stay out of

that tunnel until we could reinforce it like the other one. Seeing we had lots of time on our hands we decided to tackle that later. But then we spotted a smaller third tunnel with a pile of wood which had already been cut and was ready to put in place.

Given that we had what we needed, we went ahead and made the tunnel safe, then we decided to clear the cave-in out of the way. As we moved the rocks, we started to smell something very unpleasant. All of us had already smelt it before, we knew exactly what we would find. When we moved a big rock from the top of the cave-in, the smell hit us like a brick.

The area was well lit making it easy to see the pile of bodies just at the bottom of the cave-in. There were four bodies in all, it looked as though they had been dead for some time. Looking around it was clear they had been trying to get out but didn't make it. The cave-in was complete, it had cut off the oxygen to the tunnel beyond that point and they all suffocated.

We stopped for a moment to pay our respects, then continued to clear the cave-in. Once we had them out, we gave them a proper burial. In this case it was by fire. We built a large fire and put them on it to make sure no predators could get to their remains.

It was starting to make sense now. It had seemed too good to be true, EVERYTHING was here, the cabin, the food, the power, everything. I'd been asking myself why would anyone just leave a place like this? Why would anyone leave a nice cabin fully stocked with everything and not come back? Why had the refrigerator been left the way it was?

After finding the bodies and giving it some thought, we concluded that the four of them had been working at the end of the tunnel when the quake hit. Every other part of the mine had been well reinforced. The bracings were just a few feet away, that meant the section we found them in had to be new.

The quake also explained why the water wheel had stopped, the shaking had dislodged the boulder and blocked the channel that fed the wheel. It must have been hell in there when it happened. Not only was there a cave-in, but the lights went out too, that meant they couldn't even see to dig their way out.

One day I was wondering what it was that had the four of them at that end of the tunnel; I decided to check it out. We'd cleaned out the cave-in and finished supporting the mine but hadn't gone back in since. Even though it was kind of creepy that four people had lost their lives there, I wanted to know what they were doing.

I went to the end of the tunnel and looked closely at the back wall. There I saw a large vein of quartz. As I looked closer, I noticed there was gold in the vein, lots of it. It seemed that no sooner had these poor guys found a large deposit of gold, that the quake hit, and they never got it out.

Now everything was making even more sense. They must have found a fair amount of gold already in order to fund this operation. They'd built an amazing place with all the comforts of home. A nice cabin with hot and cold running water, heat, food, all of it. Unfortunately, the cave-in was too bad for them, but it was great for us.

Now we knew we were going to stay there. We took turns working the mine while others explored the area. One day while Floyd and I were out exploring and hunting we came across a very old and little used road. That was a bit disconcerting because we both knew it meant someone could find their way out there.

At least it was several miles from the cabin and there was no path leading to it. We figured we would be good for now. We marked the opening with a rag to find it again and decided to split up and check out both ways. We would go for one hour and return.

I went uphill and didn't get far before the road dead ended, I returned and went looking for Floyd. I found him looking out over a huge valley. We both figured it was the one we came up.

The road had clearly not been used for years and was overgrown in many places, we figured it was ok. We returned to the cabin just in time for dinner. It was great to come around the corner and see the smoke coming out the chimney and smell dinner in the air. We could smell the fresh bread and blackberry pie from a mile away. We were happy again for the first time since the quake.

It'd been at least a month since we found our little bit of heaven. During that time, we continued to cut firewood to ensure we wouldn't run out, and we conserved our other supplies as best we could. We knew that the supplies were only for four people and there were eight of us. We used it sparingly, and we continued to hunt and fish to supplement what we had as we prepared for winter to hit.

We didn't have long to wait either, after a nice Indian summer the snow started to fall and fall it did. We were snowed in the cabin a few times and had to dig our way out to get fresh air for us and the fire. There was a pen for the chickens, but we knew that was not going to be good enough for them over the winter. Instead we brought them inside the mine to keep them warm, and to keep them making us eggs, it worked out well.

We didn't lose anyone over the winter. We were lucky to find that cabin, there was no doubt, we wouldn't have made it through that winter in tents. Then one day in late winter, maybe early spring, Ed made an incredible discovery."

"Would you like to tell them about it Ed?"

Ed replied, "Sure why not, I was out exploring the site when I found a hollowed-out tree. I saw something sticking out, so I looked inside, it was a small cotton bag, but it felt like it weighed several pounds. I couldn't believe my eyes when I looked inside the bag, it was a large cache of gold. One of the miners must have stashed his gold inside the tree and it had been dislodged by the quake.

My first thought was to hide it back in the tree, but then I thought about my friends. We had been through hell to-gether and I owed my life to them, I decided I'd split it with everyone. Besides the plan was to equally split ALL the gold we found, really this was no different.

By now we had a fair amount of gold and we knew it was going to be the only real money for a long time to come. You should have seen everyone; it was like one of those old slap-stick movies. After I told the others about the gold I found, everyone started running around looking for other stashes, but none were ever found. Now if you don't mind, I'm going to let Ted finish this."

"That's fine Ed. It must've been mid spring when our worst fear happened, we heard someone yell, 'Is there any one in there?'

Mark and I both stepped out with our guns to find out who had found us. They'd called out to see if anyone was there, I said yeah there are bunch of us here and asked who they were. They said they could smell our smoke while com-ing up the road, which turned out to be the one that Floyd and I had found. That's when we met John and Edith here," point-ing to John and Edith.

John spoke up and said, "We had left a little militia con-trolled hick town about a month before then, as soon as we were able to travel. We spent the winter there; it was over-crowded, and people were killing each other just because they felt like it.

We would've left long before, but with winter coming we couldn't go anywhere. We spent the winter packing away whatever we could and took off as soon as possible in the middle of the night. We left in the dark with no flashlight and as much food as we could carry."

Someone in the room spoke up and asked John, "Where were you when the quake hit?"

"We were in New York City when it hit."

Someone else asked, "Did you feel it?"

"No, we didn't, but let's allow Hank to finish and I'll tell you about New York when he is done."

Hank said thank you and continued.

"Now where was I," he paused and said, "Oh yeah these guys showing up at our little heaven in the woods," and laughed, again pointing to John and Edith.

"They both had little with them and were hungry. We invited them in and gave them a meal, but we were still leery of anyone at this point. Now we KNEW our little piece of heaven wouldn't stay isolated forever.

We sent four guys down the road to see where it led. After several days they said they came upon a high overlook and made a troubling discovery. They'd seen a convoy of trucks. The trucks appeared to be heading up the same road but were moving slowly. They said they watched them for a spell until the convoy stopped"

Ed spoke up, "We could see that a bridge had been washed out, consequently they were setting up camp at that location. It was getting late, so we headed back. The trucks were still a long way away but not too far that it would take them long to make it up the road. We returned to the cabin and told everyone what we found.

As I described some of the trucks, John told us they were from the town they'd left. He said they had been planning on exploring the mountain in the summer but must have started out sooner with us leaving and the good weather.

John also told us that there were several places that would require them to build bridges to get past, but that he was sure they could do it. We figured we didn't have long, a few weeks at best. We knew the convoy, or a scouting party would make their way up here, we started preparing to leave.

The first thing we did was to take an inventory of everything we had. John and Edith each had a backpack, a four-man tent, their own sleeping bags and some cooking gear as well. They had time to prepare for the mountains, therefore they were well enough equipped just like the rest of us.

We collected every bit of food that was left that we could carry. We had found four rifles and four handguns with ammo for all, we even found some explosives that must have been used for blasting the mine. We left everything else because we knew how hard it would be to travel up stream.

Every effort was made to make it look like the owners had left long ago. We pushed a boulder on the generator to make it look like it happened in the quake and to deprive them of it. Luckily, we hadn't buried the miners, that way there was no sign of them.

We left the doors and windows open and threw a bunch of stuff in to make it look like it had blown in. The mine and cabin were left intact in hopes of it slowing them down because they wouldn't want to leave it. Additionally, we figured they wouldn't send people out looking when they could put them to work in the mine. It broke our hearts, but we simply trashed the place."

Henry spoke up, "What about the gold you did find?"

Ed answered back, "We still have it, well at least I know I do."

We heard, "I do too, and another, and still several more."

As Ed described the gold, and because it seemed as though everyone had held onto their gold, I was concerned. My first thought was this could be a problem. Up until now no one had anything like that, and we weren't concerned about anyone stealing. No one had anything worth stealing or worse yet anything worth killing over.

I had no idea what to do about it, or if I should do anything at all. I decided all we could do now was wait and see how it played out. About that time several people excused themselves because they had to work early in the morning and Brandon's men had lights out soon.

Hank spoke up, "I'm getting tired. I'd be happy to continue at another time for anyone that wants to hear the rest of it."

With that everyone went their separate ways and we headed back to our cabin. As we walked, I took that opportunity to express my concern about the gold to Hank. He said he understood that it could be a problem. I told him we would figure out what to do to make sure the gold and everyone was safe.

I felt a little better about it after our conversation, but I was still concerned. I just didn't want anything to ruin what we had. That night Ann and I spoke about it before we went to sleep, and Ann told me 'to sleep on it' we laughed.

The next day was much like the days before except, Floyd, Ben and I headed out to find a suitable location to build their cabin. I'd seen this nice location one day when I was exploring the area and told him I thought it would be perfect for him and Alice.

It wasn't far from ours, a bit down valley, and had a nice place for a garden. When he saw it, he said it was perfect and rushed back to the cabin to get Alice to show her. Beth, Ann and the girls went back with him and everyone agreed that it was great.

The girls started walking around it, talking, and they seemed to forget we were even there. With that, us guys made a quiet departure and left the girls to figure out how they wanted to arrange it. After all it's always the girls that have the final say on how things go anyway.

Later that day we headed over to the mill and took a nice swim in the pond, it was a hot day, and everyone was ready for a dip. It was nice to just relax, laugh and joke a bit. From there we went to dinner. Afterwards anyone that wanted to hear more met up outside the cave.

Chapter 30: The Climb Continues

Floyd continued to tell us about the rest of their trip.

"We started out walking in the stream heading down instead of up, we figured no one would go downstream looking for anyone. When we got back to the confluence, this time we headed up the other one staying in the middle of the stream. Our hope was to not leave any signs that we'd been there or that we went up that way.

As we made our way up the valley, we never started a fire during the day because we didn't want anyone to see the smoke. We lost track of how many days it had been, but it was a bunch. The stream had been getting smaller and smaller, when one day we came upon a large opening and we could see the headwaters.

It opened out into this breathtaking meadow. It was a lush plain with tall grass blowing in the breeze. The whole area was crisscrossed by a small braided stream that flowed to where we crested the valley.

Everyone just looked at each other and didn't even need say anything. We just dropped our gear where we stood and said about the same time, 'Let's stay here for a spell.'

We had been traveling for some time, we were high enough and far enough away. We figured we'd be safe making a fire during the day. After that long climb, we were hot and tired. Many of us just laid down in some of the shallow streams and let the cool water flow over us. It felt great to just cool off and rest like that.

After we got camp set up a few of us decided to check out where the water was coming from. We could tell we were near the top because we could see the pass a mere hundred feet up. We hadn't gone far when we found a few nice springs flowing from the side of the mountain.

That water tasted great, we just sat there and drank all we could and filled our water containers. From the pass we could see for miles and miles, both from where we came up and what was ahead for us. That night there was a beautiful clear sky, the stars were bright, and we could make out every constellation in the sky.

We laid around that night watching for satellites and counting them. At one point the International Space Station passed overhead and it made us wonder what ever happened to the people manning the station.

It was peaceful and beautiful there. We spent a couple nights resting after the climb getting there. When we left, we stood on the pass and looked ahead down into a lush valley below. Then there it was, we could see plumes of smoke way up the valley. We couldn't make out where because it was beyond our line of sight, but it was clearly smoke we were seeing, and we knew we had to find the source.

The valley went so far north that we couldn't see the end. We could also tell it was going to be hard to get to the bottom. It looked like it was well over a thousand feet down. By now we were off our maps, we had no idea where we were and really didn't care. All we knew was we wanted to get to the valley floor below, then head up the stream to find who made the smoke.

We came down the side of the valley, that meant water was limited save for the occasional small feeder streams along the way. At times we were switch backing down a forty-five-degree slope with the ground at forty-five degrees. Several times we're walking on shale and having it slide out from under our feet, which nearly caused several to fall.

At one point, near the bottom of the face, we decided we

needed to slide down the shale. We sat on one foot with the other foot in front and glissaded down the face. It was hell as our feet kept getting crammed into the toes of our shoes.

When we reached the bottom of the valley, we came upon another incredible location to stay, it looked like someone had made it just for us. It took one hard day to reach the bottom and everyone was beat.

There was a section of the stream that had a small waterfall with the perfect pool under it. The kind where you could sit under the flow of the water and let it run over you. Everyone took the opportunity to get a shower, we cleaned up and relaxed in the water.

A little up stream of that we found a sweet fishing hole and caught several fish for dinner, it sure was nice having fresh fish that night. We spent a few days there and explored downstream a bit. We were a good mile down when we heard a loud roar and knew it was a waterfall. As we looked at the falls, we said there was no way anyone was going to get up that, neither in nor out of the water.

The next morning, we started up the valley, hoping that this one would lead us to a safe place. We knew that by now we were deep in the Rocky Mountain wilderness and we knew there was something up stream. After seeing that falls, we were certain no one was coming up the river.

We'd traveled several more days and any time one of us asked if we were there yet, our standard answer was it's just over the hill and around the corner, it always made us laugh. Then one morning just after we got up, Tom here came walking out of the woods with his hands up telling us not to touch our guns.

I don't think any of us even thought about it. Then Brandon and Peter came out and the rest is us here now. I don't know how we can ever thank you guys for welcoming us in."

It was getting late, but no one wanted to miss what John had to say; everyone stayed up to hear him.

Ben asked John, "How did you get here from New York City and why would you have left it?"

With that John took a deep breath and let out a long sigh, and replied, "You have to understand this is hard to say (another long pause and a sigh), New York City is gone."

GASPS, that's all you heard.

"There's nothing left, it was burned to the ground, the entire city is gone," He answered with tears in his eyes.

"How?"

Chapter 31: The Fall of New York City

"I think it was almost four o'clock in the afternoon when breaking news interrupted the daily programming that a major quake had struck the entire west coast. None of us could believe our ears. The entire west coast?

Everyone knew that California was supposed to be hit by 'The Big One' but no one ever said anything about this. The newscasters were saying the earthquake began off the north coast of British Columbia and traveled all the way south to the Gulf of California."

Floyd interrupted, "Are you telling us the entire west coast was shaken at the same time?"

"Yes, the scientists said the Cascadia Fault ruptured where the Juan De Fuca Plate dives under the edge of the North American Plate. That the crust had moved over forty feet and the rupture traveled along its entire length, from British Columbia to just north of San Francisco."

Bill gasped, "Oh my god we never heard any of this, why didn't you tell us any of this before?"

"I'm sorry Bill it was just too hard, but now there are too many people to think of to hold it in any longer."

Ted asked, "How long did it last?"

"The scientists said it lasted over nine and a half minutes, they said it traveled all the way to the San Andres Fault. It was reported that Cascadia caused the San Andres Fault to rupture along its entire length as well.

They said that every city on the west coast was hit by massive seismic waves, one after another. It said that the quake was felt all the way to the Rocky Mountains. Everyone was in shock; no one expected something like this to happen.

By closing bell of the stock exchange that day, the Dow Jones had plummeted over one thousand points. All night we heard more and more news about it. Some of the western TV stations had been able to get satellite uplink by generator to get the news out. The newscasters pleaded for help from the government.

The president came on shortly after with a brief statement saying that the government would do everything it could. They said that this was an unprecedented event and FEMA had never planned on something of this scale. The next morning the Dow opened down another five thousand points, they closed trading almost as soon as it opened.

Some news had made it out about Seattle, and it said that the city was in total ruins and it could never be rebuilt. They said it was impossible to evacuate any survivors from any of the Puget Sound Region. They went on to say that the quake caused the crust of the earth to shift and that the ground under the entire region had sunk over fifty feet. That flooded the entire region for good. Scientists said the area would never be above water again."

Floyd spoke up, "Well the ground sinking explained why I couldn't reach the valley when I tried to go see the damage. I was wondering why the water hadn't receded after the quake."

"With every hour that passed, we heard more and more despair. Later that night word reached us that Mount Rainer had exploded and covered everything with ash and lava for hundreds of miles to the east. All air travel in the country was halted because of the ash cloud."

Bill asked, "How long did it take for New York to fall apart?"

That question seemed to strike a chord in John, you could tell it was hard for him to speak about it. He teared up again as he continued.

"It's not as simple as that, the west coast fell apart because of the destruction, the complete loss of life and infrastructures, and of the death and suffering.

Back east it was different, nothing was destroyed by the quake, it was too far away. The effects of the west coast being obliterated was incalculable. To start with the psychological effect was enormous. Nearly everyone in the country has family or friends living on the west coast. No one could get any information on their loved ones and the news was bad.

The economic effect was also beyond calculation. California was the eighth largest economic power in the world. Just the loss of that alone was devastating. You add in the entire west coast, no imports, no exports, no commerce whatsoever and you have a trifecta of doom.

Remember I told you the Dow dropped over six thousand points in two days, and the market was closed indefinitely. The country was still not out of the depression and the economy was hanging on the edge, as it had been for years. There was no way it could hold out with that type of destruction.

To make matters worse the government came out and said there was no way they could get in help. Anyone on the west coast had to fend for themselves. Those were not their exact words, but they may as well have been.

With the economic collapse and martial law declared nationally it was all people could take. Almost everyone now knew the world that we knew was over, the looting that had been contained in the city exploded. The cops couldn't, or wouldn't, even begin to stop it. Just like in New Orleans many of the cops joined in the looting because they figured what was the point anymore.

Entire malls were emptied in under an hour. Every Wal-Mart in town was picked clean in minutes. Sporting goods stores and pawn shops were hard hit by people trying to get survival gear and guns.

People flooded the subways only to find none of them were running, abandoned by the workers, with the windows on the cars smashed out. People were running down the tunnels trying to get away from the mayhem in the streets.

Rioting was rampant in the streets. Cars burning everywhere, first the cop cars then any car was a target. Traffic came to a standstill and the only way to get around was on foot. There was the sound of breaking glass everywhere, and the smell of burning buildings filled the air. People were running out of stores carrying anything they could manage. I remember thinking to myself how stupid can people be, what do they plan on doing with a flat screen TV.

Even while the buildings were being looted, they were set ablaze, huge fires raged as building after building burned. There was no way for fire crews to even reach them let alone fight them. In time skyscraper after skyscraper were in flames all the way up to the top.

To make it worse after it began there was no one who could help. The first responders didn't respond because they had to defend their own families. Everyone that was home stayed home to protect their loved one. And those who could leave didn't because even if they tried, they wouldn't have been able to reach anyone that needed help.

My city was literally burning to the ground and there was no way to stop it. From my twenty fifth floor condo I could see the Empire State building engulfed in fire, and rioters on the ground cheering."

"Where was your condo?"

"We lived on Fifth Street near the intersection of West 34th Street. We managed to make it out of our building before it was set ablaze. We were trying to make it out of the city as fast as possible but that was proving to be difficult. There were hundreds of fires all over the entire city, none of them could be extinguished consequently they burned out of control.

I remembered my history and what happened when America carpet-bombed the German cities in World War II with incendiary bombs. Just like those cities, New York City now had hundreds of fires raging, spread over the city. Those fires began to converge which formed larger ones then those combined as well.

We were watching the beginning of a firestorm, as the fires began to merge, they sucked huge amounts of air to the center. It created a fire vortex that looked like a giant fire tornado. The more fuel there is, the larger the fire, and there was almost unlimited fuel in the city.

We had a boat at the marina, we headed for it on foot praying that my boat was still there. On our way a woman ran up to us screaming for help, her son was trapped under some rubble and she was begging us to help her son.

We had to stop to help her. She said her name was Betsy and her son's name were Hank and that they were trying to get out of the city, when a sign fell and pinned him down. Hank was lucky that the sign landed on some other rubble which stopped it from crushing him. With some help from others we were able to get the sign off him, he only had a few scratches.

As we worked to free her son, I could feel the winds picking up, they were blowing toward the center of the city. I knew this was a sign that the firestorm was building strength and that we had to hurry.

I told her we had a boat and that she and her son could come with us, but that we had to hurry. By now the winds were picking up, it was difficult to run against the force. The winds were kicking up dust and making it hard to see where we were going. Finally, the four of us made our way to the waterfront and the marina.

When we reached my boathouse, I was relieved to find it was still locked up and no one had taken my boat. As we pulled away from the dock, we could see fires on the opposite shore as well, we knew we couldn't just cross the river. We ran with no lights and stayed away from shore and decided to float downstream and go ashore wherever we could.

We didn't need to go far before we were able to make it ashore across the Hudson River into New Jersey. By now it was dark and when we looked back, we couldn't believe our eyes. Every mile of shoreline was in flames, none of the skyline had escaped the fire. As I scanned the shoreline, I could see several fire vortices spiraling thousands of feet into the sky.

Then I saw this gigantic vortex spiraling up, I couldn't see the top even from as far away as we were. The flames reached all the way to the clouds. Ominous black clouds high in the sky were spiraling in toward the center of the fire. The fire was sucking in huge amounts of air to feed itself and created strong winds even as far away as we were. The suction was so strong you could see semi-trucks being sucked in. It was the worst thing I've ever seen in my life, and I used 'was' correctly."

John's eyes were filled with tears as he choked out his story. You could tell it was hard to tell. I told him he could finish later, and he refused. I don't think he wanted to tell any of it ever again and just wanted to finish.

"In a few short hours New York City's Manhattan, the

greatest city man ever made was finished, totally destroyed. As we looked around, we saw countless boats doing the same thing we did, fleeing the city like rats escaping the fire with no idea of where to go or what to do next.

People lined the shore with their boats and stayed there for some time. The boats were tied together making huge rafts. We waited there for the fires to burn themselves out before we left. Betsy and her son had a little luck at least, while we were in New Jersey she found some family and stayed with them. All the better because we knew we couldn't take her with us.

As soon as we could, we headed north to some property I owned, but first decided to get a closer look to see what was left of the city. It was an eerie sight, as we approached the southern shore of Manhattan, we watched closely for any signs of life but saw none.

Even before we reached the shore, we could smell the burnt flesh. As we approached, we saw burnt bodies floating along its banks, scores of them. The sight and smell were even worse when we reached the bank and went ashore.

There were hundreds of burnt bodies, piled on top each other. Row after row of bodies mostly burnt to a skeleton, it was clear they had tried to reach the shore as the fires burnt all the way to the river. As we slowly made our way inland, we found fewer bodies. What were left of the streets were huge piles of smoldering rubble.

There were countless skeletons everywhere, lying where they fell and were completely burned up. The smell of burnt flesh hung in the air even more, I vomited repeatedly. None of the skyscrapers escaped the fire, and most of the streets were impassable. The closer we got toward the center of the city the worse the damage was, the roads were melted and glass from the store fronts laid in solid puddles on the ground.

There were no lights anywhere, no sign of any life, no birds, no rats, not even any cockroaches. There was absolutely nothing left alive in the city. All that was left was the burnt out and fallen shells of some of the taller buildings, most of the smaller ones were buried under the rubble from the taller ones. The devastation was so severe that we needed to leave.

How could the greatest city man has ever seen been destroyed so quickly? How could it have not been affected by the most violent quake the world ever saw, a quake three thousand miles away. How could it fall at the hands of a minority of people? What did it really say about us all, if we could do that to such a mega-city? As we returned to the boat and pulled away, I turned around to get one last look at my home and began crying again."

By now there was not a dry eye in the place including myself, everyone was horrified at what John described.

Someone asked, "How did you get away?"

"We headed north up the East River. We couldn't believe our eyes when we saw what was left of the Brooklyn Bridge. The two towers still stood but the span was gone. One of the span cables was still intact with several smaller cables hanging from it, while the other was gone. I have no idea what happened to it only that it was gone.

We continued up stream because I had a jet at a small private airport community north of the city. As we moved north, we didn't see any life on the New York shores. But in New Jersey boats lined the shores with people trying to survive. At times we could see people trying to flag us down to help them, but we knew that was impossible, they would've overwhelmed my boat.

I always kept my jet fully fueled and ready to fly at a moment's notice just in case I needed to get somewhere fast. It was several miles north and not far from the river. We figured we would go see if it was still there and hoped it was not destroyed.

When we made it to the boat launch, I was surprised to see no boats there. The streets of the city were deserted but littered with dead or abandoned cars. We only had a couple miles to go to make it to the airport and were overjoyed when we saw my hanger was still intact. I opened the door and there she was, my jet just waiting for us to fly her out of there.

We always kept the hanger loaded with survival gear and a couple weeks supply of food and water; we were happy to be able to eat."

"What about the ash from the volcano and the no-fly order?"

"The answer to your first question is by now there was no ash left in the air where we were. The second one, well the government no longer controlled anything including the air. I didn't hear anything on the radio until I flew close to Chicago, which was when I heard I was entering restricted air space and was told to land."

"Did you land like you were ordered?"

"No way, when I heard I was entering the air space and was ordered to land I wanted nothing to do with that."

"What did you do?"

"I dropped close to ground level, sped up and turned south for a spell then I continued west."

Someone asked him where he was heading.

John paused again, "I was heading to my parents to

get them. We were to head to South America, figured it was warmer than the north."

Someone else asked, "Did you make it to your parents ok."

John took another deep breath, sighed and slowly shook his head and said, "No, I was shot down somewhere over south western Colorado, not too far from here."

The group gasped and almost as a whole asked, "How?"

John shook his head again and said, "By a surface to air missile. I saw it coming and rolled, but it clipped my wing. The landing was hard but since I'd been flying low over highways, I was able to land on a freeway."

Beth asked, "Were you or Edith hurt bad?"

John said, "No only minor bumps and bruises."

"Who shot you down, the military for flying in a no-fly zone?"

John came back fast with an answer and he didn't seem happy.

"I don't think so; my guess was it was one of the militias. Maybe some other bands of nutcases that had broken into a National Guard Armory and stole some surface to air missiles. When they saw my jet, one of them shot at me. I don't know why, maybe just because he could. After that we ended up in that stupid little hick town where your brother is your dad and your aunt is your sister too. The rest of the story you already know."

I stood up and returned to the front.

"It sounds like you have had a rough experience, but you are safe now, from what I can tell you will be a great asset to the village. We have a committee made up of representatives of different groups, I think one of you should join that committee. Do you guys have a nominee?"

"Mark gave a quick and resounding, "Yes, it could be none other than Floyd. He has led us through this stuff, we know we can trust him in this too."

Floyd replied, "Thanks Mark I'd be happy to represent y'all with these nice folks."

"Then welcome to the committee Floyd, I'm sure you will do fine." With that we adjourned.

Within a short time, the newcomers settled in and seemed like they had always been part of us. But now our little group had grown, and it was becoming difficult to fit everyone in the cave for meetings, we decided we needed a better solution. It was Patrick that came up with a good solution, we would build our own little amphitheater.

Chapter 32: Going Up

It had been several months since the newcomers had arrived, and it would be fall soon enough. Everyone pitched in to help them find a place to build their cabins. There was a garden in every field with a plethora of fruits and vegetables growing, we also had a dozen separate large wheat and rice fields.

The mill was mostly built, and the water wheel worked like a charm. The grinding stones were finished and turning on the shaft. That would grind down the high spots, before the grain was ready. The mill was turning out to be a favorite meeting spot over the summer, it gave everyone a nice place to just lie back in the water, relax and stay connected.

It also powered the ceramics studio, where a couple of potters' wheels were driven by their own small water wheel. A Step Kiln was built, and several people used them to make all kinds of useful and decorative items for their homes.

The heat of summer had passed, and everything was going great. One day while a few of us were relaxing in the pond, Fred asked me,

"How far up the valley have you explored."

"I only went as far as the big falls, I didn't see any sign of human activity, so I didn't look further."

"I think we need to scout out the valley all the way to the top, then drop down the other side of the pass."

Ben replied, "That's a great idea, count me in," as did Floyd, Bill and Ted.

"Then it sounds like a plan, we have enough backpacks and bags for everyone. We can take two tents and use fire or stoves to cook. We have plenty of food we can bring and can supplement that by hunting and fishing."

Fred said, "We even have a couple of MRE's left if we want them."

Bill responded, "Thanks but no thanks."

We laughed because we all could relate to that.

Fred continued, "The next question is how far should we go and how long should we go for?"

Ben replied, "I don't think we want to constrain ourselves with time, we have plenty of time and supplies, so we shouldn't limit our trek." Everyone agreed.

"Well then how far do we want to go?"

Ted spoke up and said, "I think that needs to be based on what we see as well. When we reach the pass, we can see down into the valley below. Figure what's in front of us, then adjust our plan based on what we find when we reach the valley floor."

Fred added, "Yeah we may find falls we don't want to try to pass or signs of civilization. If we encounter someone there, they'll want to know how we got there and where we came from. I'm not sure that's a good idea."

"That has always been a risk we face, including from someone coming up from below again, this time they may not be nice. Ok then let's do this. We need to talk it over with Brandon, but I think it might be best if he stays here."

Over the next couple of days everyone pulled together their gear and split up the loads evenly. We had plenty of jerky including fish, deer, elk and bear. We figured between the dried goods, and hunting, we could last. Besides by now we were all good at surviving off the land.

Our ranch was the furthest point up valley, therefore we

used it as our starting point. We loaded up our packs and took off early in the day. It was a nice day, not to hot not to cold, so hiking would be easy. We knew we would make it to the falls that first day, Ann and Beth went with us. It was a warm night and we could make out some stars, but the rest were obscured by the trees. The eight of us were enjoying a pleasant night by the fire.

I had found a nice stump to lean against near the fire and Ann was leaning against me. Fred was sitting on a log across from us and the rest closing in a small circle. The fire was crackling and shed this ever so soft glow on us when a piece of cedar in the fire popped out and sent an ember flying into Fred's lap, but he didn't see or feel it.

Beth was sitting next to him and when she saw it, she jumped up and started smacking Fred's lap. Of course, Fred had something to say about that.

"WHAT THE HELL ARE YOU DOING!!"

The rest of us that saw the still glowing hot coal but didn't have time to react, started laughing while Beth tried to explain what she was doing.

"That last pop from the cedar threw a coal into your lap while you were looking at the stars. I saw you didn't see it and that was the fastest thing I could do."

We were still laughing at the funny scene. Of course, Beth was not happy about that and told us all to shut up. When we stopped laughing Ben decided it was time for a story.

"Do you guys know how long it's been since we have done this, quite a bit. Hey, Peter, it's been forever since we heard any of your bullshit sea stories do you have one for us."

Ann replied, "Do we have too, I've heard them all a thousand times," as she rolled her eyes.

Jokingly I crossed my arms and blew out my lips like I was pouting.

Fred added, "Yeah come on sailor boy let's hear one."

I gave Ann a smug look and said okay. She decided she had heard enough of my stories and got up to go get some firewood and water some plant somewhere.

Beth asked, "Do you have something scary? I would love to hear a nice scary story now."

"Well I don't know if I consider it scary, but you might. I was stationed on the U.S.S. Nimitz working as a safety inspector roving the ship late one night for my duty. We were in home port, and the aircrew wasn't aboard and there were lots of empty berthing space where I was walking. I was going through an area well after midnight one night when I passed a rack, then felt this extreme cold hit me. Because the spaces were not in use the ventilation system was off, there was no real air flow, but the cold had hit me like a wave."

Beth exclaimed, "What was it?"

I replied, "I had no idea, I took a mental note of it and continued my rounds. When I got back to my office one of my co-workers was in the office and I told him about what had happened. He asked if I knew which space it happened in and I told him yes. When I gave him the compartment number, he reached over to a file cabinet and pulled out a file and tossed it to me. He told me a guy had killed himself in that berthing compartment. I looked at the file and it was in that rack where I had felt the cold."

Fred responded with a fake sneeze that sounded much like bullshit, but Beth was all over it.

"Are you saying you saw a ghost?"

"No, I never said anything about a ghost. I just made an observation, besides I never said I saw anything."

Ted replied, "Then what are you saying?"

"I'm not saying anything, but as a scientist it makes me go hmm"

Beth barked at Ted, "What are you saying you don't believe in ghosts?"

"Well daa... No, I don't believe in ghosts."

I added, "I'm not saying I believe in ghosts. But given we are all made of stardust, yet somehow, we are cognitive of our very existence. Why is that? And I'm not saying I believe in God either, just saying."

We debated the meaning of life stuff the rest of the night and slept under the stars that night by the fire.

It took us two days to reach the highest point I'd gone before; we spent the night there. Now we were in uncharted terrain and it was getting difficult to climb, and we were a fair bit above our homes.

We were staying on the edge of a small plateau, from this vantage point we could still see our homes by the day and flashlights moving around at night. I was sitting on the edge dangling my feet while looking at the little lights moving around below. I was bored, I started to flash Morse code at everyone below to see if anyone noticed it. I figured if they could, someone would respond back. I was right, someone did.

I called out, "Hey guys bring your flashlights! Check it out, I was flashing my light to everyone below and someone responded."

"Not just someone, look there is a couple more."

"Everyone line up, lets flash ours in a pattern."

Fred said, "Hey let's do a pattern like from that alien movie with the lights."

"Fred these hand crank flashlights are cool; we never have to worry about batteries."

"They are nice, aren't they?"

We loved the idea and wondered if they would respond in the same way, which they did. We spent hours like that trying all kinds of patterns and seeing if they could or would match them, again they did. The best part of it was that no one had planned it, it just happened on its own. Before I finished, I sent a Morse code to Ann that I loved her. She responded back with she loved me more, I smiled and headed off to sleep.

In the morning we continued up valley. We made good distance that day, the next night we could no longer see the fires below, subsequently no lights after that. We wondered if we would see them when we reached the pass and if the fires could be seen from there as well.

It took us several more days to make our way to the pass. It was hard going and required roping up several times to get past some steep rapids and a huge falls. It was late in the day when we reached the pass. We looked back and to our disappointment we were able to see smoke from the fires of our village. This meant that anyone that came up from the other side would be able to see them as well.

Fred spoke up, "This means it's now even more important that we go as far down the valley as we can. We need to see if there is anyone down below that we need to worry about."

Ben called out, "Guys come quickly."

We ran over to looked down the other side of the pass. What we saw was the most incredible valley below. It was a long way down and went well beyond what we could see. There was a sharp bend way down the valley, that meant we couldn't see beyond it. It was a nice clear night and there was a great place to set up camp, we stayed there.

That next morning, after planning our moves, we started down the valley, but the going was slow. It was clear that no modern human had ever passed this way before. That was a neat feeling, trailblazing virgin land. Floyd took the lead and did most of the bushwhacking while I stayed in the back.

We followed the stream from the headwaters all the way down until the valley opened into a large open braided stream. About a week in we saw smoke rising from the forest canopy. There was only one plume, that meant it was an isolated cabin and decided we would approach it carefully.

Chapter 33: The Others

We were at an overlook checking out where we saw the smoke. From our vantage point we could see a cabin, a barn, and a modern metal building with large double doors. It was clearly an old cabin, but it was in good shape. It looked like it had been there for many, many years. The metal building was new and looked like a large shop or garage.

"Would you look at that, they have pigs, goats and cows in that pasture. Can you say steak and eggs with a side of bacon for breakfast?" With this look of desire Fred let out a long deep MMM... while licking his lips.

I replied, "Funny, what are you going to do, shoot one and bring it home on your back?"

"I know, but a man can wish."

"I know I'd kill for a pork chop or some ham too." Fred could see that same look on me.

"Now that's what I'm talking about, killing one and cutting it up right where it lays."

The rational me had to come back from the dreamland BBQ I was at, "Obviously someone lives there, maybe we should just ask."

We had not been watching long before a woman came out of the cabin and rang an old-fashioned triangle on the deck for lunch. We were amazed that we were able to hear it that far away. A couple of kids came running out into the open field, we were pretty sure it was a family, but we had not seen the dad yet. A few minutes later a guy came out of the metal building wiping his hands on a rag.

We decided that only two of us would approach the house, Fred and I decided to go while everyone else watched

Xavier Bruehler

from above. Floyd is a hell of a shot; he would be watching us through the sight of the sniper rifle to make sure we were safe.

The next morning Fred and I went to visit the house before the dad left. We decided to approach the house unarmed and to announce our presence early on. As we got close Fred called out, "Hello" he paused, again he called out only this time a bit louder.

"HELLO in there, we have no weapons and do not need any supplies. In fact, we have some we can share if you need it."

We could hear voices inside but couldn't make out what was being said. Then a window opened slightly, and a gun barrel came sticking out. We raised our hands, turned around and raised our shirts to show we had no weapons. This time I spoke up.

"As you can see, we have no guns on us and we have no desire to take anything you have. We have all the supplies we need, consequently we don't need any of yours. We saw the smoke from your fire from up the valley a way and came to investigate who was here."

We heard the lock on the door open and a man stepped out with that unmistakable look of an AK-47 trained on us.

"My name is Peter and my friend here is Fred, what's your name?"

He replied, "Hooowwwdy ma name's Alex."

Alex was a stocky guy with a big full beard, he was wearing a plaid flannel shirt and overalls. He spoke with a deep voice and a strong southern accent.

"Hi Alex, we came down from the pass above scouting out the valley. We're trying to find out what, if any threats to our home, could come from this direction."

286

Alex replied, "We're the only ones in this here valley fer as I know, we got here jist after the quake. This here cabin has been in ma family fer generations, when the quake hit, we came here to get away from what was coming."

As we spoke, his wife and kids came out on the porch. I was pleasantly surprised at how welcoming she was.

"This here is ma wife Elaine and ma two kids George and Sue. Please come in y'all an make yourself at home."

Elaine was a pretty woman, stood maybe five foot if she was wearing heels. With long blond hair and a pretty sundress, she was soft spoken and seemed shy at first.

Alex continued, "I'm sorry where'd y'all say you come from?"

I replied, "We have a community several miles down valley on the other side of the pass."

"What brings y'all here?"

"We had some people come up into our community from the valley below. That made us consider that we needed to check out if we had to worry about above."

"Shoot, where's ma manners? Can we get ya something ta eat or drink maybe some coffee?"

My eyes widen, my mouth immediately started watering and I was clearly excited, Fred started to visibly drool.

"COFFEE!!?" I said in this wishful manner. "Really, you have coffee!? I can't remember when the last time was that I had a caffeine fix."

"Well I can't promise it'll be a good cup, but it's coffee."

"I don't care if it's as bad as that rut gut I had in the Navy, that we used to use to remove rust from the decks. If it's coffee, I would love some."

With that, Alex turned to Elaine and asked her to get us all a cup. As we walked in, I could smell the coffee brewing and I started to drool. As the smell drifted through the air it brought back many memories. Several minutes later Elaine brought out a tray with cups on it and a pot of coffee.

As she poured our cups, she handed them to us. It was funny, both Fred and I put the cups under our noses and with our eyes half closed and heads waving, we both took a long deep lingering breath.

"I can't believe how good that smells after months of not having it."

I raised my cup and toasted.

"Hopefully, here's to a long and beneficial friendship."

Alex raised his as well and added, "Here, here, and to new friends."

I took my first sip of coffee after what felt like forever and added.

"Hell, and it tastes great as well."

Alex asked, "How'd y'all get here? I've been way over that pass and didn't see any sign of people, but it's been more than a year. I know the terrain is unforgiving."

"It was hard, we had to rope up a few times, but we were able to make it Okay."

"Are you two alone?"

"No, we're not, there're four others up the valley waiting for us to give them the okay to come down."

"Well I think of myself as a good judge of people and you guys seem to be upfront, feel free to invite them down."

We stepped out on the porch; I waved my arms as the signal to come down.

Alex asked, "Can your friends see us from where they are?"

"Yeah, they can, we could see your whole farm from that overlook up there. Look up on that bluff, you can see them waving back."

We looked up at the overlook and we could see Floyd standing there signaling OKAY with the semaphore flags. I replied OKAY back, so they headed down.

Alex asked, "Whatcha signaling?"

"It's semaphore just like they used on the ships long ago, I learned it as a Boy Scout."

"Would y'all join us for dinner? We can get to know each other. I'd love ta hear more about where y'all came from. We have plenty of food. I bet it's been a long time since you've had some smoked ham."

"You have no idea, are you sure you have enough?"

"We're well stocked and we have more."

"We saw your animals in the field. Are you sure you can spare it?"

Alex laughed and replied, "We have plenty, I smoked a couple hams bout a month ago out in the smoke house."

"I'm sure I speak for everyone that's not here yet, when I say hell yea."

Fred chimed in, "Well I can guarantee you he is speaking for me this time."

It took about a half hour for everyone else to make it

Xavier Bruehler

down. As they approached, I introduced them.

"Alex this is Floyd, Ben, Bill and Ed. Guys this is Alex and his wife Elaine and their kids George and Sue."

"Nice ta meet y'all, please come on in."

Floyd asked Alex, "I noticed as we were coming down the valley that we didn't see any roads leading up here. How did you guys get here?" Alex laughed, "We flew here, I have a helicopter."

"You had a helicopter to get you here!?"

"No, I have a helicopter, it's inside ma hanger out back. We used it to fly in because there are no roads coming up the valley. The closest forest service road is at least a hundred miles away, and the closest paved road more than a hundred fifty miles from there."

Floyd asked, "Are there any other homes down valley?"

"No, I've flown over the entire valley and searched for signs of any and we're the only ones for at least one hundred miles in every direction."

Ben exclaimed, "You mean you have this entire valley to yourself?"

"Yep that's exactly what I mean. I started telling Peter and Fred here this cabin was built by my great, great grandfather and has been passed down ever since. It's deep in the Rocky Mountain National Wilderness and I don't think anyone else including any government office even knows it exists."

"My great, great grandfather came here over a hundred years ago and built it with his own hands. As you can see it's in great shape and I've made a few improvements to it over the years. It uses a micro hydro generator, that means we always have power. I installed modern appliances for Elaine, you have to keep the little woman happy if you want to be happy."

Elaine laughed and said, "You're damn tooting."

"The cabin has hot and cold running water and is well lit. I'm sure y'all saw the hanger out back for the helicopter, so all and all we're as ready as we can be here."

Bill asked, "Ready for what?"

"READY FOR WHAT!!? Are you nuts!? Where the hell have you been this last year? We've known for years this country was only a single catastrophic event away from failure. We've been getting ready for it all along.

Over the last few years we've been improving the cabin and stocking it with at least four years' worth of food and other goods. There's over a thousand gallons of fuel for the helicopter and gas for any other use. That's enough to keep me flying for several years depending on what I do. Ma family was super rich, I have enough spare parts here to almost rebuild the chopper, I even have a complete spare motor and rotor."

You could see Fred's eyebrows rise, he asked, "How do you keep that much fuel good for that long?"

"It's not hard to keep AV gas good for far more than two years. First when I brought the fuel up, we transferred it from the barrel it was in into a new one that was filled with nitrogen gas. We passed the fuel through a couple good filters to trap any impurities including microscopic water.

That takes care of most of the causes of it going bad, and then before we closed it up, we topped off the nitrogen to ensure there was no contact with oxygen and sealed it up. Finally, when we pump it into the helicopter, we pass it through a fuel polisher to ensure there is nothing in it we don't want."

"I flew in pigs, chickens, pheasants, goats, turkeys, and

some cows. We won't be lacking any meats here."

Ed asked, "Aren't you worried about someone trying to steal any of it or something?"

"We've been coming here for years and have never seen any sign that anyone's ever found this place. Like I said before there are no roads here, we had to fly in."

"How far UP valley have you flown?"

"I flew up to the pass and landed about a year ago; I spent two days there watching for smoke. Then I flew low down the other side for at least a hundred miles. That was why I was a bit concerned when you said you came from there. I didn't see any signs of humans down that valley either."

Fred replied, "That's because we didn't get there until the later part of last summer."

Alex asked, "How many of ya are there?"

"There's a total of seventy-one of us there, we have several farms growing everything we need to live and then some. We plan on building a large stockpile of food and seeds, just in case, and as a means of trading when we can."

"Well I may well be interested in doing jist that with ya. It shoor would be nice ta have some fresh fruits and vegetable that we don't already have. With only the four of us we are limited on what we can grow."

"Well besides fruits and vegetables we also have grains like wheat, rice, corn, oats and soy."

"Do ya have the means to grind the grains as well?"

"We sure do, we built a mill on the riverbank, driven by the water."

"Then I'm shoor we can come ta a deal we can live with."

Fred spoke up, "As a matter as a fact I think we can, we want to know what's down valley from where we are, and an aerial view would be great."

"Well Fred I certainly could fly down that way, but I'm not sure ya want me to. If we do and we fly over someone they'll know we came down from above and have a reason to go up."

"Damn, you're right Alex, what do you have in mind?"

"If we came up from below and only flew up as far as y'all searched down and turned around, anyone below would think that was where we came from."

"Why don't you guys think about the offer and let me know what ya plan."

I replied, "We'll do Alex."

Alex added, "Sometime later this year I plan on heading to a place east of here, there's a huge warehouse fer all the big sporting goods stores. Only a handful of people know about it and it's not on any main roads."

"How do you know about it?"

"Cuz I got most a these here supplies from there, I got it wholesale and picked it up from the warehouse by helicopter, that means I know we can land there. While we're out, we can head over your way and fly up valley watching for civilization. We fly as far as we need then turn around and folla the ridge back from the other direction. Then if-in someone does see us they'll come a looking for us in the wrong direction."

"That sounds great Alex it seems like you've done this before."

"That's cuz I have Peter, it's how I brought everythin here. I didn't want no one ta know I'm here, and until y'all showed up no one ever has."

"We'll have to discuss that when we get home, maybe we will take you up on the supply run, there are some things we need."

"Alright Peter you're welcome to join me, I saw that sniper rifle Floyd was carrying, it would be nice to have a gunner in case we're attacked."

I asked, "How well do you know the region?"

"Pretty darn good why?"

"I want to see if we can find an older sawmill that uses the old circular Bell saw blades. It's the one thing we can't make to mill wood for building."

"There's one down valley from here, I flew lots a wood from here to it to get milled, it was cheaper."

"Okay Alex, we'll have to work out the details but I'm sure that is the easy part."

"How bout I give you's guys a tour of the spread?"

"That would be great, from a distance it looks like you have a nice place here."

Alex led us out and showed us his barn and fields, then we headed to the big building we saw from the overlook.

For some reason Floyd was fixed on the helicopter, "Is that the hanger?"

"It shoor is."

As we entered through a small door on the side of the building, Alex turned on the lights and there it was, a big beautiful helicopter shiny and clean.

Now Fred was impressed, "Holy shit that thing is nice."

"Thanks, she's a Whitetrack EC120, she seats four and can be configured to carry a large payload."

Floyd asked, "What type of fuel does it use?"

"She runs on high octane aviation fuel, kind of like a real high-octane gas."

Right about then we heard the ring of the triangle and Elaine saying dinner was ready. As we approached the house, we could smell the ham cooking. When we sat at the table it was covered with scalloped potatoes, corn, collard greens, biscuits and the best ham we've seen in a year.

That night after dinner Alex opened a bottle of Patron and we talked by the fire long into the night about our new world and told each other's stories.

Ed was the first to spin his yarn.

"I remember one day many years ago, Bill and I were out for a night on the town heading back to the city. It was late and we were riding the BART when this girl sat down next to me and started up a conversation."

Bill chimed in, "She was clearly into him."

Ed turned to Bill and gave him that look, you know the type when your girlfriend is not too happy with something you said or did.

"I got this, it's my story you can wait your turn, but Bill is right this girl was interested in me, but she was not my type. Bill sat there like we didn't know each other, and I did nothing to lead this young lady on, but she didn't seem to take the hint and continued to flirt.

At one point she held her boobs in her hands and asked me if I liked them and said she hoped so, because they cost her a small fortune. Then she told me to go ahead and feel them. I couldn't believe it was happening. I always thought it was just a Hollywood thing, that girls didn't do that. Out of curiosity, and wondering what fake boobs felt like, I said okay and took both her boobs in my hands and squeezed them. They seemed nice, if you were into those things."

Alex jumped in and said, "You liked it, and you know it."

"Not really, I don't swing that way, Bill here is more my type."

You could see the look of realization as he figured out Ed and Bill were a couple.

"I see... then maybe not." We had a little laugh at that.

"Anyway, the next stop was ours and when Bill and I got up to get off the train we took each other's hands and looked back at her and I blew her a kiss as we departed."

Fred responded, "Figures it's always the gay guys that women hit on like that, it never happens to me."

I replied, "Aww you poor thing, there may be a reason for that Fred."

"Yeah, yeah, yeah, I get it."

Ed turned to Bill and said, "Okay, NOW it's your turn."

Bill replied, "That's okay I don't really have any good stories to tell."

"Come on Bill let's hear one."

"I'm sorry Ed, but I really don't feel up to it."

I said, "That's okay Bill, you don't have to. What about you Fred, do you have any good stories? Being ex-Army, you must have a horror story or something. It doesn't have to be funny; it can be anything."

"Well there's one I could tell, but it was not that long ago. Funny Peter, you know all about this one."

I looked over to Fred and shook my head with that I WILL kill you look.

"Don't do it old man, don't go there."

Alex asked, "Don't go where?"

"Peter here doesn't want me to tell everyone about what happened to him on our trip to Little Haven."

"That's right I don't, but if you really feel the need to have fun at my expense..."

"Okay, if you don't mind."

"I do mind, but you're going to any way aren't you?"

"I sure am. We were a few days up that incredible valley we loved so much when it happened. Peter and I were riding in my ATV and stopped the column. Everyone else was setting up for the night and Peter and I went for a walk to check the area out."

"Fred I'm warning you don't go there."

Shaking his hands like he was acting afraid Fred said, "OOOOO I'm shaking in my boots."

"Well you should be, if you do it you should be afraid, you should be very afraid."

Now Ben had to hear what had happened to me, he added, "Come on Peter let him tell us."

"All right Fred but you've been warned."

"We were a half mile ahead of everyone when Peter took a step too close to a bank with a huge mud hole below and it was really deep too. You should have seen it; he was walking in front of me talking one minute and gone the next. I ran up to make sure he was alright when I saw him.

It was the funniest thing I ever saw, he looked like a huge walking mud Yeti. I promised him as he climbed out in the stream to wash off that I wouldn't tell anyone but..."

The place broke out in laughter, everyone but me that is. I wasn't too happy about that, but I guess if it helps morale it's all good.

Fred spoke up, "Alright squidly lets hear one of those tall sea stories that squids are famous for."

"Hmmm. That is a tough one. Okay, we were in the Indian Ocean on patrol one day when I saw this mermaid swimming along with us like a dolphin riding the bow waves."

Ben responded, "Funny Peter, real funny."

"All right this is no shit, it really happened. I was stationed on a sub tender in Rota Spain when I was seventeen. We were out on a rare underway trip to Palma Majorca Spain for some well-deserved rest. As soon as we got into international waters a Russian trawler started to approach our ship. The ship kept getting closer and closer and the Captain called in the Spanish Air Force to fly out and show them the errors of their ways.

Within a few minutes a Spanish harrier screamed over us. He flew around and came to stop some distance above the Russian ship and hovered. Little by little the jet started to lower over the ship like he was landing on it. You could see the heat from his engines roaring down on the crew of their ship.

It was the funniest thing to watch, their sailors were holding their hands over their heads bent over and running for cover inside their ship. It didn't take long for the Russian ship to get the message and it turned away and took off. It was cool we were cheering the pilot for his move.

Before the pilot left, he turned his jet on its side, that way we could see the bottom of his plane and here was this huge Spanish flag painted on it. As he flew by, he waved his wings in a salute. It was cool to watch it."

Alex asked, "Okay Peter, real or another sea story?"

"Very real, I decided to keep it clean and end our fire on a good note. I don't know about the rest of you, but I'm ready for some sleep."

Everyone else went off to bed then too. We spent the night there sleeping in the barn, the next morning we woke up to an unforgettable smell in the air.

Floyd raised his head and with flaring nostrils sniffing the air he took in three deep breaths.

"Is that bacon I smell?"

Fred was already up and replied, "It sure is Floyd, I've been savoring it for several minutes now and am heading in."

"Don't eat all of it before we get there Fred."

"Hey if you snooze you lose Peter, you better get moving too."

Everybody had a good laugh and we headed in together. As we entered the house Elaine was waiting for us.

"I see y'all followed your noses in this morning, coffee boys?"

"How could we miss it Elaine, it smells great and yes please, black for me."

Everyone else echoed my request.

While we were eating, we made plans on getting back

when Alex spoke up.

"How'd ya guys like a lift home?"

Ben jumped up, "Hell yeah! I've never been in a helicopter before."

"Well I can only take three of you at a time, that means it'll have to be two flights, but It's not that far, it'll be quick."

I spoke up, "I think that's a great idea, it's nice of you to offer Alex."

Alex replied, "I must admit I have my own motives. First, I'd like ta see what y'all have going on over there, and I'd love to meet more of ya people."

"Okay then, Fred you Ben and Floyd go on the first flight and the rest of us will come on the second one. Fred make sure you get to the fort I don't want to fly over it and get shot down."

"Alright Peter, I'll let everyone down-valley know what's going on when we get back."

"Then Alex when you bring the rest of us back, we'll give you a tour of our community and you can see what we have to trade.

"That sounds great Peter."

Ben was beside himself getting to ride in a helicopter.

Excitedly he asked, "When do we go? When do we go?"

Everyone laughed at his giddiness.

"We can go any time ya want, I jist did my weekly service yesterday so she's ready to fly."

With a full mouth Fred mumbled, "I don't know about you, but I'm not going anywhere until I finish this incredible breakfast." Then he washed it down with a nice hit on his coffee. You could see the pleasure in his body.

"Besides the seating, I can carry a sling load under as we fly. Is there anything you guys could use that we can fly in on the first trip? One we can just drop and go?"

Without a second thought Fred replied, "Yeah if you can afford any of the gas, we sure could use it."

"Sure, I could spare a couple barrels, we can work it out when we get there."

"That's great, thanks Alex I'm sure we can."

It took about a half hour to get the helicopter out of the hanger and ready to fly. As soon as Fred, Floyd and Ben were belted in with helmets on, they took off. The flight only took about fifteen minutes to make it home. As my ranch came into view Fred showed Alex where to land in the field.

Meanwhile back at my ranch, Ann and the girls were working out in the fields when...

"What is that sound?"

"I'm not sure Ann but it sounds like a helicopter."

"Grab the gun's ladies and let's get under cover."

From the trees they saw a large helicopter with a net under it fly past then come back in for a landing. They were surprised at who climbed out of the copter.

"Fred!? What are you guys doing on that thing?"

"Hi Ann, our new friend Alex here gave us a ride home."

Ann asked, "Where is everyone else?"

"They're back at Alex's place, Peter and the rest stayed because the helicopter only seats four. Alex is going back to get them, everyone step back so he can head out."

We removed the barrels from the net and signaled the all clear to Alex.

"EVERYONE BACK UP SO HE CAN TAKE OFF."

As everyone backed away the helicopter took off and disappeared up the valley.

Inquisitively Ann asked, "Who was that Fred?"

"His name is Alex; he lives on the other side of the pass above us in a really nice ranch."

"Is Peter alright over there?"

"He's fine Ann, he's back at the ranch with Alex's wife and kids, and they'll be back in an hour or so."

It took about fifteen minutes to fly back to the ranch, and when they did, he had a surprise for me. The night before Alex and I had worked out a deal for some additional supplies. He gave us three baby steers that rode back in our laps and a pregnant heifer slung below for some trade to be determined later. We also arranged a trade of pheasant, ducks and chickens to ensure a good genetic mix for both of us. We loaded it up and readied to go.

Alex said, "Oh I almost forgot these are for you."

"What is it?"

"Well the large wrapped ones are steaks, enough for dinner tonight for everyone, then there's some smoked bacon and ham, this one is just for you, I bet you recognize it."

"I do, that's the way the Navy buys coffee."

"Yep it's twenty pounds."

"Oh My God I can't thank you enough for this."

"I have a couple hundred pounds of coffee, twenty won't make a difference."

"That's kind of you Alex, I'll need to find something to do in return for your generosity."

"That won't be necessary, think of it as a gesture of good faith."

After we loaded the inside, we attached another sling load with the heifer and took off. When we reached the X-Bar, we dropped the heifer then took off again for a fly over of the area to show Alex Little Haven.

As we took off, I started telling Alex about our little home, "Welcome to Little Haven Alex, our little haven in the woods."

"It's great, the name fits it perfectly."

As we flew down, we looked at the fields and the mill, it was kind of cool flying over Little Haven like that. It gave me a hell of a perspective on our little village. To minimize the impact on the area we established roads to get around. We were on our way to the fort when Alex looked down and something caught his eyes.

Excitedly Alex called out, "Is that pot I see growing down there?"

"It is, why? You're not one of those sheep that bought into the lies to brain wash everybody into believing about it are you?"

"Hell no, I think you and I have found the price of those cows and then some."

I nodded in agreement and Alex reached over to shake hands.

"That harvest down there is only the first year, next year we plan on doubling the size."

"Why do you need that much weed?"

"It's not about the weed though that is a bonus, we are more interested in the hemp. We'll utilize every part of those plants. Besides using the buds for medicines, we can also use the rest for a wide range of things. We can make clothes, paper and rope to name a few, we can also get the cannabinoids from the stalk for medical uses as well."

We passed the fort on our way down and continued until we flew over the lower outpost. We decided not to fly further and headed back up valley and hovered over the fort before we returned to the X Bar. I could see Brandon waving at me, and I waved back at him. I was glad Fred had told him we were coming I didn't want to get shot out of the sky by a .50 cal.

As we landed at the X Bar and the blades came to a stop, I could see Ann waving at me. We got out of the helicopter and walked over to everyone else. After hearing the helicopter come and go, several folks had made their way up to our ranch to find out what was happening.

"Hey everyone, this is Alex, he and his family live on the other side of the pass above us and he was nice enough to give us a ride home, I want everyone to make him feel welcome."

"Hi everyone, it's nice to meet ya I look forward ta working with y'all. From what I could see as I flew over, we'll be able to work out some nice trading."

"Oh, and by the way Alex here has given us a generous gift. He has given us a hundred pounds of beef for lunch. Henry didn't you say you were a BBQ chef in your past life?"

"I sure was, and you don't even have to ask Peter I'm on

it, and I'm sure I'll have plenty of helpers."

He was right, people came out of the woodwork offering to help. A bunch of us jumped on a couple ATVs and headed off to give Alex a better look at our little haven. We drove from place to place and Alex laughed when he saw we had named the roads. It was beginning to look like a little city with roads connecting all the areas we travel.

It took a couple hours to give Alex the dime tour of the place including the fort, and we ended up at the cave. By then it was lunchtime and Henry and his crew had cooked the beef over the fire at the amphitheater, the smell drove everyone nuts. The steaks were huge, everyone got about a pound of beef. While we were eating someone in the crowd called out.

"Alex, where were you when the quake struck?"

I had to interrupt.

"Let's let the man eat."

"It's alright Peter, I'm sure they want to know what's going on out there. Besides I've already finished my lunch."

Everyone gathered in anticipation to hear what Alex had to say, people settled in for his story and continued to feast on the meal, mostly steaks.

Chapter 34: Washington D.C.

Alex started his story.

"I was in Baltimore when the quake hit. It was 3:45 pm when the news interrupted Ellen DeGeneres with the story of a massive earthquake that had struck the entire west coast. Ma jaw dropped to the floor, the entire west coast? How's that possible?

I watched in horror as the news trickled in that the Cascadia Fault had ruptured along its entire length. They said that every major city from Seattle to San Diego was in ruins and that the Golden Gate Bridge had collapsed. They said it had triggered the San Andreas, which also ruptured completely.

As we watched it happening, I told Elaine this was it, that this was the straw that would break the countries back. I told her watch the Dow it's a fixin ta collapse, and shore unff it did. With that we finished loading our bugout bags with those last-minute items. We never filled them because we figured it was better ta do that last bit depending on what the problem was. We not only already had an escape plan in place, we had several escape routes planned out to the airport.

The roads were already crazy, and we were hearing about looting all over the country almost immediately after the quake. We made it ta the airport, fueled up the helicopter and took off. There is not much isolation from civilization within a hundred miles of D.C, but we had found an isolated spot, with no roads to it for our bug out location.

The ash from Mt Rainer had spread mostly Northeast and was not heavy were we were. We knew there was a no-fly directive due ta the ash, but what choice did we have. We jist took our chances with both the ash and the authorities and took off. We heard the control tower tell us about all air travel being halted but we pressed on anyway.

We stayed low and were heading out of town, maybe they had bigger fish ta fry, so they left us alone. Our bugout location was well stocked, jist waiting for our arrival. From our vantage point we could see the lights of Washington DC and the surrounding area in the distance.

Floyd asked, "Are you sure it was Washington DC?"

"Yes, this was our bug out location, we knew exactly where we were and what was around us. We had plenty of food and water and we were armed to the teeth, so we decided ta hang out there at least until they lifted the no-fly order, or it was safe to fly.

"I knew that even with the engines off, ash could get into the turbines. We taped plastic over every place that ash could get in and cause damage; we even taped the doors closed. A few days later we heard on the radio about New York City burning to the ground and that order had broken down. Everything was happening just as many of us Preppers said it would, if something really big happened."

Fred spoke up, "You are in good company here, many of us here right now have said the same things for years."

Floyd asked, "Why would you leave that spot if you were far from anyone, well supplied and safe where you were?"

"Haven't you heard?"

We all responded, "heard what?"

"Oh My God you don't know."

"KNOW WHAT!?" Alex looked at Elaine and with the most painful face you can imagine said, "It's all gone, everything in a fifty-mile radius of Washington DC has been vaporized."

We exclaimed, "VAPORIZED! What do you mean VAPOR-IZED?"

Fred spoke up and said, "They did it didn't they? Who was it the Russians? China? Who?"

Ed asked, "Who did what?"

Fred answered, "Someone dropped a nuke on DC."

Alex responded, "The bombs came from one of our own Trident submarines. It was around two weeks after the quake and order had already collapsed. Washington was no longer in control of anything including the Navy. Every ship captain acted in what he felt was best for him or his crew.

Before Washington lost control the Captain of the U.S.S. Florida heard about the quake and requested permission to return to their home port of New York. The Captain and crew expected there would be chaos in the aftermath and wanted to ensure their families were safe.

Washington denied their request and ordered them to stay at sea. None of the crew was happy about being denied permission to return to be with their families. The Captain was so upset when his request was denied that he lost his mind. And because his crew was pissed, he had no problem convincing them that Washington would have to pay. Captain and crew knew that life as we knew it was over and they wanted pay-back."

Floyd asked, "What does that mean?"

"The Captain launched one Trident missile with all its warheads on DC. There are ten MIRVs on each missile. Each MIRV is a separate warhead and all of them came down on the DC. area. The Captain of the sub said if anyone came after him, he would fire the rest of his missiles."

Everyone exclaimed, "Oh My God!"

Ben asked, "How did you hear about it?"

"Well we saw it happen, it was mid-day and we were still in the mountains a hundred miles northwest of DC. From our location we saw the first blast then another and another in a matter of minutes all of them had detonated. It was a sight that'll be burned into my mind for the rest of my life.

I couldn't tell how many there were but there were multiple mushroom clouds rising over the Washington DC area. It didn't take long before the outer bands of the blast waves hit us. I knew that meant things just went from bad ta worse, we already had planned to make our way out of there but had waited be'cuz of the ash, but now with DC being nuked we figured that it was time to leave."

Someone called out, "Did the radiation reach you?"

"No most of it went to the east and we were far enough away from the blast zone. We packed up our stuff and took off as soon as we could and headed west. We made it ta Chicago with the fuel we had and landed ta refuel. That was where we heard about why and what the Captain wanted.

He had only one demand, ta be left alone wherever he settled. We only stayed long enough ta refuel the helicopter and off we went. We made it here and haven't left since we got here. Have you guys heard anything new?"

We have much to tell you Alex. It could take some time to go over the stories that our newcomers have told us. Do you want to wait to go, or come back with your family and we can go over the gory details at that time?"

"It's already been several hours since I left this morning, and I'm shoor Elaine is starting ta worry about me."

"I understand, why don't you bring your family back tomorrow for dinner at our place, we can tell you about it, we have plenty of room and you guys can stay the night."

"That sounds like a great plan. I'll see y'all tomorrow evening, but we will have ta leave early because I need to deal with the cows. Hey, Peter, did you like the tequila last night?"

"I loved it."

"Well I'll bring a bottle with me when we come back."

"That will be great, we look forward to sitting down and getting to know each other better."

Ann overheard Tequila and looked at me with raised eyebrows and asked, "Tequila...?"

I'll never understand how when I say something, she can't hear me but when it comes to something like coffee or Tequila, she has killer hearing.

"Sure, we had some last night after the best damn smoked ham I have had in months."

"SMOKED HAM!? What else have you not told me yet?"

As I reached down and tapped on the top of an unopened mostly unmarked can.

"Well this, twenty pounds of coffee he gave me just before we left."

"You jerk how long were you going to hide that from me?"

"Well I was going to surprise you by you waking up to it brewing."

Fred caught the last part of that and asked, "BREWING? Brewing what?"

I laughed.

Ann responded, "Peter here has been holding out on the coffee he has."

"Oh yeah it was great, that first smell made me drool, wait did you say has? Not had?"

"Yeah, what do you mean why the distinction?"

"Oops, you spilled the beans Fred, no pun intended."

Beth asked, "What are you guys talking about?"

Ann answered, "These guys have been holding out on the coffee."

Now I felt like I was being attacked, "Now wait a minute I was going to surprise you in the morning with it brewing now the surprise is spoiled. And Alex made us some while we were there that's it."

Fred came back, "Yeah it was great we had some the first day there, before that ham dinner and had some more with a killer country breakfast of bacon and eggs."

Now all the girls exclaimed, "BACON? YOU HAD BACON for breakfast?"

Fred looked at me and said, "You need to shut up before they string you up Peter."

"I have some bacon for us, I was planning on a hell of a breakfast. Forget it now."

Ann exclaimed, "Forget it my ass, where is that stuff?"

"Right there in the corner."

Ann looked at Beth and said, "You grab the coffee from the jerk over there and I'll get the bacon. We are having some right now."

The girls went nuts and cooked two of the four packs of bacon Alex gave me and didn't want to share it.

The next day Alex returned with his family. Lucky for me besides the birds we decided on he brought me a variety of meats including more ham and bacon. Now I was out of the doghouse at least for a little while. Many of our neighbors turned out for our meeting, we talked late into the night. During that time the topic of what was below us came up.

Alex asked, "Peter, how far have y'all scouted out the valley below you?"

"We have gone several miles down on our own, down to the top of a series of waterfalls and had not gone any further. We went several miles past the point where Floyd and his people came into the valley."

"Did they come up from the valley floor?"

"No, they had seen our fires from high on a ridge down quite a bit below where we scouted out. We really have no idea how far the valley goes or if it is even uninhabited like yours or if it leads straight into the remains of civilization."

"We really need to go all the way down to find out."

"You're right Brandon; we do need to."

Sandy asked, "Why don't you fly down to check it out, it would be faster than if you tried to make your way down and wouldn't leave any trail to follow back if you find anyone."

"Let me answer that one for you Alex, if we fly down and fly over someone in the trees below, they would know someone is up here with a helicopter and come looking for us and the chopper."

"You're right Peter, but you missed an even bigger problem with that, if they have any large ammo, they could shoot us down, not something I want to happen."

"I didn't think of either of those issues, what are our options?"

"That's a better question Beth."

Alex had a suggestion, "I brought maps of the area below, so we could see how far it is before there is any known roads."

"That's a great place to start, where are they?"

Alex brought over the maps and we poured over them for hours before we concluded that we were a bit over two hundred miles above any roads on the map. We decided that it was too much of a risk to fly down, accordingly we planned on exploring it on foot.

We would use the same method as we did when we came here and try not to leave any trails to follow back. Alex and his family returned home the next morning and we began planning the trip.

The scouting party was made up of George, Allen, Susan and Floyd. Their mission was to go past where Floyd's party had met the valley. Then keep going until they either found civilization or until they ran into people. If possible, they were only to observe and listen if they found anyone and report back anything they found. They were not supposed to use fire during the day or cook any meals just MRE's to avoid detection at any cost.

Chapter 35: The Valley Below

Of course, that wasn't as easy as it sounded. They were out about ten days when they noticed smoke coming from the valley floor below them.

Sue asked, "How far away do you think that smoke is Floyd?"

"Several miles down valley would be my bet Sue."

Allen exclaimed, "SMOKE? Where?"

"Look down there, it almost looks like fog or wispy clouds."

"Well guys you know the drill, I stay here with Susan and you guys head down there after dark."

"I do; remember I was on the receiving side of it when you guys came to our camp that night."

Floyd asked, "Hey Susan, have you seen the night vision goggles?"

"Yeah they are in the pack over there by the cedar."

"Thanks, I found them."

That night they crept up on the camp hoping to gain a little intelligence, it was a good thing they did. As they approached the camp their hearts sank when they realized they were looking at scouts who were checking the valley for signs of life.

There were four men dressed in matching fatigues, from what they could make out of the conversation the men would be heading up in the morning. They were at least two days below the lowest and smallest of the big waterfalls.

Floyd didn't want these guys to see them because the

scouts were armed to the teeth. Each of them had AK-47s and Glocks on their sides. Their combat vests were hanging on trees nearby and all of them had hand grenades attached. From what our guys were able to make out they were part of an organized militia. They are exploring the valleys above their base, which was further down the valley.

It was easy to figure out who was in charge because everyone referred to him as Captain and replied, "Yes sir."

"That hike up here was brutal Captain, I wonder how much harder the rest of the valley is."

"I know Braxton, but we have a job to do and we knew it wasn't going to be easy."

"I'm with Braxton, Captain, I don't know how far we are going to be able to go, besides this is stupid."

"WE WILL GO AS FAR AS I SAY WE WILL GO!! YOU GOT THAT JONES?"

You could see the disgust in Jones' face, "YES SIR!!!"

"We'll be heading up at first light, everyone hit the sack, Jones you have the midnight to six tonight, Smith you relieve him."

Both responded with a resounding "Yes Sir" and headed off.

As the two men were heading off our scouts could hear Jones complaining.

"Man, I don't believe he gave me the balls to six again, I have had it the last three nights while the rest of you get different times."

"DUH!... Dude I couldn't believe you said that to him, he's getting tired of you talking back to him."

"Screw him, who died and made him God?"

"Well that would be our insane leader Anderson, unless you want to question him as well."

"Not a chance in hell, not a chance in hell," they both laughed.

With that Floyd decided it was time to go, they quietly moved away and returned to camp, it was almost midnight before they made it back and told everyone else the news. None of them were happy with what was heard that night.

"What are we going to do Floyd, if these guys make it to Little Haven, they'll bring back reinforcements? From what I could see of those four we wouldn't stand a chance against them. There are sixteen grenades back there that I counted, you can only imagine what else they have."

George asked, "Did you guys cover your tracks back here?"

"We did, we stayed in the stream coming back."

"Good thinking Allen."

"How long did it take you to get up here Allen?"

"About three hours Sue, but we moved slowly making sure we didn't leave any signs."

Floyd said, "Then we need to get out of here at day-break."

Allen replied, "They said they were going to head out at first light, if we leave at daybreak too, we'll be able to stay ahead of them."

"What do you mean stay ahead of them?"

"We don't want to lose sight of these guys. I don't want

them to surprise us. We're going to keep watching their camp every night until either they give up or we make it to the first outpost."

"Good thinking Floyd, we'll know even more by the time we get there."

They spent the next few nights sleeping on rocks, no fires and only eating MRE's. It was difficult not leaving any sign that they were ever there, especially with the scouts so close on their tails. At least they knew the way up the falls, Floyd thought to leave ropes that they could use to go up, and the militia scouts wouldn't have that in their favor.

Floyd's team stopped at the top of the last big falls; it gave them a good view of the area below it. Floyd stayed a bit lower so he could hear what was being said when the scouts found the falls. None of them were prepared for what was to take place when the scouts reached the area.

"CAPTAIN! I think you need to see this."

As the Captain came around the bend, he didn't like what he saw.

"HOLY SHIT"

"That's for sure Captain, look at that thing, it must be one hundred foot tall. The rocks on both sides are slimy and covered with moss. Look at this thing, there's no way we are going to get past this monster."

"Smith, front and center... you're the climbing expert here what do you think."

"I'm sure it's possible to get past it but there is another question you should be asking yourself Cap. Should we? We are over a hundred miles from the closest road and have been climbing for weeks and haven't seen even one sign of any human activity. The maps show this heads deep into the wil-

Xavier Bruehler

derness and has never been inhabited. There's no way anyone is up there."

Braxton commented, "It's your call Captain."

Then Jones asked him in a sarcastic tone. "Well Captain now what do we do?"

You could see the anger building in the Captain. He pursed his lips, closed his eyes and sort of rolled his head in a no manner. Then in a harsh, angry voice, said, "Jones, if you say one more word to me, I swear to God I am going to..."

Jones stepped up behind the Captain, and in an even more confrontational tone asked, "You're going to what... SIR..." with the sir in an even more sarcastic drawn out and challenging manner.

As the captain turned around, he had his pistol in his hand and put it against Jones forehead.

The captain replied in a deep slow voice, "I am going to blow your damn head off you piece of shit; I am sick of your snide attitude and I am not going to put up with it anymore."

No one could believe their eyes. A .50cal Desert Eagle was pressed up against Jones' forehead with the safety off and the Captain's finger on a hair trigger. Everyone, both theirs and ours, froze and watched as it played out.

Captain continued, "I suggest you not utter another word, step back, turn around and walk away and not come near me for a while."

The man slowly stepped back and turned his head as he walked away. You could see the fury stewing up inside of him, the Captain still had his gun trained on him as he moved away. What the captain couldn't see was the guy removed his Glock from his chest holster and was going to shoot him.

However, one of the other guys did. When Jones noticed the Captain had turned his back and lowered his gun, then Jones started to spin around and began to raise his weapon when, POP! POP! POP!

As Jones was dropping to the ground the Captain raised his gun again in time to see Jones hit the ground.

"What the hell just happened?"

"Jones was going to shoot you in the back Captain, look it's in his hand, and his finger is on the trigger."

"Did you do that Smith?"

"Yes Sir, I did, if I hadn't you would be dead now Sir."

"He's right Cap, I saw the whole thing he just beat me to the shot, I didn't see the gun until he turned."

"What are we going to do Cap?"

"Thank you, guys, it's nice to know you have my back, literally. What we are going to do is go home, I'm tired of this. There is no way anyone is up there. You know guys the sad thing is, I was just about to say that when he started talking smack again, what a waste."

Smith said, "I told him the other day he was out of line, I guess he figured in this new world he didn't have to follow rules anymore."

"Guys we'll never be away from someone telling us what to do. NEVER."

"What about him, do we just leave him like that, shouldn't we bury him?"

"Nope leave his dumb ass to be eaten by the critters, his body will be gone in a few weeks. Collect his gear and weapons and let's get out of here."

With that the three men turned and started down, Floyd could hear the Captain say that he was going to report there was no reason to pursue this one any further. The relief was almost palpable.

There was no reason to go any further down, they already knew they were over a hundred miles from Little Haven and they heard them say it was at least another hundred more to the nearest road.

The next morning, they started back, this time it was a bit easier because they had left ropes and vines in place to use to get back up and they didn't need to take the precautions they did the last few days. They still restricted their fires to night use only and eating MREs, but it wasn't as bad getting home.

It'd been more than a month since they left when they saw the outpost above. They decided to freak out the watches and tried to sneak up on them. Little did they know the watches had seen them first and were ready for them.

"Shhh, lets scare the shit out of them."

"You guys go ahead, I'm going to brief Brandon, have fun."

"Thanks Floyd, we'll see you tomorrow."

When the scouts went through the door to the outpost no one was there, as soon as they were in the blind one of the watches on duty released the trap door handle that collapses the roof on the shelter to hide it and trapped them inside. The guys inside could hear everyone laughing outside.

"GET US OUT OF HERE."

More laughing.

"Alright you win, you got us good, now get us out of here."

The watches opened the cover and replaced the panic trigger, now it was set to drop again if needed. After filling in the watches the two of them headed up to tell everyone else what they saw. Floyd briefed Brandon and us on what they found and later that night had to repeat it once more to everyone at the amphitheater.

After that we kept watch on the valley, but we were not as worried about anyone making their way up. The valley below the point where Floyd and his team came in was even harder than what was above it.

Chapter 36: The Flight

It was mid-summer and we had set a day with Alex to fly us on the resupply run we talked about. Just after breakfast we heard the rotors coming down the valley and knew he was on his way. Alex landed his helicopter in my yard and powered down. We met him outside and shook hands and gave each other a manly hug.

"Welcome back Alex."

"My pleasure Peter, I'm looking forward ta this trip even though it's with some trepidation. Any time I fly I take the chance of being detected and shot down. Peter, are you going on this trip?"

"Not this time Alex, this kind of stuff is for the young and strong, not the old and fat."

Alex replied, "I'm with you man, but I'm still young as far as I'm concerned."

"Well you are still young compared to Fred and me." We laughed.

"Okay ya got me there, who'll be going with me?"

"That would be Malcolm and Doug."

They're both decorated Army Special Forces snipers, each has four and six tours respectively in Afghanistan and Iraq under their belt. I can't think of anyone that I'd rather have with me, than them. These two are as good as it comes when dealing with guerilla warfare. Let me introduce you to them."

"Malcolm, Doug, can you guys come over here?"

"We'll be right there, Peter."

We were approached by two huge guys. They are both body builders and have worked hard to make sure they maintain their shape. Doug is a big black dude and Malcolm is a short stocky Mexican, and both had matching Special Forces tats. They had been a team for many tours having served in the same unit in both Afghanistan and Iraq.

"It's nice to meet ya guys. Have ya ever been in a helicopter?"

They both nodded their heads and did one of those acknowledging grunts and replied,

"More than we like to think about."

"That's good 'cuz this ain't gonna be a smooth ride."

"Trust us we can handle ANYTHING you can throw at us."

"Alright guys let's get loaded up and go."

As Malcolm was putting in his rifle, Alex noticed it and asked, "Is that your sniper rifle?"

"It sure is, it's my little baby, it's an M40 A5 sniper rifle. With this baby I can shoot a fly off a pile of shit at a quarter mile."

Alex replied, "Yea right, that I'd have to see to believe."

"It's true Alex, we were in country one day waiting for our target to arrive and he bet me he could do it. I doubted him and bet him two weeks' pay. I lost."

"Now that sounds like someone, I want with me. I can't tell you how much better I feel knowing I have someone flying with me that can shoot back if someone is shooting at us."

Patting his gun Malcolm replied, "Well with this baby, you can count on us."

"Somehow I get that feeling."

Malcom asked, "How are we doing this Alex?"

"I've configured the helicopter to only carry the three of us and cargo. I also brought along the sling, if we need it. I've removed both the side doors where you'll be sitting, that way you'll be able to shoot if ya have ta. Ya should strap in."

Doug spoke up, "That's a negative Alex, we NEVER strap in a helicopter, if it's going down, we want to be able to go without worrying about being strapped in."

"That's fine Doug, I'm sure you've done this more than me, seein how it's my first time with guards. We're gonna head up valley till we reach the ridge, then turn south and follow the ridge top. After about a half hour we'll turn east, then drop down the valley adjacent to where the warehouse, then we'll come up the valley with it."

Ann said, "Sounds like you have done this trip a few times."

"I have Ann, but things could've changed, we need ta be ready for anything. Now when we approach the warehouse, I'll fly high and slow ta see ifin we can see if anyone is there. If we think it's safe, we'll land there, if not we'll leave and decide what to do."

Allen asked, "What about the saw blade, are you still going for it?"

"We will Allen, when we finish at the warehouse, we'll continue up that valley and drop down another one to get it. From there we'll make our way home."

With that they loaded what was needed for the trip and off they went. The flight up valley was nice and the flight over the ridge was real exciting. Alex decided to be funny, when it was time to drop down the first valley, he didn't give them any warning.

Suddenly, he pushed hard on the stick and rolled the helicopter almost on its side and dropped down the valley. Doug was not too happy about the unexpected maneuver, but Malcolm loved it, Alex made several quick maneuvers while he flew along laughing every time Doug reacted to it. It wasn't their first flights in a helicopter, but Doug never liked them.

After about an hour Alex called through the headset to be ready as they were coming up on the warehouse. At first, they could see cars in the lot, but no one was outside. As he hovered over the warehouse for a bit and started to lower, they could see men running out of the warehouse, and opened fire on them. You could hear bullets pinging off the helicopter and Alex pulled back on the stick and took off almost straight up and off to the side. It was a good thing they were just outside their effective range; therefore, it didn't put holes in the helicopter.

"How many did you see Doug?"

"I made out at least ten before they opened fire on us."

Malcolm replied, "I made out at least a dozen."

Doug asked, "What's the plan now?"

"I saw a nice place some ways uphill of them where we could land and make our way back there."

Alex asked Malcolm, "How far can ya get a good shot from?"

"Quite a way from a stable platform, what do you have in mind?"

"I can fly out of their range, can ya see if ya can pick off a few?"

Malcolm replied, "I don't think that's a good idea, if we came back like that, they'll call for reinforcements and we'll be screwed. Let's go back to that spot I saw, and we can come in under the cover of darkness and see if we can take them out one by one.

Doug liked that, "That sounds like a great idea, they'll think they scared us off."

They landed in the opening and made their way to the warehouse, then watched for the rest of the day trying to figure out how many people were there and counted twelve. It looked like Doug may have been right because none of them seemed to be edgy. They didn't know if there was anyone else inside, but figured they had to try after coming this far and taking this much a chance. Alex noticed both attaching a silencer to their rifles.

Alex asked, "How do you plan on doing this?"

Malcolm responded, "We're going to shoot them as they change their guards, then more will come out to see what happened to the off going guards and investigate."

Malcolm took the northwest corner where he could see the north and west side of the building. Doug took the southeast side so he could see the south and east sides. Alex held back to be ready to approach the warehouse from the backside.

They agreed to take out the next set of guards on their next change.

It was around 2200 hour when the guards were changed. Malcolm and Doug then each took out four guards with barely any sound. Malcolm's next shot took out the antenna so they couldn't call for backup if they were detected.

With that done they approached the warehouse, Alex

and Doug entered from the back and Malcolm entered from the side.

It was dark inside because everyone, but the guards, were asleep. They crept in and looked in every room checking for anyone else. Doug noticed the light was on in one room, he opened the door slowly. As soon as he could see inside, he saw the man looking at the door wondering why it was being opened slowly. When he saw Doug, he opened fire and Doug closed the door.

Doug retreated only a little bit and turned back to the door with it in his sights, when the man came running out the door, Doug shot him, and he dropped. A few other men heard the gunfire and came running over. Doug got another one of them and the other got the drop on Doug.

"DROP YOUR WEAPON AND PUT UP YOUR ARMS," he commanded.

Doug dropped his gun and slowly raised his hands and turned toward him.

The man asked, "Who are you and what are you doing here?"

Doug replied, "I'm nobody, I just found this place and came looking to see what it was."

"Then why did you just shoot my friend there?"

"Because he opened fired on me first and I was defending myself."

"Well you came to the wrong place, you're going to die for this, but not until Pat talks to you. I'm sure he will have some questions for you. Move it that way."

The man pointed his weapon to a room in the corner.

Just as Doug opened the door to what looked like a storage room, he heard a too familiar sound. He turned and there was Malcolm, who took out the guy that had him at gunpoint. No sooner did Doug get to tell Malcolm thanks when he heard another single shot, Doug saw his best friend Malcolm drop to the ground in front of him.

Doug yelled out MALLCCOOOLMMM..., just then more guys opened fire on him. Doug was furious, he took cover inside the room and exchanged fire for several minutes taking out a bunch more. It fell quiet for a minute, then he heard a shot ring out. It was different than the POP POP POP of the 9mm Doug was using or the guy shooting at him. This one was much louder, and then he didn't hear the shooting anymore.

When Doug looked out, he saw Alex standing there with a 44 over the guy that was shooting at him. Doug heard a muffled sound in the room he was in. There were no lights, but he could make out a shape in the corner that was sitting on the floor, the person was tied up. They didn't hear any more shooting, they figured they had killed them all. Doug went to deal with his old friend Malcolm, while Alex approached the person in the dark corner.

When Alex removed the gag covering the person's mouth, he noticed it was Alfred Conrad, the owner of the warehouse.

"Alex is that you?"

"ALFRED!!?"

With elation in his eyes and excitement in his voice he exclaimed, "Oh My God it is you, Alex what are you doing here?"

"We came looking for supplies. We were hoping no one would be here but I can see we're wrong."

"Well I'm happy you did, these guys found it a week or so

after the quake and took it over."

"Where is everyone else?"

With tears in his eyes he replied, "They killed them, I cooperated, but they killed them anyway, everyone but me. The only reason they didn't kill me was because I knew the warehouse. I was certain I was going to die after they got what they needed."

Meanwhile after making sure his friend was dead and couldn't be helped, Doug took a moment to honor his best friend and covered him. He had a job to do so he continued to check out the warehouse.

"Alex come quick there is someone else over here in this office."

"I'll be right there."

As Doug and Alfred approached, they noticed a girl tied to a chair and gagged. As they drew near, she started screaming through the gag and trying to squirm and kick. Doug tried to calm her down while he removed the gag. She screamed at him to not touch her, but he continued to cut her loose. As she noticed he was freeing her, she calmed down. After he freed her, she broke down crying and fell into his arms and wept heavily.

"My name is Doug and I won't harm you; we've killed the bad guys that had you tied up. What's your name?"

Through the tears she replied, "My name is Amanda."

"Well you are safe now Amanda, no one is going to hurt you anymore, I promise you that I won't let them."

That seemed to calm her down, and she was able to get control of herself. Doug decided to question her about the place.

"Amanda, do you know how many men were here?"

"No, it changed all the time."

Alex asked Alfred, "Do you know how many men were here?"

Alfred replied, "It changed from day to day but there were fifteen today. I never knew they had a girl; she didn't work here."

"That's good because I counted and we killed fifteen, we're safe for now."

Doug asked, "Do either of you know what their leader looked like?"

Her tears turned to anger, and she replied, "I'd know that bastard anywhere. He made it a point to refer to me as his property."

As we came around a corner Amanda saw the man and started to kick him in the face and nuts. She kept screaming, "It serves you right you bastard." It was clear they found him.

After that Doug and Alex started looking for the items they came for. It took them most of the night to find everything they needed. Then Alfred told them that new people came in every morning around nine, we needed to get going.

Alex asked Alfred, "What do you two want to do?"

"I have family here and need to go see if I can find them."

"I understand; is there anything I can do to help?"

"No but there is something I can do for you. This place is an arsenal now after the men brought in so many weapons."

You could see the excitement in Doug's eyes, they got big and he quickly turned his head and asked, "Weapons, what type of weapons?"

Alfred replied, "Hell, all sorts of rifles, grenades, mines, a huge horde of RPG's and a couple surface to air missiles."

"Where did they get all that?"

"Their group took over a National Guard Armory and brought some of it here."

Doug's eyes opened even wider, "Where is this stuff?"

"It's in the secure storage in the back section of the warehouse."

Alex said, "Hey Doug I'm gonna get the helicopter while ya check out the storage?"

Doug replied, "That would be great, see you soon."

Alex headed back to get the helicopter, while Doug used the leaders key to open it and looked inside the storage area. As he looked at the stash, Doug heard Angelico music in his head and started drooling when he saw the hoard. They grabbed as much armament as they could and still carry what they came there for in the first place, this included cases of MRE's.

Once Alex was back, they loaded the inside as full as Alex dared. Doug piled the rest in the net then turned to Amanda.

"Do you have family around here?"

"No, and I have no idea where I'm going to go?"

"Well we have a seat for you if you would like to join us. Would you like to go with us, or stay here and fend for yourself?"

"I have nothing here, let's get out of this place before more arrive."

Doug explained the rules and expectations of living in Little Haven and she agreed to them. They flew for at least another half hour when Alex called back on the headset.

"Doug the mill's coming up on your side, can you get a look with your scope before we pass over it?"

"I sure can Alex."

Doug looked through his scope and didn't see any movement around the mill. There were a couple of burnt out cars and trucks but nothing that looked new. He could make out a heavy dust coating on the vehicles and no footprints in the dust. After radioing that back to Alex he came in for a closer look.

The rotor blades stirred up the dust as they got close. If anyone was there, they certainly would have come out to investigate. Since it was clear Alex put the helicopter down in the parking lot and they went into the mill.

They had gone there for one reason and that was to get the saw blade. They were happy to see it was still there. They were able to get it off in no time and loaded it into the net. While they were there, they grabbed the hand tools they could get as well, and anything else they thought would be helpful in their new home. They took off and continued up valley until they reached the ridge. Then followed that ridge for a bit when Doug hollered out, "Alex, slow down, what is that down there?"

Alex slowed the forward motion of the helicopter and descended a bit; Doug could make out a small herd of cows roaming in an open field.

"Hey, Alex, how much more weight can this thing carry?"

Alex replied, "None. Why?"

"I want to get one of those cows. Do we still have room in that net?"

Alex seemed irked, "We have room but can't take much more weight, why?"

"Because I'm going to get us some meat, hold her steady Alex."

Alex replied, "If we cut it up right there, we could take some."

Doug said, "Thanks."

The next thing they heard was a shot followed by the bolt action of his rifle being reloaded, then another shot.

Alex radioed back trying to tease Doug and asked, "I thought you were supposed to be good, why did it take two shots to get a cow?"

"Funny Alex because you moved. I told you It's not easy from a helicopter. Now can you land this thing by the cow I want to process it and load it in the sling."

Amanda looked over at Doug and said, "You're good with that thing." She smiled and asked, "Are you married?"

Doug turned to her surprised that she asked that after her ordeal in the warehouse and replied, "No I'm not."

She smiled back looking at him like her knight in shining armor.

They landed and processed the cow and loaded as much as Alex dared to load and went to take off. The helicopter struggled to get off the ground, but once it was airborne it was fine. They continued their flight changing valleys several times before they came down our valley. You could hear them coming for some distance and many were waiting at our cabin to help unload.

It didn't take long to divide up the cow and unload the helicopter. Alex didn't want to stay around because he wanted to get home to his family. In return for his services our team of crack barn raisers planned to head to his place and build a barn for him the next day. Alex left Doug to fill us in on what happened on their adventure and off he went for home. We waved as he flew away swinging his helicopter from side to side to wave back.

Doug filled us in on the loss of his friend Malcolm and on Amanda. She decided to stay in the cave while she figured out what she wanted to do. As it turned out Amanda and Doug became more than friends and they moved in together. Maybe it was his saving her life or maybe that they just really liked each other, but either way they were good for each other.

The night they arrived Amanda filled us in on where she was from and what she had seen.

Chapter 37: The Fall of Chicago

Amanda started out, "I was living in Chicago when the quake hit. We didn't feel anything, but it was all over the news. The mayor of Chicago knew that things would get out of hand real fast. To keep everything under control he immediately requested the National Guard to step in and maintain order before any looting began."

"His fast action kept Chicago from collapsing into chaos and was able to prevent any destruction at all. The Guard placed armed soldiers at every major intersection with orders to shoot with non-lethal rounds if anyone started to loot or destroy things. It didn't take many being shot to stop the rest from trying to do more damage."

Lester yelled out, "You mean the mayor just took it upon himself to declare martial law?"

Amanda replied, "Yes, he remembered what had happened in New Orleans and didn't want it to happen there."

Lester interrupted her again, "Who died and made him God?"

I couldn't let him continue and I called out, "Please let her finish, others here want to know what happened, and Lester, I want to talk to you when we're done here."

Amanda continued, "Thank you Peter, now where was I, oh so the mayor acted quickly enough so that the city escaped the fate we heard about in New York. We had also heard about Washington, DC and feared we would be nuked as well.

None of the members of Congress, the Senate, the President, or the Vice President survived the nuking, and the government collapsed. The Secretary of Defense was in Chicago with his family at the time of the nuclear attack. Back in 1991 or so the U.S. Government ordered the removal of nuclear weapons from every surface warship as part of the SALT treaty with Russia, so none of the surface ships carried them.

Most of the rest of the country had fallen into total chaos, some turned to Chicago for guidance when they heard it was still intact. After about a month it became the defacto capital of what was to be called The Eastern States of America AKA the ESA. They didn't really have any control over anything but did seem to be able to get help to some places.

By now the rest of the world knew about the fall of our government and many outside forces saw it as an opportunity. The UN was no more, and China had been closely watching events unfolding and used the collapse of the US as an excuse to move in.

At first, they came claiming to be our 'FRIENDS', they claimed to be only wanting to provide us humanitarian aid and flew in tons of food. We had no means of stopping them and many needed the food and medical supplies so badly that they didn't object when more and more of them flew in.

Then it started, they flew in flight after flight of their people to 'operate' what plants were left. They restored power to key areas so they could provide power and feed their people and did little to get any to ours. In many of the suburbs the Chinese immigrants took over abandoned homes and even a few suburbs that had been left uninhabited."

Jonathan asked, "What about the people that hadn't left them?"

"There were stories of them being exterminated, but there was no proof of it."

Jonathan exclaimed, "Oh My God is that still going on now?"

"No, but I will get to that. Many of the large militias were not going to allow China to take over what was left of this country. When the Chinese arrived in Chicago many were very much opposed to it. The food was almost gone, there were no medical supplies left and the Chinese had waited until we had little fuel left for our fighters. We couldn't stop them even if we had tried.

The new ESA government was stuck, they had nothing left to help the people and no means to fight, so they allowed the Chinese to just move in. They took over most of the federal buildings and police stations and manned them with their army. They distributed huge amounts of rice and other staples and restocked some of the hospitals but only under guard."

Doug asked, "Why did everyone allow the Chinese army to just move in?"

"Because they said the only way, they were going to bring in supplies was if their army was in charge of their security."

Doug asked again, "So everyone just gave in?"

"What else were they going to do, no one had planned for this. Our modern food distribution system failed after a few days because we set it up that way. The National Guard that manned the streets was able to maintain order for a while but that was starting to crumble. When the Chinese came in, they brought tons of food.

They flew over the city dropping leaflets about sending in supplies if no one resisted their occupation. After a few days the troops arrived saying they would be bringing in food and supplies. The catch was simple, if you wanted food you had to submit to their demands."

Doug asked, "So everyone just submitted?"

"Hell no, there were many out there that said no way. Many gangs turned gorilla and attacked the supply lines and stole the supplies for themselves. Some were successful and were able to steal large amounts of supplies and killed a lot of Chinese troops in the process. All that did was cause the Chinese to fly in even more men. Many that tried to fight back were blown to hell by the Chinese, blasted to bits by fighters.

In time they declared that Chicago was no longer the new Capital, took down the flag and replaced it with their own. It was then we knew their intentions, after that things started to change VERY quickly. They began going from door to door searching for weapons and 'unauthorized contraband.' They raped anyone they desired and forced others into slave labor, anyone that resisted was executed.

They instituted a curfew as soon as they had taken over, with kill on sight orders for violators. If you wanted to eat you would show up in line with a bucket and get a week's supply of rice. Water was your own problem, you had to find it yourself from whatever body of water you could locate. Concentration camps were built inside the naval station and the carrier was taken over with no fight at all. After that they cut what little power there was, and things started to degrade very fast.

Militias in and around Chicago started to do more guerilla attacks on the Chinese. But when they did fight, that gave away their position which told the Chinese where they were located. The Chinese were then able to bomb them to hell, sometimes using our own jets and bombs. After that many started to operate in smaller units that were harder to find and attack.

One day a group of fighters made their way to the carrier

and were able to detonate a large explosive on board and render it useless. The Chinese towed it out to deeper waters and sank it. But the messed-up part was they did it close enough to shore, and shallow enough water that it didn't sink below the surface. They made sure we would see it there as a reminder of their superiority.

As time went by the rice supplies stopped and things began to get scary. That was when we decided to get out of Dodge. We knew things in Chicago were bad and we had heard other parts of the country were not under Chinese rule. It turned out that it was easier for them to take over a large metropolis than is was rural areas. Many gun control laws prevented residents from being able to get weapons and ammo, in order to control everyone. That left us vulnerable, just what the 2nd amendment was meant to prevent.

People living in rural areas had lots of guns. Many had farms so they didn't bow down to the Chinese and their ploy to control everyone with food. Most had formed tight knit groups that blocked off roads and didn't allow anyone near them. When the Chinese came knocking, they acted like they were compliant, but took them out when they slept. Even the Chinese couldn't bomb every square mile of the country so they couldn't get to them."

"How did you get out?"

"All the roads in and out of the city were guarded by the Chinese Army. No cars or trucks could neither come nor go so that was not an option. They posted guards at the bridges watching for people leaving in boats down the Chicago River. I knew the direction of flow of the River was turned by engineers in the 1800's. The river flowed from Lake Michigan to the Mississippi River Valley and gave us a way out.

I lived in a house along its banks with my husband Bill and two kids, Billy and Samantha. As more and more people started to resist the Chinese, things started to get nasty. We witnessed the destruction of one marina when resistance fighters used it as a rally point to attack the Chinese. The Chinese blew the hell out of the marina, blowing million-dollar yachts to smithereens.

The destruction set many of the boats adrift and they floated down stream. Sometimes they would end up on shore and start fires on shore, they burnt down entire apartment complexes. We would watch them drift down stream and the Chinese guards on the bridges just watched them drift past them and laughed.

One day there was a large air raid upriver from us, we could hear them bombing one of those sites. A bit later a large boat drifted down stream and ran aground just offshore of our home. Most of the fire had already gone out, and the boat was still in fair shape, with the cabin area still intact. We found the inside was usable, and that the inside bridge was functional, so we came up with the idea that we could hide inside and set it adrift again and float it past the Chinese guards.

The Chinese were beginning to lose control and said that the next time that they were attacked they were going to scorch the city, that nothing would remain of it. The freedom fighters decided to call their bluff and planned an all-out attack on the Chinese headquarters."

As we sat there listening to Amanda my mind wandered, I imagined how things unfolded that night when the freedom fighters attacked the Chinese.

It was just after dark when snipers opened fired. In seconds all twenty-four guards dropped, the searchlights were shot out and the outside of the building fell silent. For the next few minutes there was no movement outside the building except the attack team descending on the building from zip lines above.

"Peterson you and Sampson are the lookouts, Waltman you and Head release the gas."

Waltman ordered, "Head, grab the gas bottle and let's move."

"You got it; the intake vent is over here."

"Get your mask on and let's get this going before anyone notices that the guards have been taken out."

"I'm almost there, one last connection."

"Hurry man, I think I hear something."

Just then a lone Chinese guard stepped out from behind an air conditioning unit, rubbing his eyes and straightening his uniform. About the same time, he noticed the men, Peterson saw the guard and tossed a knife at him and took him out.

"Now that is what I mean let's get this done."

"It's done; I'm opening the gas now...okay it's working let's go."

Head signaled the rest that it was a go and regrouped with the rest of his team by the entrance to the roof. They jimmied open the door and looked in, it was safe. The five men had their P90's at the ready and descended the stairwell looking for any survivors. Everyone they found was dead, the gas did its job as advertised, and no one lived. The other teams came in on the ground from all four sides and cleared the rest of the building.

"Funk, front and center."

"Yes sir Captain, I'll be right there."

"Take the flag and get the damn Chinese flag down, and get ours up."

"With pleasure sir."

Funk turned to his friend Waldon and said, "Let's get to the roof and get this up."

"I'm with you Funk."

As they were leaving, the Captain called out the all clear and that they could remove their gas masks. Waldon and Head had made it to the roof.

"Waldon would you like the pleasure?"

"I'd love it but this one's yours, you worked so hard for it for so long. You lost your family to the bastards and you deserve pay back."

"Thanks bro, I never thought two kids from south Chicago would ever be bringing down a Chinese flag from The Federal Building and replacing it with a flag of the ESA."

"Richard, I never would have even dreamed of an ESA flag, a U.S. one maybe but not this."

"I told you I hate it when you call me that, its Dick."

Laughing, Waldon replied, "I know' followed by even more laughing."

"Take the rope asshole, let's do this together."

"The two lifelong friends pulled the ESA flag to the top, then lowered it to half-staff for the lives of those that had been lost getting there."

While I imagined what had gone on that night Amanda had been continuing the description of her experience.

"The attack by the freedom fighters pissed the Chinese off. The next day they started pulling out their troops. There was partying in the streets as the Chinese were withdrawing, but we were worried that was a prelude to something bad. We figured the Chinese were pulling out, so their people were not harmed in the attack. For us it was time to go."

Someone called out "How did you get out and end up tied up in a warehouse in Colorado."

Chapter 38: The Escape

Amanda continues,

"It took about three days for the Chinese to get their army out of Chicago, then it started. As soon as we had found the boat, we stocked up on any supplies we could get our hands on and hid them in the boat. When the bombing began, we got on board and set her adrift.

There were lots of burning boats drifting down river that night, so we knew it was our best time to go. We set a controlled fire on deck, so it looked like the boat was on fire as it drifted past the Chinese guards posted on the bridges outside the city. When they saw us, they just let it drift down stream. The Chicago River is not a very fast river in that area, so it was slow going. At times we would wash ashore, and had to look out to make sure no one saw us when we pushed the boat back into the flow.

When it was dark, and we knew we were past the Chinese controlled area, we went on deck to look around. It was a horrendous sight. From a distance we could see the Chinese J-31 stealth fighters patrolling. The formation of their JH-7 bombers was in route to the city with bombs hanging from the wings.

We cheered when we saw a third generation MPAD Stinger B shoulder mounted surface to air missile slam into one of the boomers. But that cost the Illinois National Guards soldiers that fired it their lives. Having seen where the attack originated, one of the J-31's went back around and strafed the area killing everyone. But the pilot got careless and the bomber hit the ground and exploded. I was so close to where it impacted that the concussion almost knocked me on the ground. The remaining jets continued to bomb the city blowing everything up. Chicago was in flames.

The rest of the night as we drifted downstream, we heard one explosion after another as the Windy City was being destroyed. I could only think that maybe this was kind of what it was like the night Chicago died when O'Leary's cow started The Great Chicago Fire so long ago."

Tammy asked, "Did anyone ever see you on the boat?"

"Yes, many times, most of the time they just waved at us as we drifted past them. Sometimes they would call out to us to help them, but we couldn't. We only had limited supplies and we knew some of them would just take what we had.

I remember one time all too well. We were a bit more than a week out of the city, when we decided to clean some of the rubble off the deck. While we were cleaning it off, someone started to shoot at us. Bill and I each had Chinese AK 47's, and lots of rounds we had taken from Chinese soldiers that had been killed. We returned fire and took both out.

We finished clearing the deck and were able to fire up the engine. With the lightened load we made much better time. For the next month we slowly drifted down river to conserve fuel using the engines only when needed, until we finally reached the Illinois River.

There was not much difference between the two rivers except that the Illinois River was much faster, so we were able to travel more without running the motor. In our travels down river we saw many farms, some burning or long since burnt, dead cows and other animals bloated and floating down stream or washed ashore.

We passed through several cities that had been destroyed with their bridges gone and partially blocking the river. It was like a crazy obstacle course getting past it all.

Because the boat had an in-cabin helm, we stayed inside

to maneuver around debris. While at the same time trying to drift downstream unnoticed. We had a good map and were able to keep track of where we were by the bridges and the cities we passed. We traveled by night as much as possible, to avoid the people that shot at us. Whenever we did come upon a town, we would wait until dark and stay inside and look like we were just washed ashore.

There was this one town we entered, we approached it by night and noticed that there was almost no light coming from it. We were getting low on supplies, so we decided to take a chance and go ashore in one of the darker areas looking for anything we could use. We checked out a few abandoned farmhouses and collected some supplies but no food.

We had been ashore for a few hours when we heard a large truck coming. We hauled ass back to the boat and took off even though we had not found the most important thing we went looking for.

A few nights later we were on an isolated reach of the river when we saw a lone dock. It was getting light so we could see a nice house on a hill, not far from shore. We decided to check it out and were happy we did. The house was destroyed by others, but there was a nice smaller house still intact enough to use. It had been vandalized but still usable.

We figured that if the house was still useable after this long that we might as well stay. We had been living in that boat and needed a break from it, so we planned to stay if we could, and it was great. We had been there for almost a month when our ten-year-old Billy, was out back playing, and found something that turned out to be a hatch.

We opened it and looked inside, we couldn't believe our eyes, it was loaded with food. It turned out the family that lived there were Preppers, they had a huge stash of food, water and other survival supplies.

We loaded it into the boat in case we had to flee fast, we didn't want to leave it. We were able to stay there for another month before we heard a large truck coming. We figured they must have seen the smoke from our fire and came to investigate. Our first thought was to hide out in the bunker, we figured we would lose the boat if they found it so we just left the place as fast as we could."

Sandy asked, "Did they see you leaving?"

"I don't think so, because no one ever fired at us, but we did get out of there with a boat load of supplies. Now that we were resupplied, we continued downstream and eventually reached the Mississippi River."

Sandy commented, "That must have been a big relief from being on the smaller river."

"Not really, it only made things worse, now we were on a superhighway of boats. As we approached the confluence of the Mississippi, we noticed that the river was flooded, the closer we got the deeper the water was.

There hadn't been any heavy rains or anything like that, we were wondering why the flood. We knew we were coming up on Pere Marquette State Park in Illinois, and that the river chokes down small through that reach and we were worried it was the cause. We noticed that the floodwaters had covered a large sand bar between the two rivers and made a short cut. Let me tell you that was scary when the two swollen rivers met, the currents are nuts through it.

As we rounded a bend approaching Alton Illinois, we could see the problem. Debris had collected at lock and damn 26 and blocked it. There were trees, boats, trash and even the remains of a couple houses jammed against it. It blocked the flow of the river and caused it to back up as far back as the confluence we came in on.

From a distance, we could see lights on the Missouri sides of the bridge, but Alton was flooded, so there were no lights. We could make out people along the shore, so we didn't want to go that way. That was when Billy came up with a great idea. We fired up the engines and turned into the flooded city streets. We navigated the streets all the way around the downed bridge and were able to stay out of sight of everyone.

The flow of the water took us back out to the Mississippi. We traveled down river until we approached St. Louis. As we got closer, we spotted the remains of the Arch, it almost made me cry. It was sad to see it like that, because I remembered when I was younger, I was able to ride the odd elevator to the top and look out it on the river.

Seeing the destruction, we knew we had to be careful, but it was too late. One militia group had taken control of the Chain of Rock Locks and was patrolling the waterway. When they saw our boat, they came out after us. Over a loudspeaker we heard, 'This is the Missouri Militia, stand by to be boarded, or you will be blasted out of the water."

Amanda paused for a bit; you could see tears welling-up in her eyes. As she started to speak again her voice was cracked and broken. I stopped her and told her that she didn't need to continue. She took a deep breath, wiped the tears from her eye and replied.

"I know Peter, but I think I really need to talk about it, I haven't been able to do so since it happened, and I need to get it out."

Tammy came over to her and held her. Amanda sobbed for a bit more and said, "Thank you Tammy, but I think I'm ready to continue."

"Okay but I'm going to stay here with you if that is alright with you."

"That would be nice."

Amanda continued, "We were still under power, so Bill hit it and we tried to run away. They opened fire on us, and Bill returned fire as I tried to steer us around the obstacles. I wanted to die when I saw Bill get shot and fall overboard. I spun around and tried to reach him, but they overtook us. They came on board and took me and the kids ashore. They hauled us up to some guy who told me I was his property now."

Amanda was so upset she was shaking, Tammy tried to stop her, but Amanda insisted she needed to go on.

She continued, "When I told him I was no one's property he pointed his gun at Billy's head and pulled the trigger. I was in shock, hysterical and screaming at him. Then he pointed the gun at Samantha and asked me, "'Whose property, are you?'" I already knew this guy had no qualms about killing a kid, so I told him I was his property, then he shot Samantha just out of spite. Instead of breaking down I attacked him, I wanted to kill him with my bare hands. While I was hitting him, I was smacked on the back of the head and knocked out cold."

Gasps could be heard throughout the crowd, almost everyone there was crying as well. Amanda had tears flowing down her face again. With that Amanda just fell into Tammy's arms crying. We decided to call it a night and that we would continue the next day if she was up to it.

Amanda felt better the next day and decided to continue where she left off.

"When I woke up, I was handcuffed in the back of a van with a hood over my head and gagged. We rode in that thing for who knows how long. When we came to a stop, I heard the doors open and they dragged me out. Someone screamed at me to stand, so I did, that was when they removed the hood.

I looked around and saw several others around me also hand cuffed and gagged.

Chapter 39: The FEMA Camp

"A man stood on the back of a big truck and called out.

"'Welcome to our labor camp you are officially the property of the Missouri Militia. You WILL do as you are told, when you are told, or you will be shot, no warnings.'"

They had divided everyone, with the men separated from the women. The men were to be taken for manual labor and the women taken for other uses. The guy on the truck told some sergeant to take the men to their barracks and Frenchy to take us to the women's barracks.

This Frenchy guy led us along a long path to what looked like nearly brand-new buildings. I wondered what the hell they were. As we filed in the barracks, they locked the door behind us, and Frenchy stood in front of us.

What we later learned was that it was a FEMA camp before the quake. After the quake hit and things started to get out of hand, FEMA began rounding up people and moving them into the camp. They claimed it was for everyone's own good and that it was to keep everyone safe. But after the government folded, the militia took the camp by force from FEMA and made it theirs.

Soon after we arrived, Frenchy called out,

"'Alright ladies, you are now in Camp Nelson; this will be your new home from now on. Any attempts to escape will be punished by death on the spot. As you can see my men are moving down your ranks removing the cuffs. If you want to live, I suggest you don't try anything stupid.'"

I couldn't believe how much those cuffs hurt. While I was rubbing my wrists, a guard removed the cuffs from this tough looking chick. She immediately turned, kicked him in the nuts, then bolted. She didn't get far before a half dozen guys opened fire on her and killed her right there. The rest of us dropped to the floor hoping we wouldn't get hit in the crossfire.

The commotion didn't faze Frenchy, he continued telling us what was expected.

"'We are outside of Livingston, Louisiana but this is only temporary for most of you. How long you stay here will be dependent on you. When we have enough suitable women you will be brought to the main hall where you will be displayed for auction.'"

You could hear the gasps from the women, including yours truly, many of them started to cry uncontrollably.

That asshole went on to tell us, the better we looked for the buyers, the sooner we would get out of there, maybe even to a nicer location. He said the people that could afford to buy us, had lots of gold or other assets and wanted their property looking nice. If we wanted to get out of there fast, we would take advantage of the dressing room in the barracks. With that he turned, and left the room leaving several men behind with AK 47's at the doors.

Many of the women started talking. A younger blond turned to me and said, 'I'm not going to parade around in front of some fat rich guys, trying to find their next lay.'

A red head screamed, 'NO WAY, I'm not doing it, I'd rather die.'

One of the guards chambered a round in his gun and replied, "'That can be arranged.'"

Several of the women that had been captive in the barracks for some time, went to the dressing room to shower and get dolled up. I asked them if they were really going to just give in and give the creeps what they want. A girl with dark brown hair and the prettiest eyes you ever seen explained the facts of life to me.

"It's far better than what happens if you're not ready for display when they come for us."

I asked her. What do they do if you are not ready? She replied,

"It depends; if you're only slightly attractive, they may just shoot you. If they think you aren't worth the trouble or won't sell for much, then they just get rid of you."

I couldn't believe what was happening. Who were these people, and what made them think they could do it? Then this girl grabbed my arm and dragged me towards the dressing room. Her name was Angie, she said she was from Gulf Port Mississippi.

As we made our way into the dressing room, we saw naked women everywhere. Some were crying as they were forced to get dressed, while others that had been there longer were laughing as they got dressed and put on their makeup.

One girl turned to the guard standing at the door and asked if he was going to leave and let us get dressed? The man laughed and said no and that we needed to strip and get ready for the presentation.

The girl shrieked at him, so the guard slapped her in the face. One of the other guards came over and stopped him from hitting her again. He told the first guard to be careful with the merchandise and called him a moron. He said we don't make as much if they are damaged and that we didn't grow on trees.

Later that night they paraded us down a runway in a smoke-filled room, just like the ones they use for models. The lights were in our eyes, so we couldn't make out much, but

I did get a few glimpses of men at tables with booze and smokes. One by one, we had to walk the runway while we heard them whooping and whistling.

These auctions were only part of our hell. The entire winter it was cold, and we had little heat or food. We lost weight, but that seemed just fine to the men because the skinnier women sold faster and for more money.

I can't count how many of those stupid freak shows they made us put on, or how many times I was happy no one picked me. I'd been beat countless times because I didn't do the moves they wanted, or even try to look good for any of those pigs. Then one day I heard a bunch of catcalls when I went down the runway.

I could hear the auctioneer calling out something, I couldn't make it out, but I could hear the excitement in his voice. This time as I came to the beginning of the runway, one of the guards pointed for me to return and do it again. I'd seen other, much prettier women, asked to do the same thing then never seen them again. This was the first time it had happened to me. I knew this meant my time there may be at an end and I really feared what was in store for me.

That night I wasn't returned to the barracks like every other time. This time I was taken to a small room, with a large full-length window on the wall. They told me to walk around and show off, I walked but not any different than I ever do. Then a voice came over a speaker and told me to undress. I screamed and told them there was no way I was going to do that. The guard came over and poked me with his gun, but I still refused.

Just as the guard was grabbing my dress, I heard a loud tapping on the window and the guard stopped. Shortly after that I was led out to a van with a couple other women. One of those women was a blond haired, blue-eyed beauty. Her name was Jonie, and she looked like she had spent most of her adult life as a trophy wife for some guy.

They didn't blind fold or tie us up, and there was food waiting for us in the van. While we drove, I had a chance to talk with Jonie. I asked her how long she had been there, and she said just a couple of nights. While we were riding, I asked her to tell me about her experiences.

Jonie seemed happy to fill me in on the events.

"Oh Mt God, "'she said in that dragged out irritating manner, "'My husband and I were living in a house deep in the woods. I always told him he was crazy stocking up that food, weapons and ammunition, but after the quake I found out why. The first two weeks we had to fend off people trying to get to us.'"

As her tears began to fall Jonie continued.

"It was horrible. I had to shoot people and kill them, I never thought I could kill them, I never thought I could kill anyone anyone. But when it comes down to it being either them or you it's not as difficult as you think. After a month or so, fewer people came down our road until we didn't see any-one anymore.

We spent the winter there and didn't see a soul: we thought we'd made it through the worst of it. We had plenty of food and water and George always had several cords of wood on hand, so we stayed warm. One day about two weeks ago a couple of armored personnel carriers drove down the road to our house. One guy stood up in the turret with an RPG and another stood up in the other one with one as well.

Then a man stepped out of the lead APC and walked up to the house. He called out that if anyone fires on him or his men, both RPG's would be fired. George looked at me and told me we had no choice but to surrender, which we did. I don't know what they did to George because they separated us right away. The next thing I knew I was in this hell hole being sold like cattle.'

Did you say two weeks ago?!

'Yes why?'

I told her I had spent months there before I was sold and was amazed that she had only been there for a couple weeks. She said I misunderstood her, she said it was two weeks ago that they found her. She said she was sold the first time down the runway."

Laughing, Amanda continued, "I wonder if it had anything to do with the fact that I did everything I could do not to be sold, but not so little to beat me into submission."

Amanda continued describing Jonie's story.

"Anyway, even though I loved my husband he was many years older than me and very rich. I knew what I was doing going into my relationship with him. In some ways this is not much different. I made myself look hot and dressed in as little as I could and got out of that place right away.'"

I told her, oh girl you sold yourself to the highest bidder. She said sometimes you do what you have to do. Jonie also thought it might be easier to get away outside of that camp. They say you can't judge a book by its cover. That truly was the case with Jonie. If you look at her you think dumb blond, but she was far wiser than I this case.

I also asked Jonie if she heard anything about what is happening in other parts of the country or the world. She said, yes, that everything changed after the destruction of Chicago. Up to that point China had been leaving the rest of the country alone, but that eventually changed.

China started bombing militia strong holds, churches,

schools and hospitals. They spread out and tried to take over the smaller cities. That ended up being a big mistake for China, and a fatal one at that.

She heard that those attacks galvanized that part of the country for the first time since the quake. With a common enemy to remove, the militia turned their attention to the Chinese. Cries went out to the rest of the world to help get the Chinese out of our country.

It seems none of our European 'friends' could help us even if they wanted to like us they too were now living in the dark ages. They had no Army or Navy and no means to get help to us from on the other side of the pond. Jonie said it was our neighbors to the north that came to help."

I called out, "WHAT, CANADA?"

Amanda replied. "Ya that was what she said, Canada, and be respectful there, many of them gave their lives trying to free us from the Chinese."

I replied, "Sorry, I love Canadians, some of our best friends are from Vancouver, BC. I was just surprised because they're not really an aggressive people."

Chapter 40: Hail Canada

Amanda continued with Jonie's story.

"After the Chinese bombed Chicago, the rest of the world, that still had any means of communicating, condemned their actions. But that was not worth much because none of the old methods of punishing an invading country were worth anything.

Actions like embargoes or economic sanctions wouldn't work since there was no way to enforce them. But since Canada was in a better position to help, they stepped in. Still many questioned their motives believing Canada only offered to help because they knew the Chinese were on their own doorstep and they didn't like that at all.

While Canada was considering how it could help, Preppers and various militias were looking at options as well. But the problem was communications. Many Preppers had VHF radios, but they were not safe to use. They learned early on that the militias had radio tracking equipment which enabled the militia to find them.

As time went on, several of the militias began broadcasting in their own areas. Some would spew their own political bull shit while others worked on coordinating borders for mutual protection and trade.

With the increased connectivity, some sense of unity started to form. When the word about China made its way around the region. More militias joined the network of stations and use of VHF radios stepped up as well. It was close to a year before any real communications network was restored. When it was, discussions about China happened in earnest.

Meetings where set up to discuss attacks, and to contact the outside world. While the responses were disappointing, it didn't come as a surprise to anyone that few countries were able or willing to help. But when asked, Canada said yes.

In the spring, after the bombing, representatives from several unified groups attended a meeting in Oak Park, Illinois, as an act of defiance to the Chinese. Oak Park, Illinois is a suburb of Chicago. Not all militia groups wanted the unified groups to represent them, some didn't even want them to exist. Even so the meeting went ahead, and Canada sent their representatives.

The groups took no chances, many of the leaders who had made their way there had come under attack. There was heavy armament around the city, but it was worth it, because the Chinese needed to be destroyed. With a lot of effort on everyone's part, they were able to work out a coordinated plan of attack on the new Chinese foothold in Milwaukee, Wisconsin.

Jonie said she knew a guy that was in Oak Park and that he told her about what had happened in the meeting.

Jonie continued telling her story from her friends' description.

"'I want to thank everyone for coming. I know many of you have taken a large risk by being here. We understand how important it is to hash out a plan of attack as quickly as possible. I'm Ambassador Glenn Boarder from Alberta, Canada and I represent Canada. I've brought along General Louie Van Pander; he'll oversee the forces.

Before we go any further, I want each of you to acknowledge that General Van Pander is in command, and agree to support him and follow his orders, even if you don't fully understand his decisions. Let's begin by going around the table and introducing ourselves. When it's your turn, please state the region you represent and confirm that you understand and accept our requirements.

The general began, 'I'll start this out, and we'll go to my left from here. My name is General Louie Van Pander, but you can just call me General or General Pander. I've been appointed as the General in Charge of eradicating the Chinese from North America. I was born in Vancouver, BC and have been in the Army for 35 years.

Like many of you here, I lost family and friends in the quake, and can relate to your pain. I want to hear from each of you about what you think is the best way to approach this. After the meeting, we'll adjourn and I'll have each of you join me in my makeshift office, one at a time. After that, we'll meet again and go over what I think we'll be able to do given your assets and those of Canada. Okay who is next?'"

A big dude wearing fatigues in front, stood up, "'I am Captain Bill Rogers and I am the leader of the Northern Indiana Militia. We are over five hundred strong and made up of many of the citizens of what's left the northern half of Indiana. I was born a Hoosier and by God I will die one as well, not Chinese. I understand the need for one leader for this type of operation and we'll support you all the way.'"

The Captain turned to the rest of the people gathered there and pleaded with them to work together to get the Chinese bastards out of our country.

"'Thank you, Captain Rogers, I look forward to hearing your take on how to do this. Ok next.'"

"'My name is Captain Raymond Miller. I'm the leader of one of the Wisconsin militias. Now that those damn Chinese have taken over my home state, I'm already chomping at the bit to get them out of there, so Captain Rogers I can tell you we are with you. I don't have the kind of numbers Captain Rogers has but we're highly experienced guerilla fighters.

We took out several columns of Chinese, when they made their way north out of Chicago and we have confiscated every piece of Chinese military hardware we could get. We're more than ready to follow your orders, he said with a salute.'"

General Pander saluted back and thanked him.

"'My name is Colonel Jack Magee. I'm in charge of the militia out of the Great State of Missouri. I have twenty individual groups now under my command and will fight with our neighbors to the north to the death. I know you want them out of here as badly as we do, hell yeah, we understand your terms and agree to them.'"

"'Thank you, Colonel, I look forward to hearing your point of view.'"

"'My name is Gerald Transom; I don't hold a military title, but I do command over two hundred fighters out of Ohio. My parents lived in Chicago and I'm ready to kill those bastards that killed them so, yes sir we are with you.'"

"'Thank you, Gerald, and even though you don't hold a military title I'll still hold your input with just as much meaning as any of the military trained men we have here.'"

"'My name is Stanton T. Filber III.'" He said in a greater than thou manner, "'And like Gerald, I don't hold a military title, but I do command my own army. I'll share our numbers with you in private but not in this group. I do understand your orders and agree to them, but after we get rid of the Chinese, we won't be working with any of these groups again.'"

"'Thank you, Stanton, for your frankness and I hope we'll be able to work as a team despite your harsh feelings about some of your co-leaders.'"

"'Despite my feelings, we'll work with them for our common goal no matter what. The enemy of your enemy is your friend, at least until you kill them all.'"

"'Okay, thanks again Stanton, I'm sure you will.'"

"'I'm Major Frank Bear and I've been tasked to lead the Northern Illinois militia. We're based out of what is left of Freeport, Illinois which is a bit west of here. Before the quake I'd been the leader of the Northern Illinois National Guard, and the leader of the Northern Illinois Freedom Fighters. We have complete control of the guard unit and its weapons. We completely understand the need for uniformity and will throw all our assets at those bastards.'"

"'Thank you, Major Bear, I look forward to working with you. Okay then now that we have covered the pleasantries, we have much to do. I believe lunch is ready for us and I don't know about any of you but I'm hungry. Let's head into the restaurant and get something to eat.'"

The group of men agreed and got up and headed to eat. As they left, they talked with each other and started down the long road of freeing us from outside control. Lunch was a good opportunity for all to get to know each other and trade stories about their lives since the quake. Hopefully the six men would form the bases of a free country once and for all.

After lunch, they each met with the general. They told him their ideas on how to free Milwaukee and get the Chinese out of the country once and for all. It was well into the night before the men were able to make their way through the meetings.

As each finished with General Pander, he told them that he would be going over his plans based on what they gave him, in the morning. The next morning, they met at the table and he explained his plans. The general gave each of them a task based on their strengths and assets, then provided information on how he believed they should free Milwaukee.

It took a week to get the word out to the smaller groups and to amass their forces into position. Meanwhile Glenn, the Canadian Ambassador, went to Milwaukee to try to end the occupation peacefully. He found it was not going to be good. General Pander was under orders to wait on his offensive until Ambassador Boarder had a chance to resolve the matter without a fight.

The Chinese had different plans for the Ambassador, the second he entered their compound he was taken into custody. He was brought before a brigade of Chinese soldiers and made to kneel on the ground. Their leader shot him in the back of the head. They threw his dead body on the street and closed their gate. With that, General Pander ordered the offensive to begin.

Two days before the impending attack, multiple groups of people snuck into Milwaukee to warn the residents. Fortunately, many were able to get out safely, the Chinese did their best to try and stop them, but even more stayed to join the fight. The Chinese figured we wouldn't attack if Americans were still there, but they bet wrong.

It turned out it was a good thing that the gun control nut cases didn't get their way, if they had, the citizens wouldn't have stood a chance of fighting them. I'll never understand why the politicians in this country think that the guns are the problem.

Thousands of militia forces surrounded Milwaukee and closed in on the Chinese. The day of the attack the Chinese were in for a big surprise. General Pander had coordinated with The Great Republic of Texas to lead the attack. Under the cover of darkness, they brought in a Carrier Battle Group and created not only a naval blockade, but a no-fly zone for the Chinese.

Several destroyers fired precision guided low yield Tomahawk BGM-109A Tomahawk Land Attack Missiles at painted targets on the ground. The missiles were armed with low yield warheads and were used to take out their command and control as well as their communications, with minimal damage to the city. They also hit the Chinese air bases but with high yield warheads.

The aircraft carrier, T.R.S. Gerald R. Ford, enforced a no-fly zone over Milwaukee, and provided support for the forces on the ground. The Chinese thought they had a surprise for us, because they fired their carrier killer missiles thinking they would take out our carrier, but they were the ones that were in for the surprise. The Ford was armed with multiple 100w precision lasers that made short work of their missiles.

Texas, however; wasn't done with the Chinese. The night before the attack on Milwaukee, the Texans positioned and nuclear powered, ballistic submarine just offshore from Beijing. They launched an SLBM on the Chinese capital and destroyed the city before their military could even react. With Beijing gone, Texas knew that was the end of their occupation in North America. Now it was just a matter of removing them from our soil.

That day the Chinese in Milwaukee agreed to an unconditional surrender. Very little damage happened to Milwaukee and our land was free of them. The Chinese could pull ALL their forces out of the country, but they weren't allowed to take any of their weaponry with them.

It was a great day. For the first time in almost a year, there were no Chinese forces in our land. To everyone's surprise, the Canadians kept their word and pulled their forces out of the country as well. Unlike the U.S., and our, 'Helping hands', they didn't stay where they weren't welcome. As soon as the job was done, they exited the country and left it up to us to deal with the mess. Besides it wasn't like they had trillions of dollars, paid on the back of the taxpayers, to throw away on a people that didn't want their help."

Amanda continued telling her story.

"Shortly after Jonie finished telling me about what'd happened up north, we came to a stop. Two men came to the back and pulled her out of the van, they slammed the door shut and took off, that was the last time I saw her. After another few hours passed, we came to a stop again. This time they pulled me out of the van and drug me to a nearby a SUV.

Behind the SUV was a large semi-truck, as I approached the SUV a man motioned to one of the men that brought me there to get the truck. The man jumped into the already running truck and pulled away as they led me into a limo waiting for me.

As I got in the car, I could see for the first time the scum that had bought me. From what I could tell, I was sold for the truck and its contents. It made me feel like a piece of meat sold at a bazaar.

After a couple days of driving we ended up at that warehouse and I was kept there as his property. He took every opportunity to remind me of that and I was forced to do as I was told, or I was beaten and starved. I hadn't been there long when my hero Doug here, saved me."

We thanked Amanda for sharing so much with us. The tragedy that she and others experienced made us even more grateful for what we had. We were happy as life in Little Haven continued with no problems. Everyone was content, healthy, and enjoying our new lives. Some; however, had embraced their freedoms more than others.

Chapter 41: A Necessary Evil?

One day late in our second summer in Little Haven, we were relaxing in the pond cooling off after a long hot day. We had been drinking the hooch Brandon's men made, so we were a bit relaxed when we heard Roy call out.

"Hey there, we knew you guys would be here."

I replied, "You're right. What are you guys up to?"

"Judy, Lacy and I were looking forward to a dip in the pond."

Ben patted his hands on the water and called out, "Then jump in, the water's great."

The three of them stripped off their clothes and joined us in the water. They splashed around for a bit, then came over to the rest of us and sat down.

As Roy was settling in, he said, "You guys sure are laid back for a bunch of old folks."

Fred mocked him with a breaking old man's voice, "Thaank yoou ssoonnyy," and laughed; we all did, including Roy.

I added, "Well Roy I think if you hung around us, you'd see how laid back we are. You might even be in for the surprise of your life. None of us in this group go for any of that oppressive crap, that has been crammed down our throats by the cults of the world. We had to live with it all our lives and now they no longer control anything, at least not here.

Just look at Ann and I, we live with Sandy and Tammy. In the old world we'd be shunned even though the four of us don't have sex. We've noticed that the three of you live together. We don't know if there is anything else, and it is really none of our business."

"Funny you said that, that's the reason why we're here. We knew you guys were here, and that the seven of you are the ones that influence the council. We've been living together for some time, and though Lacy and I were legally married before the quake, we both love Judy the same as we do each other."

Fred handed a Mason jar with hooch in it to Roy and said, "Here have some rot gut."

Roy reached over, took the jar and threw back a nice swig of it. Then as he reached to hand it back, Fred, asked, "What about the girls, don't they want some too?"

The three looked at each other with a smile and Roy replied, "They can't have any."

We raised our eyebrows.

Ann jumped in, "Oh My God, you guys are both pregnant."

Lacy smiled and replied yes, we are. We both love Roy with all our hearts, and we know he loves us too," Roy nodded in agreement.

"And I love Judy as well. The three of us are as happy as you guys clearly are and want to be married."

Tammy had to jump on that one, "Now that's what I'm talking about, how dare anyone tell us we can't be married? Sandy and I have loved each other for over ten years, it was great when the Supreme Court ruled it was legal to get married. As soon as we got the word out to our friends, we did."

"Easy girls easy, you know how I feel. As the Chairman of our little village I don't see any reason why you can't. As a matter of fact, after the court's ruling some people interpreted it to mean that you could, have more than one spouse. I think that as the leader it would fall on me to be the one to actually marry you guys."

With tears of joy, Judy came running over to me and said, "Thank you Peter thank you; I love you."

Then she grabbed my face with both hands and gave me a huge kiss square on the lips. I looked over at Ann and she just smiled at me.

"Hold on everyone, this isn't a done deal. I think it's something that needs to be brought to the council, even if not for a vote, but at least to get a feel for their take on it."

This time Ben jumped in, "Well I can't speak for the rest of the council, but this member is for it. I'd be okay with more than one wife."

He looked over at Beth, who was looking at him with her eyebrows raised, slightly pursed lips and this almost confused REALLY?! Look on her face.

It made me chime in, "With them both being pregnant that brings up an important issue."

Now I had Ann's attention, "And what issue would that be you horn dog." She asked in an inquisitive manner,

I looked at her with that sly smile that I know makes her laugh. And replied. "There's a little thing about breeding in a small community. With a small genetic pool, we're setting ourselves up for what I call the hillbilly syndrome."

Ann looked at me, now shaking her head with an I can't believe you just said that look, then in a long drawn out manner.

"WWHHAATT are you talking about?"

Everyone laughed. Laughing too I replied, "Think about

it, with the limited number of men and women we have, and everyone living in a monogamous relationship, there'd be in-breeding in just a generation or two, including the problems that come with it."

Fred had to jump on that one, and spoke up, "I have to say he is right guys; I don't know about you, but I don't want any buck tooth, deformed kids running around here calling their sister mommy."

Ann replied to that, "Really Fred, are YOU going to stereotype people like that?"

"I don't know if I'd call it stereotyping. I just know I lived with a hillbilly for some time and met her family, conse-quently I know what I've seen."

I had to interrupt, and spoke up, "All right guys, that's enough. I'll take this to the council and see how it flies."

Roy continued, "It's not like we're the only ones living like this. Crystal is living with Jason and Braxton, and there's no question what type of relationship they have, and there are several more as well."

Judy jumped in, "Look it's not like we are hurting any-one. We just want to get married."

Ben turned to Roy and the girls and said, "Well guys trust me, if I have anything to do with it you will get your mar-riage."

Ann decided to really join in on this one. I think she thought it would make me change my mind about it and asked me.

"Let me get this straight, you are ok with me having sex with another man?"

I stood there for a long moment then replied, "CLICK...."

Ann smiled and replied, "Not this time sweetie, it's safe, no land mine here."

I paused again, then with that cheesy smile I'm known for, I replied, "If you were trying to have another baby then yes."

"Talk about double standards, so because I can no longer have babies then I'd be stuck with just you, and because you can, it's okay for you?"

"If it means I'd be doing my civic duty, sure." I smiled back at her.

Ann replied, "You're so full of shit, just admit it you're just a horn dog."

All I could do was smile and shrug my shoulders. Now Tam had something to say about this.

"Let me get this straight. You believe that the women, should sleep with the fertile men, to stir up the genetic mix."

"Not necessarily all but..."

Surprisingly Sandy stopped me from digging myself deeper and said,

"I have this one sweetie. The answer is sort of, any child-bearing woman should have only one child by any one father, be it their husband or someone else. After that when or if they are ready to conceive again it should be with a different guy."

"But what's to stop the husband from being the one that gets her pregnant again?"

"That's easy, when they are trying to have another baby, they don't have sex with their partner. But if they do, it's not like it's a crime."

"That's just crazy Sandy, and you guys would be alright

with that?"

Ben replied, "Sure why not, while I can't have sex with Beth, I'd be able to have sex with someone else, maybe several someone else's. All's fair in love and breeding."

I decided to end it, "There'd have to be a lot of things worked out if we decided to go down that road. However, for now let's just keep it simple and get this marriage thing dealt with."

Later that week, I broached the topic with the council. I was surprised to find almost no disagreement from them, only one member objected. It was decided that with something this important, if there wasn't a unanimous vote by the council, then it'd have to go before the village. We called for a meeting during the next potluck, to go over the topic. After everyone had eaten, we gathered around the amphitheater to address the issue.

"Hi everyone, welcome and thank you for coming. I know most of you know why we're here. We have an important topic to address tonight. It affects several residents of our happy village. I feel we need to support them in their wishes, the same as we have everyone else.

Roy is already married to Lacy and both want to marry Judy. We knew that Wendell, Megan and Lucy were an item, and no one seemed to care. There are several other larger couples here tonight as well.

Before the quake, marriage was a religious sacrament, that for whatever reason, was required to get government benefits for your partner, and had other things tied to it. We don't have those constraints anymore, therefore it's not an issue about benefits, nor it a religious sacrament for many, at least not for us here.

But these guys love each other. They want to shout it

to the world so why not let them. Tonight, we're going to have our first real vote. One on something that'll affect Little Haven for years to come. We're going to hold our first official vote.

A long time ago, the Greeks brought democracy to the world. They were the first to give the people a voice, on what they would do. In their case, the question was fight or capitulate to the Persians. To do it, they invented voting, they did so by each person dropping stones in a basket, white for yes and black for no.

Our vote tonight, needs to be done in an anonymous manner. Everyone will be able to vote what THEY feel. Without feeling as though they must fit in, or be influenced by others. In that light I've placed one hundred white stones and one hundred black stones in the baskets below me.

I want each of you to take one of each stone in one hand. Then proceeded to the last basket and drop in the stone for your vote, then throw your other stone in the creek below. This way no one will know who voted what. Are there any questions about how this will go?"

After a pause no one spoke up with any questions.

"I see there's no questions. I'll start this out, I'll take my two stones and vote."

I took my stones, voted, and threw my other stone in the creek. One by one, each member of the village filed through and voted. When the last person finished, I had Alex count the stones on the table in front of everyone, because he was an outsider. When he was finished, he handed me the count and I stepped out to tell everyone else.

"Can I have everyone's attention please; I have the results."

Sandy yelled out, "TELL US, TELL US."

"Give me a chance Sandy, okay the vote is overwhelming...."

"Get on with it, tell us what it is."

"The vote was fifty-seven to four...."

Bill yelled out this time, "Peter if you don't stop messing with us and tell us the result, I'm going to come up there and sock you in the nose."

Everyone laughed, and yelled, get on with it. I laughed too and called out, "The vote is yes, if you feel the need to marry more than one person, you're free to marry anyone you want."

Everyone was ecstatic, they were crying, and hugging and then we heard Phil Hudson yelled out.

"NO! We do not feel that marriage should be between anyone but one man and one woman, anything else is a sin. God forbids such unholy acts and will strike us down if we allow this type of sin to happen."

It was clear, most of the people didn't like what he was saying. They started shouting out all sorts of hypocrisies, like Noah had multiple wives. The more they shouted, the more Phil got upset. They started screaming, you know the rules, no one tells anyone how to live. Now his followers were getting scared. I fired my pistol in the air, to get their attention and called out.

"That's enough. Everyone has the right to his or her own opinion and beliefs. That includes Phil and his followers. Most of our village is in favor, so it is so. We're free to marry who ever we want, within our own belief systems. NO ONE and I mean NO ONE has the right to tell anyone else what we can do or believe."

With that, a large cheer went out, you could see tears running down the faces of Sandy, Tam, Bill and Ted. As I looked out over the crowd, I could see lots of hugging and crying going on. Maybe the open relationships were more prolific than I knew? Phil yelled out again.

"God won't allow it to happen, you will all be damned and go to hell."

Anderson yelled out, "We've already been there, now we're here. It's that kind of attitude that we're happy to get away from. What makes you think you have the right to tell us how we, HAVE to live?"

Now I was concerned, "Alright I want the council members to meet with me. Phil, could you and your followers, join us in the cave please. We need to resolve this and not let it become a mob thing."

Phil replied, "Alright Peter, we will be right there." As they headed in, I turned to the group and called out.

"Everyone else, you're welcome to continue to celebrate as long as you wish. The council and I'll adjourn to the cave."

I turned to Alex, I'd asked him and his family, to fly in to count the votes and asked him to join us in the cave. Phil and his followers, followed us into the cave to discuss the predicament we're in.

I started out, "Phil, do you really believe you'll be able to convince anyone out there to change their mind."

"I am sorry to say Peter, I don't. However, we can't just stand by and live in this kind of environment. You never said anything about living like this, before we left the lake camp. I must stand up for my beliefs."

Ben spoke up, and said, "Why do you think it's your job to tell the rest of us we can't, just because we don't believe the same thing as you do?"

I interjected, "Okay guys we need to resolve this now. Phil you understood the rules before we came here. I know you did because I was the one that went over them with you before we ever left the old camp."

I could see Phil was truly torn about the whole thing. A now calmer Phil replied, "I did Peter. I did believe that we all had those rights, but when I met Andria, she showed how to see things in a different way."

"Well then Phil, that leaves us with a problem. What are we going to do about it?"

Alex spoke up, "I know I'm not a member of this village. I have no place to say anything, but I have a possible solution to your dilemma. I can take Phil and his followers away from here, somewhere they'll be happy."

Becky Lou, one of the council members, spoke up, "I think that's a great idea, but you won't just leave them with nothing will you? We love you guys; we wouldn't want to see harm come to you."

Alex replied, "No Becky Lou, you can provide em with the supplies ya can afford or fit in the chopper. I'll take em someplace safe, well as safe as can be in this dangerous world."

"Phil, what do you think of that idea, are you okay with it?"

Phil stood there for the longest time thinking. I reminded him that if he stayed with us, they'd have to live with the new policy. He finally asked, "Where would we go?

Fred chimed in, "I'm sure Alex can find someplace safe for you. We'll give you everything we can, seeds, food, and other supplies."

"Phil stood there going over what had unfolded, then he replied, "I know it is not our place to tell any of you that you can't live the way you wish. I also know we can't live in that kind of environment without feeling unhappy about it. I think the only option is for us to take you up on your generous offer Alex, we will go."

Up to this point, everyone was just listening closely to everything being said. Scotty, one of the followers decided he needed to speak up, "Whoa, wait a minute here, I never signed up for this. I have no problem letting others live their lives, I dropped in a white stone, look I still have my black one."

He held out his hand with the black stone in it.

"I only joined up with Phil and Andria, because they had a bible. I love it here and have no desire to leave."

Three more of his followers chimed in, they were okay with the way things are and didn't want to leave.

Andria exclaimed, "WHAT!? What are you saying?"

Amber, another of their followers replied, "They're right Andria, no one gave us the right to tell the village how to live their lives? Besides I also voted yes. I'm staying here if everyone will have me."

It seemed it was worked out. Phil and Andria would be heading out, while the rest wanted to stay and live with the vote. I turned to them and said,

"You, and any of the rest of your followers, are welcome to stay. As long as you have no problem with the way things are; and can let everyone live their lives as they wish."

Andria turned to them and said, "You can't just abandon us like this."

Scotty replied, "I never believed we had the right to inflict our beliefs on others."

"Alright, let's make sure everyone understands. Phil, you and Andria, are okay with taking Alex up on his offer. While the rest of you, want to stay, and can live with things like we agreed to?"

Phil replied, "Yes Andria and I will go, but we ask you guys to come with us."

Nicky spoke up and replied, "I'm sorry Phil, but I love it and have friends here. I wish you the best."

I took Phil and Andria aside, the three of us talked by the fireplace. As we did, Andria admitted it was for the best for them to leave. It was a good thing we had a means to take them somewhere safe. I don't know what we would've done.

"Guys, why don't you head home, now. Get everything you can, packed. In the morning we'll help you get whatever we can, to make your life as comfortable as possible. If we can't get everything you'll need before it's time to leave, we'll wait a day; this insures you are ready. I'd like for us to part on good terms."

Phil replied, "Thank you Peter, Andria and I never wanted to create any bad feelings. We just can't live with what you have decided to do. I hope we can still be good friends after this. Even if we never see each other again."

"You'll be allowed to get whatever you can fit in the chopper, in the morning, but for now, you'll be held here for the night, I'm sorry."

With that, they headed home. The rest of us, returned

to the party to enjoy ourselves and inform everyone else what was happening. We stayed until late in the evening, before we called it a night.

Before he left the party, Alex found Doug, he had a request for him.

Alex called out, "Hey Doug, do ya have a minute?"

"Sure, what's up Alex?"

"I need to ask ya a favor. I'll be flying Phil and Andria out of the valley in the morning. I need someone I can trust to have ma back from threats from the ground."

Doug replied, "Sure Alex, I can handle that for you."

"I'll take off straight up, then south, watching for signs of life ahead of us. We're heading for the Carson National Forest in New Mexico. It'll take several hours to get there. I need you to know we may be heading into some dangerous territory. We could easily be shot out of the sky. Are you up to it?"

Doug tilted his head slightly and replied, "I'd think you know by now, I'm all for the danger."

Alex laughed, "I know, that's why you're my first pick. I'll need ya ta be watching and be ready for a fight."

"Alright, I'll be there in the morning."

That night, Phil and Andria, went home and packed what few things they had. Alex landed his helicopter in their field, they loaded everything they could carry. Their followers were there to show them off. They wanted to wish them well, along with a few others. There were tears by many as they loaded into the helicopter.

"Are you ready to go Alex?"

"I am, Peter, we have their stuff loaded and some extra

fuel in the sling, I wanted to have enough to get back."

"Are you going far enough to need that much fuel?"

"I don't think so, but I'd hate to run out. We'll refuel when we land with them."

Doug asked, "How long do you think we'll be?"

"It shouldn't take us more than a few hours, another hour ta refuel, and a few more to get back. Let's say six hours ta be safe."

I added, "We'll keep the radio on, and listen for you, if you need help. Not sure what we could do but..."

"Thanks Peter, I'll remember that. Hey, it's possible that we may be forced to land. If that happens, I'll key up ma radio three times in a row, then I'll wait for you to key yours back once. When I hear ya reply, I'll wait one minute for each day we'll be delayed, then key it once, then twice more to close. If we're delayed more, I'll repeat the same signal."

"That sounds like a great plan, good luck my friend, happy flying."

The flight was uneventful all the way to New Mexico. As they flew over a wooded forest, Phil saw an old house below, that looked empty. They landed without being shot at, then unloaded. The place was clearly abandoned and showed no sign of recent use. They refueled with Phil's help, said their goodbyes, and off they went.

The flight back was a different story. Shortly after entering the Rocky Mountain Republic, they heard a transmission on the scanner.

"Mayday, mayday, to the pilot of the helicopter who just flew overhead, we need help do you read us?"

They looked at each other with distrust with what they heard. Then again, they heard a voice that was clearly a woman and she sounded distraught.

"Mayday, mayday we're in trouble, please help! PLEASE."

Alex looked at Doug and asked, "What da ya think?"

"No one could find us that fast, so I don't think it can hurt to answer."

"Alrighty."

Alex turned his radio to the frequency on the scanner, and replied, "This is Alpha Romeo Victor four, I read your transmission what is your emergency?"

A few seconds later, they heard a frantic female voice, "We're in the farmhouse you flew over, we've been out of food for a long time, we're starving. Can you help us?"

Alex replied, "Are y'all under attack?"

"No, no one knows we're here."

Alex and Doug discussed it for a few minutes, then decided to check it out. They flew high, then located the farm by the girl telling them when they were getting closer. Doug was able to see the farm in his sniper scope, long before Alex.

"I see them Alex, there's two girls standing in the yard of a farmhouse, waving their arms."

"Keep your rifle on em while we hover for a bit, look for signs of others in the woods or in windows."

After looking and not seeing anyone else, Alex told the girls to stay in sight. He slowly brought the helicopter in for a landing, while Doug kept the rifle trained on them. With the rotors still turning, Doug jumped out and searched the women for weapons and found none. He quickly went through the house and barn, found no one, then motioned to Alex it was all clear. With that, Alex shut down the helicopter and joined Doug and the ladies.

Chapter 42:
The Damsels' in Distress

The ladies were clearly in bad shape and in need of help. Doug gave them each a couple of MREs, which they attacked, while Alex and Doug asked them about their story.

"Howdy ladies, my name's Alex, and this here is ma friend Doug, what's y'all's names?"

An emaciated blond replied, "I'm Lydia, and this is my best friend, Nina. We found this house just before winter and stayed. There was enough food here for the winter, but that ran out some time ago."

Doug asked, "Why didn't you move on, when it ran out?"

Nina, also clearly malnourished, replied, "Because when we found this place, it was still intact. For whatever reason no one had ransacked it, we figured it was safer than anywhere else we had found."

Alex asked, "How did y'all call us?"

Nina replied, "When we searched the house, we found a radio that worked, we left it off to save the batteries. When we heard you coming, I got to it about the time you flew by, overhead. We didn't think you heard us when you didn't respond."

Doug replied, "We didn't think we were going to, it's not safe to take chances like this."

"Then why did you?" Lydia asked.

"I don't know, I just felt like we should. In this crazy world we need to help when we can, and I could hear the desperation in your voice."

Lydia walked over to Doug, then hugged him tightly around the neck, she thanked him as she started to cry.

"Okay ladies, you've been here for a few months and no sign of any soldiers or marauders?"

Nina replied, "No none, it'll be late soon, you should get some sleep here tonight and fly us out of here in the morning."

Alex spoke up, "Whoa, I never said anythin about flying y'all out of here."

Lydia came back, "Then why are you even here?"

Alex answered, "We can leave ya some food."

Doug shifted his head and eyes and motioned to Alex to go talk privately.

Alex turned to the ladies and said, "We'll be right back ladies, it seems we need to talk."

"We can't just leave these ladies here they'll starve."

Alex took a deep breath, sighed and replied, "I know we have ta help em."

They went back to explain the village, and the conditions of going there. Both said it sounded like their kind of place and would love to do their part. Alex and Doug headed in to search the house, looking for anything that could be used in the village.

As they approached, Doug said to Alex, "Would you look at this place? It's huge, I bet it's a half million at least."

"I think it's more like a clean mill, let's go check it out, my bet it's full of stuff we can use."

Excitedly Doug threw his fists in the air away from his head and swung it out in a joyful manner and said, "**SCORE!** It looks like we hit the jackpot. We need to stay here as long as we can, or at least as long as it takes to get whatever we can fit in the helicopter."

"I think you're right Doug, we need ta pick this place clean before we go."

Doug turned to the girls and said, "Okay ladies, how about you show us around your mansion."

The ladies took each of the guys' arms, they continued talking to them as they walked. As they entered the house Nina said,

"Welcome to our humble abode, please make yourself at home, we did," and laughed, they all did.

Doug answered with the worst fake British accent, "Why thank you my lady, I think we will, I do think we will."

Even more laughter, and even more lame fake British talk, as they looked through the house.

The girls led them to the kitchen. Even before they got in, the smell assaulted their noses. As they entered, the sight was disturbing, Alex almost lost his lunch. There was trash piled high throughout the kitchen, dishes in all three sinks, and mold growing everywhere.

"Sorry it's a bit messy boys, it's not like we have running water or electricity."

"It's alright Lydia, we've seen worse since the quake."
The two of them, rifled through the modern gourmet kitchen. They were looking for anything to take back. A bit of the twenty-first century would be nice, even if it's only a little. There were two Viking, wall mounted gas ovens, they decided to take them. One would be for the cave, and the other for the fort. The six-burner drop in stove, would also be a great addition to the cave given its community use. In the end, they picked the kitchen clean to give out to whoever needed it.

"I know most of the village doesn't have power, but I do

know that Peter does. He has plenty to run a few electrical kitchen appliances. I'd bet any money he'd like most of these appliances, but I think Ann would like it more."

"Ya might be right Doug, grab em, they're not very big or heavy and have so many uses. We need ta be looking at the bigger picture Doug, sure we can bring stuff for ourselves and others in the village. We need to think about trading too at some point, we need things for that as well."

"Alright I will keep that in mind."

They continued going through the house, they put aside a bunch of stuff that they thought would be good to take. When Alex stepped out the back door he almost dropped to the ground. There was a large greenhouse, made with UV resistant greenhouse plastic, sitting intact.

"Well Doug, it looks like we'll be staying here for a bit, we CAN NOT leave that here. We have ta take it apart and bring the panels back. You keep looking around out here, I need to go check in and let them know we'll be at least a week.

Lydia exclaimed, "A WEEK?!! We're starving here."

Alex replied, "Don't fret Lydia, we have lots of good fresh food, plenty for more than a week."

Nina drooled, "Fresh fruit?"

Alex smiled, "Yes Nina, why don't ya come with me to the helicopter. Lydia can hang with Doug, while we radio in. Then we can get some food for a couple nights."

"I thought you said it's not safe using the radio?"

"It's not Nina, but we're not going to talk. I'll key the radio three times and wait. If our friends hear it, they'll key back once. I then wait one minute for each day we're delayed and key once, then twice more to close. That tells em how long we'll be delayed so they don't worry about us."

Nina stepped up close to Alex, and in a cooing voice said, "WOW! That's smart; you're a smart man Alex," as she took hold of his arm and pulled him close.

Alex knew exactly what this young girl wanted. He knew that she was just trying to manipulate him with implied sex. He also knew he was a happily married man, and unlike the rest of us, he wasn't free to have more than one partner.

"I'm flattered Nina, but I'm married."

As she held him even closer, she asked, "Are you happy?"

Alex took her hand, and held her away, and said, "Thank you, I'm flattered, but yes I am. Doug's girlfriend recently left him. I know he is looking for a new friend, but that don't mean he'd be opposed to more than one."

"What do you mean?"

"Like I told ya earlier, we live in a different society, without those restrictions."

"Oh, I guess I didn't fully understand that part, I can assure you, Lydia is already hitting on him in the same manner, I told her you were mine and he was hers."

"Again, I'm flattered Nina, lets you and I get this work done and head back, I'm sure Doug would be happy for your attention tonight. Well okay, let's get this food inside and make something with it."

Nina said, "I'd love to make us dinner."

"Why thank you, that'd be great."

"It's been a long time since we've had fresh food."

After sending their message, the four of them had a nice dinner, and relaxed by a fire in the fireplace. Lydia opened a bottle of wine and poured some for everyone. They'd been talking for some time and Alex was getting tired.

"Well you guys enjoy yourselves; I'm going to sleep in that nice bed I found up there, I'm tired."

"Alright, good night Alex. We don't have to get up any set time, tomorrow do we?"

The three of them, stayed up late that night, drinking a couple bottles of wine. Maybe it was because the girls were no longer hungry, or the wine talking, but the three of them spent the night together.

The next morning, Alex woke up first, he made some bacon he'd brought and eggs they found in the coup. The smell must have wafted through the house, because Lydia came running down the stairs wearing only her panties yelling.

"IS THAT BACON I SMELL?!!! Oh My God it is bacon, how the hell do you have bacon?"

Not really shocked, but a bit taken back by her display, Alex simply replied, "Yes, it is, now could you go put on some clothes please."

Embarrassed Lydia replied, "Sorry I'll be right back."

When she returned, she again asked, "Now where'd you get that bacon?"

"I have a ranch with all the farm animals I need. We knew something was comin and were ready for it. That's also why I have that helicopter and fuel out there."

"Was Doug with you guys for the quake?"

"No, I met him in their village, on the other side of the pass, from our ranch. They have a village that I think you'll love."

"If everyone there thinks like you guys do, I'm sure we'll love it. Nina and I have not had so much fun for a long time."

"TMI...TMI."

"No, it was not like that silly, we are just friends... EWWW."

Stuttering Alex replied, "BA...BA..tha..that was not what I meant?"

She giggled and said, "Yes you did."

Then she smiled and gave him a hug, "Oh and thank you for telling Nina about Doug, she would never have joined us without knowing that."

Meanwhile back in the village, on the first day, Randy heard three clicks on the radio. He knew it was Alex keying his radio.

"Peter come quick, I think its Alex."

"I'll be right there...okay Randy key it back one time and start the timer."

Randy keyed it and waited. One minute, two minutes, three ... seven minutes passed, another key, then two more.

"That's seven minutes."

"Great, I guess that means that they found something that will take them some time to get. Keep me informed."

They spent the next week stripping the farm of everything they could, and still carry the girls back. They topped off the helicopter with gas, and figured they had plenty to make it home and loaded more in the sling below. The helicopter was loaded with every pound Alex thought he could carry and off they went.

A week later, back at Little Haven, "Is that a helicopter I hear?"

"I think it is Sandy, it should be Alex heading back, he is due in today."

"I hope it is Alex, it would suck if someone else was flying in here."

"Look you can see it now and that IS Alex, I would recognize it anywhere."

As it drew near, you could see all sorts of stuff poking out the netting. As Alex landed, he released the net and landed next to it. The first one out was Doug, but we were surprised to see two women step out of the helicopter as well. After the rotors wound down then Alex stepped out. I watched as the group made their way toward me.

I asked, "Welcome back guys, and who is this you have with you?"

Doug motioned to his left and pointed.

"Peter this is Nina, and this is Lydia. Nina, Lydia this is Peter he oversees the village."

"Hi ladies, and welcome to Little Haven."

Nina replied, "Thank you Peter, I'm sure we'll be happy here, Doug told us all about it."

Lydia also replied, "I don't know how much longer we would've lasted there, without having to leave and find food. As soon as we left the house, we could've been found and killed or worse."

"Well ladies, I'm sure you have much to ask, and we'd love to hear what the two of you have seen since the quake. But before we go over that we need to get you settled in."

Doug spoke up, "I've already taken care of that Peter, they'll both be staying with me. Amanda and I split up some time ago, so I have an empty house."

With a sly smile, Doug added, "Besides we have become good friends since we met."

"I see Doug, I take it you've already gone over the rest of the rules as well, besides our liberal relationship philosophy."

We both laughed.

"I have; I was beginning to think that I was going to be one of those guys, that ended up with no one."

Doug reached his arms around both the ladies, they reached theirs around his lower back, and the three stood close. Doug smiled and continued, "But now... not so much."

I told the ladies, "All right then, with that already dealt with, we'll have a potluck tonight and the village can hear your story."

Doug replied, "If it's all the same to you Peter, I'd like to get these two to my place and get them settled in, we'll come by the cave tonight for the potluck."

"That would be great, we'll see you there."

The three of them headed down valley to his place, and Alex and I started to walk around the helicopter and the haul.

"I'm glad you made it back safe Alex, your family has been waiting for you and should be up here shortly, they were down by the cave."

"I'm glad ta be home, it's been a busy week."

"I can see that Alex; what do you have in here? I can see the handle of some big garden tool sticking out of that netting."

"That's a large roto-tiller trailer."

"Hell yeah, that'll be great, we can use it this year for the fall seeding, we already have the gas to run it."

"But that's nothing, compared to some of the things we found where we got the ladies. This place was huge, and untouched. That's the reason we stayed so long. It took some time to figure out what to keep, then load it on the helicopter.

Among the things we found, was a large greenhouse, that's what took us so long. We dismantled the building and took the plastic panels. We also took the ventilation system, to keep it cool in the summer."

"We'll find the right place to build it. When it's done, we can setup an aquaponics system and raise fish and grow vegetables, it works much better than dirt."

The two of us watched, as everyone unloaded the helicopter. Alex directed them as to what to put where, and what to leave for his home. I couldn't believe the stuff they found. It would make life much easier for many as it's disseminated.

"Are you guys staying the night, to hear what the ladies have to tell us about their encounters?"

"No, I want to take Elaine and the kids home, they already told Doug and me about their experiences, but I'll leave that for them to tell you."

"That sounds like a plan, you get going. I see them coming up now."

"Thank you, Peter, I'm sure Doug can fill you in on the details of our trip. If you need more from me just let me know, I'll be happy to fill in any gaps."

We waved as they flew away, now our village had lost two of our friends and got two new ones back in return. That night we had a huge potluck, everyone was there, and they were dying to hear about the outside world.

Motioning toward the ladies, "I'd like to say welcome once more to our new residents Nina and Lydia. They came from the house in Colorado, that we found the stuff that'll make our lives better. I know you don't want to hear from me, I'll hand you over to our guests."

Motioning to our new members, "Ladies..."

Norm said, "Thanks Peter, you're right we don't."

"Funny Norm."

Chapter 43: The Mile-High City

Lydia and Nina, both stepped up to the front of the amphitheater, to tell everyone their tales. Everyone fell eerily silent very quickly. It had been some time since we got any news from the rest of the country, or world for that matter.

"Hi everyone, my name is Nina, and this is my best friend in the world Lydia. We've been buds since we were in grade school in Denver. We lived there all our lives and were horrified when the quake hit."

Someone called out, "Did you feel it?"

Nina continued, "Some said they did, and others said they didn't, neither of us did. Every channel on TV, interrupted their programming to tell the world what they knew, but it wasn't much. The most ironic thing, was that we had just watched an episode of 'Doomsday Preppers', about being ready for a major earthquake when they interrupted the show we were watching."

"Being long time Preppers, we looked at each other and knew this was it. The funny thing about it, was that at the end of the episode about a killer quake, the supposed experts said, 'The chances of it happening were low', it was just a few minutes later it happened."

"After that evaluation, Nina told me that their experts were full of shit and sure enough she was right."

"Thanks, Lydia, for the confidence. Anyway, we'd prepared for anything and knew what to do in this type of situation. We debated, do we stay and bug in, or get the hell out of dodge. We figured that given how far away we were, that we might have a few days before the shit hit the fan. It only took one day before things started to go haywire.

But we didn't wait, we geared up as soon as we heard about the quake. We hit REI and got every freeze-dried item they had. It was funny, the clerk asked us why we bought them out, we told her the truth, and that she needed to get ready, but she just looked at us like we were insane.

When I looked back the dumb bitch was shaking her head and pointing to us with another casher and laughing. We sure got the last laugh.

We knew we needed to get the hell out fast, we maxed out our credit cards and went nuts getting better gear. That included a lightweight tent, and negative fifteen down sleeping bags that we could zip together. It wasn't even four hours later that we started seeing things crumble, then we hauled ass out of there.

Because we'd been Prepper's for a long time, we were already ready. We'd mapped out our escape route, and practiced it many times over the years. When it came time to go, it worked like clockwork. We knew precisely which forest service roads to take. We had a Jeep 4x4 with nice clearance, towing our Can-Am Commander with lift kits and the full tilting windshield to get us way beyond the roads.

We got out of Denver around five that night, then headed up I-70 toward the Eisenhower/Johnson Tunnel. The traffic had already started to slow down, but we still made it to our favorite overlook. We both cried when we looked back at our hometown. There were huge plumes of smoke rising from the city.

We sat and watched for some time. As the sun set completely, we could see the glow of the fires below; I hated I was right. But at least we got out before it came apart.

We turned south heading for Salida. It was our jump off point where we had more supplies stashed, for just such an emergency."

Someone called out, "It sounds like you guys were set for bear. How'd you end up in a farm in the south?"

"That's getting a bit ahead of ourselves. We made it to our bug-out location just after dark, then settled in for what we expected to be a long camp out. We had tons of food, and years ago we bought a cabin on an incredible lake, teaming with fish.

The only road to it was overgrown years before, and we didn't use it to get there. We figured we would be isolated from anyone indefinitely. We also figured we could go in occasionally to see if there was anything new.

We had satellite TV for the news, until it went off air. We were saddened by what we were hearing. When we heard that the government had fallen, it was too surreal. One day in late fall, we returned to the cabin after fishing, and found the it had burned down. We have no idea how, or why, only that we lost everything. The only thing left, was our Can-am, which we had hidden away from the cabin.

We decided to move on, seeing how we had lost our food. The exception was what we had stored in the Can-am and our backup stash. We left our tent and sleeping bags in the ATV as well as other things. We figured we would need it if we had to bug out from the cabin.

Over the course of fall, we traveled south on forest service roads and off road. In time the gas ran out. Now we had to pack everything in our packs. We continued, on foot, until we came across the house, where they found us. By then it was just a bit before winter. We couldn't believe our luck when we found it and realized it was untouched.

The rest of the story is, now we're here with you guys, looking forward to our new life in Little Haven."

There were few questions for the ladies, and it was getting late, therefore we decided to call it a night. Before he got away again, I asked Doug if he was up for a chat.

"You did an incredible job again Doug. Fred sure knew what he was doing when he picked you for his team."

"Thank you, but it's great to be home."

"You sure found a bunch of cool stuff. It was nice of both of you to donate so much to those that need it. I hope you kept enough for yourself, to make your life more comfortable."

"We did, and I'm looking forward to having a few of the comforts of the twenty-first century, without the rat race that came with it before the quake."

"Good for you, I understand I have you to thank for those appliances."

"I just showed them to Alex. He's the one who grabbed them for you."

"Well anyway, we'll put them to good use, just wait for the next potluck. I make some killer baked beans with a crock pot; they'll make you drool."

"I can't wait Peter, I'm glad you'll be able to put them to use."

"I understand that you also found a complete solar power system."

"I did, my plan is to give it to the village to use with the greenhouse."

"That won't be necessary, we have plenty of panels to run the greenhouse without the power system. I know you and your ladies don't have power, why don't you install them on your place, That way you can have lights for your family."

"Well for one thing, I'm a ranger not an electrician. Give me a target and I'll take care of it; but installing solar, is out of my league."

"I'll help you install your system, it's the least I can do for you after watching over Alex for us. You guys made quite the haul this trip, its great how much you just gave to the community."

"It's my pleasure, there's still much more left at the house, but I'm not sure it's a good idea to return. We were lucky to have made it out without any troubles."

"What were those green sheet-looking dirt things, I saw removed from the helicopter?"

"Oh those, they're two foot by two-foot bamboo mats. Alex saw the bamboo and said we needed to cut them. There was a huge field of bamboo growing at the farm. Bamboo is a major asset if we plant them right, it can be used in many ways."

"He's right, there's many uses for it. What do you say about making that your crop, for anyone that wants to use it?"

"That would be great, it'll give the girls a good job. Alex told me how easy it is to grow and about the many things that can be done with it."

"Perfect I'll get them down to your farm on the ATV."

With that, we both went about our day.

Chapter 44: The Transmission

Georgia was on radio duty one day, when the normal silence was broken. Everyone in the room sat in silence as they listened to the voice on the radio.

"Attention, attention. This is the Rocky Mountain Republic broadcasting on 1345.450. We are broadcasting to announce the first regional swap meet located in Aztec, New Mexico at the county fairgrounds. This is a safe zone, and security will be provided by the United Aztec Militia.

We will have all sorts of items available for sale or trade, including food, ammo, and comfort items. We welcome all who can hear this transmission, we will have a huge BBQ cook out for anyone that attends.

If you hear this transmission and wish to attend, feel free to respond acknowledging your intention to attend. A generalized list of items you can bring will help others know what to expect. If you are maintaining radio silence, we understand your need to remain isolated. The date and time will be on a separate message as well as more details about the event. There will be a meeting after the cookout for the leaders of any settlements to discuss what is going on around us.

This message will repeat itself.

Attention, attention..."

Randy exclaimed, "Everyone come quickly, we just received a radio transmission from someplace in New Mexico. They're having a swap meet and are looking for attendees. Marty go get Peter, Eugene can you go get Brandon, they both need to hear this."

"I'll head up and get Peter."

"Thanks Marty."

Eugene replied, "Okay I'll get Brandon and anyone else along the way."

It didn't take long, before the cave filled up with people wanting to hear the first voice we have heard over the radio in a long time. They were even more excited to hear that some semblance of civilization was out there, it was incredible.

By now I had arrived, and the place was packed. Everyone was hollering, laughing and talking about what they wanted, and what they had to trade.

"Hi everyone, this sounds like quite the event."

"Peter you need to hear this, it's about to start over."
"This message will repeat itself."

"Attention, Attention. This is the Rocky Mountain Republic broadcasting on 1345.450, ... there will be a meeting after the cookout for the leaders of any settlements to discuss what's going on around us.

This message will repeat itself."

"Well Brandon, we knew the day would come, when we'd hear something on the radio. It wasn't what I expected, but it's good news anyway. Fred, I see you've made it; I think we need to go."

Fred replied, "We need to talk about this, and figure out who will get to go because we can only take three people in the helicopter."

Brandon spoke up, "Well Alex is a given, I think one of them should be you Peter, as you would represent us at the meeting."

There was a loud agreement among the large crowd that had gathered.

"I want to go; I want to go."

We heard it over and over from all over the crowd.

Brandon spoke up again, "We're going to have to figure out who gets to go, what we can bring and what we want. How the hell are we going to do that, so that everyone feels it is fair?"

Chloe came up to Fred, Brandon and I with an idea.

"Why don't we have a lottery? We can put white rocks in a closed bag for everyone that wants to go, and two black rocks. We each reach in and take a rock and the two black rocks get to go."

"Hold on everyone, we'll have to wait for more info about this before we start drawing stones. The council and I will have to sit down and go over whether or not we even want to respond to the broadcast or just show up."

The discussion went on all day long, it didn't stop until well after the last of the transmissions. Many good ideas came up about what we could bring including lots of our food stock. But Floyd had one truly intriguing idea.

"Hey Peter, I have an idea that I think you will really like."

"Okay you have my attention Floyd, what do you have on your mind?"

"I've talked it over with the rest of the people I came here with, and we have decided to donate most of the gold we found. We each only want a small amount to keep as a reminder of our experience, and we want the rest to be used to get something for the good of the village."

"Wow that's a really selfless act. I'm sure that gold will be the number one item of trade there."

Brandon joined in, "That'll make things much easier, and we can send less food for trade."

Days went by and no transmission, when the silence was broken again.

"Attention, Attention. This is the Rocky Mountain Republic broadcasting on 1345.450. Plans are still on for the swap meet; it will be held on the thirty first of October starting at eight A.M. Booths will be free to sellers, and there is no admission fee for this event. Check in will be at seven A.M. the morning of the meet, and sellers will be assigned a location based on what they have for trade.

All, firearms will be checked at the gate, and will be returned when you depart. The meet will last three days, and there is space to set up camp on the same site as your booth. Water and toilet services will be available, but not electricity.

Representatives from the Rocky Mountain Republic will be present to talk with any interested settlement. Meeting with them is NOT required for attendance, and there won't be any high-pressure sales pitch to join.

If you are planning on attending, key your microphone once at the end of this transmission, at four o-clock tonight. Please one key only, to tell us how many groups will be coming.

Attention, Attention..."

I said, "Well now that we know more, we need to figure out who is going. Let's have a meeting tonight and we can use Chloe's idea with the stones. That will be as fair as can be."

"I'll get the word out Peter."

"Thanks Rodger, I'm sure we'll have a good turnout tonight."

That night, I informed everyone about the details, I told them about Chloe's idea. She had already made a bag of rocks to draw from. To my surprise not everyone showed up for the drawing. Many had expressed concerns that it was a setup, and that we shouldn't attend. Some feared that if any of us were captured, they would torture us to tell them our location.

I started it out, "We know why we're here, let's get this underway." An overwhelming resounding cheer went out by all.

"Chloe can you join me down here."

"Coming."

"While she makes her way here, I want to say I'm happy to see all of you. I want to thank Floyd, and his people, for the generous offer to give up most of their gold, it'll be a great bargaining tool. I'm sure this'll be a great experience, and that we'll find something good. I know that if we could, meet with a new central government, we should at least hear them out. Okay Chloe's down here so I will hand you off to her."

"Hi everyone, this is my first time down here. I'm not used to being in front of you. We had each of you drop a white rock in a bag if you're interested in a chance to go to the swap meet. I know many of you here tonight decided to not drop in a stone, but you're still more than welcome to stay and see the results. I have two black rocks to drop in the bag. Whoever draws a black rock will get to go on the flight to Aztec for the meet."

Chloe dropped the stones in the bag in front of everyone and handed the bag to Fred. He didn't want to go; therefore, he was a good unbiased person to hold it. One by one each person reached in the bag.

Elated, Bill yelled out, "I GOT ONE, I GOT ONE!" and held his black rock in the air.

More rocks were removed when David simply raised his hand with a black rock and nodded his head. I made the third passenger, so the lottery was over.

"It looks like we have our three passengers. If you two can join me here, we can go over the details of our trip tomorrow. Alex will be flying in tonight; he'll land in my field and stay with us. We already have everything that we'll be using to trade, and Floyd will bring the gold up in the morning as well. If you guys can be at my place by 0800 we can be on our way by 1000."

The next morning, we loaded everything in the helicopter, and got off right on schedule. The flight to Aztec was uneventful, and we were shown our spot.

Chapter 45: The Swap Meet

It took us a few hours to fly to Aztec for the swap meet. As we approached, the radio crackled to life.

"This is the United Aztec Militia; you have entered our controlled air space, please identify yourself and state your purpose."

"This is Peter, I'm the leader of a group coming in to participate in the swap meet, and the regional meeting for the Rocky Mountain Republic, we request permission to land."

"Have you received the expectation regarding your weapons, and do you accept those restrictions?"

"We have received the message and will comply with your restrictions."

"Then you have permission to land, look for the man directing you into your location."

"That's affirmative, request permission to do a fly over to get a lay of the land, before landing, in order to ensure our security."

"Granted, you are cleared for flyover and landing."

To be safe, we did our flyover to get a feel for the area, and to make sure it looked legit. We could see camps set up, and all sorts of wares spread out in front of them. We were confident now that it was legit, then landed where we were directed. As we exited the helicopter four armed men approached.

"My name is Sergeant Ramos, I am here to collect your weapons, and ensure you do not have any on board except for what you may be looking to sell. Those will be rendered safe until you, or your buyers leave the area. You are free to hold onto your knives. Are there any questions?"

"Nope, and we don't have any weapons to sell or trade. The weapons we have on us are all there is."

We handed over our weapons.

"Alright, we landed you in your sales location. You are free to set up any type of camp, and sales area you wish, provided you do not go beyond the roped-out area on the ground. Who is the leader of this group?"

I stepped forward and put out my hand.

"That would be me, my name is Peter and I'm the leader." The sergeant stepped up and shook my hand.

"It's nice to meet you Peter, if you can come with me, the rest are free to get set up."

As we walked across the fairgrounds to the headquarters, we had a chance to talk. It was nice to see the Sergeant be so open and frank.

"Thank you, sergeant it's nice to meet you too."

"Where are you from?"

"Well that's a little hard to answer. We have a little village that we built, deep in the Rocky Mountains in what used to be Colorado. It never existed before so there is no way to really describe where, other than coordinates."

"Strange, before the quake that would have sounded odd but now... not so much," we both laughed.

"We are heading to the headquarters, you can get registered, and meet the people that put this gig on."

"That would be great. How long have you guys had this level of security and normalcy?"

"It's only been about six months, ever since we took out the tyrant that had control over the area. He was one of those people that thought with the fall of the U.S. government that he was going to take over this region. He had been successful for some time, but we took him out."

"Hoollyy sshhit. Was it bloody?"

"Amazingly no, it was more like a coup. Many of the men here today, were more than happy to turn on the asshole. They went in while he slept and killed him. Now we have a local government running Aztec, and many of the smaller cities have rebounded, and have their own as well."

"We haven't been in contact with anyone since the quake. We live in an isolated location and haven't heard any news about what is going on out here. We scan the ham radio frequencies and the FM bands as well, listening for any new transmission; but had not heard any until yours."

"That's because up until recently it was not safe to transmit, people like that clown we just defeated would come in and take whatever you had."

"Yeah that's why we didn't reply to your broadcast. We don't want anyone to triangulate in on our position."

"What is the name of your village, and how big is it?"

"We call it Little Haven, it's our little haven from the crap that's been the rest of the world. Currently, we have a hundred people living there. We walked over a hundred miles ever deeper into the wilderness looking for the right place to set up. We found the most incredible location and have made quite the home for ourselves."

"Are there any militia there?"

"Nope, we do however have a well-prepared bunch of

Preppers. It turns out we were right." We both laughed.

"Well Peter we're here, I'll be moving on to the next group to help. You head inside,
the others will take good care of you."

"Thanks, Sarg, I hope to chat more with you."

"I would like that, maybe I can make it to your camp tonight."

"That would be great, we'd like to hear what you have seen."

"All right then, I'd love to hear more about Little Haven."

The outside of the building was beat up. Many of the windows were covered with plywood. The walls were covered with graffiti, and you could see there had been a fire. A barricade surrounded the building with long barbed razor wire. Guards, armed with AK-47's, and full hard-plate reinforced personal armor flanked the gate as I entered. Even the stairs showed clear signs of the battle that happened here. Yet among it all were planters containing tomatoes, growing tall on a large trellis.

As I entered the building, I had to pass through a metal detector. There were some helpful people ready to guide me where I needed to be. They brought me over to the sweetest little thing, I have met in a long time.

"Welcome, my name is Eve, and I'll sign you in and help you get set up."

"Hi Eve, it's nice to meet you, my name is Peter and I'm the leader of Little Haven. Where are you from?"

"It's nice to meet you to Peter. I was born and raised right here in Aztec. Did you find your site okay?"

"Yes, we landed on it."

"Oh, you guys were that helicopter I heard fly over."

"Yeah that was us, we wanted to see what was here before we landed. You guys have one hell of a setup going here. How many groups or booths are there?"

"You guys make fifty outsider groups, and we have another 25 more local reps. So how many in your group?"

"Four counting myself."

"Okay here are four tags, the red striped one is for you as the leader. You need to have them on while you are here. That way we know everyone here has been screened."

"Do you need all our names?"

"No, you're welcome to put yours on the registration, but given the state of things it's not required. But a first name would be great if you will."

"Not a problem."

I spent a few minutes filling out the form, relieved to see no questions about who we were or where we live. We spent a few more minutes doing paperwork, and she gave me a printout of the schedule.

"Well I hope I've covered everything okay, and that you'll enjoy your stay here in Aztec."

"I'm sure you have Eve, and I'm sure others will be able to assist me if I need it. Thanks for your help, let's hope things stay calm here."

I was impressed by how many people were in there getting signed up. There was a sign-up list for the republic's meeting, so I signed up for that. I was looking forward to learning what was going on out in the rest of the world.

Xavier Bruehler

As I made my way back to our site, I saw several things I wanted to take a closer look at. I was expecting to help set up but was happy to find it was all done. We already had many people standing at our table, waiting for their turn to talk to someone.

I stepped into the pop-up gazebo, and saw Bill approached by an older woman. Her face told me that she has lived a tough life, clearly having worked in the sun. Deep wrinkles covered her face, but still the nicest smile. As she walked up, she put out her hand and introduced herself.

"Hey there, my name is Jamie, where'd you guys find this wheat. There's none to be found for a hundred miles around here?"

Bill shook her hand and proudly replied, "Hi Jamie my name is Bill, we grow and mill it ourselves. As a matter of fact, I was the one that ground that very bag."

"It's nice to meet you Bill."

The woman held the ten-pound bag open under her nose, then took a deep breath. Her eyes lit up, and a pleasant smile of recognition came to her face. She took a second deeper breath, and with an even bigger smile exclaimed.

"Oh My Gosh, this smells soo fresh."

"That's because we milled it two days ago, just for this meet. We keep most of our grain whole, until we are ready to use it, it stays fresher that way."

Jamie exclaimed, "I don't have any gold or silver, and I'm afraid I can't afford to trade any of my ammo. Would you be interested in some quilts for flour?"

Bill is one hell of a trader, I left it in his capable hands to work out a good deal.

"I think we can, Jamie. I know several families that would love a warm quilt."

"They're made from scraps I've collected from abandoned houses."

"How many do you have?"

"I have ten with me here. And can get twenty more, if you're interested."

Bill looked over at me, raised his eyebrows with that should we look. I nodded yes, and then he mouthed, "All of them?"

Again, I nodded yes. He turned back to her, "We'll take all of them."

Elated, the woman said, "I can have the rest here in a few minutes."

I could tell Bill was excited, but he's a master at hiding it from others.

"With that done, let's talk turkey, all thirty quilts for..."

Bill turned to me unsure of what I wanted and asked, "How much should we charge?"

"You're the one that put your sweat into making it, who better to know what it's worth."

"Thanks Peter," he turned to the woman, "How about all thirty quilts, for fifty pounds of fresh ground flour?"

"I think that's a bit low for thirty of them, how about one hundred pounds?"

"Yeah that's too much, let's say we sweeten the deal a bit per se, how about sixty pounds of flour and we throw in ten pounds of sugar."

"WHAT!! You have sugar?!!"

Showing her excitement was a mistake. Now Bill knew he had her where he wanted her, even though he'd never take advantage of her.

"Sure, we have rice and soy too."

"Alright, let's say fifty pounds of flour, twenty pounds of rice and ten pounds of sugar?"

Bill paused for a few, scratched his Goatee a bit, looked at me (I shrugged my shoulders in an okay manner) he put his hand out and said, "You have a deal, and I'm going to throw in a ten-pound sack of soybeans, do you need help getting the rest here?"

"No, I have a few sons that can do that. My husband will be so happy with what I got for the quilts. I told him it wasn't a waste of time making them all."

Bill said, "You tell him sister."

She was back in ten minutes, with three-wheel barrels filled with quilts, which she used to haul away the grain. It didn't take long for our food stock to be traded off. It came to little surprise, that the hemp products sold out even faster than the grains, especially the medical stuff.

We didn't want gold, instead our trades were for commodities, things we could use. David had an agenda of his own. Well it was for all of us, but David was looking for hardware. He was able to find a booth that looked like a hardware store. He found boxes of switches and other assorted electrical items, along with spools of wire and all sorts of pipe and fittings. Though we had many of those items from the motor homes, we needed more. In the end, we had made one hell of a haul on this trip.

Since we still had a few odds and ends left, and we still needed to spend the gold, we stayed one more night. We were able to trade for various live, laying hens and a couple roosters from different farmers. Handfuls of various clothes, and an assortment of foods to eat while we were there, including my favorite, donuts. After we had sold everything we could, we went looking at what there was to get with the gold.

We were on the outside edge of the swap meet, when we approached what to the untrained eye, would have appeared to be a big pile of steel, but not to David.

"Peter is that what I think it is?"

"If you think it's a thresher David, you'd be right."

The man must've heard us because he chimed in, "I see I have a couple men that know what they're looking at. You're right, it's an old horse drawn thresher, with metal wheels that won't go flat. Only a handful of people knew what it was when they saw it."

"That's because David here was a farmer before the quake."

I still am, remember Peter, "We both laughed.

I put my hand out and introduced myself.

"Hi, my name is Peter, and this is David he is our best farmer. Could he check out your thresher?"

"Sure, my name is Charlie, be my guest."

"David, seeing how you know more about this than I do, I'll leave you to work out a good deal."

David stepped up and did a thorough inspection of the thresher. The man had it on blocks so we could turn the wheels, that ensured it drove the rest of the parts. It needed the wood replaced, but that part would be easy. As David looked it over, he kept nodding his head slightly, mentally noting what he saw.

Then David turned and asked, "So Charlie what are you hoping to get out of it?"

"Well I have all the food that I need, but I'm low on ammo."

"I'm sorry to say, we don't have any ammo, we need some ourselves. But I did see a guy a few rows down, he has a large hoard of a variety of calibers."

"Yeah but he is only looking for gold to trade, and I don't have any gold."

David smiled as he looked at me with a sly look, then turned to Charlie and said, "Well you are in luck tonight, gold is what we have to trade, and we would be interested in the thresher. The only thing is, can we come to a deal that works for both of us?"

"I'm sure we can David."

The two men went at it for what seemed like the longest time, and in the end, they came up with a deal that got us a functional thresher. Even better we still had enough gold left over to get the ammo we needed, and even a mountable .50cal and plenty of ammo for it.

Now it was time for me to attend the meeting. I was both excited and apprehensive, as I entered the hall. The security was high, and there were armed men on either side of a man standing near the pedestal. He stepped up and tapped the mic.

Chapter 46: A New Map

"Welcome everyone, my name is General Richard Cline. I am the general in charge of the four corners region of the Rocky Mountain Republic. I have been tasked to inform you that we have established a new central government, it covers what used to be Colorado, Utah and the northern half of both New Mexico and Arizona.

We have stopped the advance of Mexico into New Mexico and Arizona, and stopped dictators throughout the region. We have tried to give you some semblance of a normal life, like this swap meet tonight.

We have control of the military bases within our boundaries, as well as the National Guard Stations and their arsenals. We now have over five thousand troops in the entire area, and are always looking for more soldiers, men or women. As you can see by the lights, we have provided power for some areas.

We have an elected Governor for the region, and hope to include all the cities, towns, and any little settlement within our borders. If any of you out there represent one of those places, and have not heard about us, feel free to come see me after this meeting. We can go over more of what that means for both you and the region.

I'm sure it is not news to anyone, that there is no single central government running what used to be the United States. But there are a few other regions like ours that have formed for strength and safety.

For a time, Chicago was governed by what was known as the Eastern States of America, which went halfway to the east coast. Unfortunately, it had fallen into Chinese hands. Since the Canadians didn't like having China on their doorstep, they teamed up with Texas and several militias to kick out the Chinese, then they returned home. When the Canadians left, there was a power void in the region and from what we can tell, that void has not been filled.

There is little left of the west coast, but what is left, is inhabited by small bands of roving bad guys. There is nothing left of the Pacific Northwest. There is hope, though, that after a few years' people can return to parts of the region. Eastern Washington and Montana still have major fighting between militia groups. Since the quake, thousands have died as the competing groups have fought for control.

In case any of you don't know, New York, City was burned to the ground, and DC was nuked by a rogue sub captain. The Calvert Cliffs Nuclear Power Plant melted down, making the entire Northeast uninhabitable, the fallout spread all the way to the coast and beyond. The southeast was heaviest hit and Florida was invaded by Cuba.

With the loss of federal control, Florida became a mecca for the Cubans. Many came that already had family, friends, or relatives in one of the Cuban neighborhoods. Eventually anyone that could get out of Cuba, flooded into Florida, then on to parts of Alabama, and Georgia. They brought everything with them, food, clothes, whole households of possessions.

There was no border control, Coast Guard or Navy to stop them. Castro loved the idea and made ships available to take them there for free. Even now there is still heavy fighting along the new Cuban borders with Alabama and Georgia, making it not a good place to be.

Mexico too, knew a good thing when they saw it, however they were not as lucky. They attempted to take back Texas, but that turned out to be a bad mistake. As soon as the federal government collapsed, Texas immediately declared themselves as The Republic of Texas and once again their Republic flag flew.

Many Navy Captains, especially the Texans, pulled their ships into the Corpus Christi Naval Base and joined the Republic. All personnel onboard the ships or on base, were given the choice to join the Republic. Anyone that left was provided free passage out of state and ample supplies. Most of the cities in Texas didn't implode after the quake, not even the large ones.

That gave Texas a fair size naval fleet, which they used to kick the Chinese out of North America. One of their subs nuked Beijing, to make sure they didn't come back. Texas also controls the Air Force, Army and National Guard bases within its boundaries. The Republic has unlimited power and oil. Sections of several states have trade agreements with them, they provide power and fuel in exchange for commodities they don't have.

The Mexicans didn't know any of that, and decided they wanted Texas back and tried to move in en masse. It was a short-lived battle; a couple of destroyers fired a few Tomahawks into the Mexican President's Palace. They gave up that idea real fast. The Mexicans were, however, able to move into the lower half of this state and most of southern Arizona, before being stopped.

"We have a treaty with them, or at least an agreement, to hold the ground we both already have. Anyone living in the New Mexican territory, that wanted out was able to leave without a problem. The Mexican's didn't really want them there anyway, and scores of Mexican immigrants that lived in the U.S. before the quake, flooded into the New Mexico."

"Beyond the Texas Republic is a sort of no man's land, there is no government, no control of any sort. If you venture out that way you will likely die. It's like that most of the way to the western shores of Lake Michigan, north to Canada and south to the southern half of Georgia and Alabama. I hear that the southern part of Louisiana may be making a comeback, but I have not got any confirmation about that.

In case any of you here don't already know, there is no west coast to speak of. Few still live there, but I am sure there are some folks out there eking out an existence. But the truth is, none of us know how long any of these new borders will hold. I don't know anything about the rest of the world.

These are the realities of the new world today. That's about all I can tell you about what is left of our once great nation. If you are interested in joining us, feel free to see me after this meeting and we will go over the details."

He continued to tell us about the pros of joining them, he made it clear it was an option and that no one would be required to join. He also pointed out that without joining, they wouldn't be able to call for protection if someone came in trying to take over. I returned to our campsite that night and told everyone else about what I'd learned. I'm sure it won't be taken well when we tell everyone else.

Later that night, we were relaxing by the fire, enjoying some of my favorite elk and venison hot dogs on homemade buns. While we were sitting around someone came to our camp. As he approached, he called out to get our attention.

"Knock, knock."

We jokingly replied, "Who's there?"

Unaware that he had become part of a knock knock joke he replied, "Sergeant Ramos."

"Sergeant Ramos who?"

"No, it's me Sergeant Ramos...oh I get it, that was funny, is this a good time to come visit?"

We all enjoyed a laugh.

"For sure Sarg, come on in and have a seat."

"Thank you, and please call me Samuel."

David spoke up, "Alright Samuel come on in and have a seat. Would you like an elk and venison hot dog, roasted over the fire?"

"A what!?"

"They're hot dogs, made from elk and venison. Ann, Peter's wife makes them, and they are incredible, especially roasted over a fire."

"Sounds great, I don't mind if I do."

David brought him one on a bun, he put the dog to his nose and took a deep breath. His eyes rolled back, and he exclaimed.

"Wow! smells great", He took one bite; his eyelids raised, his eyebrows became big, and we heard a clear, ummm.

"Holy cow, these are great. I've never had anything like it before."

"Samuel where have you come from?"

We could tell that hit a cord. He became quiet, lowered his head, and looked away.

"It's okay, you don't have to answer if it brings back hard memories."

"Sorry I will, it's just hard to think about it, but maybe it will help to vent some."

"Only if you want to. We could talk about the price of tea in Albuquerque if you wish."

That helped snap him out of his mood and made everyone laugh, including Samuel.

"I was living with my parents in Boulder, when the quake hit. I only heard about it on the news, but my sister swore she felt it. We eagerly watched the news for any info we could get, and we were shocked when we heard what had happened. Boulder is not a large town. It's mostly a vacation spot for the rich, and for skiers in the winter. As things deteriorated around the country, we didn't have much looting happening there."

"What happened to get you here?"

"That's the hard part. It had been about a week after the news of the quake, when a militia rolled into the city. They had tanks and APCs. Soon after they arrived, they killed the Sheriff as soon as he stepped out to stop them. They rolled into the town square and started making demands. A short stocky red head guy, the type that has a temper as short as him, stepped up with a megaphone in his hand.

'I'm Captain Richardson and I run the militia ya see before ya. As ya can see we are well armed and will kill anyone that tries to stop us, or that doesn't do as they are told. My men and I need a resupply of food and drink, so ya will all go get whatever you have and bring it to us... NOW.'

Everyone looked around in disbelief. Then Captain Richardson looked at the tank and with a nod of his head, the tank turned the turret on the courthouse.

He looked at the gunner and nodded and yelled, 'I SAID NOW.'

KABOOM. The courthouse exploded, with everyone still in it looking out the windows. The blast sent a concussive wave we could feel as it went off, it knocked many on the ground. Then everyone started screaming.

'You will have your food here by 0800 in the morning, and I want all able body males over sixteen here as well. They will have the privilege of serving in my army.'

The mayor stepped out, 'I'm Mayor Evens of Boulder and I can tell you we won't cower to your bullying.'

The man didn't hesitate, he pulled his side arm from its holster, and shot the mayor in the head. "Now who will be the next to step up...no one? I see, then all of you go and return with my demands....GO!...NOW!'"

Samuel continued, "Everyone slowly walked away talking, the next morning we returned to the square, carrying all sorts of food and drink. It was then, that I knew things were not going to be good.

That asshole stepped up on the APC and exclaimed,

"I see you have brought the food I requested, and I see many young men out there. All of you boys that are over sixteen, step forward."

Many in the crowd stepped forward. I had no desire to go, besides I was the only one to help my parents work the small garden we had. I tried to step back out of sight, but he must have seen me.

"You, boy, the one trying to hide back there get up here."

Timidly I replied, "Me?"

"Yeah you get up here now."

I went up.

He asked, "What do you think you were doing?"

"I can't go with you, I'm the only male left in my house besides my parents, and they can't do the work that needs done."

"I don't give a shit about any of that."

"But I can't, they need me."

"I want your parents to come up here now."

I watched as they approached, they were clearly scared for both me and them. It was then he did it. He said if they were the only reason, I couldn't go then he would fix that. He shot both in the head in front of me. I was horrified, I was 20 when that happened. Then two of his men came up behind me and hit me in the head.

When I woke up, I was tied up and left that way without any food or water until I agreed to serve. I vowed to kill him if I got a chance."

David asked, "Did you get to?"

"No someone else beat me to it. We had traveled to southern Colorado with the militia. Then someone killed him, and his militia fell apart. Afterwards the men went their own separate ways. I made my way here, then joined the fight against the local Colonel and we won. Now the rest is what you see here."

Bill said, "That sucks, a young man like you shouldn't have been forced to fight like that."

"It sounds like you guys are safe and happy, and there's no fighting?"

I replied, "No Samuel, we live in peace and happiness. No one needs anything, and we're happy most of the time."

"I want to go with you guys, do you have room in your helicopter?"

Bill answered, "I'm so sorry, but no we don't. We had to

draw straws to see who could come on this trip."

Oh well, at least I asked, hey if you come back and can leave a seat open for me, I would love to return with you."

Alex added, "Maybe we can make sure to have an open seat on our next trip to the flea market."

"That would be great. I'll be ready to go at a moment's notice."

Before he got to excited, I decided I needed to let him know about our rules. "Sounds great Samuel, but there are a few things you need to know before you decide to join us."

I explained the rules, and benefits, about living with us and he agreed. I figured that was that, until the next time we returned, but it turned out I was wrong. We had planned on staying two nights, we had a good day the second day. That second night by the campfire we heard.

"Knock knock."

Now we really had no choice, I answered.

"Who's there?"

"Oh no, you're not going to catch me with that again. Are you guys busy?"

Bill answered, "No Samuel, what's up?"

"I have an important question for you."

I asked him, "Do you want to talk alone?"

"No, this effects everyone. You told me yesterday that I was welcome to join you but that I'd need to wait for an open seat. Correct?"

I replied, "I did, then the rest of us talked about it after you left, and we're good with the idea."

"What if I told you I had access to a helicopter?"

"I'm interested, how?"

"I have a close friend that I owe my life to, he's a helicopter pilot. When I told him about your village, he asked if I'd introduce you to him."

"Well bring him by."

"I hoped you'd say that."

Samuel turned around and called out, "Jason, come on in."

A rather large guy stepped out of the darkness. He had a long full beard and mustache and a few extra pounds. He wore beat up dirty camo's, that made it look like he had seen his share of action.

"Guys this is Jason; Jason these are the people I was telling you about."

"Hi Jason, my name's Peter and I'm the leader here. What has Samuel told you about us?"

"He said you guys have a village somewhere up north, and that you live in a hidden valley."

"That's a fair description, we live in the Rockies, and have had no contact with the outside world until now. This is our first trip out, where we've contacted others that we didn't have to shoot at. Tell me Jason, how is it you have access to a helicopter?"

"I was the private pilot for the late Colonel, and with him dead, I ended up with the helicopter as mine. I helped the guys that killed him get to him, long story short I helped them, in return they showed their gratitude by giving me the helicopter. They knew I was looking for a way out of the war, and that it would be my way out."

Bill asked, "Then why are you still here?"

"Because there's a lot of people out there that'll shoot you out of the sky, if you fly over them. I've been hit that way several times. If you don't know where you're going it can be difficult to find a safe place to fly to."

I added, "You're not the first one to tell us that. You said Samuel told you a bit about our village, did he tell you about the rules we have?"

Jason replied, "He did, he said that you have a simple outlook when it comes to justice. That most offences end in death."

"Well that is a simplified explanation but sort of."

I explained it to him, and he agreed to the conditions. Bill had a few questions for Jason.

"My wife and I have seen a lot of deception, by people trying to take advantage of others, why shouldn't we expect that from you?"

Samuel seemed offended, by the question of his friend's intentions.

"Jason is a good man; I owe my life to him. I'd stake my life on him."

I replied, "It's alright Samuel, it's a valid question. We don't REALLY know you either. You, vouching for him doesn't help much. We need to make that judgment on our own. Bill has an uncanny knack of being able to read people, it's what he did for a living, consequently I trust his skills in that area."

"I understand Peter, sorry Bill."

Bill continued, "Actually Samuel, your reaction told

me a lot by itself. I was already convinced we could trust you. It's my experience that people of good moral character don't tend to get along with those that don't. But I do have a couple more questions for you Jason, if you don't mind."

Jason turned on his log to face Bill and said, "Fire away."

Bill started out, "Tell me Jason, why would you want to leave Aztec? I'm sure you have lots of friends and maybe family here. There's access to all your needs here. I bet you could even have a job with the Republic if you wanted it. Why would you leave this behind to traipse off into the unknown? You know nothing of us, or our lifestyle, some would call what we have a socialist society, at least one has."

Jason sat there for a long moment. You could see he was thinking about how to answer such profound questions. Then in a deep soft voice he replied.

"Bill, that's both easy and hard to answer, first off why leave Aztec? That would be because I don't have anything to keep me here. My only family is my wife and kids and our dogs. My only other friend here is Samuel, if you guys took him away when you came back, that would be the last time I'd see him, and that would hurt.

But why leave Aztec? You've seen a controlled Aztec, you see the Republic guards everywhere, there's a reason for that. It's not just Aztec we have to contend with here. There still are people out there that will rob you blind if given a chance, both in and out of Aztec. We don't live in fear every minute of the day but it's also not all roses. I don't want my kids living in a semi military state. I want my kids to grow up in a nice safe place with the same morals my parents instilled in me.

I want my kids to grow up knowing where their food comes from. I want them to grow up knowing right from wrong. I don't want them growing up in the tiny piece of crap house we have now. Also, with no means of taking care of them, except by me going out and killing more people. I spent far too much time having to do that for that asshole I worked for. I want nothing to do with killing others, unless they are trying to hurt me or my family.

I'm sorry Bill, I started to rant there. The easy answer is, I want to get the hell out of here the first chance I get. You guys seem to have the kind of place I'd be happy to raise my kids. If it'll sweeten the pot a bit, besides having a fully armed gun ship on your side, my wife is a schoolteacher. From what Samuel said you guys have kids there too."

Bill leaned back and took a big breath and replied.

"Let me first say Jason, you have nothing to be sorry for. I was hoping to elicit an emotional response from you, it's part of what tells me more about your character. Believe me, I can understand how you feel about living here. If I was living here and heard about Little Haven, I'd be the first in line to sign up. As for sweetening the pot, I'm sure Peter would love knowing he had a gun ship at his disposal."

They looked over at me and saw me nodding my head yes.

Bill continued, "Now your wife's skills, are a different story for me at least. There are several kids in our village, and we have talked about getting some sort of school started for them. Many believe that living in our lifestyle, teaches them everything they need to know. Personally, I don't see it that way. Does your wife, what was her name, have any books for teaching?"

Jason replied, "My wife's name is Kim, and yes, she was able to save a lot from the school before it was burned. The old school is where the meeting was held. She risked her life to get them out of there. She went back in the burning building several times, before I had to hold her down to stop her from going in again. And before you ask, Aztec has no desire to open a school."

Bill laughed and replied, "I was."

As far as I was concerned, I'd heard enough, I could tell by Bill's reactions to his answers, that he was okay with him too. I told him the good news but with a small caveat.

"Thanks Bill, those were some hard questions; I wonder how I would've answered them. Jason, we've allowed several people into Little Haven, we've always brought in people from the cold. I don't see any need to change that now. If you and your wife, are okay with the way we live our lives, you'll be welcomed there.

I do, however, have one thing I'd like to ask, to make me feel better about bringing a fully armed gunship to Little Haven. I'd like to ride shotgun with you if that's okay."

"That'd be great Peter, it would give you and I, some time to talk man to man. But I can assure you, that you have nothing to worry about, remember I'll have my wife and kids with me. I'd never take any action that would put them in jeopardy."

"I didn't think you would Jason, to be honest, I just wanted to ride in an Army gunship."

With that we laughed, it helped break the slight tension that I felt. I figured we'd taken in many people already, and that we could use more to help make our community stronger.

"Great, what time do you plan on leaving tomorrow?"

"We'll be leaving shortly after it's light."

"Okay, we'll be ready to take off at first light as well. I'll see you in the morning. I'll be landing in that field next to you."

Off he went, but Samuel stayed behind.

"Peter, I have another request, I have a close friend that I won't leave behind either, can I invite her as well? I trust her with my life."

"Sure, as long as she understands the conditions."

"That's not a problem, I think she'll like some of those alternate lifestyle things you talked about."

Off he went as well.

That night, we packed away our goodies, so we'd be ready to go in the morning. The next morning, as we were finishing breakfast, we heard the helicopter coming in. It was one hell of a sight, here this fully armed gun ship lands next to us. After the blades stopped turning, Jason jumped out and came over.

As I neared the helicopter, Jason put out his hand to shake, and with a sly smile said, "What do think of my little toy?"

I replied, "I like it, what is it?" Jason replied, "It's a UH-1/ T700 Ultra Huey and she is fully loaded."

I replied, "Nice, I flown in a Navy helicopter before but never an Army one."

Jason replied, "It's better than theirs." we both laughed.

Samuel jumped out of the helicopter. As we passed, he turned and asked me to watch out for his girl for him. Just before I jumped on board, we recovered our weapons and took off for home. I was happy to have a chance to meet Jason's family, and his two dogs, one of which was a wild dog from Af-ghanistan named B.

The ride home was uneventful, and everyone was happy to see Alex's helicopter come over the ridge. I had radioed in that we were coming back with some friends; everyone knew to expect the second helicopter. I knew they got the message because I heard the three quick keys I was listening for when I did it.

Fred made sure there were ample people at our ranch, with the ATVs and their trailers, to help unload the heli-copters. This was the first chance Brandon had to check out Jason's aircraft. The bird was decked out with .50 cal's mounted on each side. When it landed it was loaded with ammo and the family's possessions.

That night we gathered at our ranch instead of the cave. Jason and his family brought a large military tent and cots for his family, they just set up in my field. Once they were done, the community came together for a huge cookout and Jason told us about his experiences.

Chapter 47: The Destruction of LA

"I know everyone's eager to hear what Jason has to say, about where he came from and what he saw. I'll let him go first before I fill you in on what I learned. Jason it's all yours."

"Thanks Peter, hi all, my name is Jason Badik and to my left is my wife Lindsey, and our two kids Ben and Tom. The first thing I wish to say is thank you for allowing our family to join you here in Little Haven."

A loud you're welcome came from the crowd.

"Before the quake, I was a pilot for a helicopter tour company in LA. I was also an apache helicopter pilot in both Iraq and Afghanistan. My family and I, lived on the edge of the Angeles National forest in the hills above LA. Our house overlooked the city, and we loved the view of the city lights at night, it kind of looked like fire.

That fateful day, I was standing on our deck looking down on LA, when the ground started to shake. This quake was not like any we had felt before. We could tell it was from a long way away and different. It seemed to last forever. I could see the earth rolling from our vantage point and was horrified as we watched the devastation unfold.

Our house was built to withstand an 8.5 quake, I was pleased to see it fared well. Then, just as we thought it was over, the ground shifted under our feet. The sideways movement was so sharp that it took my feet out from under me. I knew this one was closer, and it felt much like many other quakes we had experienced, except this one was huge. It lasted several minutes, it was crazy.

When it had stopped, we looked out to see the city in ruins, we couldn't believe our eyes. The city was in flames, there were explosions going off everywhere and smoke filled the air.

Every now and then we could see the skyline through the smoke, and we weren't surprised it wasn't the skyline we were used to seeing. Most of the tall buildings were gone, we could make out some of them, toppled over and laying like dominos.

There was one thing I never understood about most Californians. All we ever heard for the last few decades, was that it's not a matter of if, but when, the 'Big One' was coming. Yet few in California, took steps to be ready for it, they called the Prepper's movement nuts. Hollywood made a show that portrayed being ready as a good thing, but all they succeeded in doing was making the people look like idiots.

We knew this was an end of the world as we knew it event, and that the Zombies would be banging at our door before too long. Our neighbor to the north and I had spent years planning our action. As soon as they got home, they came over and we put our plan in action."

Someone called out, "They weren't home when it struck?"

"No, they were at a local store when it happened. As soon as the quake was over, they made a beeline home. They grabbed their go bag, and everything else that was important, and came over to our place. We set off the charges in the drive to our homes and dropped trees across the beginning to hide it as best we could, then waited and watched."

Sam asked, "How long did it take for the first people to find your place?"

"That's a good question, we expected it to happen before night fall of the first day, but we were surprised it took two days before we saw the first people on our road."

John asked, "What did you do?"

"When we saw them on the road, we set off one charge a bit in front of them, that scared them, and they turned tail, and ran. The next ones were not dissuaded, after setting off the rest of them in the road, they left the road thinking it was safer.

Unfortunately for them, we set trip wires along the road, as soon as they hit the tree line, claymores went off and killed them. After a week of on and off attacks we had to re-place most of the traps. When we knew we weren't going to be able to hold the house any longer, we headed for the bunker.

Luckily for us, money was no issue, everything we did was with that in mind, right down to which piece of property we chose for our home. We made sure the backside of our property was on National Forest land. Before the house went up, we built a two-story bunker under the house, it was even larger than the house. The entrance to the first floor of the bunker was hidden and designed to withstand several pounds of C-4. The lower access was also hidden, and it was where we stowed our food and the entrance to a second escape tunnel."

"How long were you able to stay there?"

"We lived in the house most of the way through the first winter and only needed to use the bunker if someone came. Every time someone took over the house, we used the bunker to hide. We then used the upper escape tunnel to get out and take out the invaders from a safe distance with a sniper rifle with a suppressor."

Nathan asked, "When you started killing them off why didn't they come looking for you?"

"Oh, they came looking for us, but when we built the bunker, we made sure there was no outward sign it even ex-isted. One of the air intakes went through the roof, there was no sign of it on the ground. The intakes had a diversion fitting in them. If someone found it and tried to flood us, the water just went into our storage or carried away. There were several hidden air intakes, if someone tried to cut off our air, they had to find all of them.

Our exhaust; filtered everything including cooking smells. We got our power from the solar panels on the roof. If no one ever looked up there, which no one ever did, we would still have power. Our water supply, was a secondary well under the bunker, it could be pumped by hand if necessary."

Sandy asked, "So how did they find you?"

"The only thing we could come up with, is that when we kept taking out their guards, they figured we had to be in a bunker, they started looking until they found our entrance."

Someone asked, "How did they get in?"

"Well the first to try, didn't make it. The entrance was inside a two-door air lock, when we saw them inside it, we set off gas and killed them. That, of course, pissed off their buddies and they really came at us. We didn't have enough gas to stop all of them, in time we ran out of defenses.

Thing is, we used that weakness as a weapon, after we killed them in the trap, we went into the lower bunker. They thought we escaped out the upper exit, so they thought they won. When several of them moved in, thinking they scored a nice bunker, we set off a second line of gas defense and killed even more.

We knew that would really piss them off, and that it would only be a matter of time before they got in. As soon as they found our last air intake, they covered it up, they also cut the wires from the solar panels, meaning it was time to go."

Sandy asked, "How did you get out?"

"We used the lower escape tunnel that took us deep into

the National Forest. After night fall, we made our way out and disappeared into the forest. They looked for the exit but never found the second one. No one thought to look deep into the forest.

We had a stash and an ATV some ways in, and more stashes including gas at regular intervals, we headed deeper into the forest. It took us a few months, but in time we made our way to New Mexico and the group you met."

"Damn it sounds like you couldn't have been better prepared. It's too bad they found you, you could have stayed there a lot longer."

"It did suck to have to give up our place like that, but we knew it would be impossible to stay there forever. We hoped to be able to stay long enough for things to settle down out here."

It was getting late; everyone dispersed and went their way. Over the next few weeks both Jason and his family and Samuel and his girlfriend, found places and had a couple simple cabins built. They had become valuable assets to Little Haven and carried their load with hunting and farming.

Chapter 48: Getting Ready for Harvest

It wouldn't be long, before we'd need the thresher for the harvest. One day not long after they got back from the swap meet, Allen came up to our ranch and wanted to talk. I was in the barn doing my chores when I heard, "Peter where are you?"

"I'm in the barn, come on in."

"What ya up to?"

"Not much, just trying to figure out how to fix this damn thresher. As far as I can tell, the metal parts are here but none of the wood is left. I can see where it belongs, because you can see the screw holes and a little wood left on some of the holes, but nothing else is left. Do you know much about them?"

"Yeah it cuts the wheat from the ground, then separates the seed from the plant. Then it drops the wheat into a hopper on the back, it seems the hopper is gone. I tell you what Peter, I can replace the wood parts, and I know that Fred's mechanic Jordan, can get the rest of it going. Why don't you let us take care of this thing, and you go about doing what we hired you for?"

"Hired? Funny, real funny, what IS my pay?"

"The love and gratitude of the people."

"Alright, I'll go for that, thanks the job is yours. Do you need me to ask Jordan?"

"No, I'll take care of it, he owes me anyway, I made a cedar chest for him and his wife Sue."

"Do you want us to move it to your place?"

"No, I think we're better with it here; you have more resources for repairing it."

"That's even better, because I want to help refurbish it. Besides, we have the torch Alex brought back from the mill. We'll need it to break some of the bolts on this thing."

We continued our talk, we had a few of the newly brewed beers that Rodger made. It was good stuff for home-made brew, and it had a hell of a kick. That's when we heard Ann calling, "Peter, can you come in, I need some help."

Allen quipped, "The boss is calling."

"That she is, I best get and see what she needs."

"Alright Peter, I'll catch you later." He made a cracking whip sound as I walked away.

"Good one, of course you know I owe you one now."

"I wouldn't have it any other way, later."

I made my way in to see what Ann wanted, the surprise I got almost made me drop. Tammy and Sandy where sitting at the table with Ann talking. When I came in, they just looked at me with this strange look, one I'd never seen before, that made me nervous.

"Hi sweetie what can I do for you?"

"Well to be honest it's not me that needs you, the girls have something to ask you."

"Sure, what can I do for you ladies?"

They both paused and looked at each other, Tammy was the first to speak up.

"We want to have a baby."

"I'm sorry to tell you about the birds and the bee's ladies, but that requires a guy and a girl, and even if one of you plays that role that won't get you one."

Xavier Bruehler

"Funny Asshole, we're not here to joke, we have a serious request for you."

Sandy decided she didn't want to wait anymore and blurted out, "We want you to get both of us pregnant."

That almost dropped me to the floor, not something I'd ever even thought of. I looked over to Ann and she was smiling back at me.

"You knew about this? How long?"

"Yes, and no, they just came to me now while you were out there with Allen and brought it up. I think it's a great idea. Remember you were, one of the ones that championed the whole community breeding thing. They're part of the community, and want to do their part, and have babies. Who better then someone that lives in the same house; besides you can't tell me that you don't love both."?

"No, you're right I can't. How long have you two thought of this?"

"We have been since shortly after the vote. We've been talking it over for some time and decided that you were our first choice. Will you do it? Will you try to make the two of us pregnant?"

"At the same time!?"
"No."

"You do of course know, we don't have any of that medical stuff, to do it that way, other than a turkey baster, we would have to do it the old fashion way. Your choice ladies and remember that it doesn't always happen the first try."

"Of course, we do silly. We've talked about that; we both love the both of you and can't think of a better choice of who to try it with."

I looked at Ann again, then both the girls, they stood there with this...well? look, until I said, "Okay I'll do it."

Both the girls came running over and through their arms around me and kissed me, Sandy said, "Oh Peter, thank you we can't tell you how much we appreciate this."

I couldn't resist the perfect opportunity, I looked at the two of them, then the bedroom then raised my eyebrows, smiled and motioned to the bedroom. The four of us laughed and Tammy replied,

"Not now you horn dog, we need to wait until we're ovulating, and what if I choose the turkey baster anyway. Our periods have been synced for a long time, so it should fall on the same time for both of us, but you never know, it might not."

Ann looked at me with this evil look and said, "Do you think you are up to this Peter, or should I say Peter Rabbit."

The three girls thought that was hilarious and couldn't stop laughing.

"Why do you ask?"

"Because when you are trying to get pregnant, the guy needs to be ready to service their needs, several times a day. In this case it could be twice as many times. Are you, pardon the pun, up to it? Besides you ARE getting older, it may not work as well."

Again, the girls had a good laugh at my expense.

"I guess we'll see won't we."

Over the next few months, life was a bit hard for me, or not as the case may be. Life in the village continued as normal and I spent many nights with the girls, but still only slept with my sweet wife. We only did it when either of them was ovulating, accordingly it was not too bad, but it sure takes the fun out of it.

Over that time, Allen and Jordan, had been working on the thresher and had completed it. It was just in time because harvest season was close upon us. Even though we were using a turn of the nineteenth century thresher and living in a mostly nineteenth century village, we still had many of the twenty first century comforts.

Allen and Jordan made sure that the thresher was no exception. I'd been busy on the other everyday things, and it had been some time since I was out in the barn. One day after a long day at work, I heard Allen call out, "Hey Peter can you come out here?"

I made my way out to the barn, the two of them had covered up the thresher with a tarp.

"What's up guys?"

Allen replied, "While you were busy doing whatever you've been doing, that's more important than this, we finished the thresher. Pull the cover off Jordan"

Jordan pulled on a rope they had placed in the rafters and showed me their handy work.

"Woo, there's no way that's the same machine we brought back from Aztec."

"Yes, it is, besides getting the thresher they were smart enough to get plenty of paint for it. Alex and Doug had brought every nut and bolt and nail they could find from the mill. We had everything we needed to completely rebuild the thing."

"It looks like you did more than just rebuild it."

Jordan proudly replied, "That's because we did, do more

than just simply restore it. We modified it to work even better than it did when it was built. We made it so we can reconfigure it to harvest all the grains grown in the valley. Before, you had to walk behind it to control it, which would have been hard work. We designed a seat so two can ride it, one to steer and one to control the hoppers."

"Holy shit you guys have really outdone yourselves."

Allen smiled and replied, "Thanks Peter, who's the first one to get to use this thing."

"Well I guess that depends on whose field is ready to harvest first."

Jorden asked, "Are we going to let just anyone use it?"

"Well I think I'll leave that up to the two of you. If you allow just anyone to use it, you may find yourselves fixing it again. If you're the only ones to use it, you'll be very busy fools real soon."

"What should we do, because I don't want to have to be the only ones operating this and I sure as hell don't want to have to fix it all the time?"

"You could teach a few good men or women to operate it."

Allen responded to that, "I like that idea."

"Good, then I'll leave that part up to you two."

It was harvesting time, and the thresher worked like a charm. It made it so easy to harvest the wheat, and corn, that we decided to double both fields next year. Before we were limited on how much to plant, by how much we could harvest, but not next year. That also meant we could bring in twice as much supplies to the swap meet.

We already had several customers that we sold to, that

placed orders for next harvest, and they had a shit load of ammo to trade. We planned to meet most of them at their settlements instead of having to go to the swap meet to make our trades. Only a couple wanted the safety of the meet to trade. The fact that we had a gun ship, to both escort our run and carry even more cargo, made it more efficient.

Things sure were looking good for us. We were living the life our forefathers lived. A simple life, living by the land, yet we had many of the things we grew to love about our old lives. When the quake hit, I don't think any of us could've ever thought that we could really have our cake and eat it to.

There was no crime, no violence, no nothing, to give us that stress that we were used to before the quake. Things were perfect... for a while.

Chapter 49: Murder in Little Haven

It was a Friday night, right after harvest, when Paula was walking home from her friend Kris's house. It was a hot Indian summer night, and she was walking alone along the path between their houses, when she heard a noise.

"Is that you Robert?" Robert was her husband.

In a deep angry voice, she heard, "Yeah, it's me, where the hell have ya been?"

She replied, "I was with Kris, why?"

"I don't think that's where ya were. I think ya were with that Craig fellow that you screwed last month supposedly trying to get pregnant."

"Don't be silly Robert, I only went there once, while I was ovulating, and didn't even do it. I didn't like his smell, I told him sorry and came home. I told you that, that night, it was why I returned so soon."

"Well I don't believe you."

"If you don't believe me, go ask Kris and her friend Tim, he was there too."

"Oh, then you were doing them too I see."

It was then that she smelt the booze on his breath.

"How much have you been drinking Robert?"

"That's none of ya damn business bitch."

"That's it, you won't talk to me like that, I'm going back to Kris's and spending the night there, while you sleep that rot gut you've been drinking off."

"Oh no you're not; you're not going to sleep with that

bitch or her husband."

With that, Paula turned to walk away and go to Kris's house. That's not something he could stand. Robert picked up a log; and hit her on the back of the head. It didn't knock her out, then when he turned her over, she scratched his face with four of her fingers, unbeknownst to Robert, she ripped off his necklace. That infuriated him, he hit her with the log again, this time it killed her.

The next day, when Kris was heading to see Paula for their morning tea, she found her friend lying dead on the forest floor. She screamed, Kris's friend Tim heard her scream and ran to see what it was. As Tim approached Kris, he saw her kneeling over with her friend Paula in her arms.

Tim asked, "What happened Kris?"

"It's Paula, she's dead."

She couldn't believe that her friend, who had been with her the night before, was now lying dead in her arms. Others heard her scream and had come running to see what was up. Tim turned to Roger, and told him to go get me, and Mark to get Brandon.

It didn't take me long to get there. Brandon was already checking out the scene, when we heard a noise in the brush next to us. It was Robert, Paula's husband, waking up from a drunken stupor. He was covered with blood and stinking of booze. We'd already seen the blood under Kris's fingernails, and there were large scratches on his face. It didn't look good for him.

In a still drunken, angry voice, Robert yelled, "What's going on here?"

"It's Paula, Robert, she's dead."

None of us could believe our ears when he replied, "She

sure is, I smashed in that cheating bitch's head last night with that log over there."

I looked at where he pointed, and sure enough, there was a bloody log lying on the ground, not far from his wife's body.

"Let me get this straight Robert, you're telling me you killed her with that log?"

"You're damn right I did. That bitch was cheating on me with that other bitch Kris over there, and her boyfriend. And look she even scratched my face."

Kris just about came unglued over that, she started screaming, "How dare you call me a bitch, you piece of shit drunken murderer; Paula and I were just friends. You killed her, now I'll kill you." With that she lunged at Robert, she was fit to be tied.

I said, "Tim, get a hold of her while we sort this out."

Brandon spoke up, "I don't think there's anything to sort out, we heard him say he killed her. He never once said he didn't, and you can see the scratches on his face where he even said she scratched him. It sounds like he has already tried and convicted himself. We know what that means."

Kris started screaming again, this time she was saying, "Give me a gun. GIVE ME A DAMN GUN NOW!!!"

I knew she and Brandon were right. The law was the law, it was the first one we wrote. We didn't even have to prove if he did it, he did that job for us in front of a dozen witnesses. Robert, still drunk as a skunk, still didn't even realize what was happening.

We had no choice; everyone was saying give her a gun. Brandon did, but as he did, he told her to wait one minute. She said ok and I walked over to Robert and asked him one last time if he killed his wife.

His reply was, "I sure as hell did, I killed that cheating bitch."

"Robert you were one of the first to join us, you helped write the very law we're about to enforce now, do you understand that?"

It was only then, that he realized that he was in deep shit, he tried to stop what he knew was coming.

Robert exclaimed, "I deserve a trial,"

Kris screamed, "YOU DON'T DESERVE ANYTHING BUT A BULLET,"

Brandon replied, "The only ones that could do a trial, if we felt there was even a need, would be the counsel. We have a quorum of the counsel present and Peter, that should be plenty."

I replied, "I agree, let me see the hands of the counsel that feel he is guilty and should be executed here and now?"

Brandon was the first to raise his hands, two more members also did, and I did as well.

I continued, "Then it's unanimous."

About that time Kris found Robert's necklace in Paula's hand. She recognized it because she had given it to him for Xmas last winter.

Kris yelled out, "Look, Paula has his necklace in her hand, it was clearly ripped from his neck."

Robert reached down for his necklace only to find it not there.

"Well Robert, you've left us no choice. Kris, as Paula's closest friend, the decision on who does his execution, is on you. You can ask someone else or do it yourself. What do you say?"

With that she turned to Robert, "I want to hear you say you're sorry for killing my best friend."

"That only infuriated the drunk, his reply was, "Kiss my ass you whore."

That was it for Kris, she put the gun to his head, and pulled the trigger killing him instantly. That was the first time we ever had to deal with something of that manner.

Chapter 50: The Community

It was ten years ago today, that "The Great Quake" rattled our world. Since then our little piece of bliss has endured, unlike the first camp at the lake. In fact, it has flourished, there are dozens of farms, scattered down the valley. As our community grew, we set up an area near the cave to build houses.

That was easy after we built the mill; and brought in the nails needed to complete the work. We even built a couple stores at one end of the village. Little Haven was beginning to look like an old west town with a twenty-first century twist.

We've had a surplus, of our grains and seeds, every year since our first full harvest. We traded that surplus at several swap meets, and various farms within a short flight's distance. In return for those supplies, we got every farm animal we wanted. On one of the trips, we even found a veterinarian who wanted to join us. He set up shop, in one of the first store fronts we built. He was also one of the first to enjoy our community electricity. We produced enough power that we were able to put up lights down through the middle of town.

We met more people at those meets, several wanted a new life, and joined us. In all our community has grown to well over two hundred. Now the number of women to men was almost fifty percent. We knew it was a danger every time we added to it, but we also knew we need more people to make it work. We've also concluded that we're approaching the limit we want to bring here.

We came hoping to live our lives in peace, with a roof over our heads, and ample food to eat. Everyone came with the understanding that we help each other out, in return would get help when needed. We have literally built our community on that premise and must continue to do so.

The cave is a perfect example. With everyone's help we were able to build a structure that has been used by residents and as a community center. We gather there for meetings, potlucks, and various other get-togethers. It provided shelter for the first to arrive, and later for new members of our village. We're proud of our cave, we will continue to use it for new-comers and community events.

Our cave now offers six bedrooms, and a community kitchen. There's a large dining/meeting area, and lots of room to just relax and read or work on projects. We installed one of those Viking ovens and six-burner stoves from the mansion. Additionally, we have another range with an oven that we got from the swap meets.

The outhouse was a bit of a hike from the cave, but after a couple of winters, the walkway was enclosed. Now no one had to go through the cold to get to it. The outhouse was eventually repurposed for storage. We were able to acquire two composting toilets from the swap meets and install them inside the cave. They work well and use no water.

With the tub finished, everyone would be able to get baths with hot and cold running water. In the first summer, the tub drain was directed into a dry well to ensure it didn't make it to the stream or used to irrigate.

Every effort was made to provide the comforts of homes we left, while keeping everything simple enough that nothing required much upkeep. I think it was the second summer that the wood floor was laid, to keep it clean, and heat from the fireplace was piped into it to help keep it warm, and to protect from heat loss to the ground.

Everyone helped construct the assorted cabins and stores throughout the valley. They put their love, and in some cases their blood, into the construction. Everyone did something to help, whether it was lifting logs, or bringing a sandwich to someone scraping the bark off the logs, which by the way led to several marriages and lots of babies.

That type of involvement reinforced the type of community we've grown to love. It's made for strong lifelong friendships, that anyone living in the pre-quake world would've died for.

On one of many trips to the swap meets, we were able to get a forge, to work steel. Rodney found his calling, he picked up on being a blacksmith in no time.

We added a second set of grinding wheels to the mill to extract oils from the grains. Besides making corn and soy oil, we even made hemp oil. The pond was used to irrigate several fields for planting.

The shaft of the wheel turned several things, a generator shaft so we had power for both cabin and the mill, and the grinding wheels. That required shaping two large stones and mounting them on a shaft connected to the whole thing.

A potter's workshop was improved with several more potter's wheels, driven by a second shaft to throw clay dug from a deposit not far away. The wood fired Climbing Kiln, was based on ancient Japanese techniques.

It was built in steps, with the fire at the bottom. Objects fired on the lowest level were the hottest, like ceramics, and simple pottery was fired in the upper cooler cambers. Additional oxygen was injected into the fire chamber by a bellows, turned by the water wheel to get it hot enough to fire ceramics.

We're happy in our little haven, and hope that the old habits of our pre-quake world don't find their way into ours. We've taken every precaution to ensure that doesn't happen, so far so good.

Chapter 51: New Orleans

We never joined the Rocky Mountain Republic, and it was a good thing. In their sixth year, one of the larger militia groups brought about a coup and took them over. One of their first actions, was to go to the registered settlements and impose their rules on them, fortunately they never found us. The rest of the country is a mixed bag of hope and despair.

The Northeast Region has held together well despite the nuclear plant that failed. They still have a working government, who've been able to hold their border to the west. They only did it because of overwhelming force. Philadelphia had been looted, but after the post-apocalyptic zombies had left, the people that had bugged in, were able to take it back and restore order. All the Urban Preppers, that people had made fun of, turned out to be right. If they had not built up their own arsenals, they could never have retaken the city. Take that gun control nuts.

The Southeast was a different story. Cuba continued moving north, they took over most of Georgia and Alabama before the Northeast Region stopped them. The Midwest is still a large no man's land. After the Chinese were run out of Chicago, that left a huge void that was never filled. The uncontrolled area; spanned from Ohio's eastern border region to the east border of the Rocky Mountain Republic. After the Rocky Mountain Republic fell, the militia was unable to control the east border, consequently fighting rages still today.

The entire west coast was obliterated, that meant order was never restored from the Canadian border to Mexico. There were reports that after the dust settled, and the ash washed away, that large areas of the Northwest were repopulated. Small pockets of people moved into the area. These adventurous few, found a lot more of the land was still useable then anyone ever could have thought possible.

Many of the new settlers lived in downed buildings, sewers, and even in the remains of the aqueduct that used to bring water into southwest California. The area east of the Sierra Nevada's and the Cascades, was spared the destruction of the quake, but not the rioting or militia control.

Montana had always been a hot spot for large militia groups, those groups were able to secure new borders and declare their independence from any other rule. Before the quake a huge number of the population of Montana had belonged to militias. Because of this, the only real fighting in the state was between the various groups. Militia groups fought between each other, and smaller groups fought the bigger ones who wanted control of their territory.

Texas was doing well. The Republic of Texas expanded into part of the no man's land of the Midwest, as well as all of New Mexico after the fall of the Rocky Mountain Republic. Texas played a big role in protecting parts of the south, they partnered with other states to benefit themselves and those they joined forces with.

At first, New Orleans didn't fare well after the quake, just like after Katrina, gangs took over the city. When the famed hurricane had roared towards the coast, the population had plenty of warning and large numbers had evacuated. New Orleans ended up unprotected, and open to gang rule. That wasn't the case after the quake, instead, when the rioting began, people took shelter and bugged in to wait out the chaos.

When the gangs started to go house to house, trying to get whatever they could, they found people waiting for them. These people were armed to the teeth and ready to take back control of New Orleans. Bit by bit sections of the city were retaken from the gangs. Gang members that fought back were killed, and their bodies were hung from bridges to show other gang members what was coming.

Eventually it was the harshness of winter, no electricity, and no heat that broke the hold the gangs had on New Orleans. By the first spring after the quake, New Orleans was back in the hands of its citizens. But unfortunately, they still had no power, gas, or any means of doing anything to rebuild.

The newly elected leaders, of New Orleans, knew Texas had declared their independence and that Texas was making trade agreements with their neighbors. Up until that point Texas wouldn't have even considered talking with them about any kind of deal. The recovery opened them up to negotiations with the Texans. It showed what could be done, and several other cities in Louisiana were bolstered by their example.

Pearl River, Slidel, and several other smaller cities joined forces. The people of these small communities were hell bent on taking their cities back, by keeping the gangs out. They barricaded roads and put up signs saying looters would be killed on sight.

With gangs under control, the leaders of the lower Louisiana Coalition, were able to offer Texas access to the Gulf ports and unmolested access to the Mississippi. They were also able to offer seafood and other commodities to trade for power and fuel. The bond between Louisiana and Texas was strong enough that citizens of Louisiana were offered jobs in the Texas Defense Forces. They were deployed to protect Texas's assets.

The arrangement between Louisiana and Texas worked well. Louisianans were able to stay close to home and defend their own homes and land, and Texas didn't have to send their citizens to man remote areas. The people of southern Louisiana were especially grateful as they had work that was close, that allowed them to provide for their families'.

As New Orleans fought back gang violence and worked at providing for the needs of their citizens, they also had to deal with Mother Nature. Early in the first spring after the quake, several storms slammed the coast and almost overwhelmed the levees. In the past, the Army Corp of Engineers would have worked to keep the floodwaters out of the city, but without their assistance, areas of the city had flooded again. While the floods were not nearly as bad as those experienced after Katrina, city officials knew it was only a matter of time before another storm would come along and cause more damage.

With that in mind, the leaders of the city came up with a radical idea. Instead of fighting nature and trying to keep out the water, they decided they would allow the city to flood. But they were going to take steps to deal with the flooding BEFORE the water began rushing through the streets. Planners looked at the many buildings, which had been looted and destroyed. They decided that rather than trying to rebuild the structures they would instead repurpose the materials to further their new proposal.

Materials salvaged, from buildings lost, would be used to reinforce the ground level of still valuable buildings expected to be flooded. Places, where erosion would wash away the base of a building or destroy the foundation, were covered with the rubble from the destroyed buildings. The extra reinforcement was further enhanced, whenever possible, with concrete foundations. The plan was to ensure that the buildings would have a solid foundation even under water.

Reuse was a key component of the plan. Instead of making more concrete from quarries, blocks of concrete were broken up and remixed into new concrete. Any building that couldn't be made safe, was dismantled and used to make something new.

After the city had removed unsafe buildings and reinforced those that they could, they began working on a walkway system. Bridges were built between buildings, connected on the second floors and built as arches for strength and to allow water travel underneath them.

The plan to dismantle unsafe buildings, and to reinforce or create new, stretched beyond the core of the city and branched out to the French Quarter and other neighborhoods as well. Entire neighborhoods were rebuilt using repurposed material, and a new way of thinking. Rather than asking for trouble by building houses on stilts, the approach was to build houses that would float when the water started to become a problem.

Using GIS disaster planning software, planners were able to predict the flooding. The data allowed them to map out where the water would be an issue, this provided information on the best places to construct new roads and bridges that would ensure ease of transit. Additionally, areas expected to be covered with deep floodwaters, were circled with huge piles of concrete, which were designed to create a fish habitat. When flooded, fish from the Mississippi would migrate to the area and thrive in the habitats.

As construction continued, all gasoline storage tanks were removed from the ground. When possible, the tanks were relocated, but the requirement was to prevent any fuel from leaking into the water. The city learned from past mistakes, they wanted to protect the environment from future contamination. For those areas already damaged by fuel leaks, the city covered the ground with layers of clay. This created a barrier, and then added concrete rubble on top of the clay.

It took almost five years to change the face of the city. When all the buildings were built and reinforced, the walkways were completed, and the area was deemed ready, officials then slowly began to allow the water to flood the city of New Orleans. The process was slow in order to make sure nothing was missed. People all over the city and suburbs watched to ensure there would be no surprises, problems were dealt with before the water flow could continue.

After several weeks of slowly raising the water level, it eventually matched that of the Mississippi River. The process forever changed the landscape; the city of New Orleans would never look the same again, and the French Quarters was saved and ready for their new lease on life. New Orleans became the Venice of the south and everyone applauded. Parade floats became boats that really were floats.

Not only was New Orleans the showcase of the south, it also provided lessons on how a society that pulls together can succeed. Because of their deal with Texas, the city had the fuel they needed. The fuel had been used to run the heavy equipment needed for the dismantling as well as for the new construction. And as the city began to take shape, everyone that wanted to live there was given a home with electricity and water. Food was distributed at work sites, subsequently everyone had their needs met in return for the work they did to rebuild their city.

No one got rich on the backs of the workers. Every able body was put to work, if they were not involved in the build-ing, they provided other services needed like childcare, and sorting and distributing supplies as needed. If someone didn't work, they had to leave. That kind of incentive kept people motivated to work. More importantly most of them loved their city and wanted it to thrive. No one could stay if they didn't carry their load.

As New Orleans rebuilt, the mobs in the north con-tinued to leave the region alone mostly because The Texas Re-public was protecting it, in order to have use of its ports. The Republic of Texas had made a treaty with Cuba to stay out of Louisiana and any other area of its interests. They also made a trade agreement with Cuba for more of its commodities.

As time went on, Texas was shaping into a leader in the country, but didn't want the responsibility of areas that were still in chaos. The bad part is that even now, ten years later, there's still no single stable government to control order. You never really know when, or if, some rogue Navy Ship Captain will fire another weapon at someone.

Chapter 52: The World

Most of the Northern Hemisphere was not much better off. Europe had no central government but at least chaos didn't still rule the continent. Many of the small isolated little hamlets faired okay. That was because they didn't rely on the insane trade infrastructure that led to an inability to provide food for more than three days.

How Asia faired, depended on which part you were in. After Texas and Canada beat the Chinese in Milwaukee, and after Beijing was nuked, China fell. With the fall of the Chinese government, maintenance on the Three Gorge Dam ended, that left it susceptible to the ravages of nature. Several years ago, something snapped in the climate and storms became much more violent. A group of massive storms converged over the headwaters above the dam. With no maintenance, and a massive amount of water entering it, the dam couldn't hold back the water.

The dam failed; it flooded every mile of the Yangtze all the way to the China Sea. Oddly enough the failure of the dam, was a good thing for anyone that survived. The flood washed away or covered the industrial plants, and their waste, and left a new fertile plain perfect for farming. And because the Chinese population had dropped below a hundred million, it became much easier for them to feed themselves.

Australia was one of the countries that never lost control of their people. They were smart and stayed out of the chaos and kept to themselves. However, they too had to change the way they provided for themselves. They were also lucky that the changes due to climate change brought more rain to their desert and started to provide more farmland for them.

The governments of South America fell, and many died

in fighting, but when the dust settled most of the people that survived fared well. Unlike the U.S. most of their population were subsistence farmers who were able to provide for their families, they never went as nuts as their North America counterparts.

Oddly enough Vancouver B.C. was mostly abandoned but it didn't stay that way. It's now inhabited by wild animals and many resourceful people who survived the mayhem, they prospered by taking only what was needed from their environment. Many live quite comfortably in the ruins of the city, amazed sometimes at what they find.

In the end almost six billion people died. After the initial loss of life to the quake, many more lives were lost to mass killings, famine, and disease. Even with that many dead, there are still too many people living on the planet, but at least it has a chance to repair itself. Oil no longer rules the world, as people found new ways to live and get around after the supply was cut cold turkey.

Even though some areas were able to restore power, it's not as reliable as it was before. With the world population much smaller it stands a chance of repairing the scars that us humans have inflicted on it. It still amazes me that so many cannot believe that we had affected the planet on such a large scale, probably the ones that raped it in the first place.

Chapter 53: What's Next

Life has been good to us here in Little Haven. Even after ten years we've had little crime and haven't lost a soul in five years. Our population has grown a bit more than any of us ever thought it would, but as word of our village spread so did the number of people that wanted to live here. I wasn't surprised by how many changed their minds when they learned they had to carry their weight, but we didn't want them anyway.

Fred is happy in his retirement, sitting on his dock fishing with his dog next to him. He and I go there almost every day to enjoy a pipe and not catch fish. Catching them is too much work, that's why we never bait the hook, but I hope Ann never finds that out.

We lost George the cook, a few years back; we think it was his heart. The rest of us original eight have settled in and love life. Living deep in the wilderness has been the best thing in our lives. Now as we sit around the fire, we look back at the last ten years and I'm content to live out the rest of my life right here. I have no desire to go out into the hell that still boils so long after the quake. I've made some incredible friends here. I know that things can only get better.

We've been able to keep the location of our village mostly secret; we hope that never changes, but we're ready either way. We've rigged multiple layers of booby traps down the valley to the big waterfalls, just in case someone decides to venture up even further than before. We have our own military helicopter with twin .50 cal machine guns and a large arsenal, but we hope we never have to use any of it.

No one in Little Haven lacks for anything, we have all the food we need. We have many of the best parts of the twenty-first century and have cast off the crap that supposedly made our lives better. We've built a community that is as close to a utopia as we could ask for.

We do still head out into the rest of the world, but only on a limited basis. A couple of years back we saw the first of only a few flights over our heads. We figured they must be pilots with their own plane and airfield. Every now and then we hear something on the radio, mostly ham operators talking between each other. Generally, what we've heard are reports of more violence and death and destruction. Because of that, we have maintained radio silence and won't change that until we think it's safe to come alive.

Sandy gave us twins, a girl and a boy. Tammy only had one, she gave birth to a boy, a week after Sandy's twins. The three of them have grown up as best friends and time will tell what is ahead for them.

In all, dozens of babies were born over the years, which has insured a generation will grow up not ever knowing the horrors of our past, except what we teach them in school. After the third year, a nice one-room schoolhouse was built, that needed an addition added on only a few years later.

It's getting late and the girls are calling me in for dinner, I think it's a nice honey roasted ham with all the fixings, that means it's time for me to go. There's much more to say, but that will have to be a different time. Live free and enjoy our crazy new world.

The Beginning...

I hope you enjoyed the book. I will be making the characters of the sequel from the people that have given me feedback. If you wish to be in the sequel come visit my Facebook Group page https://www.facebook.com/groups/WhenTheFaultBreaks/

Reviews area always welcome. http://amzn.to/1SVKLp9

CPSIA information can be obtained
at www.ICGtesting.com
Printed in the USA
FSHW021944130619
59055FS

9 781520 145280